Praise for
Precious

"Sandra Novack's novel *Precious* is surprising, partly because it never becomes what it appears to be—a novel about a missing child—but rather brilliantly develops into a powerful story about another family in full-tilt crisis. It is surprising as only the best debut fiction can be, showing a new writer already in full command of her gifts."

—*Atlanta*

"Novack has a strong sense of the inner lives of the female characters. . . . A sense of foreboding lies beneath the lazy summer suburban surface of their lives. . . . Haunting . . . Novack infuses the suspense of a thriller into her close observation of a domestic drama."

—*The Columbus Dispatch*

"Astute observation and incisive writing . . . authentic voices . . . blindness, loss, rage and forgiveness form a powerful dominant dynamic with the fallout scrupulously shown."   —*The Free Lance-Star*

"Suffused with grief and an unsettling, cooly observed nostalgia."
—*The Atlanta Journal-Constitution*

"A sharply observed, lyrically detailed story of love, loss, and the perseverance of families . . . The novel's narrative richness and focused energy baffle conventional expectations, and Novack's frequent use of the present tense adds a chilling sense of urgency to her tale, driven as much by character as plot." —Allentown *Morning Call*

"An ideal book for a book club . . . [There are] echoes of Joyce Carol Oates and Anne Tyler in the themes Novack explores. . . . A powerful, gracefully written, subtly startling work of art."
—Huntington News Network

"Arresting yet engaging . . . Novack's characters are so sharply drawn you expect to look up from the book and see them walking down the street. . . . Novack engineers her plot so flawlessly that the reader is swept up in the flow of the story. Her fine writing holds your attention to the end. . . . This is a very good book." —Baton Rouge *Advocate*

"Haunting . . . told with emotional honesty and a unique grasp of the sometimes searing complexity of human relationships, this novel manages also to convey some depth about the very randomness of life and fate." —*Library Journal*

"Trouble simmers beneath the surface of a bucolic Pennsylvania town in Novack's dramatic, elegantly rendered debut. . . . In this accomplished first novel, [Novack] writes tellingly of the complex relationships among families, lovers, and friends." —*Booklist* (starred review)

"Lyrical and finely crafted . . . graceful prose . . . Novack takes the massive distance between friends, husbands and wives, and makes it her home." —*Publishers Weekly*

"The characters come alive in the details. . . . [A] precise, often beautiful debut." —*Kirkus Reviews*

"This has everything I want in a novel. The Kisch family—and really, all of the people who inhabit this wonderful book—seem so real that I feel I've literally met them. The everyday setting is made haunting by the heart-stopping plot and by the novel's exact and understated prose. This is a novel about an era, a world, and a neighborhood, but at it's core it's about a family struggling to understand, and to be understood."   —LAURA MORIARTY, author of *The Rest of Her Life*

"Exquisitely written, *Precious* is about all the vanishings in our lives—family, love, trust—and the stories we tell ourselves and each other to fill the subsequent holes left in our hearts. So haunting that I haven't been able to forget a syllable of it, *Precious* isn't just spectacularly special—it's truly one knockout punch of a debut."
                    —CAROLINE LEAVITT, author of *Girls in Trouble*

"*Precious* exposes the connections of fearful hope, and weighs the cost and ultimate endurance of love. Written with compassion and grave grace, this lyrical, nuanced book establishes Novack as a significant novelist from whom we will hear much more."
                    —ERIN McGRAW, author of *The Seamstress of Hollywood Boulevard*

"Like Natalia, just one of the unforgettable characters in this novel, Sandra Novack understands 'the small, complicated spaces that exist between people.' But she also understands, as Natalia learns to, how people can close those spaces, how they can return home to a love they thought was lost. *Precious* is a beautifully written, moving, and wise novel from one of the best new writers to come along in years."
                    —DAVID JAUSS, author of *Black Maps*

Precious

RANDOM HOUSE TRADE PAPERBACKS NEW YORK

Precious

A NOVEL

SANDRA NOVACK

LIBRARY OF CONGRESS CATALOGING-IN-PUBLICATION DATA
Novack, Sandra.
Precious: a novel / Sandra Novack.
p.   cm.
ISBN: 978-0-8129-7837-7
1. Missing children—Fiction.   2. Fathers and daughters—Fiction.
3. Runaway wives—Fiction.   4. Family—Fiction.   I. Title.
PS3614.O925P74 2008   813'.6—dc22   2008023472

Book design by Mary A. Wirth

For Carole

author's note

Although a few events in *Precious* are based very loosely on incidents from my personal life, this story is, and always has been, a work of fiction. Events have been altered and radically changed to fit within the context of the story, and so, in their finality, bear no resemblance to truth.

one

1

Sissy is too old to be telling anyone she dreams of Gypsies. She is too old to speak of women who crawl through the window to snatch her from bed, too old to be frightened by their long faces, their pellucid eyes and wrinkled, drawn skin. *Baba,* they call. *Little doll. Come with us, Baba,* they insist. The Gypsies sing: *Child, you are ours.* They linger at the brink of her waking, at the border of her dreams. Sissy is too old to confess that she wakes with a sharp start still, or that when she awakens, she calls instinctively for Eva, and then waits and waits yet a moment more before turning on the light atop her bedside table. Hunched down in the sheets, she imagines the mist that hangs outside her window, phantom shapes that emerge from darkness. Her mind races over the always-present dream.

In the moment Sissy awakens, there are no clutching fingers but the disconsolate hurtling of a black bird against the window, the sound of beak hitting glass and then a flutter of wings. Sissy knows this is wrong, that birds and Gypsies have no place together. But, between her dreams and her waking, they are still there—bound. Then, suddenly, nothing: magically, both bird and Gypsies vanish.

Sissy is nine—an unlucky number—and she is too old for such nonsense. She knocks five times, a *bumpity-bump-bump* rhythm, a language she and her sister, Eva, share through the walls at night.

Where are you? the knocks urge. *Can you come here?*

It happens in a small town in Pennsylvania, one known for the predictability of its days, in a neighborhood with faint yellow light and tree-lined streets curved like crescent moons. Here the houses are spotted with roses around the mailboxes and peopled with working families who tend to crabgrass on weekends and gather afterward on front lawns for idle talk and an occasional cookout of burgers and franks, Miller and Bud. This happens in a time when peeling burns, shiny knees and flip-flops are preferred to practical shoes and sunscreen, and children practice Travolta *Grease* moves in the driveway—a little hip, a little lip. In the evening hours, these same children roam the streets with flashlights in hand, playing lightning tag and hide-and-seek in the neighbors' hedges. Years from now, the remnants of their days will still speak through the markings on tree trunks and pledges of love and forever. It happens on a Tuesday in late June, during a summer of abysmal heat, a summer when, after a thirteen-year silence, cicadas crawl out of the ground and set about their buzzing, shrill hums and calls from trees. You can hear them everywhere you go, drowning out the robins' chatter. Here, in this town, aboveground pools litter backyards. Flowers scent the air.

The first girl who goes missing: Vicki Anderson, known to Sissy Kisch but hated after the horrible incident involving Precious. Vicki: ten years old with braces and a clever, round face, a girl with a habit of twisting a curl of cropped hair around her index finger. Last seen wearing mustard-colored slacks and a white shirt embroidered with bees.

She vanishes only four blocks from Ellis Avenue, where her house is the third on the left, a yellow house with a picket fence lining the yard. On the day of her disappearance, Vicki is just leaving the park down the street from her house. She has just freed her bicycle from the bike rack, kicked back the stand, and mounted the Desert Rose for home.

Vicki: thin-boned, boyishly tall, with a sloped nose like her mother, Ginny's. It is Ginny who, suddenly concerned with the time and a cooling dinner, drives her paneled station wagon down the skinny road that leads to the park. In an hour or so the sun will turn red and set. Neighbors will draw the curtains. Porch lights will burn and fireflies luminesce, and crickets will sing. The cicadas will cease their calls, their tymbals silenced. Now the sky appears not lustrous but a dull blue, throwing off a shade of lavender, a trace of pink.

The park is much like any park you might find in a small town: cracked, dusty asphalt; a basketball court, its metal fence curling back like a question mark; the tennis nets grown haggard from use and sagging in the middle. Swings line the playground, the ground packed solid beneath them. To the right, a baseball field. When the boys and girls slide into home, clay and dust float through the air, and their screams and laughter carry to the bleachers. Behind the field, the dark shapes of trees rise up—cypresses, maples, birches, pine—tearing through the sky. Quick currented, Monocacy Creek cuts through the woods and winds through town, the steep banks ridden with ferns and cattails and limestone.

Ginny looks around. "Vicki!" she calls. The smell of tar drifts up to her, the paved surface below still holding the day's heat. As she walks, she feels the tackiness of her sandals against the ground. She finds Vicki's Desert Rose lying on the asphalt, the wheels stopped, the wicker basket adorned with plastic flowers still holding the scraps of the day's journey. Indecipherable to Ginny: a twig shaped like a slingshot; a rock with a depression in the center, as if a finger worried it there.

Alarm shoots through Ginny as she indulges, first, the worst of all possibilities. She calls out again and tries to calm herself with thoughts of her foolish child, her unpredictable, headstrong child. Vicki is the type of child, Ginny tells herself, who instead of coming home might walk off with another girl to go to another house, or go in search of more treasures: a penny with a worn patina left lying on the pavement, an arrowhead nestled in the dirt, a sprig of laurel. This is the child who, after all, jumped from a tree branch ten feet high and sprained an ankle, the child who, on a dare, pushed her own fist through a window and then tried to hide the jagged lashes on her knuckles and wrist. "Daredevil stitches," Ginny remembers explaining to the doctor, a young man with reddish hair and a careful walk. His stare pierced through her, as did his questions. He noted her responses, dressed the wounds. "Be careful," he advised, looking more so at Ginny than her daughter. How angry Ginny was. She didn't speak to Vicki for the rest of the day and sent her to bed early, without television. Now she glances toward the long line of swings and tells herself that Vicki *is* the type of child who might leave her bike without concern. She's the type to get a good yelling at for worrying a mother so. Thirty years ago (when such a thing was acceptable) Vicki would have gotten a good thrashing for this, which is just what Ginny's own mother would have done to her.

"Vicki!" she yells, irritated that her daughter might play a foolish game at her expense. A breeze moves the swings and sets the chains squeaking. She calls louder as she walks by the slides and monkey bars. She jogs toward the tennis courts. There she sees the Kearnses' sons, from down the street. Tall and muscular, courteous and smart, these high school boys make honor roll. They make prepubescent girls blush. They hire themselves out for yard work and give bored wives a quiet pleasure, a secret thrill and recollection of their own lost youth.

The boys swing their rackets back and forth, their faces stern with effort. The ball lets out a sharp pucker. A solid stroke from Brian, the older boy. Agile, smooth movement from Josh, his normally feathered hair plastered against his face and sweatband. Vicki often fawns over Josh and lingers around the courts, though this is something Ginny has not learned from her daughter's lips but from her diary, the countless entries strewn with chain-linked hearts. Ginny can pick the lock with a bobby pin.

She calls to them, her voice shaky. Sunlight hits her chestnut hair, highlighted with streaks of blond. "Boys," she says. "Boys, have you seen Vicki? Has she been here with you?"

When Josh glances over, he misses the ball and curses under his breath. He adjusts his sweatband, positions it higher on his forehead. Mrs. Anderson lives a few blocks away from his house; she once paid him twenty dollars to paint her fence, a task that took two days and left a sunburn on his legs and arms. Her daughter leaned against the porch rail, her hands propped against her chin. "You're gorgeous," she said. Then, embarrassed, she laughed and ran into the house. He didn't see her the rest of the time he was there, nor has he seen her today.

"Well?" Ginny asks again. Her face is pinched and sharp, etched with worry. She remains, to all who see her, a lonely but attractive woman, someone once pretty in those years before her husband's death, in that time before gin in the afternoon and cigarettes that have dulled her skin. She wears black shorts and sandals, a red tank top with loopy ties at the shoulders that show off her arms.

Josh ambles over to the side of the court, lifts his thermos, and takes a long drink of Gatorade before approaching her. When he does, he notices her glassy, bloodshot eyes, the thin lines that spread like small fingers around her mouth, the faint sourness on her breath. He laces his fingers through the fence, determined to look Mrs. Anderson in the eye and not be ashamed for her.

"It's time for dinner," Ginny explains carefully. She leans forward, as if she is going to whisper a secret, but Josh rights himself. Gradually, so she won't notice, he inches back. She tries to stay calm but is aware of a frantic quality in her speech, a slur, a certain pointedness that cuts forth, accusing, though she knows these boys would do her daughter no harm.

Josh runs a hand through his hair. "Haven't seen her all day." He squints from the sun. He adds, "Mrs. Anderson, are you okay?"

"Of course I'm okay," she says. "It's just that she's late, and you know Vicki. My God, that girl, if you don't have an eye on her, she just does what she wants, all the time."

"I'm sorry," he says, and he is. "But I haven't seen her."

She lets Josh's statement register. Does this mean the boys have been here all day and Vicki hasn't walked by the tennis court? Or that she might have walked by, and the boys, engrossed in their game, didn't notice? But Vicki, seeing Josh, would have surely stopped and lingered; she surely would have sought this boy out. Still, both boys have been here all day and have not seen Vicki. And yet, the Desert Rose lies on its side, the red tassels fanned out against the ground.

Her thoughts run as dry as the baked pavement. Brian looks at her strangely, and she feels suddenly ashamed by her inattentiveness. Ginny's gaze moves beyond him, beyond the tennis court to the woods, to the rows of cypress and Scotch pine, slippery elm and black oak. "Thanks," she says. She walks and then sprints across the scorched grass, the sharp blades scratching against her sandals. The air presses down on her skin, thick like metal. Beads of sweat form on the nape of her neck and brow. When she reaches the ridgeline, blackbirds scatter from the canopy of branches, and, panting, Ginny peers into the dense underlay where mountain laurel grows. She smells earth and pine. She bends for a moment. She places her hands on her knees.

Ginny threads through the maze of trees. At the place where the cypresses give way to oaks, at the place of the brambly bushes and the swimming hole that children have dammed over the past decade, she stops. There the current swirls, and dense trees rise up on the other side of the creek, the brush and ferns more difficult to navigate. She scans the woods. There on the banks, wet leaves smell of rot and mud. The sound of trickling water floods her ears, washing over everything. The cicadas hum—shrill, resolute.

She did not want this to happen. She did not want to come out this evening. She did not want to leave her home already snookered, nor did she wish to face the boys and see in them that dread that made her ashamed.

What those boys must think, what they must tell their mother. They must have so many stories, so many lies, passed from house to house.

She did not want to be out searching for Vicki. She wanted nothing more than to feed her daughter dinner and feign interest as Vicki showed her the treasures of the day: the rock, the twig, the flowers already wilting from the heat. "Guess, Mom," Vicki might say, turning her head, pushing a stray curl behind her ear. "Guess what each means."

"I don't know," Ginny might respond. "You tell me."

And Vicki would smile wryly, keeping from her mother the significance she placed on each, turning over each item in her hands as if they held magic. Ginny might have felt good then as she settled back and flicked on the news, the voice of the anchorman spilling out into the room: the threat of layoffs at the steel plant, the union workers picketing; a lawsuit filed against the company for pollution; the plumes of smoke rising above the south side. The world would all be so distant then, with her daughter sitting on the floor, Indian-style, happy enough despite everything. She did not want any problems at home, and now even her stomach betrays her. The world spins. Light-headed and dizzy, Ginny feels the weight in her legs like stones. She sinks to earth, falling upon it on bended knees. She grips at leaves that break apart in her fingers. The light filters through the branches overhead and then down through the water. The algae-covered rocks catch a floating leaf. A dragonfly touches down on half-submerged debris. It flutters to the creek's edge, a buzz of translucent wings.

Victoria, her girl with a sweet face and a grizzly bear's courageous heart, is gone.

By the end of the evening, Ginny will call her neighbors: Milly Morris, Edna Stone, Matt Brandt, Ellie Green, and Jenny Schultz, despite the rumors she knows this will instigate. "Have you seen Vicki?" she will ask dumbly. "Did she stop by your house, any chance? No, I don't know where she is; that's why I'm calling." Within days, police cars will frequent her driveway. A sturdy-looking officer with a crew cut and glasses that pinch his temples will file the official report. When they see flashing lights, neighbors will emerge from their homes to check on mail that has already been retrieved. They will linger on their sidewalks. Concerned, Frank Kisch will call late at night, after work. "Are you okay, Ginny?" he'll ask. "My God," he'll say, "is there anything I can do for you, anything at all?" Police will search the park and will find a lone clog in the dirt, a piece of rope, a strap that might belong to the Desert Rose. They will scour the woods, search the old stone house at the corner of the park property, the one built during the Revolutionary War. Eventually neighbors will organize a community search, Matt Brandt and Edward Morris deciding to take matters into their own hands. The children will mimic with their own search, a game, flashlights in the bushes, tales of woe. "Vicki," they'll say in a whisper, "are you there? We're coming for you!" Canines will track scents. There will be rumors of a bark, an alarm call, a half-mile trek through the woods, the dogs alert to a smell, and then—suddenly—nothing.

This will mark the first disappearance, in a town in Pennsylvania where nothing ever really happens. This will mark the beginning of fear.

But now, with the Desert Rose piled in the back of her station wagon, Ginny speeds along her street.

The Morrises, who own a purple house—"that eyesore," people say behind their backs—are sitting on their front porch tonight. Milly notes Ginny's speed and glances over at her husband in a knowing way. She leans forward, causing two rolls of flesh to appear in her midriff. A mass of short gray curls hugs her broad face. She tells Edward, "That woman could kill someone, driving like that."

"We've no need for gossip, Missus." Edward feels as easy and calm as the night itself and loves the stillness of evening, the stars that form a wide canopy above them—Orion, lazy on its daggered side. "Does the gossip really matter?"

"Oh, I'll say it does." But even so, Milly laughs a little foolishly.

They look out to the street. For the first time in the town's nearly two-hundred-year history, local officials have issued water restrictions; hoses lie coiled like green snakes against the houses, limp and useless. The lawns have turned gold and then brown. No one is to wash their car, but Edward snuck out in the middle of the night, bucket and sponge in hand, laughing like a teenager. Even in the near dark, his Ford gleams, the gray smokiness catching the moonlight. He stands up and checks on the potted marigolds that he bought as a gift for Milly. "Dry," he says, and heads into the house.

She calls in, "I'm just saying that maybe that woman should lay off the liquor."

"As if the poor woman hasn't been through enough," he calls back.

Milly shakes her head. "I'm just saying that if she doesn't watch it, she'll have a death on her hands."

Three days after the disappearance of Vicki Anderson, and the June heat settles over everything—the tree in the Kisches' backyard, the stifled song of the ice-cream truck as it passes down the street, cranking out a jaunty melody. Children flock around, money in their fists; they purchase Creamsicles and Nutty Buddies that melt as soon as the paper is torn off. They laugh and drop sticky napkins onto the sidewalk, pitch some into a nearby yard. The heat resonates and throbs, creating a yellow glare, a pulsating tenor.

Three days, and life pushes on, despite. In the afternoon, Eva and Sissy are left alone while Frank Kisch goes off to work the three-to-eleven shift, first gathering his lunch pail and then making his way out the back door. Today he tells Eva to make sure the dishes are washed and dried and put away. He tells her to pick up her clothes and to vacuum the rug. Standing in the kitchen, he delivers these instructions in a voice that is perhaps sterner than he intends. At the doorway, Eva lingers, her dark hair falling over her shoulders. She's seventeen and almost always ignores him, and there is, between them, a tension he cannot bridge or fix. Frank regards her and thinks again how Eva is like her mother, right down to her temperament, her slight frame and hair. And that look she gives him now—her expression crestfallen, a crease forming between her eyes—is so much like Natalia's. He doesn't know when Eva managed to grow up, when his once ungainly child stretched in the arms and legs.

There was a time when, as a child of nine or ten years old, Eva would slip into bed between him and Natalia after having a bad dream. Her small voice would call, tentatively at first, into the darkness, and he would hear Natalia turn and sigh before lifting the covers. "Come here, little one," she'd say, kissing Eva's forehead, and Eva would lace her arms around Natalia first, and then crawl over her mother and bury her head under Frank's neck. She had always smelled to him like honey and milk. There was a time when Eva adored him, times when, in the summer, he'd lift her and toss her into the pool, and she'd swim underwater, darting away from him before she'd reemerge and squeal, "Again, Daddy! Again!" Thinking of this, he grows irritated with Eva even though she has done nothing wrong, even though her only fault is growing up. She watches him, arms folded across her chest, the line of her jaw hard. He turns his attention to the backyard and glances out the screen door, past the empty pool, to the maple tree that he suspects has a fungus—the leaves have wilted and dropped months earlier than they should, the trunk turned black. He adds: "And I thought I told you already to rake up the goddamn tree leaves."

"I got busy," Eva says, shrugging. "There's a lot you want."

Frank ignores this, though there is something faintly conciliatory in his tone. "I don't want you two going out today, either. I don't want you near the park at all. The police have been down there. I don't want Sissy to get upset. Watch your sister."

After Frank leaves, Eva calls Sissy down from her bedroom. The girls rake. Or rather, Eva rakes. The blanched afternoon passes over her. There are leaves, so many leaves—they drift and float around Eva. She yells at Sissy to come down from the lip of the aboveground pool and help. She loves her sister as much as she did when Sissy was a baby and Eva would carry her around, pretending Sissy was hers, but there is bitterness, too, that trumps everything on days like this, a resentment that shadows her love. Eva wants only to be rid of Sissy, rid of responsibility. Today, Eva wants only to see her man.

She rakes. "Personally," she says now, "I think the Anderson girl had it coming to her because she didn't listen. Do you hear me, Sissy? I said she never listened, just like you. I told you to get down now. I told you to get down and help."

"You're wrong," Sissy says, "about Vicki. And you can just forget it if you think I'm going to help. Dad told you to do work, not me."

Eva's eyes slant. She rakes and gathers, stuffing leaves and pieces of bark into a trash bag, carrying it with an outstretched arm so as not to ruin her skirt. It is her favorite skirt, one that looks good against her sunbaked legs. Catlike, she strides down the walkway, dramatically, with a flair she only half believes she possesses. She opens the back gate and walks past the carport to the bins in the alley that smell of rotting fruit—thick, sweet, already drawing flies. She dumps the trash. She smacks her hands together and tosses her hair back over her shoulder. She glances up and down the street, waiting to be noticed.

Back in the yard, she finishes her wicked stories, tales involving knives and torture, and Sissy, if Sissy is not careful. Satisfied by the look of horror spreading across Sissy's face, she ends with a moral: "That's what happens to girls who don't do what they're told." She makes a slicing motion across her throat. Then, the dreaded evil eye. It is a game, a lark, though Eva sometimes feels that even if made-up stories were true they wouldn't surprise her. She's a bit too world-weary at the age of almost-eighteen and sometimes believes she has seen enough for a lifetime.

All this makes Sissy wince. "I don't believe you," she says, indignant. "I don't believe any of your stupid stories."

"Would I lie? Have I ever lied to you?"

"Still," Sissy says. She extends her arms, her body perched on the metal lip of the pool that her father hasn't bothered to fill this summer, the hottest of summers. She could fall to her death now with that evil eye, she could live a damned life where no wish earnestly wished for would come true. Over the past months, more so since their mother left, she has begun to think of Eva with dread, a sudden unfamiliarity that disarms even her most tentative attempts at connection. That her sister also has the capacity to be kind—to braid her hair or allow her to eat ice cream or let her sneak into bed at night—only confuses Sissy, only makes the summer stranger.

She closes her eyes and tries to ignore Eva's stories. *One more step,* she thinks, *and everything can change.*

"Get down!" Eva yells, exhausted.

One scuffed Converse poised in front of the other, a lace dangling precariously off the ledge, Sissy does not get down. Too much is at stake to come down now. The metal rim sags under her weight. One step, then two. She pretends that she is walking high above the world, on a wire. She feels distanced from everything—Eva, her tales of Vicki's disappearance, the demand of chores, the pull of gravity. She tells herself: One pirouette at death-defying heights and she will bring back not Vicki but her mother. One pirouette and she will return her life to normal.

"Are you listening?" Eva asks. "I said get down, Sissy. Get down now." Irritated, she stands with her hands on her hips. Could she demand, *Obey?* Could she tell Sissy that occasionally, and more so since their mother left, she has wanted to break Sissy into pieces, rip apart her limbs, devour her in anger? Or worse, could she confess that on those days when she leaves Sissy, she wishes she'd come home to find her sister gone, not quite like the Anderson girl, but gone nonetheless? If their mother were here, none of this would happen. Their mother, Natalia, misses everything, of course. She chose to leave in the cold and snow, preferring it to warm goodbyes and sunshine. She has left Sissy to tears in the nighttime and Eva choking on her sense of sisterly duty.

Sissy holds her arms up high in the air. She thinks only of the next step, the turn she will ease into, her life afterward transformed. When Eva calls again, Sissy ignores her.

And this—this more than anything—angers Eva more. She is not Sissy's mother; nor does she wish to be. If Sissy does not want to sleep, Eva will not make her. Nor will she run in the middle of the night to comfort Sissy when she wakes from dreams of old women, her head filled with the sound of scraping fingers, her forehead beaded with sweat. She will not check the closet for monsters and sinister men. And if Sissy somehow falls from the lip of the pool and cracks her head, Eva will only say it serves her right. Today, under the weight of chores and the expectation of her man, she is in no mood. She picks up the rake again and digs into the grass. "It's not funny," she says.

"I'm not laughing, am I?" Sissy questions.

If Eva does not find Sissy's actions amusing, neither does Sissy. Dreaming, she knows, is serious business. At nine, she already senses the world outside her is treacherous, easily broken and shattered. She closes her eyes and conjures the world of her mind and heart. She fills the pool with water, sees the light reflecting off the surface—brilliant, forgiving.

Another step forward. She balances herself and feels a discernible risk. If she comes down, she will be simply herself: a square-bodied girl with unruly split-ended hair the color of blanched cocoa beans, breasts that refuse to grow even though she stuffs her shirt with toilet paper and admires the pretty lie. Plain-looking compared to Eva, more the owner of her father's build, Sissy, if truth be told, pales in comparison of beauty, just as she often pales in courage. She hates to be alone, unlike Eva who always wants away from the house, away from Sissy.

"Get down!" There is a nastiness in Eva's voice that surprises Sissy. "Grow the fuck up, will you?"

Up and down, Sissy thinks. *Get down, grow up.* The water she conjured just a few moments before disappears, leaving only the sagging liner speckled with fake pebbles, the peril of falling. The part of Sissy that is afraid (the part of her that is always afraid) is certain her pirouette will lead to a sudden, spectacular death. *A blaze of glory.* A fall, a crack against the empty pool liner, the spilling of blood. Her funeral: well attended. Strangers mourning her, wailing into the long night. Carnations laid atop her casket, a stallion to pull her coffin, a feathery plume on the horse's harness.

But despite the obvious risk at five feet in the air, she tells herself that one turn can undo time. One death-defying pirouette and the world is hers. Eva will stop being agitated, quick to anger, and return to simply being her sister. Her father will fill the pool. Her mother will emerge from the back door and stand on the steps. Tall and lean, her hair long and wavy like Eva's, though pinned back loosely from her face and sprinkled with gray, her mother will wipe her hands on a kitchen towel and call Sissy in for lunch. Maybe, Sissy reasons, even Vicki Anderson will find her way home, though this is something she throws in begrudgingly, to assuage a lingering tie in her heart that comes from once being friends, from those long days together, from the many sleepovers where the girls transformed an entire room into a pile of blankets and then scurried underneath them like moles. She can still see Vicki's face, her dark eyes illuminated by a flashlight, the shadow under her chin. Vicki asked, "What do you want to be when you grow up?"

"I don't know," Sissy confessed. It seemed pointless to plan her life when her desires changed from day to day.

"Well," Vicki Anderson told her. "If you don't have ambition, that's not my problem. I'm going to join the circus. Or ride on trains. Or dissect a heart. Or be a famous ghost detective and end up on TV. Watch, and you'll see my name around."

"Anything is possible," Sissy said, shrugging.

And today, with the light spilling over her, everything does seem possible if she stays up here, away from the ground.

"I've got another story for you," Eva yells. "A doozy about a sister who kicks her younger sister's ass."

"Quiet!" Sissy says, daring, arms raised. She doesn't need Eva's stories; she has her own. Tucked beneath her bed is a shoe box that contains her favorites—Nancy Drew and *Ringling Brothers* and *Circus on Rails* and *Ghost Detectives.* Also in the box she keeps a stolen photograph, yellowed at its scalloped edges, of her mother as a young girl—Natalia with Frank, her head tilted back, a dark dress with a bow around her waist, a daring V-neck. Under that lies a diary filled with secrets and stories—stories that avenge Precious and murder Vicki Anderson five times over. Stories of old women with gnarled fingers and broken teeth. Stories of birds in the night, their iridescent eyes watching everything. Stories of Eva, who Sissy often refers to as Darth Vader, the Evil Overlord. Stories of her mother, to which Sissy has added fantastic twists: instead of leaving, her mother grew white wings and flew away. Instead of not saying goodbye, her mother sent many regretful letters, pages damp from tears. In one tale, Sissy even made a knife tear at her mother's flesh, but after she penned those lines, she immediately regretted them and blackened out the entire passage with a marker.

A sullen ache settles in her, and she misses what is gone. She flails her arms forward before catching her balance. Her pulse races. To soothe herself, she begins a familiar refrain: *Once upon a time.* Once upon a time, she tells herself, there was a girl perched five thousand feet in the air on a pool top, the daughter of a woman who danced around fires in a country with no name. Sissy strains to complete the story. She does not remember all her mother's words spoken before bedtime and will, in fact, never remember them entirely—those tales of lost women, wanderers; those who disappeared in ash and dust and were forgotten; a woman left on a street corner, peddling trinkets and reading palms; bits of the stories told in fragments of other languages. *My real mother threatened to sell me once because I didn't listen,* Natalia once said in a bedtime story. *She could be a real* Kurva *who shape-shifted like an animal.*

Sissy remembers to breathe. She adjusts, readies herself. She begins a turn. She hears crunching leaves, smells almonds and coconut butter. Then, a yank. Her legs wobble and strain, pulled by gravity, and then, she alights—flesh and bone hitting the ground.

Eva stands above her with a look that says it all: She will brook no foolishness. "Queen of the morons," she says sharply. "I told you to get down and work."

Sissy rises and brushes pebbles and dirt from her knees. She wipes away blood and rubs a welt that is already forming. The moment is ruined, the day is ruined. Nothing will change. She will only be herself, an inconsolable girl.

Sissy's bottom lip protrudes slightly, and Eva knows that a serious tantrum is about to come on, as quick and violent as a summer storm. *She's been brewing this,* Eva thinks. *She's been brewing this up all day.*

Sissy gives an exasperated kick, one directed toward Eva's shin, and one that lands, miraculously, squarely where she intends. A wave of pain travels through Eva before she swoops forward and smacks Sissy's face. Then she catches herself. She steps back suddenly, saying, "I'm sorry, baby. I didn't really mean to do that."

Too stunned to answer, Sissy wipes her nose with the back of her hand.

"For Christ's sake," Eva says, bending over, "don't cry."

But it is too late, and crying is exactly what Sissy does, although this is not what she wanted to do at all. To cry is to admit that you are wrong, or that you have managed to find yourself somehow terribly alone. When she cries, Eva tells her to toughen up. When she cries, her mother is leaving again. When she cries, she hurts all over, for everything. She chokes back her tears, and, indignantly, says: "You're *trying* to kill me. You're trying to goddamn *kill* me."

Eva rights herself. It is senseless, she knows, to argue. "Goddamn kill you, Sissy Kiss?"

"Goddamn it all to hell," Sissy says, and kicks at the ground. She notices a cicada crawling there. She stomps it with her foot, feeling a guilty pleasure.

"Goddamn it all," Eva ventures, "to *mother-fucking* hell."

Sissy's eyes widen, and Eva senses Sissy will not press the limits of foul language as far as *that,* despite however much Eva might encourage it behind their father's back.

Eva takes Sissy's arm and pulls her closer. With her free hand she straightens Sissy's KISS T-shirt; it has managed to crawl up on one side, simultaneously scrunching Gene Simmons's face and revealing skinny flesh and rib. "If I were trying to kill you, Sissy, you'd already be dead by now."

"Thanks a lot, jerk."

"Don't be a Neanderthal."

"Don't use big words."

Eva steps back again and looks Sissy over. Something in her chest constricts and she feels it then—obligation, a pestering love. "You'll be fine," she says. "No permanent damage." She sighs the sigh of the ages and looks over Sissy's shoulder, down the yard, and out to the alley. "Forget the chores," she says, finally. "I'll make up some excuse with Dad. Just go—go inside. There are franks in the fridge. I'm going out."

"Where?" Sissy asks. "Are you going out with Greg?"

"Absolutely not," Eva tells her. "And where is none of your business. And God no, not Greg. He's a juvenile delinquent, practically. Just because *you* adore him—"

"I don't," Sissy says. But she has already daydreamed what she has deemed an inevitable wedding: white streamers and pink frosting on the cake (peonies, perhaps, or roses) and Greg's light blue tuxedo trimmed with velvet, Sissy in tulle, and her father in the back of the reception hall, passing out cigars.

"Earth to sister," Eva says.

"What?"

"Good God, never mind." She heads inside, and Sissy follows.

"Eva?"

"What?"

"Is it him? Are you going to meet *him*?" She has come to think of him as the mystery man, the man of magic—lean with a pleasant, wide face and smile. Only a week ago, he pulled up in the alley, got out of his van, and hugged Eva, who was waiting for him. He presented her with a flower he had hidden behind his back. "Is it him?"

"I told you that's a secret," Eva says quietly. "You promised not to tell."

"I won't tell. I'm just asking."

"Not him," Eva lies.

"Are you mad at me?"

"Do you know you drive me crazy with questions?"

"Are you mad?"

"No, not really. Are you going to tell?"

"No."

In the kitchen, Eva pulls out a soda from the refrigerator, opens the can, and pours a glass of Coca-Cola. "You know what to do if anyone calls?" Eva asks, leaning against the counter. "If Dad calls on break? *Especially* if Dad calls. I'm indisposed. Say it."

"I'm indisposed," Sissy says.

"Not you. Me. I'm indisposed. I'm counting on you not to tattle. Tattletales get their just due." She hands Sissy the half-finished glass and watches as Sissy drinks the soda and holds it in her mouth for a moment, leaving it to fizzle.

"I already told you I won't," Sissy says finally.

"Good. I'm sorry for what I did before."

"Do you really mean that, or do you just not want me to tell?"

"I mean it."

"Okay."

"How much do you love me, kid?"

"Tons," Sissy says. "I love you tons."

"You always say that," Eva tells her. She crosses her arms. "You're too easy."

Sissy sips her soda. "Eva?"

"What?"

"Why didn't Dad fill the pool?"

"Because he's an asshole, that's why."

"Eva?"

"What?"

"Did Mom go where Vicki went?"

Eva squats down, to eye level. "No," she says plainly. "Mom didn't go where Vicki went."

"Maybe Mom was kidnapped."

"Don't be ridiculous. Why do you conflate things?"

Sissy looks at her strangely. "Maybe," Sissy says finally, "Mom was kidnapped and that's why she hasn't called."

"You've got it all wrong," Eva says, impatient to be on her way, and, at the mention of their mother, annoyed again. "Mom's probably still in Italy with Dr. Finley, like she was when she wrote to us. That's the truth, Sissy. Mom is gone and she isn't coming back, so you might as well just forget about her."

Sissy follows her sister down the hall. Eva picks up her purse from the living room chair and opens it. She stands in front of the mirror and applies a coat of orange lip gloss.

"Eva?" Sissy lingers in the doorway.

"Jesus Christ, *what*?" She smacks her lips together.

"Do you ever get lonely?"

"Don't be ridiculous."

"You don't?"

Eva primps her hair. Her chest constricts again, though this time she ignores it. "Everyone gets lonely, I guess."

"What do you do when you are, then?"

Eva checks the clock—just about three, just about the time he'll finish—and takes her keys from her purse. "I don't know," she says, heading out the door. "I just pretend I'm not."

Sissy does conflate everything; it's a mark of her character and disposi- tion, one that she will not rid herself of in all her lifetime. Gypsies and

birds and ghosts, her mother and Vicki. What she cannot fully understand becomes a mass of threaded contradictions within her, dancing
around in her mind until they form a lover's knot.

After Eva leaves, the day grows as long as a shadow. By four the
house will begin to feel ominous. In the kitchen, the basement door will
become a gateway to a place filled with cobwebby terror, unspeakable
dread. In the living room, Sissy will be certain someone lurks just outside the window: a mystery man, a murderer. Upstairs, the shuttered
closet in Sissy's room will suddenly hold too many secrets; each slat will
cause her worry. She will find refuge in Eva's room, the room that is, according to the red-lettered sign on the door, STRICTLY OFF-LIMITS! On
Eva's walls there hang posters of exotic places—Italy, Spain, France—
Eva has always wanted to travel to, though she laments frequently that
she'll never get away from this town and from these people, though
what people she refers to exactly is mostly anyone's guess. Clothes cover
the carpet, piles of books litter the bureau. The room smells of cinnamon and lemon candles. Eva's jewelry box stands always open. Black
and white with two silver clasps on each side, the box holds a dancer, a
ballerina dressed in a white tutu and frozen on pointed toes. Sissy will
wind the back of the box and listen, absorbed, as the ballerina turns in
circles.

She stays away from the open window in the hallway and the attic
door. She races down the steps. In the kitchen, Sissy quarters an onion
and places each wedge at a corner of the living room, an act designed,
her mother said, to keep away evil. Natalia performed this ritual every
time there was misfortune—a fight with Frank, a tiff with Mr. Schultz,
the migraines plaguing Edna Stone. Worry, Natalia warned, has no
sense of boundaries or distance; it simply lurks, waiting to find you.
There were constant rituals, in fact—digging a hole in the dirt and filling it with coins to bring money, rubbing vinegar on foreheads to chase
away headaches—all designed to keep disaster at bay.

Not quite satisfied with the onion cutting, and the tears it has caused, Sissy crosses herself, throws salt over her shoulder. There will be no worry, not in a near-empty, vulnerable house.

She eats a hot dog, makes a mess with the ketchup.

She turns on the television to *Scooby-Doo*. This much she knows, even when she is alone: If she had a dog, the world would be better. If she had a dog, she wouldn't ever feel lonely.

In the living room, the light filters through the curtains. Dust floats in the air. It will be after dark when Eva arrives home, if she arrives home at all, her hair mussed, the smell of a man all over her, though this will not register to Sissy until years afterward—the deceit, the lovely lies of summer.

Unlike Rocky, the mutt down the street who nips at the neighbors and who used to scare Natalia half to death, Scooby-Doo is a bona fide coward; still, he chases a phantom.

Sissy yearns for her mother. She thinks of Vicki, despite—

Last summer, the girls were inseparable, which made the mothers happy. Both women didn't do well with many of the other women in the neighborhood, those who wanted to sit and gossip over iced tea and talk about how they loathed their children's teachers, or their mothers-in-law, or their husbands. Natalia would have none of that public airing of grievances. She preferred a certain measure of appearance, of not saying too much to any one person. Natalia was that sort of woman—whatever awkwardness she may have once felt as a youngster had transformed itself into a formality that often grew more pronounced when a neighbor showed up, inexplicably holding a crumb cake. "Strangers," she often said. "I don't know why they would want to sit and talk."

Except for Ginny Anderson. They met at the school's bingo night, and the women hit it off. In the weeks following, Ginny would stop by for coffee and they'd talk while the girls were left to solidify their friendship. "Go outside," Natalia would say, patting the children on the back with her palm, nudging them forward. "Go play."

Last summer, the girls hunted the neighborhood. They transformed themselves into private eyes and schoolmarms, Indians and cowboys, wardens and prisoners, dancers and thieves. They were sharks who circled around in the pool. They were dead swans, floating on the water. They were divers, plunging down to the bottom of the sea in search of gold doubloons. They planned routes, drew maps, knew shortcuts through alleyways and hedges and broken fences. They worked out elaborate rescue plans. They brought chalk to mark trees.

They shared blood and claimed sisterhood. They told stories until they erupted in laughter and Eva had to bang on the wall and yell for them to be quiet.

Together they made entire worlds from nothing. Throughout the long summer, they were always running away, always finding a way home.

But Precious! Sissy will never get over the incident involving Precious, one that led to the dissolution of friendship. A gift from her mother, a porcelain doll that had traveled as Natalia's first mate on a boat years before, Precious was Sissy's most beloved possession: her peasant dress the color of pumpkins, her lips painted red, her hair long and black and still smelling faintly of ocean salt and faraway places. When Vicki wanted to play with Precious, Sissy adamantly refused, and when she refused again, Vicki engaged the doll in a tug-of-war, until it broke, literally, in two.

In her anger, Sissy threw her half at Vicki, missing, hitting the wall. And then on the floor was Precious's shattered face, her tiny hands disembodied. In the middle of the night, to avenge the horrific incident, Sissy snuck into her mother's sewing room, unsheathed the metal scissors, and lopped off Vicki's hair as she slept. How her hands trembled as the blade went down, catching the moonlight; Vicki woke, felt her head, and screamed so loudly the entire house woke up. And this was followed by Vicki leaving at three in the morning, and by Mrs. Anderson's anger. Sissy's punishment ensued: three days alone in her room, like a common criminal.

A secret Sissy holds: She saw Vicki on the day of the disappearance, and this is a thought that, despite her hatred, she worries like a strand of hair. If Vicki is really gone, if she didn't just run away, could Sissy have stopped any bad luck and misfortune? Could she have called out, offered reconciliation, a game of hopscotch on the pavement? Instead, she let Vicki ride by the house and watched, resolute, angry, as Vicki stood up on the pedals and popped a wheelie with her new bike, the Desert Rose. "Later, Gator," Vicki said, and Sissy stood with a cocky expression as Vicki disappeared down the hill, out of sight. How her thoughts circle around what might have been, what was and is. She wonders if what she saw was a real or a phantom girl.

Maybe Sissy's mother, that Gypsy soul, stole Vicki away, and all of this and none of this makes sense in Sissy's mind, and all of this and none of this seems real.

Scooby-Doo shivers in fright. "Scooby-Dooby-Doo!" he says.

Sissy finishes her hot dog.

The light filters low.

She steps outside and heads to the park.

2

"Fucking children," Eva says to no one but herself. She flips on the radio to drown out her thoughts, to drown out Sissy's incessant questions. She tires of having to engage Sissy in what their father deems useful summer activities: 4-H, which resulted in Sissy practically reduced to a catatonic state after witnessing the birth of a breached goat; reading days at the library; and, before the Anderson girl's disappearance, trips to the park, where, overwrought with boredom, Eva languished while Sissy ran around the monkey bars like an animal or dreamily walked off on her own, away from other children, as if the day weren't able to sustain and bolster her. She is tired of Sissy, tired of chores and this too-domesticated summer, which is not the summer she imagined at all.

Eva rolls down the windows. She fans her skirt and lifts her thighs from the seat; they release like duct tape. She can feel the moisture between her legs, the heat. She touches herself, briefly, wondering if she should have showered again, but then dismisses this thought. She has no intention of going back into that house. Eva drives out the carport and down the alley, refusing to be magnanimous and rescue Sissy from loneliness. To do so would make Eva lonely, too. To do so would be like scurrying into a dark hole.

This is not to be the summer of tears. This is the summer of Eva and her man. This is the summer she will follow advice bestowed upon her the day her mother left, when Eva's pleading became so urgent Natalia stopped packing and thought to explain. "Don't give up your freedom," Natalia said. "The day you give up your freedom, the day you lock yourself away, is the day you disappear. In your own skin, you vanish."

Perhaps her mother was also thinking of Sissy, who was, after all, the accidental outcome of birth control gone awry. That day, as Natalia lugged her suitcases down the narrow hallway on the first floor and into the kitchen, she thought to add: "And for Christ's sake, Eva, please make sure you use some protection." She paused then, and her voice softened. "Whatever you think of me, I still worry about you."

With that, she left Eva stunned and broken, barely able to speak.

Since that day, Eva has joined countless women in America and gone on birth control. She has developed a reputation in the process. The girls at school know Eva. They have heard rumors that Eva struts around ready to straddle most of the boys. They hold a polite distance that Eva interprets as simple jealousy. The boys know Eva, too: Alex and Greg and Ralphie and Brian Kearns, George and Yusuf, the exchange student. She and George did it in the boys' locker room, Eva distributing her weight on a flat wooden bench while he fumbled with her bra and slathered her neck with his mouth. At the park, she and Alex did it missionary-style. Alex's back seemed to carry the weight of the stars, a celestial, magical boy. She and Yusuf did it under the bleachers, her face touching the support beams, the smell of dusty wood seeping into her nostrils as he pushed from behind. Brian, the boy who confessed he masturbated to his mother's Sears catalog—his favorite was on page eighty-seven, a blonde in a blue teddy—did it with Eva behind the eighteen-wheeler at Orr's department store on Main. In a manner of speaking. *He may be thinking of the model,* Eva thought; *he may be wishing for hair that is flaxen instead of dark chocolate.* He touched Eva once, quietly convulsed, and then made countless apologies.

Each boy has taught her something about control, the lack of it, the getting and keeping of it. She must feign recklessness with the stoner, be sensitive with the shy one, a beast with the foreigner, whatever is necessary. It has somehow become a mark of survival to know when to hold a distance, when to move closer, and when to stay away altogether. She has not yet had the thought that Natalia has had a hundred times: People, even those in love, push and push their bodies together and still find themselves exhausted, consumed—after everything, they can only right themselves, put on their clothing, and walk out into the world again, alone.

But Eva won't be with any more boys as foolish as her sister, as naïve-sounding and young. Thoughts of her man absorb her; they leave her breathless and wet. The road stretches past lawns fierce with heat, so fierce that it is as though everything—the houses, the pavement, and Eva herself—might simply burn away. The sunlight spills down, pressing against everything, and she wants her man even more. He has asked her many times to simply call him Peter. He has asked and she has promised not to tell, and he has sealed all this talk with kisses and has extended his arm around her shoulder and said, "That's my girl."

She rummages under the seat and pulls out a pack of cigarettes. She takes a deep drag, exhales out the window. She says his name now, keeps it on the tip of her tongue, the aspirated, breathy *P: Pete, Pete, Peter.* And yet she cannot help but think *Mr. Fulton.*

A horn sounds. Eva glances over to the oncoming lane of traffic. She stumps out the cigarette and brushes away smoke before Mr. Nealy, their neighbor, sends up a wave. His hunched posture is evidence of a man too old to be driving without the aid of glasses, if at all, and his habit is to lick his lips as he pushes down on the gas pedal. As he passes, he turns briefly and squints, as if his face weren't already wrinkled like a cabbage. He drives ten miles under the speed limit, his boat of a Buick chugging by Eva's Honda Civic. It was Mr. Nealy who spoke to her father at a neighborhood picnic a few weeks ago, that day when ants bit ankles and Sissy was tortured and outcast from a group of children who had taken to calling her Mr. Ed. Eva listened as Mr. Nealy prattled on about *Dallas,* and how all the actresses strutted around braless. "The paper decreed it's a jiggle show," he said grimly. "Girls running around today, all wanting to be noticed. You can't *not* notice." He seemed to wait for her father to agree and hold fast to wholesome values, but her father remained silent. Later, at home, her father demanded that Eva not swagger so.

Eva plans a necessary lie. If Mr. Nealy should see her father and mention that he saw her on this day when she was told to stay at home and watch her sister, Eva will say she only went to the grocery store for milk, butter, and eggs, all of which they are in dire need of getting. She cannot bear the thought of her father taking the car keys as punishment. Nor can she bear the thought of irritating him more. She has spent most of her time staying out of his way. How angry he often becomes with the girls, how bitter when things aren't just right, when chores aren't done and the house is left a mess. His outbursts happen with greater frequency and seem directed at what Eva hasn't done correctly: Sissy hasn't been wearing sensible clothes, or Eva has been wrong to let Sissy excavate only the toffee bits from the ice cream, or dinner wasn't nutritionally balanced, or she has once again managed to turn his T-shirt a shade of pink. It is as if, in Natalia's absence, Eva is supposed to become Miss Manners, Betty Crocker, Ann Landers, Mrs. Brady, and Alice the maid, all rolled into one. And when she fails, when things aren't the way they should be, she must work through the winds of her father's moods, only to have them replaced with a silence that clamps down to the bone, forcing Eva to gnaw her way out of it.

He would be happy if she never left the house. He would be happy if she were just like Natalia.

Eva winces. Mr. Nealy's car is barely visible in her rearview mirror, and she changes the radio station, opting for the Beatles. She taps her fingers on the steering wheel in time to the music.

Pete, Peter, Petey. No, she decides, *not Petey.* Petey suggests a fumbling boy, like Brian with his fantasies and George with his sloppy fingers. She thinks of Peter's broad face that is more complicated than attractive—a pronounced nose; round glasses that accentuate his green eyes; a mass of wavy hair; pale skin that suggests he spends all his days indoors. He is a man with political convictions, a man who lived through the protests of the sixties and came out on the other side wiser, and, according to him, only mildly cynical and scathed. "The country," he told her over the phone one night, "is going to hell. We were better when we were younger. We never thought our ideas would collapse under us."

"You're at your best now," she assured him, and she was surprised— genuinely surprised—when he laughed. "Maybe you are," he said. "But I'm not."

She checks her face in the mirror and wonders what Peter sees that she cannot see yet in herself. She smudges her eye shadow—copper and rose blend. Satisfied, she sings. She passes homes of those she knows, parents of students who attend Watson High. She passes winding streets: Brandywine, Ellwine, Copeland, Main. She passes the firehouse. At the light by the 7-Eleven, she turns and drives over the metal bridge and holds the wheel tighter as the car judders. Below, she can see the rows of dark buildings, long covered with soot, the blast furnaces that spew out an orange-red flame. She scrunches lower in her seat. Somewhere below, her father is checking pipes and lines and fixing damaged equipment. She speeds up, exits the bridge. "I am going, I am gone," she sings. She waves her hand out the window, feels bold again.

She loops around the public library with its wide, squat steps, its functional design and brick columns. The sight of the library still thrills her, the thought of that early June day when she first ran into Peter outside of classes, how everything started from that brief encounter, when he held a copy of Kerouac's *On the Road* and told her his baby had destroyed his copy, crayon marks on half the pages.

How did I get so lucky? she wonders. *How lucky to be able to pick be-tween the boy's love and the man's love and pick the man, with his expansive thoughts and reading!* He has told her things, such things! He speaks of Thoreau and Emerson and Donne, Nixon and Johnson. In conversa-tion, he has treated her as an equal. He thrills her, he alarms her, when he whispers, "Here, like this," and "Go down." He appeases her when she, feeling brave, speaks tentatively of home, her father, but never of that night. He almost never disagrees that institutions are oppressive to today's youth, that they obliterate every imaginative thought. Once, over Sunday dinner, Eva told her father "The ozone is a factor," and Frank Kisch responded plainly, "What kind of shit are you learning in school?"

Watson High remains as it has throughout its many years of exis-tence: an uninspired four-story building, its boxy formality consistent right down to the hedges that run along the base of the building. Even now, with school ended, there are summer classes under way, and signs of life. She spots Jeremy Reed, the boy Eva let into her mouth, the boy who later, during study hall, ignored her while Eva sat rigidly next to him, penning eyeballs into her notebook. He leans up against his Fire-bird and gives her a lazy grin. When she gets out of her car, she strides by, ignoring him.

Down at the field, the coach runs drills, and Eva sees Greg, her boyfriend from the days of sweet kisses, her now good friend and pur-veyor of pills, weed, and beer. He stands by the sidelines, waiting for the players to finish. Even at a distance, he has an unmistakable slouch, an easy gait, his thumb frequently hooked into his belt loop. She waves, but he doesn't see her, so she turns her attention to the bus that remains parked near the building, ready to deliver students home from the shame of summer school. A group of girls congregates at the front entrance: Brenda Armstrong and the Armstrong sisters, or as Eva refers to them, the Mafia sisters, the Brenda wannabes. They wear platform shoes and summer shades, tops tied in knots just above their belly buttons.

Eva does not want to feel this way—a pull, a small panic when she sees the girls. She wishes so desperately to be prettier—taller, more graceful, smarter than she pretends. She does not want to think of these girls as competition. But she can't help but remember them all seated in Peter's class in the spring, their moist lips slightly parted, their legs crossed. She's seen the way they smile at him, the way they sometimes look at him as they answer questions about Shakespearean sonnets, as if they actually cared about Shakespeare at all.

Her strides grow more brazen. When the girls see her coming, they trade such knowing glances that Eva raises her shoulders and holds her head higher. A stiffness settles in her, one that she has had too often of late, when anyone stares at her for too long. She calls upon reserves of vanity, the knowledge that she has been told over and over again that she is beautiful, but which she never successfully embraces. She hurries more than she wishes to, feels adrenaline pour through her legs.

Brenda Armstrong, who is homely despite being a shoo-in for prom queen, smiles as Eva nears, exposing a row of perfect teeth that were only recently released from the stranglehold of wires. Eva supposes it is Brenda's smile and oddball humor that make her popular. It surely isn't her nose.

"*You've* been around," Brenda says casually. She flicks the underside of her painted fingernail.

"A lot," a Mafia sister says, the one with the short hair and full cheeks.

The girls all snicker. Eva's look grows steely. It is a look she learned from her mother when she'd turn militant, irritable with the girls, with Frank. Eva is certain there's a crease etched between her eyes and that her left eye is squinting in a mock curse. She pushes the door open. "Cheerleading is really kid stuff, don't you think? Rah, rah." She leaves them standing there, Brenda's jaw slightly dropped.

Eva hears the buzzing fan in the principal's office, set strategically to catch cross breezes of air. The hallway stretches on either side of her and gives way to classrooms and labs. In front of her is the gymnasium with its double wooden doors and stale smells. A water fountain is positioned neatly outside, a testimony to the fifties with its pea-green base and creamy knob. The tiles beneath her remain mottled and dirty-looking, though Mr. Wood, the janitor, mops them several times a week, his head down, oblivious to the students.

Eva sneaks by the office and ascends the steps to room 312. The lights are on, the door closed. She peers through the opaque glass, but it is as useless as peering through an icy window. She abandons the door and opens the nearby lockers instead, to pass the time. Most are empty, but on her fourth try, she finds a key chain that says BORN TO BE WILD, and a pack of pens. She places both in her purse as she rehearses a conversation designed to make her seem older than she is, so that she doesn't get tongue-tied as she often does when she is nervous. She will tell Peter about the local college she wishes to attend. She will say she has no desire to push papers at a doctor's office, as her mother did when she finally was able to seek part-time employment, wearing skirts that were too short not to be strategic. Eva has plans. She will travel first—Italy, France, London—before attending school. She will appear talented, poised. Ready to take on the world. Things are changing, she might say. Does he have any idea who taught her to embrace such freedom?

Eva is a reinvented woman.

If the mind has its own atmosphere, today the weather in Peter's head is cloudy and foul. He glances out the window and wishes for rain instead of sun, for pounding thunder and cracks of lightning. He blames his mood on too much starch. Because Amy is trying to perfect her role as housewife, because she seems bent on reminding him that, in light of the baby, she has turned over a new leaf, as it were, given up smoking and cursing and even so much as an ounce of alcohol, she has seen fit to have Peter included in the general betterment of the house and so has had his shirts professionally dry-cleaned. He feels like his neck must stretch to accommodate the confines of polyester and cotton. Such shirts remind him of his banker father, that depressed, fidgety man who spends his days sitting behind a mahogany desk, mulling over lending applications.

Peter scratches at his collar. A line of sweat gathers at the base of his neck. Under the fluorescent humming lights, his class takes on a bleary existence. He regards them all, this motley crew of eleventh graders who have failed English literature. Someone told him to take it easy on himself and use multiple choice instead of essay, but Peter is not a drill-and-kill type of teacher. Instead he tries to inspire these young minds. When they cover plays, he discusses Hamlet's troubled and erratic moods, as if Hamlet might encourage them to move beyond their own angsty depression and indecision, to embrace what Peter calls the "alternate path of action," one that is decisive and swift. He has encouraged conversation that too often falls short. He has implemented Elbow's theory of teaching without teachers, but he does not know finally whether it's really gotten him anywhere, or done any good.

"Is there any point," he asks them now, "to rhyme and repetition, beyond mere churlishness, of course? What lies buried under the surface of a Donne poem, what voice lives in the negative space?"

No one answers, of course. No one cares about Donne. These kids care about their wasted summer, their waiting friends and parties. Peter isn't even sure *he* cares that much about Donne, either, at the moment.

"Is it the heat that's getting to you?" he asks. His eye wanders as it always does, across the faces, not holding on to any for too long. They, his students, this group of latchkey kids and future consumers of pay-by-plastic, ask nothing of him. Irritated, itchy, quite possibly depressed and suffering from what he fears is a premature midlife crisis, Peter lingers in the silence. Things happen, he wants to say. Poetry fails. Art is forgotten. Governments go corrupt and cities are bombed. People eat, drink, and screw only to die uncomfortably in bed, alone, waiting for those they love, remembering times that are all but gone. "What is the speaker's voice in this Donne poem? How might you characterize it?" He picks it up, reads again.

Sue Kidmark pops her gum and then peels it off her face. Peter regards her as one might an experiment—he is distant, clinical, with a now detached curiosity. His gaze moves again. Some in his class will go on and negotiate their way through the maze of school, only to be confronted by more complicated mazes. Others will simply give up. They, like he, will stop scrambling and say, *Fuck it. I refuse my part.* And those who exercise the smallest defiance of the system, those who go on to be thieves or bums or even people—Peter suddenly thinks—who just have good old-fashioned affairs, will be forsaken and left to their own quiet regrets. Gone are the days of free love for all of them. In the eighties they will turn to punk rock. In the nineties they will be bankers, their fathers' children. A grayness will settle on everything just as this graywalled room settles on them now, confining, restricting.

He wishes he had another shirt.

He calls on Ethan Fritz, a boy who is sure to never run the rat race. Ethan glances up from his book, looks around to his peers, and then regains his hip coolness. He taps his pen on the desk as if the action itself is more significant than words. He makes a sudden, airy noise through his nose and gazes out the window. "I think the speaker in the Donne poem is gay, man. I bet he likes disco."

"We should probably stick to the text," Peter says. "There's no disco in the text, at least not in this version. There's sex, though. I'd think you'd all be interested in sex."

A few students laugh uncomfortably. He glances up to the clock over the door. Five minutes left and still this excruciating irritation. He notices the way the second hand speeds around, the odd way the long hand jumps ahead by minutes with a click and then jumps backward—still running, it seems, always too slowly.

He pulls at his collar. He could strip now, just as he did one summer night when he and Amy lived out on the West Coast and frequently took late-night walks at the park by their apartment. Amy pulled away from him, and then waded into a granite pool of water, lifting her skirt as she did. He remembers how the park lanterns flickered on one by one, along the line of idle trees, and how Amy swayed under a marble statue of Pan—the lifted skirt revealing her pale calves; her long hair flowing around her shoulders. "What are you doing?" he asked. "Come in," she said, splashing the water. He stripped off his pants and went in after her, and she laughed as she pulled off his shirt and tossed it over the statue, just out of his reach. Thinking of this—of the warm-scented air and Amy's unexpected actions, her youthful fancy—Peter shifts his weight and puts the book down.

"All right, a free-write," he says. "I want you to compose a poem, or offer some meditation on why John Donne is gay. Either is fine. You've got five minutes, so make the most of it."

He sits at his desk and glances around to the stacks of books, the reports and take-home assignments. How did he get here, to this place of bland conformity? What happened to those cherished nights, to the always-new conversations, to the laughter hiding in everything?

At least the morning didn't start this way. He woke from a dream in which he was soaring over a canyon, the sky a pale blue and violet, the burnt-orange crevice below streaked with white and gold. He felt such bliss that everything about the morning seemed pure and perfect. He thought to share the dream with Amy, who had always seemed to him, in their six years of marriage, to be fascinated by dreams and their hold over people. She had studied Jung in college, where they'd met, and she'd majored in psychology. There was a time when she wanted to be a therapist. This was before Peter was offered a job after graduation, teaching on the East Coast, and Amy, succumbing to new pressures of money and house expenses, decided against graduate school and got a job working at a clothing store instead. She was good with people. She told him she liked the work.

Still dressed in boxers, Peter walked into the kitchen. He wanted to ask Amy if she still remembered Jung's theories, and if she still thought she might eventually go back to school and do those things she had often talked about. He held out his arms like a bird in flight. Amy watched but said nothing. Peter took no offense to this; he figured she had probably been awake for hours. Sophie's teeth were cutting through, and, before going to bed, Peter had suggested a little brandy rubbed over the tender flesh. Amy would hear none of it. "That's not something you do to a kid," she said, but it was clear she had debated for a moment. It seemed to Peter that she wore her motherly duties with too much uneasiness. He hated to think in that way, but she had become so different after Sophie's birth. She'd suddenly embraced family values, reconverted to Catholicism, and gone off birth control. Whereas she had once loved the spontaneous and impractical and flawed joy of each day, she now seemed to regard with annoyance anything that might disrupt an orderly life. In Peter's approximation, the only aspects of her former life she clung to were her abhorrence of beef products and an almost sacred veneration for brussels sprouts, which she still called, to Peter's surprise and sadness, her *petits choux.*

However wonderful his dream might have been, it was only ill-fated in daylight. "I had an amazing dream," he said.

"Oh, really?" Amy picked up a spoon and returned to feeding Sophie.

"Good morning, Peanut," he said, kissing Sophie's head. She sat perched in her high chair, slapping her dimpled fists against the tray.

"What about the dream?" Amy asked casually, and by then it seemed to him she cared little to hear of it. He wondered if at night she fell into a nothingness—no images or color or motion.

"Nothing." He sat down next to her. "It's nothing at all." He regarded her, thinking that at twenty-nine and even in a ruined nightshirt, she was still pretty. Her face held the memory of the girl he met in his senior year. In college she was an earthy sort, pleasantly wide around the hips. She was self-assured, aware, vivacious. In those days, she shared almost anything that was on her mind. He still loved her, but sometimes when she became sullen and impatient, he felt as though she'd become a stranger.

They sat in silence for the better part of breakfast. Peter drank his coffee and read the paper. Finally, Amy put down her cup of tea. She took a spoon and stirred it idly, the metal hitting the ceramic cup. "I'd like to talk, if you don't mind."

"I don't mind," he said, looking up, surprised by the vulnerability in her voice. "Talk. What is it? What do you want to talk about?"

"Lear," she said.

Peter glanced down to where their cat sat under the high chair, licking his booted paw. A black tiger, Lear's eyes were so large and golden that Peter often became transfixed by them, particularly on nights when he snuck a little weed. "Okay," he said, smoothing the paper. "What about Lear?"

"I know he's your cat. I know you've had him a long time."

"*We've* had him since college." Peter remembered how Lear had sat on the dashboard of his van and slept most of the way as they'd driven, three days, across the country.

"I'm worried about Lear and Sophie."

"You're joking."

"I wish," she said. "I was reading this story in a tabloid, where a house cat sat on a kid as he slept. The kid turned blue. *Blue,* Peter."

"If it worries you, then at night shut the door of Sophie's nursery."

"Then I can't hear her," Amy said. "I don't even think Lear really likes Sophie; it's like he feels replaced, like it's a competition."

"Lear is fine." He leaned in for a moment, toward Amy, and was about to say something more—something to the effect that he believed she was being ridiculous—but he stopped himself. He wished he could wean her off this new-mother syndrome, the fretting about every little thing when in fact nothing bad had happened to Sophie at all. Finally, he said plainly: "The odds of a cat suffocating a baby must be one in ten million."

"Still," she said, "that's one possibility I don't want. It's not just that, either. It's the work involved with cleaning up after the cat, the time I don't have and don't want to take. You're out teaching, and I'm left here, with everything else."

"I'm out," Peter corrected, "making extra money. I'd like to be home more. It's not that I don't want that."

"Sophie tried to pet Lear yesterday, and he hissed at her."

"What did she do to him?"

"What do you mean, what did the baby do? She didn't do anything."

"You're overreacting."

Her shoulders stiffened and she sat quietly for a few moments. She smoothed her hair out of long habit, even though now it was short and permed. "Please," she said finally. "Don't tell me I worry too much. Just don't."

Were it not for her tone, which, at that point, seemed genuinely hurt, Peter might have laughed at how overly sensitive Amy was to the issue; they might have shared an amused chuckle. But he realized there was nothing he could say to rid her of her fear and of her anger at him for not understanding. The concern was real enough, and that was all that mattered. He knew she felt the way he did—that unexpected rush of pure love, a desire to protect the child at all costs—but he didn't see the practicality in being obsessively paranoid about Sophie's well-being. Life was there, all around them, and whether either wanted it, eventually something would happen. Sophie might sprain a finger, break an arm, fall on the pavement, chip a tooth. It bothered him, yes, but he saw it as inevitable. Part of being human meant eventually getting hurt. "Of course you're right," Peter said, finally.

"You don't mean that. You only ever mean that you're right."

Peter ignored this comment and read about Ted Bundy's recent escape, his half dozen murders in the Rocky Mountain area, and his subsequent arraignment in Florida. "Did you know," Peter said, trying to change the subject, "that Bundy campaigned for the Republican Party. He planned a career in politics—that figures, doesn't it? A serial-killer Republican? Did you know he volunteered on a suicide hotline and authored a book on rape prevention? How fucked-up and hypocritical is that?"

She picked up her cup of tea. "I thought you were trying not to curse anymore."

"No," Peter said, without looking up. "You were trying to get me to stop cursing, as I recall. The newspaper says that Bundy bit some poor girl's ass. Why is *that* fashionable to report, the violence? Why the attention on Bundy, like he's some superstar?"

"Another debate?"

"I'm trying to have a conversation. I thought you wanted to talk."

"I get tired of these kinds of conversations."

"You told me what bothers you; I'm telling you what bothers me."

"Bundy is a sadist," Amy said. "Why would I want to hear about *him*?"

"I'm just trying to talk."

"You're *reading* to me from the paper. That's not talking. It's not. And I hardly have the time to think about every single thing you *read*. Last week you went on about beavers, dams, and the health of forests. You don't even understand what's important."

Her words hit him, and they seemed to finalize something. He was angry but he kept his voice perfectly level. "You can tell a lot about dams and about the health of a forest by studying beavers, and I happen to find that important."

"Sometimes I don't know what's happened to you." She got up and placed Sophie's bowl in the sink.

"Me?"

"Us, then. Us," she said without turning. "I don't know what's happened to us."

And then later there was the shirt. When he complained, Amy stood in the bedroom doorway, and he thought he saw a flash of victory in her. He pulled off the shirt, intent on finding another.

"Don't bother," she said. "They're all like that."

"Who's the sadist?"

"Apparently that would be the dry cleaner," she told him. "Life gets you in more mundane ways than serial killers do."

It was only a few weeks ago that he ran into Eva at the library when he was browsing through the aisles, looking for a copy of *On the Road*. He was killing time, really—there was a woman with wavy hair, a friendly conversationalist, who worked the stacks. He'd been secretly hoping to bump into her, having already decided that she was a good candidate for the affair he knew he needed to have. But that day she wasn't working, and, while Peter stood there and contemplated what to do next, self-pity crept up on him. He was so engrossed in his thoughts that at first he didn't realize Eva was standing at the end of the aisle, watching him.

"Mr. Fulton?" she said, peering down a bit, uncertain.

He looked up, momentarily surprised. She was a tall, lean girl with a mass of hair difficult to miss. He caught himself staring, and she shifted uncomfortably and smoothed her skirt. She almost always wore skirts that made her look attractive. He could admit that—that she was very attractive. Embarrassed, he joked with her as he might with any student he saw, musing over her confusion and curiosity, as if she couldn't quite fathom that any of her teachers had a life outside the classroom, or interests other than Watson High. "I'm not Mr. Fulton," he said, changing his voice. "It's Alien Fulton to you." He held out a stiff arm and made a motion, like a robot.

It was a lame joke, a foolish attempt at a conversation. He could admit that, too, but she indulged him anyway.

"You seem different," she said, smiling. She looked around. "I mean, I guess it shouldn't surprise me that much to see you here, should it? It's a library after all. Where else would teachers hang out?"

Peter laughed. "Of course here. You know after school all your teachers turn into vapor. They only rematerialize in time for homeroom the next morning. *We live and die for Watson High!* It's a motto we keep

pinned up on a banner in our secretive teachers' lounge." He raised his
eyebrows a little, watched as she took a book and opened it. "Reading?"
he said. "For goodness' sake, why do that?"

"It just so happens I *like* to read. Now, if you're going to be mean
about it . . ." Eva pushed her hair back so that he could see the sharp
line of her jawbone and her star-shaped earrings. Then she looked over
to him and bit her bottom lip.

This pleased him, her defiance, her bit of flirting. "I'm only mean
when I'm at the library and talking to a pretty student," he said. It
slipped, and he regretted it, but she didn't seem to mind. She edged forward and read aloud. Peter felt the weight of possibility bloom in him.
It all had a slightly treacherous quality to it, a moment alone in a quiet
aisle with a young girl, reading. After all the nights Amy pushed his
hand from her thigh, after all the times she didn't want to talk and
squirreled herself away in Sophie's room instead, rocking the baby back
and forth, he found the thought of screwing in a library both titillating
and frightening. It flashed before him: sex against books, the smell of
dust all around. Afterward, a heartfelt discussion on the beat poets.

"My sister is downstairs," she said, interrupting his thoughts. "It's a
madhouse down there, twenty kids at story hour."

"Ah."

"I'm glad you're here," she said. "I was getting bored."

"Don't feel bad," he told her, smiling. "I'm almost always bored."

The next day, Peter found a handwritten poem, left on his desk. It
was awkward free verse and contained two typos. During study hall, she
came up to him. "I had to ask," she said, her face expectant, her voice
so intimate it sent him reeling. They already shared a secret then, didn't
they? Her poem, his confession that he believed she was attractive.

"Ask me what?" he whispered back. He leaned forward over his
desk, pushing the papers forward as he did.

"Was it awful?"

"The poem? No, it was fine," he said.

"I'm not very good," she said, suddenly bashful. "I know that."

"I write sometimes, too."

"Poetry?" she asked. "Can I read them?"

"You don't want to read my poems."

"I do."

The next day, when they met after class, he said that he'd forgotten his work. He felt boyish as he said it, realizing that he was frightened of what she might think, that she would see he wasn't as good as she believed him to be, or that his poems were doomed to a drawer where they'd gather dust and where someday his daughter might stumble upon them and realize that her father once had aspirations beyond what she knew or believed.

He began to meet Eva that last week of school, and then beyond that. He told himself he had time, that he was helping to nurture a young student who seemed to need from him something he could offer—conversation, a bit of fun. It seemed to him they shared a common desire for life to be different, more than a day-in and day-out routine. They both wanted something magical, he told himself, even if that magic were fleeting. It might eventually come to an end, but he didn't want it to. The feeling it fostered in him was too grand, too wondrous.

She always dressed up, and sometimes he found himself wanting her to want him. He began to fantasize that she was, as he'd often heard the boys in class say, *that girl who didn't wear underwear, that girl who would do anything on a dare. You can fill her up like a car,* they'd say, *in and out.* All the teachers had heard the rumors. Mrs. Stiley would talk about Eva over doughnuts and coffee in the lounge, saying she was worried that a girl like that was a bad influence on the entire female student body. "One takes a turn for the worse, they all do," Mrs. Stiley said, snippily. "Have you met her mother? She's a real piece of work."

"I met her father," Peter said, recalling a parent-teacher night that had taken place in spring. Eva's father had waited in the back of the room, letting all the women who had gathered around Peter's desk go first, listening as they asked questions about next year's curriculum and their children's progress. When the mothers finally shuffled out to other rooms, Frank Kisch sat down at one of the desks in the front. "I have to get back to work by eight," he said, and it was clear he felt awkward, lumped up in the chair the way he was. "Eight-fifteen at the latest. I took a long break."

"That's fine. It shouldn't take long."

"I'm Eva's dad. Frank Kisch."

Peter looked over a sheet of paper. "Usually your wife comes, doesn't she?"

It was innocuous on his part, but Peter remembered how Eva's father had shifted uncomfortably. He couldn't judge if Frank Kisch was irritated or was simply made uneasy by his question; he imagined that the gruff man in front of him wasn't used to such conferences and perhaps had come as a favor to his wife. What he hadn't thought was that there were problems at home, or that Natalia Kisch had left the house entirely. There were too many students to keep track of, too many reasons to not press the moment beyond the peculiar lapse in dialogue. "Well, then," he said.

"Eva," Frank said. "Does she seem okay to you? Is she doing a good job in school?"

"She's fine," he assured him. "A's and B's and an occasional C. The normal stuff."

In the teachers' lounge, after discussing his interaction with Eva's father, which he also deemed normal enough, Peter thought to add, "Eva's probably just going through a stage. I wouldn't believe all the things the football team says. They're not exactly credible sources."

Mrs. Stiley tsked him, and he thought of the name students had given her—Old Ironsides. "Four sources on the football team," she said, "seems credible enough to me."

After school ended, Peter and Eva continued to meet when Amy would visit her parents, who had recently relocated to be closer to the baby. When summer classes started, he'd see Eva on his way home, sometimes meeting her at an out-of-the-way park or the usually vacant lot behind the grocery store off Main. Once, wanting to see where she lived and perhaps wanting to imagine her there, waiting for him, he picked her up from her home, though soon afterward he regretted this action. He didn't remember who had first suggested meeting after school ended. He might have said, "We could still meet if you want," knowing what would happen, but when he thought back, he preferred to remember Eva making this request. He preferred to think he was obliging her in some small way.

"I want to," she said one day, kissing him suddenly. She stepped back, waiting, and it was as if something were about to burst in her.

"Want to what?"

"You know."

"Here?" he asked. They were in his van.

"No," she said. "A bed. I'd like to have a bed."

He rented a room at a motel on the other side of town. He paid in cash to the clerk, a woman with dull blond hair who asked if he wanted an hourly rate. Although he wanted it to be perfect for Eva, the bed sagged and the room smelled of smoke. He felt an abject guilt come over him, a sense that he was beyond absolution. "We can go someplace else," he said. "Someplace nicer."

"It's fine," she told him, but then she sat on the bed for twenty minutes, deciding.

These days they usually meet in Peter's van, peace stickers half scraped from the back, feathers dangling from the mirror. The shag mobile, Eva sometimes calls it, referring to the carpet that lines the floor, walls, and star-shaped windows in the back. "You're hiding me," she told him once, after their first few romps there. He responded, "You require hiding, don't you think?"

When the dismissal bell rings, Eva waits until all the students exit and then slips into the classroom. She closes the door, flicks off the lights, and turns. She bites her lip. She walks over to where Peter stands, by his desk, threads her arms around him, and buries her head in his chest. "Finally," she says. "I've been waiting *forever.*"

His body tenses as he eases away from her. "You shouldn't be here," he says.

"I wanted to surprise you. You're not surprised?"

He hears the hurt exasperation of a child, the disappointment. Although a part of him would like to soothe her, the larger part of him sees this as a dramatic entrance, a girl's naïveté. He rubs his neck. "I am surprised," he says disapprovingly. "But we could get in a lot of trouble. That's the point; I'm not supposed to be surprised, and you're not supposed to be here. We plan these things, remember? I call, say I'm a boy from school if anyone else answers but you."

"I *know* the drill. I thought it would be good to change things up a bit. I thought you'd be happy to see me. You come over. My sister's seen you. It's not like you're invisible or anything."

"I shouldn't have done that," Peter says.

"And besides, I thought—"

Peter walks away from her. He stacks the free-writes on Donne and then sits down and folds his hands on top of the desk. He might ask what she really expected. He pulls at his shirt and thinks, irritably, that she's going to get him fired. Or worse, she will further disrupt the already frail condition of his marriage. "Thought what?"

"That you cared. That you wanted to see me."

"It's not that simple. You know that."

"No one noticed," she says. "I'll make it up to you if you're angry. What do you want?" She swings her hips a little, then leans on the desk. She traces her finger over the grain in the wood.

"This isn't a game."

She walks over to the blackboard and takes a piece of chalk. "Fine," she says. "I'll leave." On the board she writes, "I will not be seen at school anymore."

"Don't be difficult," he tells her. "Don't make things so complicated by acting like a kid."

She writes again, "I will not be seen . . ."

"Fine," he says. He throws a pencil onto his desk, gets up, and walks around. He leans back, crosses his arms. "A hundred times, then," he says. "Don't stop until you're exhausted. How's that? You want to act like a kid, I'll treat you like one."

She looks over at him, plainly hurt. Something in her face grows smaller. He isn't sure if, on Eva, that means she's remorseful or only planning an insurrection, as if she might throw the chalk at him and walk out the door, leaving him to wonder about her for weeks.

"Keep going. Don't stop." The tone in his voice unsettles him and reminds him of his own father when, as a child, Peter would do something wrong.

Eva pauses.

"I didn't say to stop." Such stern formality might be a cruel thing—*possibly it is sadistic, like Ted Bundy,* he thinks—but he is feeling cruel, he is feeling sadistic, and he is angry not only with Amy, but now with Eva as well, for coming here. He watches the movement of her skirt as she writes. Her hand presses down harder on the board, causing the chalk to shed copious amounts of dust. She postures, one leg bent, her skirt now quaking with each loop she makes. After several minutes, his anger wanes. No one has come through the door asking questions. Eva is correct—no one has noticed at all. Her handwriting is loopy, childish, and it scrawls downward on the board. Her outstretched arm holds his attention—honey-colored, the smooth layering of dark hair, small wrists, fingernails painted the color of amber. She will not condescend to turn now, nor will she speak to him, and when she ignores him so completely, he feels a boyish longing return. That day they talked in the library, didn't he feel the same way as she turned to go? Didn't he suddenly want to give Eva what a girl like her so desperately wants—to see herself through another's eyes and to find that she is precisely as she wishes but never quite believes—beautiful, full of possibility? Didn't he want, even then, to go down on her? And that day, and days after it, didn't she make him feel differently than he normally does—less cynical, more vibrant, his senses blissfully alive?

Finally, he says, "Stop."

"I'm doing what you want me to," she says. "A hundred times, until my hand gets tired."

"Eva."

She puts the chalk down and turns.

"Look," he says. "It's been a shitty day. It's not your fault." He extends his arm and she takes it, pulling back first so that he must lean forward. Then she pulls him toward her hip, as if she has been waiting to take him to herself, to feel bone against bone.

"Me, too," she says. "You have no idea what it's like at home." She places her leg around his, so that he can feel the heat from her skin.

"You always say that."

"I always mean it."

He runs his hand over her arm. "Beautiful."

"These arms?" She looks down. "They're invisible. I'm not seen at school, so these arms can't be touched." She shirks away, but now they're both playing. She edges closer a second later, takes his hand, and places it under her skirt, on her thigh.

"No," he says absently. He looks over her shoulder.

"I locked it. I'm not an idiot, you know."

"I know."

She pulls at his belt loop. "Anyway," she says, "I love these jeans. I can't believe they let you wear these jeans to school, like you're a student. I bet every girl in class likes to see you in jeans."

She unbuttons his shirt, slowly. His hand drifts from her thigh upward. He kisses her collarbone. He thinks of telling her he loves her breasts, that her breasts have quite possibly undone him, and he thinks, too, that he is glad there isn't a baby attached to her breasts, but this thought leaves him displaced, and he stops, thinking of Sophie.

"What did I do wrong now?" she says, pulling back again. Her mind races over her planned conversation, even though a part of her realizes it is futile. Her imagined conversations with people are so rarely called upon in the reality of the day.

"Nothing," he says.

And it begins like this: Another button undone, a pull at his jeans, a kiss, and him giving in to all of this, his hand threading through her hair, which he has come to think of as a mane, and his finger then traveling under the wire of her bra; and now she props herself up on the desk, and the room seems to close around him, and he is in the process of forgetting—forgetting his anger, forgetting his guilt, forgetting Amy, even forgetting for this moment and for the next several moments Sophie. Eva opens her legs. The smell of her. The cotton fold of her skirt drapes between her thighs, and he sees this and feels this, and for a moment he convinces himself that he has found true passion—and there is, in that, a beauty, and there is, in that, terror that he tries to shed, and there is behind the moment a brief, fleeting thought of Amy and a rush of emotion he chooses not to examine too closely. He tells himself that, Yes, this, here in front of him, is love—he need only grasp it, the moment, and that, Yes, love disappears only to reappear in another face, and it is this thought that both destroys and resurrects him. The saltiness of skin. The coarse hairs under his fingers, the stickiness. He is struck by a moment of possibility, that moment when something unfolds in the world.

His hand moves deeper, and there is this—a rush, a breath. She swells under his fingers.

If someone comes, he thinks, *if someone should see—*

She edges forward. Another button, a zipper. She pulls him, moves her hips slowly, draws from herself. And this is the way it continues until he, inside her now, feels her muscles tighten and release, a spasm. A rush of wetness. And then, a moment later, his own spasm, and his movements slow.

Eva puts her fingers to her lips. Embarrassed, her eyes widen. She slips off the desk, repositions her skirt and adjusts her bra. "That's never happened before."

Peter says nothing. There is a cynical thought creeping in already to ruin the moment, but then Eva laughs—a sudden burst that causes him to laugh, too. They fall into a comfortable silence.

"I don't want to leave," she tells him, finally. "I don't want to go home."

"I know," he says, zipping up his jeans, "but we can't stay in this room forever."

"If we wanted to, we could."

"Eva," he says.

"Miss me?"

He hears in her voice something that reminds him of Amy and years ago, something soft, expectant. "I already miss you," he says.

"It was perfect," she says. "Perfect timing." And she supposes it is perfect timing and that the moment continues to advance perfection. There are moments when she is left to bare-boned stillness and moments like these—filled with unexpected laughter—when Eva permits herself to dream. There are moments she eases into joy.

3

Natalia taught her girls that peril lurks just in the next room, just around every corner, in unexpected places. There was always something waiting to assail you. The girls were taught to register absence, to find the bad hiding in the good. The trick, Natalia taught, is to keep moving. The trick, according to Natalia, was to not slow down long enough to feel the hindrance of danger, or loss, or memory.

The trick, Sissy thinks, is not to be afraid, to be a daredevil in your own skin.

Twenty steps out the front door, down the sidewalk, Sissy stands for a moment. She looks right and left, to the curving row of houses and the trees that shade the street, the garbage tins already out for the next morning's collection, the flies that buzz around the trash. She catches sight of Mrs. Morris down the street, hunched over at the mailbox, watering flowers. There are playful screams down the street from Michael

Massit's house, the boy who tortured Sissy at the Brandts' picnic weeks before, calling her, to her chagrin, Mr. Ed. Across the street, the schnauzer barks. All of this should offer the comfort of familiarity, and yet, in the wake of Vicki's disappearance, in the wake of the heat, and in the absence of her mother, the entire world seems changed, irreparably harmed and damaged. Mrs. Stone's white picket fence laced with wilting ivy, the hedgerow that borders the Kisches' house, the corner riddled with trees, all might shelter a madman who is only waiting and ready to lurch out and grab Sissy when she least expects it.

This is the way the story goes: *Watch out, children. Peril lies around every corner.* This is the way the story goes now, too: a slicing motion across the neck.

Sissy doesn't know anyone who has died. The idea of death seems plainly absurd, outlandishly impossible. Sissy should never have listened to Eva's stories—hard, biting, dire to the end. Eva talking about the man who came and grabbed Vicki. She doesn't understand what being abducted entails. Being swept away in the winds, perhaps, or living in another place entirely.

She shakes her head, refuses to think about it, though thinking about it is exactly what she will do. She mounts her granny bike, which is an ugly blue bike with a worn seat. She throws her book on ghost detecting into the attached basket, remembering days when she and Vicki Anderson would ride down to the corner store for Swedish fish and ice cream. Once Sissy completed the ride while wearing Natalia's heels, an incident that later earned her a quick smack, a day alone in her room.

They were friends for more than a year, since the end of the third grade, when Vicki transferred from out of state and Mrs. Nash, Sissy's social studies teacher, announced the new girl's arrival. Vicki stood in front of everyone and gave her name and favorite hobbies, which were animals, sticker collecting, and traveling. She hoped, she said, to one day be an entertainer, moving from city to city, dazzling audiences with live performances and various acrobatic feats. Mrs. Nash placed her arm around Vicki's shoulder and squeezed gently before directing Vicki to the desk adjoining Sissy's. Pleased, clearly a soon-to-be teacher's pet, Vicki flounced down into her seat, tossed her strawberry-smelling hair over her shoulder, and sat up perfectly straight. By lunch, she was telling stories of her father to a group of attentive classmates. Her father, she said, had won a Purple Heart in the war after his chopper had been shot down in Vietnam and he'd pulled the pilot through the jungle. When she spoke, she swelled with pride. Sissy later found out that Vicki's father had taken his own life after the war had ended, a fact Vicki herself often left out of most conversations. Sissy was shocked the first time she heard this; she couldn't imagine what it was like to lose a parent. She couldn't imagine it at all.

She rides now, alone. She will not look back, or dwell on what might lie around the corner. She will not be afraid. She comforts herself, imagines words flashing in her mind:

SISSY KISCH
World-Famous Ghost Detective!

Then she amends:

SISSY KISCH
*World-Famous Ghost Detective
with her sidekick, Scooby-Doo!*

She imagines Scooby-Doo sitting in the basket, coating it with drool every time he tries to communicate, because, as Natalia often said, he never learned to enunciate. Sissy has a vague belief that nothing is permitted to happen to a heroine, and that surely nothing bad has ever happened to Scooby-Doo. Still, she doubts, holding in mind a reservation that children often have when they are of two minds and worlds: that which is real, and that which is imaginary. How that line for a nine-year-old, in any day, blurs. Not everything is so pleasant, not every harm is kept away. Just a year ago, on their way home from the park, a squat-looking man approached her and Vicki, and then followed them in his car, and the girls hid behind bushes while he circled the block.

When he first approached them, he exposed the hard flesh of his penis. "My God," Vicki said later, and laughed nervously. "Did you *see* that?"

Sissy hadn't. She had kept her eyes closed. She lied and nodded. "That was wild."

If Vicki were here now, Sissy might pretend to be brave, and in pretending, she might find her bravery. If Vicki were here, Sissy would have no choice but to be brave.

There is still the task, the truly awful task, of making her way past the hedges, past the fence, to the park. And yet she is compelled. She is compelled and she is bored and she is lonely, and the house, the empty house, is unbearable, worse than the torture of the outside world. She holds her breath and counts to ten, but it doesn't rid her limbs of their shakiness, or her mind of its worry. If she pedals, if she rides hard, she will not die, and if she does not meet the face of a murderer, she will not be killed, and if she does not come across any bad thing lurking in dark places, she will not disappear. She breezes past the hedges, past the fence. She closes her eyes and reminds herself there are no such things as lunatic madmen or bogeymen, or Gypsies who steal children away.

And yet, she believes in all these things.

This is the way the story goes: peril, at every corner.

She barrels down the hill to the park, follows familiar paths, and does not turn when Milly Morris calls out to ask her what's she doing, and where Eva is, again. She pedals until her mouth is dry from the heat and flat air. At the park, she abandons her bike. She walks across the baseball field toward the woods, and at the place where the tree stands with its low branches spread wide like arms, she takes the secret path—wide enough for a single-file line, worn from trampling feet, each side riddled with bramble and packed with mosquitoes that nip and suck on flesh. A sting, a bite. One, two, three. A swat at her ankles, her knees. A welt. She hears the wild hum of cicadas, already dying. Gnats dart back and forth. Sissy trails toward the creek until the woods open up. She walks to the water hole that, over the years, was dammed by those who told and told others, those who lugged sandbag after sandbag across the muddy banks. Ivy covers the grounds. Moss grows around the base of old trees. Here, the ground is moist and cool. Water bugs race across the stilled water.

Sissy searches, hunting for clues—a bundle of sticks tied with a ribbon; a piece of bubble gum; a message written hastily in the mud; a vine that tightens around the base of a tree trunk, possibly signaling a knot, a noose. She performs a ritual, snapping off a branch, sticking it in the mud, to bring back what is missing. She waits. Across the river, under the trees, ferns slope up and form a natural barrier. She looks around. There is no one. If Vicki came here, she might have swum across the creek. She might have passed over the lacy plants and climbed up the banks, intent simply on running away from everything that bothered her.

Sissy breaks another branch, sticks it in the mud. The gloominess of the task, the possible peril and injury, consume her, and soon an hour has passed, and what Sissy wants to find, she does: a broken twig that might have been used to ward off threat, a place where rocks seem to form an arrow, moss that may hold an imprint of a hand, a stone shaped like a heart. She notes all these things. She picks up another stone, curls her index finger around it for luck, and then skips it across the water while the sun sinks deeper in the sky. She imagines the stones are Vicki, skipping across the water. She imagines the other side of the bank is another, secret world.

She does not know when, exactly, she first hears laughter. Possibly seconds after skipping the first stone, maybe minutes. She freezes, stone in hand. On the other side of the creek, at the place where large limestone juts from the ground and a thick tree branch extends over the water, she sees Vicki just as she imagined her, her bedraggled hair crowned with flowers. "I didn't really believe you're dead," Sissy calls out. "I knew I could find you." Watching her, Sissy can hardly contain her heart, its joyful leaping. Before she can think that she will be famous for her detective skills, and that she will win if not the love of her mother then the love and adoration of Vicki's mother, all while Vicki is chastised for running away and sent to her room for a month without dinner, before she can think any of this, she blurts out, "People are worried about you, you know. You can't just leave like that."

Vicki says nothing. She bends down and inspects the water, then wades in, disappearing below the surface, a flower floating first in a circle before winding down with the current.

It is a game of play, a game of magic. Sissy calls out again and waits. She pulls off her sneakers and socks, the cool water pooling around her. Her feet sink into the mud. Instinctively, she kneads her toes. She moves gradually, until her shorts and shirt take in water, until it seems that water is all around her, and that it has always been that way, so much so that water drinks her up and gathers her in.

She sees her face in the water—her long cheeks, her hair that is pulled back in a ponytail. She sticks her tongue out at herself, scrunches her face. Ugly, perhaps a bit of a horse-face. She squints, trying to see below to where Vicki is hiding. Above her the clouds have grown wispy, the sky a shade darker. Her feet lose the ground and she swims. She goes under once, quickly, and reemerges. She spits out water. She pulls in a deep breath of air, holds it, and submerges herself into the murky depths, the pool of diffuse light around her. She imagines the water is not four feet deep but bottomless and ancient. Her task is simple: to find an old friend. So much can happen in an hour, a moment. She adjusts, refocuses, moves deeper.

There, at the bottom of the swimming hole, she sees a canopy the color of swirled peppermint, and animals: horses with black marble eyes, dark as night, their manes a cool gray, some spotted with flecks of white, and others with cream-colored bodies, all attached to opalescent poles. They rise and fall. She remembers a story her mother told her once, of a magical carousel that protected children. And there is Vicki, having taken up residence in a chariot pulled by lions. Vicki laughs, breathes in water, and in the moment, all of this is real, and all of this comforts Sissy.

If she strains, Sissy can almost hear a dreamy pulse, a melodic rhythm of pipes, a surge of music and the whirl of a hollow pulse. Everything is in motion. One of the lions turns his head toward Sissy and roars. She expels a short breath, holds back air again. She feels her chest tighten and swims upward, toward the light, toward the waiting air, to cut through the surface of water and into the world again.

No one would believe such a story, not even Natalia with her tales of ghost children and caravans and Gypsy camps. At the age of nine, what Sissy Kisch already senses—what she already knows—is that most people are lonely and that when they are lonely, they are prone to make up a story. What might Sissy say—really—if asked? That Vicki lives, protected, at the bottom of a watery hole, that she is fine and well there, in that place of waiting? That nothing can harm her? That she is protected by animals and loved?

People would laugh at her. They would send her to the loony bin. Still, she might insist, no one disappears without any trace. There are always clues. There is always a story.

No one leaves forever.

Later, Sissy lies in bed, distressed by the almost-quiet, the fingers of women tapping on her window. She is not unaware of the larger world around her. *Tap, tap, tap.* In the smallest recesses of her mind, in the tiniest crack in her heart, Sissy believes the events of the day to be true—Vicki, the lions, the horses. She bites her nails, though it doesn't do her any good because they are already a knobby mess of flesh and tortured cuticles. She is so engrossed in thinking about Vicki, in thinking about an underwater world, that she fails to notice the moon that brightens the room.

Just after ten—an hour to spare before their father comes home— Sissy hears Eva climb the stairs and quietly shut the door. Sissy lets go a series of frantic knocks through the wall, and she is more than grateful when Eva knocks back and says that yes, it's okay to come over.

Blue light drenches Eva's bed. Eva lifts the sheets and lets Sissy settle in next to her. "Hey, bugaboo," she says lazily. She still feels the wave of a dreamy high, the sweet musicality of the day. After Peter, she spent the evening with Greg, getting high in his bedroom, laughing about the Mafia girls but saying nothing—nothing at all—about Peter and saying nothing about all that has bothered her in the past months.

"Nightmare?"

Sissy shrugs, and Eva draws her closer, letting Sissy form her body to the shape of a spoon against her long frame. She covers them up. "We could live under here," she says, musing.

"After a while we'd suffocate," Sissy tells her.

"Maybe." She puts her chin on Sissy's head, notices that her hair is damp and smells vaguely of leaves and mud.

Eva will not ask. She will not encroach on Sissy's time alone any more than she wishes anyone to encroach on her time, on her meeting with Peter, even more perfect now that it has slipped into memory. Let Sissy have her secrets, Eva decides. She is sleepy, she is tired, and she can and will ease into dreams.

"Eva."

"What?"

Sissy tries to form the words for the day, for all she hopes for and all she questions. She wonders if Eva believes in heaven, or God, or if there is another place people go to, another world just out of reach where they watch, wanting to be remembered. She threads Eva's arms around her instead. Finally, she says, "Never mind."

"Go to sleep, Sissy," Eva says, yawning.

"Tell me a story first."

"I don't know any," Eva says.

"Try."

Eva thinks for a while. "When you were little, I used to carry you around and pretend you were mine. I'd sing to you."

"That's not a story," Sissy whispers. "That's just something you remember."

"Once when you were a baby, I dropped you."

"Really?" Sissy turns.

"You landed on the carpet but you didn't cry."

Sissy pulls the covers closer and thinks about this. "Knowing myself," she says, "I have a hard time believing that."

"Well, you didn't cry," Eva says, nearly drifting off to sleep. "You didn't cry at all—you laughed, actually. It wasn't the end of the world."

4

As so often happens, each of the girls, as well as Natalia, would remember the incidents around Natalia's leaving differently, and they would conjure their memories in the days and months afterward but would never compare, never use the other's recollections to temper the emotions. Eva would think about events despite not wanting to, always with a feeling of dread that first left her numb and then turned to anger. For her, the entire exchange was brief, fleeting, and reminded her, as did the incident after Christmas, of how quickly things could change. That day, snow fell earlier than expected, a snow that would, over the days before Christmas, shut down businesses and blanket the town and gradually recede into ice. If the record shop where Eva worked part-time hadn't closed early, if elderly Mr. Matthews, her supervisor, hadn't been worried about Eva driving home, she might have missed Natalia's departure entirely. Once home she was quick to assess the situation: the open bags, her mother's plane tickets to New York City on the table. She'd known of the doctor as the elderly man who'd hired her mother the year before, a man with a dry sense of humor and a love of sailing. Her mother had spoken of him not with fondness but with simple gratitude. Everything seemed to fall into focus: the late days at work, the low-cut dresses. It was last minute, Natalia told her, not bothering to look at her daughter directly as Eva stood on the other side of the bed, dumbstruck. When Eva's demands for an explanation turned into frantic pleading, when her mother denied Eva the possibility of going, too, Eva felt as if her world were suddenly fracturing. This grew more pronounced with each blouse Natalia pulled from the closet and with each pair of high-heeled shoes she placed on the bed. Even the worn, brocaded suitcase lying open on its hinges seemed to indicate that things were resolutely over, the dissolution of marriage inevitable, the loss of a mother absolute. Eva might have forgiven her mother for leaving her father. Her father, everyone knew, wasn't an easy man. He was prone to stoic silences, outbursts of anger. He was complicated by the sheer fact that you might never know what he was thinking, and yet he always had expectations for the girls, for Natalia. Leaving her father, Eva might have understood. But that Natalia wasn't taking the girls—that she could be that sort of woman—was something Eva couldn't fathom. There had been fights, of course, made worse by her mother's return to work and her father's complaints that the children, particularly Eva, needed more guidance, less leeway and freedom.

If the truth were known, Natalia herself felt that, in just over twenty years of marriage, she had taken care of others so well that she had no space for herself anymore, no sense of what she might have wanted if asked or given the simple opportunity. Natalia might have said that she caught sight of herself one day—her face longer, the network of lines, the downward turn of her lips—and that she didn't know where the time had gone to. This realization produced in her an inexplicable irritability with Frank, with the girls. A feeling that everything was wrong often came over Natalia, a need to run ahead and leave everything behind her.

"It's not you," Natalia managed to say, though in that moment she felt as though saying anything might cause her to change her mind and stay. She stopped, realizing her error: Eva stood, red-faced, the skin over her chest suddenly blotchy, a desperate look shadowing her normally smooth face.

"It is, isn't it?" Eva asked. "Because you fight about me?"

"No," Natalia said again. "You're too young to understand what it's like to lose things." She knew that whatever she might try to frame with words would fail and be subjected to Eva's scrutiny. Her older daughter, like her youngest, was versed in scrutiny. She loved them both, but Natalia had to admit that she often felt burdened by the girls, too, by their needs and problems, their worries and fevers, their desire to be at the center of everything, and by their questions—why a beloved fish had to die, why God would let that happen, why someone might leave. Because, she'd say, things die. Because God lets everything in the world happen, bad and good. Because God's eye wanders like a Gypsy, and bad things pass by. Because that's the way life is.

Children only ever wanted more. They had no sense of mercy. They had no need for it.

There was never a good way to say "I'm leaving," never a way to make it not hurt. She opened her mouth, but no words came out. In that moment, she remembered a day long before, when she had been only a child and new to the country. That woman who was still a stranger—her new mother—had made Natalia stand onstage and repeat words she'd learned from *Hansel and Gretel,* words coated in such a thick accent no one listening could understand. Natalia, only eight or nine, stood still when the lights came on, thinking first not of English or German but Hungarian—"*Az erdö mélyén élt egy szegény fávagó, a feleségével és két gyermekével.*" "Hard by a great forest dwelt a poor woodcutter with his wife and two children." She fell silent. The performance was a spectacle. Such a spectacle, as if the world were turned suddenly upside down. Crying, she'd marched offstage, away from the lights and people.

It was like that with Eva, too. An awkward silence, a terrible dread. There was nothing she could translate—no emotion, no truth. To compensate, and because she hated silence, and because Eva, on the other side of the bed, was already indignant, Natalia said, "Make your own choices; at least you can try to do that in life, whether people understand or not. At least the choices are yours."

Eva said nothing.

There is always more to say, Natalia thought. *Always those things that can never be said.* If she told Eva she loved her, would it ever convey what she needed it to, fully? "I'll write," she said instead.

"That's great," Eva said, wiping snot from her nose. "You'll write."

"I will."

"What about Sissy?"

Natalia concentrated on the shirt she held, the slippery texture, the creamy sheen. She indulged the thought of turning over the suitcase and letting all the clothing fall to the bed and ground. "Sissy? She's with Mrs. Morris."

"That's not what I mean." Eva crossed her arms. "It's almost Christmas."

"She'll be fine," Natalia said, though she was no longer certain of anything. "She has you."

"And what about me?"

"You and Sissy have each other. And your father—"

"You don't even care."

"I feel shame when I look at myself," Natalia said suddenly. She looked up. "But I've never been the type of person to cry and sob and scream, if that's what you want. You can't know a person and know what's inside them. A person's heart doesn't shed itself like a tree in winter; it doesn't bare itself just because you want it to."

It was true, after all. It wasn't that Natalia didn't feel pain at the thought of leaving. For days she had turned in sleep and felt her stomach grow sick with worry. For days, her chest had grown tight, constricted, every time the girls or Frank was in the room. It wasn't that she didn't feel the terrible wrenching away from her own life, the prying away from family like one pulls away skin.

The moments dripped. Natalia zipped the suitcase.

"You lie," Eva said finally. "You don't feel anything, not even shame."

With that, Natalia felt her resolve take hold. "A few months, and I'll send for you and Sissy. I'll get you both."

But Eva turned her head, and Natalia knew that she'd never be forgiven.

If with Eva it was a full-blown argument, then, earlier in the day with Sissy it had felt subversive and deceptive, simply by virtue of age, a task made easier by lies and stories. With Sissy, Natalia acted as if everything were normal, that the day were just like any other—the two of them in the kitchen, the afternoon sun invisible behind clouds. Frank was at work, as was Eva. Sissy prattled on, happy for Christmas break, happy for the reprieve of getting picked last for basketball in gym, while Vicki Anderson got picked for captain. She was eager for snowballs and the cold on her tongue.

Sissy noticed but ignored how her mother often looked over from the sink, watching her as she sat at the table, peeling off the crusts of her sandwich. If Sissy noticed her mother was dressed up on her day off—slacks and a creamy cowl-neck sweater, hair up, a pin above her right breast: gilded holly leaves with red-beaded berries—she didn't seem to think it odd. Down the hall from her, in the living room, the plastic tree was shored up against the bay window, the lights on since nine in the morning, the silver tinsel draped over the long branches, the trinkets, made by both girls, hanging from wires—cutouts of children, little bells, beaded and sequined balls—the pointed, severe-looking star crowning the top of the tree.

Natalia couldn't bear to think of the holiday, and so did not think of it at all. She had tried, earlier, to read the bottom of her cup, but she saw only a mess of garbled tea leaves and nothing more. The house was clean, at least, short of the dishes, which tired her to look at, for it seemed life was an endless succession of small tasks, a repetition of simple rituals.

"I'll tell you a secret," Natalia said. She sat down at the table, searching for the similarities between them, the lines of recognition, the lilt of the brow. She leaned in. "Are you ready to hear something shameful?"

Sissy beamed. How she longed for access into the adult world, into the hushed conversations and suppressed laughter of women and men, into their secretive languages that unfolded over drinks and games of pinochle and Parcheesi. How often Sissy tried to sneak into the room, to pass unnoticed. How often she lingered at the top of stairs when there were arguments about Eva. Was it possible that her mother was finally willing to grant her entry to this world? Was it possible that, in sharing, she would learn some terrible secret, something *shameful*? Her heart delighted. She sat up straighter and scrunched her nose, anticipating. "A secret, really?"

"A secret." Natalia whispered, "Your father can't touch his toes." She leaned back in her chair and drummed her hands on the table.

"That's it? That's the secret?"

"That's it. I said it; it's true. Your father, Sissy, is too fat." It was a cruel remark, but she was still feeling cruel, remembering that the night before Frank had told her, plainly when she'd asked, that yes, she was looking older by a good measure, weren't they all. She had told him that if she were old, at least she wasn't fat. "What do you want?" she'd asked bitterly. "For me to be a girl again, like that, poof, magic?"

Sissy took on a look of disappointment. Did it matter if her father could touch his toes or not, or if he loved butter too much? She didn't care particularly what time did to bodies. Unlike Natalia, she never thought how time increased the burdens of some and lightened those of others so that, as they walked down the street, some seemed tethered to the ground while others, conversely, seemed to float and drift apart from everything, like leaves, like feathers. To Sissy, her father was normal enough—a stomach, yes, but flesh that seemed lived in and worn, like a favorite chair. *Does it matter that he might be fat?* Sissy wondered.

Judging from the seriousness that marked her mother's face, she concluded it did matter and that, in fact, it was of grave importance. She responded plainly: "I can touch my toes. Want to see?"

"I'll take your word," Natalia said. "Sometimes I think your father has never been happy and that's why he can't touch his toes. When you're not happy, your body crunches up on you." She sat up straighter and breathed deeply. "You see? I'm crunchy, too, these days, but at least I can touch my toes."

Sissy stretched her legs absentmindedly under the table. She kinked her head.

"You're nimble. You could probably run a marathon."

"When I run in gym," Sissy said, "I get cramps."

"Well, if ever that happens again, try some vegetable juice. It might help."

"We could give some juice to Dad," Sissy said.

"It's not the same thing." She got up and returned to the sink. She took a dishcloth from the wicker basket on the counter and looked out the kitchen window to the backyard. A light snow fell, mottling the ground, and coating the tops of the metal fence. The sky was gray. By late evening, temperatures would slide below freezing and whatever moisture the sky still held would turn icy, pelting the skin of those unfortunate enough to be outside. Natalia would be delayed at the airport, arrive a day late, though no one in the Kisch family would know this.

"Do you think I look old?" Natalia asked without turning. "Ponce de León thought there was a cure for aging, but for men that only means a younger woman. There's no good juice for stripping away time."

"No," Sissy said. "You don't look old."

Natalia looked up and, seeing her daughter's expression, she stopped. Maybe Sissy was thinking, Natalia reasoned, of that woman years ago in Atlantic City, that short blonde with the nice smile, how Frank sat on the beach and talked with her while Natalia and Sissy bobbed in the ocean, the day ablaze with children and activity. She suddenly felt ashamed again. That was only a flirtation, wasn't it? She was the one who was leaving with the doctor, not Frank leaving her for some girl. "It doesn't matter, anyway," she said.

"Are you okay, Mom?"

"I'm okay," she said. "I'm fine." The dishes sat in front of her, waiting, as they always did. She thought perhaps she would make a pie if there was time, though after their recent argument, a pie seemed like an insult to Frank's waistline, and, after all, maybe it was. She had an old thought of hunger and need: how she came to this very country, to this very region, without any choice to do so, and how after a time, in high school, she met Frank and life gradually seeded itself, without her ever seeming to make a definitive choice, one way or the other. It was peculiar to Natalia how much of life was thrown upon us: lucky or unlucky.

She mulled over her plan to meet the doctor, Ronald Finley. It was only a week before that he'd come up behind her as she was filing away his papers. He laced his arms around her waist. They'd been seeing each other for two months, since his divorce had been finalized, and he told her that he needed a change of scenery and was going on holiday for six months, to Italy. He said, "Come with me."

"I can't," she said. "You know I can't."

He held her tighter, and she could smell the lemony aftershave he wore that day. "I don't ascribe to *can't*. Not for me, or you. You're an exquisitely beautiful woman," he said, kissing her neck. "Your bone structure is lovely."

Natalia couldn't think of a time she'd ever been called *lovely*. In her youth, she had been awkward and a bit harder than she'd wished with people, difficult to know. She had been self-conscious of her looks, of the thin line around her neck that she often covered with scarves, a line that now, after years, looked only like a trapping of her age—a wrinkle. Dr. Finley had walked into his office then and returned with a gift of winter pears set in perfect rows, three by three in a wooden box, each pear wrapped in green tinfoil that was so festive she could not help but be delighted. But there was the small thought that nettled her—that Ronald Finley, unlike Frank, did not yet know that she hated pears, their gritty sweetness. She would have preferred green apples, freshly picked and stolen from the farmer's orchard, juicy and bitter on the tongue, sweeter, though, for all the sneaking around and laughter.

She watched now as the flakes fell outside the window. She washed a dish, ignoring the numbness that set into her hands from the hot water. "My mind today," she said. "It wants to jump from thing to thing, Sissy. It must be the snow."

"Why the snow?" Sissy asked.

"What?"

"Why the snow?"

"I don't know," she said. "Just because." She ran a sponge over the plate, rinsed it, and set it into the drying rack. "I could tell you a story if you want," she said.

Sissy's eyes lit up, not only in anticipation of the story itself but also of the changes that she knew would assail her mother's face as she spoke—the way her lips would turn downward when the story became grim, the way her eyes would widen when something surprising unfolded, the exaggerated movements of her hands when a detail struck her as amusing, or times when she was made so angry by her own tales that she'd let go a barrage of lamentations and curses spoken in another language. *(Tolvaj! Megállj! A fenébe!)* When her mother told a story, her face became transparent, mutable, and subject to fanciful twists of emotion. There were so many stories given to Sissy and Eva over the years: the campfires that kept the darkness at bay and burned down to cinders in the morning; travels through the barren countryside, made in intricately carved caravans with stained-glass windows. *Many Gypsies,* she once said, *were kings, their fingers adorned with rings, their voices filled with laughter.* In the telling, the caravans grew majestic, as stately as the mountains behind them, golden harps crowning them like jewels. There were stories of traded horses, stories of bears that could dance on their hind legs, chains of bells around their necks. There were tales of women who married men that turned magically into animals—a wolf, a crow, and once even a rooster. There were charms, conjurations. *(Fever go away!)* Spells against toothaches. A coin for luck. A stone to worry in your pocket. A reading of cards. A song for the dead. A wish that everything precious be given back to you. Stories of Budapest, stories of Hungary, stories remembered from Natalia's mother that Natalia passed to Eva. And then, when Eva no longer cared to hear the stories, when she was busy dating and picking out outfits and buying records, Natalia told Sissy the stories instead. They were all she remembered of her life back then, in that place, all she remembered of her *kompánia,* her family. They were, truth be told, only bits and fragments that, over time, she added to, letting her imagination fill in the holes. She had no stories from her adopted German mother. The woman was fastidious with numbers.

As it often happened when trying to recall her mother's stories, Sissy would later massacre the tales told to her. The specificity of detail and the ordering of events were ruined. It was like stars blurring into one vast woven blanket. In imagining a hillside Sissy might feel the dirt crumble in her fingers and grind under her nails, or the dancing bear might be transformed into a man searching for his lost family.

A harp. A cymbal. A violin.

There was always music.

"Okay," Natalia said, her face changing. "Let me think of one."

Sissy waited.

Maybe it was the snow, the feeling of her mind wandering, moving backward and forward and backward again, further, to more unreachable places. She tried to push the thought away, but it was there, suddenly, as fresh as the day itself. "Sometimes in life," Natalia began, "you breathe even when you don't want to. Sometimes in life, you take in the bad along with the good and rub them together until something, however small, shines."

Sissy nodded, and Natalia grew annoyed with her daughter. "Don't nod if you don't really know." She glanced up at the clock above the door frame, calculated the amount of time it would take to usher Sissy off to Milly's house and finish packing. She turned her attention back to Sissy.

"I'm telling you this story not so much for now but for when you're older. Do you forget the things I tell you?"

"No," Sissy said. "I never forget anything."

"You forget all the time," Natalia said, almost tenderly. "I tell you to clean your room and listen to your father, and you act like you don't hear me. I tell you to be nice to your sister and to try to be kind and to not be so frightened, and you don't listen at all."

"I do," Sissy insisted. "I don't forget."

"Well," Natalia continued, "this story takes place in 1944, when Gypsies lived in a camp outside Kraków."

The name Kraków sounded foreign to Sissy, silly like the word "cracker." She could not picture a Kraków in her mind and so called upon the thing she could picture instead, another camp, Camp Paupac, where she sometimes spent a week in the summer. "Like Camp Paupac?" Sissy inquired, happy to think that she might be someone who understood things her mother spoke of without question.

Natalia considered this, then she shrugged finally, already tired. "You can imagine Camp Paupac if it helps you see things. Only imagine it gray and dry, at times bitterly cold with never enough food and clean water unless you ate the snow before it started to smell funny. When I was a girl—a little younger than you—I lived there. I don't think of it often. It wasn't a very nice place."

Sissy closed her eyes and imagined Camp Paupac with its tranquil skies and hemlocks, its tethered boats undulating on the glassy lake, its cookouts with burgers and franks, the smokiness that often stung her eyes. She thought immediately of quests for frogs and fireflies through the woods, down the paths that smelled of dirt, of traps laid to ensnare unsuspecting raccoons or to douse bears with pepper. Then, in her mind's eye, she painted the entire scene gray. She drained the lakes as one might a swimming pool at the close of summer. She pulled out the bits of color from the grass, but color kept seeping through, and soon she saw only a sky the color of a robin's egg, damp grass that glistened like jewels, and so much water.

"You see, yes?"

"Yes."

"In camp the children, they were ghost children, really—very thin. Sometimes they were so thin they would disappear entirely, and you would look for them but they were gone. That's how we lived there, waiting to wake up and find that someone we loved was gone. We all waited. It didn't seem to matter how many medallions were buried, how many chants were said, how much ground was spit upon—waiting only meant the end of time. So we'd tell stories instead of waiting. The children would say, 'Ah, you need shoes? You want leather shoes, tooled and polished? Here!' We would stomp around in our shoes until they were dusty and covered in ash. We would polish them with a make-believe brush. We would tie and untie the laces of the shoes. We would unthread the laces and turn them into moths that flew around us, unexpected, magical. A hundred, a thousand moths flittering around the camp, you see? We wished we could be moths, floating atop the metal wires. We said, 'You're hungry? Here is bread!' We brought bread to our mothers and fathers, bread that was as light as the air. Once, though this was nothing we even wished for, there was a merry-go-round in our camp, a gift from soldiers. This is true. Our mothers fussed so much. They complained that the children had nothing. I rode a donkey. The other children rode bears and lions. The soldiers lifted some of us and carried us around, dancing in circles. There was real laughter that day."

She stopped momentarily. She pushed away the memory of rumors that were whispered ear to ear, the snicker from one soldier who allowed the merry-go-round to be erected—rumors of bodies floating in vats of water, occasional screams from buildings, the impending massacre of the Gypsy camp, the worried looks that sometimes assaulted the guards, those who smuggled food into camp out of a last bit of kindness and hope.

"A merry-go-round?" Sissy asked.

"It was magical. One day in a thousand." Natalia looked at the clock. The faucet dripped. She could not tell Sissy the rest of the story:

that within a month of that day, the women and men and children would all be gone. Her mother. Her father. Her younger brother. Killed, all of them. And gone with her mother and her father were the memories of them, their stories. Sometimes she told herself it didn't matter, to be stripped so suddenly of your history. Gypsies had such little historical memory anyway: only that of the eldest among them, and those remembered by them. They didn't even have a creation story. It was as if the world had always been there, and they had always been in it, turning across generations, cursed to wander, cursed to forget.

In life, if anyone survived, it was luck. If anyone found a loved one after losing them, it was luck. If anyone found a way home, it was luck. Her escape, too, was luck. In camp, in order to live (or to be promised life), family members were often made to hang one another, mothers hanging children, brothers hanging brothers. Natalia thought of her Gypsy mother's round, grieving face, and her father with his thick hair and mustache, how he yelled and screamed at the guards and pushed forward. If you screamed, you were shot. If you moved when you weren't supposed to move, the guns would fire. And there was blood—a pool of blood on the ground—and then it was the guard who, before Natalia could take any of that in, put a rope around her and pulled. A burn. A flash of blackness. And, sometime later, movement beneath her—the wheels of a cart hitting stones, the uneven holes in the ground bouncing her awake. And that long-ago day was in the present again, suddenly—the twitching of fingers, the rolling of eyes, a gray blur of sky and ash—Why is there always ash? It falls like snow but is graceless, without any hope—and then there is a moment of being aware of men and women under her, and children as young as she, and younger, staring blankly, watching without seeing, their faces twisted in pain, and it is that man again, that skinny man with the shovel, the tired man with the look of a bird, and he takes pity on her for having died once in the day. And then he gathers her in a blanket and smuggles her out into the night, through the woods, past the barking dogs, the *kutya,* to the blare of headlights and the German couple, childless. But the bird man; she will never see him again except in memory, where she will always see him, this bird man with his big German nose, who tells her, "You will not die twice today." Or perhaps he says, "You have done enough dying for a lifetime." Natalia didn't know German very well at the time.

What she knew was that sometimes things and people lived despite the world not wanting them—dianthus that managed to root in the gutter of their house; a dog crawling off to the side of the road after being hit by a car; a man searching through trash cans for food; a child who, despite not being yearned for, grew in her belly and brought with her a sense of surprise—and what Natalia knew was that people did what they had to, to get by, and that in the face of death there was so often a brute defiance, that most would give anything—absolutely anything—for a few more moments of life.

She once rode a donkey.

She once had a noose around her neck.

She died once—at least—and found her life again.

And, after recalling this, Natalia took in a sharp, involuntary breath.

She felt, in response, a pull on her sweater and looked down to see Sissy's fingers—the shape of them squarer than hers, the child who was destined to have her father's body. "Mom," Sissy said again. "What's wrong?"

"Nothing," Natalia said, recomposing herself. "The dishes. They need to be done even if no one wants to do them." She started in again on the breakfast plates. Without turning, she said, "The thing about stories is how one leads to another. How about you tell me a story instead. You tell me a story you remember, while I wash and dry."

Sissy finished eating her sandwich and thought on things her mother had said, stories her mother had told. But it happened—as it so often did—that Sissy could not call upon a single story when under the pressure of request. Even her mother's stories would never be her own. After a few moments her mother turned, and seeing the thin impatience she wore, Sissy's face scrunched up more. She gnawed the inside of her cheek until she tasted coppery blood and until her mother, noticing, said, "Jesus, Sissy, don't be a cannibal. I only asked for a story, not blood."

"I don't know any."

Natalia's lips went straight. There was a fleeting moment when she was assailed by the thought that if she left, the stories, too, would leave, and eventually there would be nothing left of her in this house at all. "What do you mean, you don't know any stories? None? I must have told you hundreds, thousands of stories. Don't tell me you don't know. Don't tell me you watch so much television your brain is a turnip."

Sissy tried, beginning a familiar refrain and giving in to the moment to inspire her, to open her mouth and pour out a story—one uncomplicated and fluid—and yet, with her mother standing there, dishrag still in hand, her face expectant, time seemed to eke by, and there was, in the place of a story, silence. She began again. She told her mother something she would later forget.

Natalia listened until Sissy finished. She rinsed a dish, set it in the rack. She squeezed the rag. She checked the clock again. "It's time to get ready to go to Milly's. A few hours, maybe more."

"That's too long."

"Time's relative," Natalia said. "And besides, it wasn't a request."

"She smells like VapoRub. She has a stuffed cat in her living room that's a hundred years old and a *fish* hanging on her shed." She made a face. "She and Mr. Morris kiss *all the time.*"

"They're happy," Natalia said, shrugging. "Mr. Morris plays with you. I saw him pull a quarter from your ear."

"He's crazy," Sissy said, but she smiled thinking about Mr. Morris and how kind he was.

"It's settled, then."

Sissy sat up straighter, kinked her neck again, remembered to enunciate. She said, "No, it's not settled. I *would rather* not go. I *would rather* be with you instead. I don't want to be alone."

"You won't be alone. You'll be with Mr. and Mrs. Morris."

"Same thing," Sissy said. "Mostly. Mr. Morris will probably be out playing golf with his friends. I'll be alone."

Natalia came over to where Sissy sat and bent down, and Sissy noticed her mother had plucked her eyebrows so thin that they looked like line drawings. She smelled that day of spice, a hint of vanilla. She pushed her hair back over her shoulder. "I love you. I love Eva, too, and your father. But the truth is, Sissy, you should never imagine a life where you couldn't bear being alone. Eventually, we're all alone. It happens to everyone at some point, whether we want it to or not."

5

Sunday is Frank Kisch's day off, and the morning is his favorite time. It is the stillness of morning that most agrees with him—its utter and succinct compliance before things set to spinning kinesthetic motion. Soon the girls will rise and take to bickering over who will wash and who will dry the breakfast dishes, Sissy on a stool smashing the sudsy water with her hands, tormenting Eva, who stands next to her, grousing about getting wet, sometimes even going so far as to push Sissy from her stool. Their arguing manages always to escalate to the point where Frank himself must intervene in a crashing crescendo—there is no one else to keep them in line, though he wishes Eva would be more mature and accept responsibility around the house and with Sissy. And then the girls will take to a stony silence, and Frank will yell more, even when he does not wish to. At forty-two, he is a bulk of a man—thick black hair, long sideburns, a strong body, broad nose and forehead, his eyes coppery like new oil. His voice booms when he's angry, suddenly charging

the air and frightening both his girls, frightening even himself sometimes, reminding himself of his own father, which is almost the last
thing he wishes to be reminded of at all. Beyond the girls, beyond the
house, people know him to be dependable, the person to call when the
car light goes on, or when the water heater fails to climb to the necessary temperature. He is liked well enough, perhaps more liked than Natalia, for it seems that neighbors might forgive a man with a temper but
not forgive a woman who refuses to gossip. "People," Natalia once said
after she tried her first potluck and Parcheesi dinner, "drain you with
questions. Did you hear that woman, Stacy, ask why we didn't keep trying until we had a boy? What right did she have to say that, with two
boys of her own?"

"She didn't mean it the way you took it," he told her. "And all people want is friendship." He was surprised when she huffed irritably in
response.

He doesn't know what anyone wants, really. He never did understand what Natalia wanted, or the girls.

When he yells, Eva will not look at him, and he feels her accusations, along with his regret. The girls hush themselves midsentence
when he walks into the room and then resume where they left off when
he leaves. In the Kisch house, it often seems there is a battle of wills, a
constant tension. When there should be order and obedience, a proper
show of respect, there is chaos. Now, since Natalia has been gone, this is
especially true. He looks at his girls—Eva, who is so much like a
woman, and Sissy, who is so flighty—and they each seem to require a
delicacy he lacks. When he cannot think of what to say, when they stare
at him blankly, he goes outside and works on the grass, or on his car, a
beautifully restored Chevy.

Sitting in silence outside on his front steps in the early-morning
hours is Frank Kisch's church and religion. A quiet hum settles on the
tree branches and rooftops and electrical wires.

This Sunday, though, when he steps outside to the glare and
warmth of the summer morning, he finds Ginny Anderson sitting on

the steps, three used cigarettes already at her sandaled feet, pressed against the sidewalk.

"Ginny," he says, still holding open the screen door. He sips his coffee, waits for her to turn, but she only stumps out another butt and exhales. Out earlier than usual, the dog across the street barks, perhaps at him. "How are you? I was worried."

"I know you called," she says, turning. "I'm sorry."

"You have a lot on your mind." He sees the lines of worry, her normally fine hair unwashed, her eyes bloodshot from lack of sleep, or booze, or both. Still, he wishes he might do something for her, ease her burden in some way, as she did his in the months of Natalia's absence, telling him that it would be okay, that she'd come back because people do come back, because sometimes people regret things and change.

"I had to get out of the house," she says.

"I'm glad you came."

She turns away then, looks across the street. "Yappy dog," she says.

"The yappiest."

"I figured you'd be up already."

"I've been up. You should have knocked."

"It was early. It's still early. I didn't want to wake you."

"You didn't wake me," he says.

She doesn't look at him again, though he wishes she would. He wishes he could gauge what she's feeling after having gone through the past five days, since her daughter went missing. "People keep coming by," she says. "I feel like I'm saying the same thing over and over. I feel like I'm saying it for them more than me, that it's okay, that no news isn't bad news. And all I keep thinking is, '*Thank you, thank you, really, but I don't want another fucking casserole.*' I want to say, 'I'm sorry, but please understand, I'm not even hungry.' "

"Do you want some coffee?"

"I'm not thirsty, either," she says. "Not for that."

"Okay," he says, sitting down beside her. He is grateful she at least seems calm.

"I was up all night. I can smell her on her bed, so I try and sleep there, but then I can't sleep so I get up again." Her voice trails off.

Frank sets down his coffee. He doesn't get the morning paper at the end of the sidewalk, though he thinks a simple action would be the easiest thing to do and might break whatever tension exists in the moment. He can smell the leftover booze on her, knows more about Ginny than he should, perhaps, first from Natalia and then from their own conversations that continued after Natalia left: Ginny's love of gin; the disability she collected after her husband, Ron, shot himself; the problems she had with her daughter, ones that almost everyone knew about despite her desire for privacy. He remembers Natalia once saying, *For God's sake, if she's going to yell at her daughter, at least she should shut the windows.* After six months of conversation and Ginny's tentative trust in Frank, she still does not come inside the house to sit, as she might have with Natalia. It is as if the house is somehow off-limits for Ginny, as if being alone with Frank, in the domain of more private exchanges, would somehow betray her friendship with Natalia. Maybe, Frank sometimes thinks, it is a sign of respect to Natalia, who was, at forty-two, Ginny's senior by eight years. Or maybe it is something else. Maybe she doesn't trust him. She never really asks anything of him, not even to clip her hedges, though he often does anyway and believes it's a start.

"It was strange in the house," she says. "I never realized that before—how empty the house could be. Vicki was such a chatterbox. Half the time I just wanted her to shut the hell up, you know. I hate to say that, but it's what I thought. I can't just say that to most people, though. I regret even thinking it. I know it's wrong to have thought it at all. She was just doing what kids do; she was just telling me about her day, about the silly things in her day, half of it she just dreamed up."

Frank takes a sip of coffee. "Sissy gets yappy, too."

"Girls," she says.

"I know." He waits, thinking. Finally, he says, "Any news?"

"No news is good news," she says. "That's what they tell me, anyway. The police put up flyers on store windows, around the neighborhood, too. They questioned some guy over on Ellwine. He has a record, minor stuff. But the guy was in Jersey that night, visiting his sister or something. They said they confirmed his whereabouts. They talked to people in the neighborhood, too, but you've already heard that."

"I know," he said. "Eva and Sissy were talking about it."

"They talked to people who live by the park, asked if they saw anything."

"Did they?"

She shakes her head and removes a fresh cigarette from her pack of Slims and holds it out to him.

"No, thanks. I'm trying to quit."

"Yeah, me too." She holds it to her mouth and lights it. Her hands shake. "No one ever sees anything. You'd have to be fucking God to see everything, wouldn't you? That's what I tell myself."

Frank picks up the pack of cigarettes and taps one out. He takes her lighter, flicks it. He inhales, remembering all too quickly how good a cigarette can be, how it gives him something to do with his hands when he's restless.

"The police," she says, her voice shakier now. "I went to the park, too. I drove around town, looking. It seemed better than being in the house. It seemed better than just waiting, but then I started to think, *'My God, what if I found her? What if I found her and she wasn't—'* "

"I can help, if you want. We can go together, today, and look."

She looks over to him, her eyes welling up. "It's like if I don't think about it, she might be upstairs, reading or writing in her diary, you know, writing about boys and school and friends, or maybe writing about me, writing about how awful I am."

"You didn't do anything wrong," Frank says. He keeps his voice as steady as possible. He wants to take her shaking hands in his and press them tight. Still, he also knows there is hardly anything he might say, hardly anything he might do to take away a mother's grief, the sudden loss of a child. He remembers Natalia, how she carried a son, their first-born, through the early months of their marriage. The baby died three days after birth. Natalia went into shock in the operating room from losing too much blood. She almost died with the baby. After that, a depression eclipsed her for months, and Frank, seeing this all, felt rubbed raw. She blamed herself, her body's unwillingness to support life, to root something. "I wasn't ready," she told him. "And look—bad luck." They didn't talk about their son; even the girls didn't know. After Eva was born, Natalia would sneak into the nursery at night and check to make sure everything was all right. Her vigilance lasted for years, until Eva's first day of school. He remembers how Natalia followed Eva's bus, how she watched Eva, small for her age, her long hair pinned back, how Eva lumbered down the steps with a yellow book bag slung over her shoulder. Natalia recounted all this to Frank, though of course Eva herself would never know that Natalia watched her at all. It is the mothers who are left to the more complicated, tenuous things; it is the mothers who find themselves waiting on their children, imagining them rushing in through the door.

He studies Ginny now without her noticing. Her look is faraway, quiet. "You didn't do anything wrong," he says again.

"I should go," she says, not moving. "I know you don't have much time to yourself. I know you probably wanted to be alone."

"No," he tells her. "It's fine." He thinks about Ginny, about her girl, how awful it must be, and how awful it would be for him if it were Sissy or Eva.

She tilts her head, listening to the sounds of the day, the noises erupting in the street. "She might be hungry. She might be thirsty. She might be in pain, Frank. She might be somewhere, all alone, and she might be hurting, she might be wondering where I am, why I haven't found her."

"You have to hope for the best," he says.

"You believe that? That she's okay?"

"Yes." He doesn't know if he believes it or not, but he knows the moment requires that he say yes, that he affirm the best possible outcome. He knows it is more about keeping his voice as steady as possible, just as he did after the baby died, when he said, "It's not your fault." He tries to make his voice like a heavy anchor, one that can still her. There is always one person who anchors another, one person who keeps another grounded. He tries to steady himself, *For Ginny,* he thinks. Still, his mind travels to Natalia.

Ginny's face shifts again. "I should go. I didn't want to bother you."

"I put on coffee," he says. "The girls aren't up yet. Stay."

She debates, and then takes another cigarette out and lights it. "The officer said that two Puerto Rican kids ran away from home a few days ago. The police asked me about Vicki, if she hated me. They didn't say 'hated,' but that's what they were asking. They asked if Vicki might ever do something like that, just run away. They asked about Ron, too; it was like I had to explain my entire life all of a sudden. Who wants to do that? Who wants to talk about everything bad that's ever happened? I mean, would you want to talk about stuff like that? Would you want to have to be suddenly responsible for everything in your life, whether you did anything wrong or not? But I felt like I was wrong. I felt like everything I did was wrong."

"You didn't do anything wrong," he says. Across the street, the dog pisses in the yard. "The police, that's their job. They're trying to help. They're trying to rule things out."

"What did they expect me to say about Ron? About Vicki? That things were bad in seventy-two, that when Ron got home he wasn't the same, that he drank, and then I started to drink? That he kept everything inside him, woke up screaming? Would that have helped?"

"It's not your fault, Ginny." A car passes by, idling down the road, the windows open, the car radio playing. A lawn mower hums to life. How easily the day can pass, how easily so much can be lost.

"I keep thinking," she's saying now, "if I had just looked at the clock. Maybe if I had just gone down to the park sooner, maybe she would have been there."

"Don't," Frank says, shifting. "It won't do you any good. It won't do Vicki any good, either."

"The police," she says, "asking if Vicki has ever run away."

Frank takes a sip of his coffee. He grows silent, thinking. Across the street, Jim Schultz comes out of the house, calls in the schnauzer. "Has she?"

Ginny says nothing.

"Ginny? Has she?"

"Do you ever regret things?"

"I try not to," he says, even though he does. "It's a waste of time to look back too much, to beat yourself up over the things you can't change, the things you can't take back."

"Once she ran away. Last fall, Natalia found Vicki at the bus stop with her backpack full of clothes. That was it. It was nothing. It's not like she was really going to go anywhere. She was pretending, trying to upset me. She was angry because I grounded her, but she broke the god-damn window, Frank. What was I supposed to do? *She broke a window.* That officer, he doesn't know us, he doesn't know our life. No one lives up to scrutiny if you're going to look at everyone's flaws."

"No," Frank says. "And kids do that sort of thing."

"Do your kids do that? Does Sissy? What's the worst thing she's ever done? Chop off my daughter's hair?"

"Sissy wakes up crying at night," Frank confesses. "Eva's been mad at me for months. Sometimes I think they're being raised by wolves."

"Natalia used to say that."

"Well," he says irritably. "Natalia is a wolf."

"Don't let them outside. The park isn't safe."

"Sissy isn't supposed to go to the park by herself," Frank says. "I told Sissy. I told Eva."

"I keep thinking if I had just looked at the time."

"Don't."

But she is so absorbed in her thoughts that she has fallen into a place where his voice can no longer reach her. The silence, the waiting for her to say something, to hear him, amplifies, and then what Frank wishes not to happen does happen, and Ginny's body shakes and slumps, and whatever composure she has relied upon is suddenly gone from her. "I'm sorry," she manages, and what he hears is her apology not to him but to her girl, to Vicki. He feels a rush of emotion. He touches the concrete step, places his hand next to her. He thinks about touching her, yet anyone he touches seems to drift from him. And so he refrains. He can do things. He can fix cars and mow her grass. He can climb a roof for her, nail down shingles. But to comfort her now, in an unmanageable grief, is beyond his prowess, beyond where they are together, in the moment. He has never been good at allaying tears. Natalia seldom cried, maybe once or twice in the history of their marriage. Even when his own mother sat on the couch in their living room, the day his father was buried, even then, when his mother cried, Frank left her with Natalia and got up, went outside, and mowed the grass. He simply doesn't know what to do with hurt, with anger, even in himself. He has no place to put it.

"She'll come back," he says, choosing to believe it. He places his arm around her. He leans toward her more, whispers, "She'll find her way back."

By late morning there is a drop of rain, then a few more drops on the sidewalk, making Frank feel that the sky is always holding itself back. The haze is discernible, the air full, ready to break but not breaking. After tinkering with his car, he heads back to the kitchen. Holding his mug of coffee, he gazes outside and thinks the morning is almost entirely lost. Ginny, suddenly uncomfortable, had slid off the step and left abruptly, without a word. Though he called to her, she didn't look back. How had he failed Ginny in the moment? He could only guess. He knows her to be the type of woman who doesn't ask for help, the type of woman who, like Natalia, prefers to keep emotion in check when she can. There was nothing in that moment that he could say to set things right. He couldn't give her girl back to her.

Soon, he will yell upstairs for the children—Eva and Sissy, safe in bed, thank God; for however miserable they are, for however much they fight, at least they are mostly together. It's well past their time to be up, but both girls, in Frank's estimation, are lazy: Eva, living in the squalor of her room, Sissy, too dreamy to be useful, her thoughts frequently distracting her when she's doing a chore. He worries that Sissy is a good candidate for accidents, for running out into the road without thinking and then getting squashed under a car tire. That she hasn't already is only because of her luck; at Sissy's birth Natalia told him that she would be lucky. "Look at her face," she said. "It's a face that wishes." Still, it frightens Frank that he could have a daughter like that. And Eva, he can barely think of her, of how unpredictable she can be, how moody, how she has blossomed so suddenly—the blossoming bright, unexpected. He dismisses this. He reads the morning paper: an article on the steel plant, measures taken by the EPA regarding pollution; a piece on an emigrant family from China. He finds the article about the two boys who have gone missing, the Puerto Rican kids Ginny spoke of. How many children go missing a year, he wonders. Five? Ten? Two? These boys and their story have made the paper, though, because the younger one is diabetic and is without medication that is crucial to his health.

Upstairs, directly above the kitchen, he hears the rustling of feet in Eva's room.

He takes eggs from the refrigerator, discards one that is cracked, and looks around the cupboard for canned tomatoes and onions. He performs this feat with a cigarette dangling from his mouth—the pack left by Ginny. He breaks the shells, mixes the eggs in a bowl, and adds water before pouring the mixture, along with the stewed tomatoes, into the pan and blasting the heat. He seldom cooks. That was always Natalia's job, and now it is bestowed upon Eva most days, and this is the reason why all of them are thinner. He wonders, briefly, what people even eat in Italy for breakfast, for dinner; wonders, too, what types of things Natalia is putting into her mouth these days, and then he thinks, immediately, *That slut.*

He calls Ginny. No one answers. He hangs up, tries once more after five minutes have passed. By the time he is halfway finished making breakfast, the girls are still not downstairs and the bottom of the eggs are scorched while the top is too wet. He serves up two plates, one for Sissy and one for Eva, and leaves them steaming on the table. He waits, leans against the counter, and then finally yells upstairs. Eva comes down first, her hair up in a high ponytail. She is dressed in shorts that are too revealing for Frank's taste, and a halter top that plunges. "Why don't you put on some clothes?" he asks.

"These *are* clothes," she says. "How about if it bothers you, you don't look."

"How long are you going to be like this?"

"Like what?"

"You know damn well like what."

Eva glares at him but says nothing. If there were a moment more between them, they would surely get into a disagreement, an outright fight, but Sissy comes down, happily, still wearing her nightshirt with her favorite rock band emblazoned on the front. Frank stares at the clownish faces, the outlandishly long tongue. "Hey," he says.

"Hey," Sissy says, yawning. "What's this?"

"Breakfast." He looks over to Eva. She is sitting at the table now, her jaw set, her arms crossed over her chest.

"You made it?" Sissy asks Eva. She pulls out a chair and settles in.

"I made it," Frank says.

"You?"

"Eat," Frank says, his cigarette still dangling, a spatula in his hand. He runs his free hand over his T-shirt, stained from working under the car. "There's kids starving in Ethiopia."

A familiar refrain whenever the girls are fussy with food, one that originated with Natalia after she saw a documentary on television, then took to a quiet, desperate mood and to eating only bread and butter for days, as if trying to punish herself.

"There are kids who are starving in America, too," Eva says.

"Let me guess," Frank says, "more words of wisdom from that English teacher who got you thinking about the ozone."

Eva says nothing. She pushes her plate forward.

He had hoped cooking breakfast would coerce them all into being together, a family sitting down at the table. "Eat." This through gritted teeth.

Reluctantly Eva pulls her chair into the table, picks up a fork, and pokes at her food. She samples it, and then glances over to Sissy, who has, since picking up her fork, eaten only two bites before doing what she always does when she thinks she is fooling her parents: pushing the eggs to one side of the plate and stacking them so they appear to have less surface area.

"Salty," Eva says.

He breathes deeply. "It's not salty."

"Whatever, then." She throws her fork down onto the plate. "You eat it." She pushes her chair back from the table, gets up, and goes upstairs. A minute later, Frank hears rock-and-roll music blaring from her room.

"Your sister is impossible."

Sissy pushes her eggs across the plate. "Tell me about it."

"Has she said anything to you?"

"About?"

"Anything."

"No."

"Are the eggs salty?" Frank asks.

"No."

"Are you lying?"

"No."

"Don't lie."

"It's a little salty."

"Then, why didn't you say that?"

"You yell."

"I don't yell."

Sissy pushes the eggs, so they begin to look like a small mountain.

"I don't mean to yell."

"Okay."

"People yell sometimes. People do a lot of things they don't mean to do. It doesn't always mean anything, Sissy."

When the phone rings at three o'clock, Eva jumps from her bed to answer it. She picks up before she turns the volume down on the Bee Gees, so automatic is her reflex, so acute is her anticipation.

"Hi," he says in a low tone. "Glad it's you."

"Me, too." Eva practically dances, hearing him. She pulls the phone cord across the room and checks to make sure the door is locked. Then, nervously, she flits to the window, glancing furtively to check if her father's legs still stick out from under the Chevy. He is there, his head and torso buried under the front end, like a car wreck. He did not hear the ringing through the screen door. He has not emerged from under the engine to come inside. There is no one else to worry about, more or less. Somewhere downstairs, Sissy, who earlier came up to complain that she wasn't allowed to go down to the park without Eva, is probably still moping on the couch, her legs draped over the arm of the sofa, her head buried in a book on ghost detecting.

"Eva?"

"I'm here," she says, relaxing. She lets the curtain fall back to its place. She climbs onto her bed. "Just covering bases. Speaking of, where's the wife?"

She hears a pause, senses that Peter is smoking dope, so easy is his voice.

"The wife," he says finally, exhaling, "is out at her mother's. And the father?"

"Under a car," Eva says. "Are we meeting?"

"Do you work today?"

"My hours have been cut. Too many summer employees, and the boss hired a full-time person last week. We could meet, though. I could make something up."

He seems to debate, as if the offer is tempting but perhaps not tempting enough, leaving her to wonder if he might prefer time alone to time with her. She hears him shift in his chair; his voice muffles. "I'd like to," he says finally. "But there's not enough time today, not for that."

"I could get out," she offers, her hope dwindling with his every word. The room seems to close on her more. She listens for any sound from outside but hears nothing. Finally she says, "I need to get out. I'm like fucking Rapunzel up here in my room."

"Just a call today," he says. "I've missed you."

She leans back on her pillow. "So prove it."

"Can't."

"I could go out with Greg then, I guess. Would that make you happy?"

"No," he says. "I don't like to think about that. I don't like to think about all the guys you've been around."

"Don't believe everything you hear."

"Lies?"

"Exaggerations."

"I see the way the boys look at you. It's hard not to notice you."

Eva grows quiet, thinking about how she sometimes desperately wished people wouldn't notice her at all, that she could become suddenly invisible. Outside she hears a car engine start. "I don't want them to notice me."

He laughs. "Spoken like a pretty girl. It's always the pretty girls who say they don't care to be noticed, and they say it because they know they always are."

"No one notices things that matter."

"Relax," Peter says. "You don't need to be huffy."

"Easy for you to say."

"I meant it as a compliment, anyway. Truthfully, I would be jealous if you and Greg were together."

"We're friends," Eva says. She gets up and glances out the window. Her father sits in the car, letting the engine rev. "My dad." She watches as her father shuts the car off. He walks to the shed and reemerges, a few moments later, with his toolbox. She breathes. "Do you get along with your dad?"

He pauses for a moment. "We didn't used to. When I was younger, we didn't get along at all. He wanted me to go into business, but I didn't. He thought teachers didn't make enough money, that they didn't get enough done, and that anyone who had the summer off was lazy. I disappointed him."

Eva twists the phone cord, listening, wanting him to say more. It is the secrets that she most wishes she could share, things she might speak only to him. Who else does she have to talk to? Greg? Sissy? Still, she hesitates. She wants to tell him about that night after Christmas, how upset she was, how confused, just barely awakened from sleep. If she told, would he think something bad about her? That she was the one to blame? Was it even real? She was so sleepy. She felt as though she was floating, and then yelling, the screams and more afterward. And yet despite any confusion, despite any disheartened doubt, she has changed since that night, regardless; the house itself has changed and she has felt broken, within it. "Peter?" she asks quietly. "Do you get along with your father now?"

"We talk now," he says. "It happens."

"Oh."

"What's wrong?"

"Nothing."

"After a while you learn to forgive most things. After a while you learn to talk."

"How long does it take?"

"I don't know," he tells her, shifting again. "Until you wake up one day not wanting to feel angry anymore."

Outside, Frank breathes slowly, taking in the smell of oil and grease. He shuffles back under his car and squints, his eyes adjusting to the pronounced difference in light. He turns on a fixture that is clamped to the underside of the car; it beams with sudden radiance. He checks the newly positioned jack to make sure it is holding. It calms him to have the world reduced to machinery—fixable, unlike people and situations. *At least metal doesn't shrink away from you,* he thinks. He turns a bolt. It gives with a squeak. Sometimes parents can do stupid, idiotic things that they then regret for a lifetime. He knows this. Still, there was a moment when, listening to Ginny, he wanted to tell her that perhaps she shouldn't have been drinking, that booze can only lead to a succession of problems. It was like that for him when he was a child, when, as a young boy, his parents would leave him in the car while they ushered each other, wide-stepped, gait askew, to the local bar with its dim light and crimson walls. The blood room. That was how he imagined it, with all the fights that erupted across the stools and in the dark corners. Sometimes he would crack the window and listen to the explosion of voices coming from the door each time someone entered or exited. While he waited, he would eat chips or pretzels that his parents left him and lick the salty residue left on his fingers. Sometimes he would fog the cold windows with his mouth and draw circles and trees, or crawl up to the front seat and pretend to drive, put the *pedal to the metal.* His mother would check on him every hour or so, less as the evening wore on. She would check to see that the doors were locked, and the more she drank, the sweeter she became, cooing and kissing his head and calling him by her pet name, her little Cracker Jack. How he still remembers her leaning over him, remembers the smoke that clung to her skin and masked the smell of talc. He regarded her with such affection. He waited for her voice to soothe him with its thin register. But then, at home, his father's temper fueled by drink, there were maddening arguments. Once the old man took a sledgehammer to the door and split it in two. Once, he hit Frank's mother, cracking her nose and causing Frank himself to intervene with a yawp and tangle of fists. Frank seldom thinks of this. If asked about his parents, he would say, simply: *They were fine; they did what they could.* He knows there are many parents who *are* fine—good, decent folks who take their kids to Walt Disney World each summer and check on their children each night before bed. He knows the world isn't filled with bad parents. But of his own, he says little out of respect. And with Ginny, he wanted to tell her, for her sake, for her girl's sake, to lay off the booze.

He might have told her then about his own downfall, that night in December, that moment that meant nothing but that caused irreparable harm. He doesn't like to think about that entire week after Natalia left, the terrible approach of the holiday, the necessity of planning for Christmas when no one in the house felt like celebrating, the explanations given to neighbors who dropped by with soaps that smelled of lavender and oranges, gifts born of neighborly obligation. There was Ginny's offer to help shop, which Frank politely refused. In the end he settled on quick hard cash. He stuffed money at the bottoms of knitted stockings, under bits of frayed yarn and chocolate and candy canes. When it seemed to him the tree looked markedly bare, he made a last-ditch effort and shopped on Christmas Eve, bringing home food baskets filled with cheese, sausages, crackers, and small jars of marmalade. The next day, Sissy received hers with a look of desperation but took quickly to opening the sardines, inserting the key and rolling the metal back. She sniffed and quickly discarded them, and then took to the sticky cheeses. She sat patiently, licking the foils, waiting for Eva to open hers. But Eva only shook her head and said, "This is unbelievable."

He had done what he could, he wanted to say. He'd looked at clothes but had had no idea as to sizes. He'd browsed through the record and eight-track-tape selections but hadn't had a clue what Eva or Sissy might like. Eva left the basket of food unopened. Frank sat down in his recliner. He rubbed his temples. He folded his large hands while Sissy announced that she could retrieve the *real* presents from the closet. Without waiting for a response, she bolted upstairs and returned with packages wrapped in Sunday comics. "You didn't know?" Sissy asked, going back for a second round. He responded irritably, "If I knew, don't you think I would have had them under the tree?" Eva fell silent through the opening of dolls and cosmetics and clothing and nylons and new purses. Within the hour everything was opened and stacked in piles, and there was one gift left, for Frank: a bucket of fresh apples.

In the following days Frank contacted an attorney, determined to get everything he'd worked for, but when the day of his appointment came, he didn't show up and called his buddies from work instead. They drove across town, to where the row homes were stacked on top of one another and all the alleys smelled of rot and trash and plummeted sharply downhill. They drove past the old house that was his childhood home, sold long ago and then later condemned as this part of town grew dilapidated, worn out like rusted metal. They drove to the same bar his father used to go to—"The Ho-Ho," they called it, "to drink, to get smashed, to get toasted, to toast that bitch farewell," they said. There they sat under the dim lights, eating peanuts and hammering back shots of whiskey. Afterward, they drove around, looking at the girls who lingered on the streets, their legs bent, their skirts hiked up stockinged thighs. His buddy Jimmy, the young kid from work, laughed and said that the last order of business was for him to get laid. Frank grinned, knowing that none of the men would actually go through with anything, even drunk off their asses, and he was right: The jeering escalated first but then diminished to silence. He came home, finally, at four in the morning, still hammered, still reeling, the world spinning around him. In the dark, he bumped into the mahogany table in the hallway, knocked over the figurine there, a statue of a man piping a flute, and Eva, hearing the ruckus, hurried downstairs, her white nightgown hanging eerily over her. "Dad?" she whispered in the darkness. "Is that you?" She turned on a light in the living room and stood, watching as he staggered forward again and then finally leaned against the wall for support. How surprised she seemed to see him that way—slurring his words, practically in tears. "Here," she said, reaching forward. She looped her arm around his waist and helped him to bed. In his room, when she turned to go and he saw the length of hair swaying as she walked, he thought of Natalia. "You look like your mother," he said, and, without thinking, he moved toward her. He placed his hand on her shoulder, kissed her neck, felt the warmth of her body— how inviting it seemed in one moment and then, the spell broken, she pulled away, wrenching, her entire body reacting like a bird suddenly caught. He stopped, realizing his error. "Don't you ever," she said, her hand up at her neck. "Don't you *ever* do that again."

He regrets this moment more than any moment in his life. He regrets that night when he saw Natalia everywhere, in everyone. He doesn't want to think of it, though Eva will not let him forget. *And why,* he thinks, *should she let me?* He has offered a thousand quiet apologies—all unanswered.

He feels around the ground for a wrench and unscrews another bolt. He hears rain, a sudden downpour hitting the hood of the car.

Upstairs, off the phone and thinking about Peter and all that she wished to say, Eva sits by her window smoking a joint. Rain pounds the sidewalk, splashes in the empty pool. In the living room, Sissy closes her book. She opens the front door and peers out, expecting, in an irrational and fanciful way, to see her mother. When she doesn't, she turns and runs upstairs. "Rain!" she yells.

Mr. Morris, outside enjoying the day, calls in to Milly. He dances for her like a child, tapping in puddles.

It lasts only a few minutes. A few moments, yes, but some moments can seem endless to the heart and make it leap and skip beyond itself.

And, in the space of the heart—invisible, silent, surprising—something rises. Ginny, who an hour before took the phone off the hook and poured a tall glass of gin, who just a moment ago was thinking that it isn't really a question of what would drive someone to lay out a row of pills—the world offers a thousand reasons, a thousand losses—leaves the pills on the table and steps outside. "Vicki," she says into air made fresh and new again. "Is that a sign from you?"

two

6

By mid-July the afternoons are impossible to bear. The doctor generally sets about drinking Scotch at three, then takes to talking about his ex-wife, Katherine, and how much he absolutely loathes her and how abysmal it is for a woman who never commandeered a boat to obtain, in their divorce settlement, the doctor's yacht that he had christened his *Little Baby* before sailing it on the Caribbean four years ago; and isn't Katherine such a mean-spirited bitch, to strike at him that way all over a little indiscretion, and isn't it wrong, he'd always say, that it was done through letters, those prepared by her four attending lawyers, and really, isn't Katherine such a homely little whore on top of everything else?

"Why," he asks today as he and Natalia sit on the veranda, listening to the rain, "did I ever love that wretched woman?"

Natalia leans back and thinks again how conversations too often grow repetitive, the mind always circling over the past, to times that no longer exist. She stares out to the cobbled streets of Florence and takes in the aroma of bread that drifts from the bakery across from them, the old stone building with its windows always blank-looking, open to cool the heat from the ovens. In the people here there is a tiredness as old as the city, and in Natalia there is a growing tiredness, too. This life is not her life after all, nor could it ever be. This is not her home. She considers first her circumstances, which she dismisses in her mind as too painful to think about or discuss: her children back home in the States, left to Frank, his moods. In twenty years of marriage he hasn't even managed to cook a decent meal; the children would be reduced to bones already, no doubt, probably living off pumpkin paste and canned tomatoes. When she thinks about Frank and the girls, she feels a heat rise within her and she grows irritated and finds all the doctor's talk distressing; but when she sighs in an effort to indicate that he is being a colossal bore, and then sighs again when he stops his reverie but won't look at her directly, he only asks her to pass the ice bucket—black, trimmed with silver. He adds three cubes to his glass, and that seems to settle whatever disagreement between them there is, if any.

"Silence between people," she says after a while, listening to the rain hit the terra-cotta roof, "is its own story, isn't it?"

The doctor says nothing. A maid mills into the room to refresh the ice, a young girl, no more than twenty with sleek black hair cut at the line of her jaw. Natalia notes her full, tender lips. When the girl takes the doctor's drink to refresh it, he smiles, and Natalia nods as the maid leaves.

Finally, he says, "We'll make this a good experience yet, my dear." He tells her, "Take note of it," reminding her that she is, after all, still his secretary. "It's been difficult to forget," he says, apologetically. "Especially about the boat."

She makes no note at all. There has been rain in Florence for five days, and down the street the flowers set in buckets hang their heads, and the women hurry by blindly, their heads also hung. Watching them, Natalia remembers women in the camp, that time when she was only a child, and she can no longer say she is sure of her own footing. She inhales, feeling a familiar hunger, wanting to stuff her mouth with bread, wanting something in her complicated heart to take hold and rise.

She chastises herself for her whimsy and childish belief in starting fresh again, one that moved her to forsake everything. *How foolish,* she thinks now, *to believe that I could leave things behind.* At first, when they arrived in Florence, there was a steady succession of activity: trips to the market for vegetables and bread, bright smells that bloomed in the air. There were decorators who furnished the space the doctor had rented— a finely woven rug was laid, fused with gold and black thread that fringed on the edges; pillows were placed on a leather seat in the main room, the seat squat and boxy, with its ends curved, like cupped hands. There were daily walks through the city, a newness to everything that made Natalia forgetful. She and the doctor discussed the architecture produced in the Renaissance, the dome of the Church of San Spirito, the pre-Baroque style of Michelangelo's Laurentian Library, the voussoirs of the Palazzo Strozzi. He was versed in all this, articulate in a way Frank never was. He'd chat happily as they walked narrow streets and meandered between the buildings, thrilled to be released from his practice. Natalia admitted that she, too, was happy to be away, that she had always held an irrational fear of hospitals, but that she'd ended up working for him anyway because, of the twelve applications she'd completed—the doctor's done in desperation—he had been the only one kind enough to offer Natalia a job at all. Still, she told him, every time she entered the building, she would cross herself and kiss her fingers.

After a few months in Florence, though, Natalia found she no longer listened to the doctor's musings and banter. Instead she listened to the voices of people lifting from the streets, language that was fluid and unknowable as it drifted by her. She remembered reading once of two brothers who spoke the same dying dialect—the brothers were the only ones left in the world who shared the language, the only ones left of their kind—but they hadn't spoken after fighting over the same woman. Their language went dead within them and was lost entirely. To her surprise, she often thought of Frank then. She thought of the girls, too. She'd expected that after she settled in with the doctor she would bring the girls to her, but that hadn't happened. She wrote to them once and, at a loss for words, told them only about simple things: the trips to the market, the crumbling buildings, the fading sunsets.

Her efforts to enjoy the time dwindled. A certain incompatibility grew then between her and the doctor. Petty disagreements arose between them. Natalia didn't like the arrangement of the living room and didn't see the practicality of a white leather sofa that she could never sit on; he didn't like a dress on her and thought it the wrong color, unpleasing to his precise eye. "Gray," he told her, "makes you look foppish and, if I might add, slightly malignant."

At night, too, Natalia began having nightmares that startled her from sleep, the subversive maneuverings of the mind, the firing synapses of the brain sneaking up on her like silent soldiers. Some of the dreams had a quality of old habit: She and Frank were young again, childless, and they drove down a stretch of abandoned road to a region of coal, to a town that had an underground fire burning in the mines. How eerie that town was to Natalia with all the empty houses, the windows boarded, businesses closed up, bicycles abandoned, the residents having fled quickly, and yet the houses and buildings still marked the traces of those very same people. In her dream, the sky was unnatural like sea glass and there was a tranquillity that Natalia sensed was easily broken. Up the road it turned dark, and a crack of thunder sounded like a shotgun. Rain pelted down on the windshield, but Frank stubbornly refused to turn on the wipers. She looked over and told him, "We need to go back." He turned his head and calmly said, "You're on fire, Natalia." And she looked down at her blouse; it peeled from her skin and broke apart, floating around the car.

She'd wake with a start. Although she seldom thought to seek comfort in others, she would turn to the doctor and nudge his mottled back. She would begin to speak, but he'd shift and settle into his own dreams without argument or care. Natalia would lie awake for hours, breathless, waiting for light to bobble through the window slats.

After the rain, there are four gorgeous days when the sky stretches, uninterrupted, and Natalia decides to leave. *Seven months,* she thinks, *is too long to be away from family.* She packs only a few items: a green silk blouse the doctor bought for her, two pairs of pants the color of cream, a clingy red V-neck, a few shirts. It's a trick she's learned in life. A light packing, one glance behind her as she walks away, but only one—and in that glance the old story is certainly proven false: We do not turn to salt, and no God proves us inexplicably wrong.

There are so few things we can actually hold on to. Love, maybe. The remnants of it, our memories, the scraps of ourselves we hold on to, despite our journeying.

She wonders if her home with Frank and the girls will feel the same now, after she's been gone from it. She has no idea when things changed, when Frank became more distant, opting to spend days out under the car, which Natalia took to mean that he was somehow avoiding her. She could blame work, she supposed, the long hours, his need for quiet, but it still made her feel inconsequential and inept, left to the girls and the house all day. At times she wonders if it is only her own flaw: to never quite feel at home anywhere, to always be on the periphery of things, just enough to feel a nagging sense of displacement that exists on the edge of inclusion, on the fringes of love, to realize nothing is entirely familiar.

Natalia has always been traveling. Her first trip to America was by boat. After the barking German shepherds (how their bared teeth frightened her, their alert ears, the saliva that dripped from one of the *kutya's* mouths), and after the fences and barbed wire and the two headlights illuminated in the dark woods, the old German, Clara, a woman already in her early fifties, scrubbed Natalia's face and body clean and put her to bed as if Natalia were a plaything. "I don't mind that you're a Gyp," she said as she pulled up the covers. "I always wanted a little girl, a little girl just like you." Although Natalia's parents and her brother were dead, and although in one moment her life had changed for the worse, and then in another moment, changed for the better, she dismissed everything the second her face pressed against the pillow. She moaned with pleasure. She had survived. She was the moth that had flown over the barbed wire, unnoticed, suddenly freed. If she was cursed, that must have marked the moment the accusations were hurtled from graves: the second she drifted off to sleep, the second she forgot those left behind and abandoned herself to the care of strangers—without burden, without thought to their histories and rooms.

Within months of that night, she made the journey to America. It was a terribly clear day. As they embarked from the port in Germany, Natalia smelled salt water and fish. Her new father, a former messenger in the army (how he feared the occupation), was a man with a smooth face and gray eyes and legs that were swift, made for running. Clara, who was much heavier, less demonstrative with affection but competent with meeting basic needs—the bed, the fresh linens, the roasted pork and peppers on the table—looked back at her homeland for a long while and then whispered, suddenly, "*Deutschland Erwache!*" After they fled, it was Clara who always held fast to her reimaginings of history. She often spoke of her belief that the Jews and the Gyps had lied, spoke of her denial that people were turned into soap and ashes, their blanched hair sold at markets. Even if Natalia protested, even if she spoke of the stench that hung in the sky, Clara would hear none of it. After Clara's beloved Dresden was bombed, she spent considerable time penning letters to Churchill, ones she'd send once a month, from a mailing address belonging to someone else.

On the boat it was Natalia's new father who held her closely so that she could see over the rails to the turbulent water below, and, in the process, he pinched her skinny sides and caused her doll's head to press into her rib cage, up under bone. He danced with her while her new mother leaned over the railing and vomited with great regularity. Clara glanced over to them, her hand holding her stomach, her face yellow. She pleaded with the fates to give her a reprieve from motion. She hated it all. She hated having to sell her silver and rings, to barter for passage. She hated having to give up her servants and the house. In America, when they took up residence in their small house, she hated having to give up her language, a language Natalia had always thought too harsh, too guttural—a language of spit.

Natalia didn't hate America. She embraced it as best she could, with an always cautious distance. She told herself she was lucky enough to have a life, even if Clara did fret too much over her, afraid perhaps that what had been stolen might be stolen back. Years later, during their last phone call, she told Natalia that she prided herself on her care, on keeping Natalia safe and close, on teaching her to read. "I never took my eyes off you," she said, and Natalia responded, "I know, that was the problem."

A young Natalia found comfort in the daily rituals: school, the predictability of afternoon chores—hanging out laundry on pleasant days, folding the crisp towels and sheets afterward—the need to please both of her new parents even as she quietly snatched provisions from the cupboard to store under her mattress, just in case. Her father would come home from work as a night watchman and let Natalia pick through his coat pockets for candy or change. "Gypsy thief," he'd say, smiling, touching her under her chin. "My little Gypsy girl." In school, she learned the language with the help of a well-meaning English teacher who tutored her over lunch until her accent gradually lessened, and then mostly disappeared. She later met Frank and married. After their boy died and Clara suggested the child suffered from weak blood, Natalia would stop talking to her parents altogether, even her father, whom she always missed.

Now Natalia makes the second trip to America by plane, her ticket paid for with the doctor's weekly allowance. She looks out the double-paned glass and tries to ignore the man next to her, whose fleshy sides spill into her seat. However tired she is, she can't sleep. Below, the ocean stretches for miles and hours, under clouds too thin to hold anything. *Eighty percent of the earth is made of water,* she remembers from school. Also, *eighty percent of a person's body. A tear is salt water. A tear is an ocean.* Once she heard that if you press deeply into a person's stomach, you can unleash a flood of tears. Natalia always wonders if that is the place in our bodies where our histories and memories and hopes are stored. What in a person's mind and heart and body holds on to what went before? What clings to the nagging ghosts—the memories of others, calling their shrill, ecstatic songs that speak of belonging and making everywhere a home? What parts of her brother and her mother and father, what parts of those people never known still passed through her, their blood coursing in her veins? What parts of Sissy and Eva? She tried to ask the doctor this once, but he shrugged and said, "According to science, very little."

Just as she teases herself into thinking the entire world is made of water, she spots umber and chartreuse and citrine-colored patches of land that stretch out like a grid below her, the tops of verdant trees and smooth mountain ridges, and then, as the plane descends, the roofs of houses, the bright blue pools and roads that scrape in every direction. America, a land that, unlike Florence, is always content to reimagine itself, a Gypsy nation.

She leans back, her lips slightly parted, emitting the soundless words she might say to Frank: *I'm sorry. It was a mistake,* she will say, simply. *I've missed you.* And as she says it, she realizes it's true. She has missed Frank. She has missed him perhaps more than anyone. He was, after all, the only one who knew her, the only one who knew the secret of the crease at her neck. He was the one who shared her history. She will say, *The time away from you, the time away from anyone or anything loved is always a mistake. They are difficult things, families. It's hard not to feel incidental. It's hard not to feel forgotten about, eventually; I'm sorry,* she mouths. *It was a mistake.*

By two in the afternoon there is a tiredness Natalia attributes to jet lag, to the hours spent with her legs crammed against the seat in front of her, the conversation with the man beside her about weather and food, and the subsequent wait for the luggage and taxi. When they drive by the house, Natalia hesitates, struck by the stark clarity of the white paneling, the burnt-looking grass. "In the back," she instructs the cabdriver. "In the back, please."

The cabdriver nods. He takes her money, makes change. He offers to help with her bag, but she declines politely, not wanting to draw attention. Even on a Tuesday, and even at this time of day, there will be at least a few neighbors out walking their dogs, or chatting in front of the mailbox, or shredding up weeds with their gloved hands. She can't bear the thought of announcing her return so publicly, that Milly Morris might know she is home before Frank, before her children, and that seeing her, a woman like that might march over with a disapproving look and demand an explanation, demand pay for extra hours of sitting. If that happened, Natalia would feel caged. She would simply slump and scream.

Thank goodness the back door is unlocked. The knob turns without hesitation. Natalia puts her suitcase down by the kitchen table. Out of old habit, she sorts through mail that has been left to pile up on the counter all week: a water bill, a phone bill, an advertisement from Orr's for the summer basement sale. She notices a new can opener fastened under the cabinet and notices, too, that the framed needlepoint she made years ago—a lavender-colored house with thin hearts stitched under it—no longer hangs on the wall next to the basement door. Frank, she supposes. He probably threw it into the trash.

If the girls heard her enter or saw the taxicab in the alley as it drove off, they still haven't come downstairs. There is no patter of feet, no on-rush of questions. She walks down the hallway, cautiously, past her and Frank 's bedroom. In the living room, she pauses by the steps and places her hand on the cool metal railing, realizing (as if she hasn't felt it a thousand times over twenty years) that the metal isn't smooth but coarse and grainy. Unsettled suddenly, she listens, still unsure if she should call out. Her younger child, and certainly of her two the more open, would come rushing down the stairs like a tolerable breeze if Natalia did call. She would be easier, Natalia believes, if not a bit persistent, interrogating, probing in a way that would eventually exasperate even the Buddha. No doubt, too, Sissy would eventually become quiet and hypervigilant, burning a hole through Natalia's back with her gaze, as if a sigh or a sneeze or a raised voice might be an indication of disaster, every minute gesture significant. Still, Natalia could withstand that. Eva would be harder, Eva who holds grudges like her father—relentlessly, with words that fall like glass. There has always been something about Eva, an unsettling assertiveness that has left Natalia on the verge of—dare she say it?—jealousy. Eva will lash out, as she often does when she feels wounded or angry. Eva will cast immediate judgment: cruel pretension, sharp disdain. Is it these traits she envies in her daughter, in addition to fearing them? Or does she simply envy Eva, her youth, her defiance that draws such attention, that moves so many eyes? Regardless, Natalia already feels that her nerves today are stretched to the point of elasticity.

She listens anxiously and hears a hushed conversation upstairs, a murmur, then laughter from Eva's room. Always on the phone. Across the hall from Eva, the television whirls with the rise and fall of cartoon voices. Natalia remembers the argument she had once with Frank, how she warned him that Sissy would spend all her days locked in her bedroom if she were given the old black-and-white. Frank relinquished to Sissy's pleading, though, the television a compromise since Natalia didn't want a dog. It all seems distant now, spent. Still, she misses those petty arguments and snubs. She misses her family.

There is no other movement, no opening of doors. They do not know she is here, listening. They haven't sensed her at all.

She doesn't call. She tells herself, *Not yet.* Just a moment, she thinks, to orient herself to the house again. Every house has its own vibrations, its own smells emanating from the kitchen, its own secrets hidden about, its own stories told at the table. She looks around, as if she expects everything might be changed, shifted out from under her. The living room rug shows the girls' constant traffic. She can see the dirt, the dust on the edges of the throw rugs, the cobwebs in the corners, the smudges on the bay window and front door. The colonial blue walls appear less vibrant than she remembers, the wallpaper beginning to curl at the corner behind Frank's chair. Discarded newspapers lie on the floor. The marble statue by the fireplace, a naïve-looking woman and man held together in an embrace, stands where it has for years. *National Geographic*s are on the coffee table in disarray. A photograph of a tiger stares at her, angrily.

At her bedroom, she breathes and closes the door behind her, gently, so that the girls do not hear. She takes in the room, the paneled walls and dim light, the painting hung above the bed of a boat on an ocean. She takes the ashtray from Frank's nightstand, opens the window, and dumps the charred remains into the row of hostas below. She looks over to Mrs. Stone's house, to the rosebushes planted years ago, a tangle of thorny blooms.

Her hands shake, and it's like a test, a foolish test that a child might think of as a game of he-loves-me-he-loves-me-not. She debates, rubbing her thumb over the slight indentation on her ring finger: bare, smooth. She opens her jewelry box and rummages through cheap pearl necklaces and clip-on earrings and pins, until she finds the plain gold band. She doesn't put it on.

Under the bed, Natalia gathers Frank's *Playboy*s and *Hustler*s. They make her feel so outdated and worn, made invisible by time. She places them in Frank's underwear drawer, under his boxers. Still unsure, still feeling as if she's misplaced something, something beyond the room, something deep in herself, she sits on the bed and hears a familiar squeak from the springs as they sag, the same worn sound she always worried about when they made love—the walls in the house are so wafer-thin. Sex needed to be quick, silent. She lies down and turns her head onto Frank's pillow. It would be within his right, she supposes, if, in her absence, he'd had other women in this bed, if Frank's chest hair, ample and wavy, had pressed against another woman's breasts.

The pain caused by this thought hits her bluntly. She tries to dismiss it and tells herself she can rest peacefully for one moment without worry. She feels strange and heavy. There is something so tantalizing about being undiscovered. She closes her eyes. Just a moment to herself, a last moment before she takes to the children. Then she will call to them and persuade them and answer whatever questions they might proffer. She will hear about the months she has missed. Eva's prom was surely successful. She could have had any number of dates, far more than Natalia might have had at the same age. Sissy probably still struggled with science and would never have a head for concrete facts. She probably also still refused to shower after gym class, even though she'd been told a hundred times she must. Natalia closes her eyes. She sleeps.

To find someone suddenly gone, to see them one day and not know that this will be the last day you see them, to not have the moment register until hours, days later, or years, is never easy. How we catch ourselves as life moves forward, thinking about that last moment and about what we might have done differently, if only we'd known.

For Sissy it is admittedly painful to remember a friend bicycling off, down to the park—to see her again, in the mind's eye, standing on the bike pedals, *bragging*, as she always did. The new Desert Rose—bright gold with a blaze of red flowers curling down the frame—was startling against the houses and sidewalk as Vicki whizzed by, larger than everything. Sissy might have stopped her, after all. She might have kept any-

thing painful from happening. It is difficult for her to remember that
she silently leveled an accusation against Vicki, that she held her responsible for the destruction of Precious, yet again, that she blamed her for
the subsequent chastisements, the yelling of the mothers, the confine-
ment to her room, as if *Sissy* were wrong, as if *Sissy* deserved to be pun-
ished, when in Sissy's mind she had been *taunted* to action. It infuriates
her. Even now, after all these months, in the haze of guilt, she is reluctant to admit that as she saw Vicki disappear over the hill, her thoughts
weren't *Come back* (as she now amends) but *Good riddance*. She refuses
to admit she fantasized a hundred times about Vicki suddenly being
gone, about Vicki being dead (what *is* dead?). Sissy had a goldfish once,
the only pet her mother ever allowed, one that, over time, Sissy often
forgot to tend to properly. She came home one day from school to find
it gone, and her mother told her that she saw it grow wings, breathe air,
and fly out the window and into a tree. "It perched there for hours,"
Natalia explained. "Puckering its fish-bird lips." Only Eva told her that
their mother had flushed the fish down the toilet after finding it belly-
up in its bowl, an egg smear of white over its upturned eye. Still, after
that, and perhaps only to assuage her guilt, Sissy imagined death as a
grand transformation—the body shifting to another shape entirely,
changed but certainly not gone forever.

All of this is difficult for Sissy to reconcile. But in the harsh reality
of the day, in a house that only knows stubborn realities, to see her
mother sleeping exactly where she should be sleeping—in her bedroom,
on the right side of the bed—to know that she, Sissy, has passed this
door a hundred times and a hundred times has turned the knob, each
time hoping against hope and seeing nothing, and then finally to see
her mother—right here! *corporeal!*— is nothing short of overwhelming.
Yet here she is, in linen pants and heels, her mass of hair, salt-and-
pepper gray, pressed against a pillow.

Sissy blinks hard, feeling suddenly that she cannot breathe. To
breathe, she thinks, would destroy the moment, making her mother
disappear. She inches forward, releasing the door without realizing. It

drifts to the wall and bumps against it, a hollow sound. Her mother awakes abruptly—she has only been here a moment, only taken a five-minute nap—and sits up, collects herself. She says, dumbly, "Baba," the name her real mother often called her as a child. "Hello."

Sissy says nothing. Disbelieving, she bows her head slightly and bites her fingernail. She turns and runs upstairs. There is a trample of footsteps, the ascent, a call for help, a frantic call not for her mother but for Eva instead. "Eva! Eva!" she yells.

"Fucking Christ, Sissy, what?" Eva pokes her head out of her bedroom door, ready to holler more, but immediately she sees Sissy's dismay: her pallor and excitement, the thin wash of worry falling over her face. Sissy shakes her head, unable to speak. She grabs Eva's arm and pulls it violently.

"What?" Eva asks again. "What is it? What's wrong?"

Sissy mouths, "Mom."

Eva rights herself. "You're lying."

Still bewildered, Sissy shakes her head. She crosses her heart, but privately she doubts what she has seen, as if she might have imagined it all, as if she dare not call upon the confidence to validate things, not if she wants them to be real. Perhaps it was her mind playing games, wishing things into existence and then placing them where the mind and heart expect. She has no time to doubt, really, no time to find an answer for Eva. Eva storms downstairs, and then there is a reality Sissy can hold on to: Eva's shrieking—persistent, high-pitched rancor filled with obscenities. She listens a moment, tentatively, until she hears her mother's voice rise to match her sister's. She scurries back downstairs. Eva stands in the hallway, angry tears running down her blotched cheeks. "You have no right," Eva is screaming. "You think we need you now? You think you can just come and go?"

Eva lunges forward, then, in a way that an animal might—angrily, unpredictably—but Natalia holds her back, firmly, by the shoulder. She tries to soothe Eva, an action that produces in Sissy an inexplicable confusion: her mother's new reserve, her attempt then, when Eva's words fail her, when Eva is left to angry sobs, to reach for her older daughter and embrace her. "It's okay," Natalia says, composing herself as well. "You're angry."

Eva steps back and frowns before another insolent look comes over her. If she could know what to do or say, she might stay there in the hallway and let the reality of the moment settle in. She might explain how missing someone can produce not more love but resentment and hate. Instead, she can only think to mumble "Bitch" under her breath before storming off again. She slams her bedroom door in a defiant way, with such force that Sissy can almost feel a breezy current travel down the steps.

"Well," Natalia says, too loudly. She places a hand on Sissy's shoulder, cupping it, but she does not attempt this time to draw her child near. "That went well, didn't it?"

Sissy nods, still not moving closer. "I guess."

"I missed you," she says. "I missed all of you."

"Okay." Sissy doesn't know why she suddenly feels reduced in this moment. Nor does she understand the hesitation in her that this utterance causes, the newly formed doubts.

Natalia eyes her in a questioning way. "Do you think I should go upstairs and talk to your sister?"

"I wouldn't," Sissy says quietly. She slips her arm around her mother's waist, the feel of her at once familiar and strange. "If I were you," Sissy says, "I'd stay right here instead."

When Natalia feels out of sorts, when she feels nervous, she tends to want to order things, to cull satisfaction and comfort from the knowledge that everything is in its proper place, that a cosmic sense of order pervades not only the universe but the immensely complicated world of one kitchen. There is a benign satisfaction that comes from scrubbing the stove, from performing a task that requires only her hands. Later, when she finishes the stove, she washes out the Brillo pad and wipes her hands on her jeans and work shirt. She moves to the refrigerator next, throwing out an old container of sour cream layered with mold, wiping away milk rings. She throws out a wilted head of cabbage. She would give anything to make *töltött káposzta* now, to bury her hands in meat and rice and garlic, to press the meat into balls, roll them in the steamed cabbage leaves, and submerge them in tomato broth and vinegar.

"You're burning that hole through me," Natalia says, feeling rattled again. She can sense Sissy behind her but focuses her attention on the empty lunch-meat tray instead.

"Eva says she won't come down as long as you're here."

"She seems different," Natalia says. "Does she seem that way to you?"

"I don't know," Sissy says.

Natalia hears the hesitation in her voice, the obvious lie. If she turns now, she will likely find Sissy's lip slightly raised, an involuntary action she performs whenever she engages in untruths. "Are you hungry?"

"No." Another lie. Sissy shuffles into a chair, draws her knees up to her chin, thinking.

"Good," Natalia tells her. "Because there's nothing to eat anyway. We'll have to go shopping." She removes all the jarred items: the pickles and relish and marmalade, as well as the cans of Coca-Cola, and places them on the countertop in a neat row.

"I have a question," Sissy says.

Natalia turns her head slightly, just enough to see Sissy's stern, unhappy look. "Yes?"

"I want to know why you left."

Natalia searches for an explanation that will soothe her daughter, but she knows of none. Her heart stills for a moment as she thinks. She pulls out the vegetable drawer and submerges it in sudsy water. She takes a dishcloth and wipes the surface, her free hand gripping the metal lip too tightly. She rinses it with scalding water that reddens and burns her skin. When she turns again, Sissy is still watching her intently, rolling the plastic place mat, and then unrolling it.

"It was a mistake to leave," Natalia says.

"But then *why* did you leave? You didn't say goodbye. I spent all day with Mrs. Morris and her dumb stuffed cat."

Natalia shakes her head slightly.

She takes a towel embroidered with a pineapple the size of her thumb and dries the drawer. Upstairs, her daughter has locked herself away in her room in an angry, silent protest at her presence and at having left, having—Natalia shapes the word for the first time—abandoned her. She knows of no mother who would do such a thing—certainly not her real mother, who, although once threatening to sell her, later clawed at a soldier's face to keep Natalia from being taken away. Even Clara wouldn't have left Natalia alone as a child. And now here, in her kitchen, her younger daughter burns holes through her for such carelessness, her daughter gifted with an evil eye. Outside, the day is crisp and bright and birds sing. She thinks of that day in December when she snuck out of the house like a negligent thief, her body slumped over her suitcase. "I was self-centered," she says, finally.

Sissy says nothing. She lowers her legs and kicks at the chair adjacent to her until it moves.

"Sometimes you just don't know why you do the things you do. You just aren't thinking at all, I suppose."

"That's not a good answer," Sissy says, her tone suddenly brooding.

"There aren't good answers for things like this."

"Why weren't you thinking of us?"

"I was thinking of myself. I was thinking of what I wanted."

"Well that's just great," Sissy says smugly. She folds her arms and kicks the chair again.

Natalia sits down at the table. "Once," she says, "a long time ago, there was an irresponsible girl who wandered away from her family, all of them, in the woods. The girl slept on a bed of moss that was as soft as fur but comfortless. At night she climbed the trees and tried to touch the empty moon, not realizing how high it was, how far away. You see? Then one night the woods caught on fire and the fire swept over the trees, burning everything. The girl ran and ran. After a time she wandered out of the forest and through a city where people busied themselves on the streets, selling bread and cursing at one another over pennies. No one spoke her language—they were all strangers to her. And it was then that she realized she missed those known to her—her family."

"So," Sissy asks, frowning, "what happened to her?"

"She searched for those she remembered. She decided home was a place you choose, not a place you have to be. She found a home again."

"We're not strangers," Sissy says.

"No," Natalia responds, feeling something in her throat catch. "You're my family."

"I'm not going to Mrs. Morris's house anymore."

"Fine. That's fair." Natalia brushes crumbs from the table and into her waiting hand. "Who cleans here?"

"Everyone."

"I see." She gets up, opens the cabinet, and takes out vinegar and paper towels. She wipes the window above the sink, scrubbing it until it squeaks. She removes the small vase with dried flowers. She brushes the dust from the bachelor's buttons, wipes down the sill. "When I was young," she says, "I buried bachelor's buttons in the ground, to find true love. And then I met your father."

"You did that for *Dad*? I doubt it."

"Ah," Natalia says, eyeing her. "It's hard to imagine that your father and I were ever that young, right? That we were ever different."

"How different?"

"We laughed more."

"Do you still love him?"

"That isn't the question. The question is, does your father still love me, or will he look at me like a stranger?"

Sissy's face clouds over. "Mrs. Anderson comes over," she says, tentatively.

"Oh," Natalia says. "I see." She concentrates on the window, which reflects back a face she does not wish to see at all.

"I don't like her, though. I don't like her at all. Vicki Anderson," Sissy says finally. "She got lost in the woods, too, at the park when her mother was *drinking*. Eva says she was probably *sloshed*."

Natalia stops cleaning. "What do you mean?"

"A month ago Vicki Anderson disappeared. I think she ran away. Eva thinks she's *dead*."

Natalia listens as Sissy relays what details she knows, mostly things overheard, the events that shaped the month, the abandoned bike, the policemen who for weeks patrolled the neighborhood, the sniffing dogs. She lapses into events, fusing in details as they come to her, in a random sort of order: the unfilled pool, the Desert Rose and investigations, the searches the children conducted and clues they found that went largely unrecognized by uncaring adults. The summer comes out in a flood of stories, each intricately mixed with the next—Eva's terrible speculations, the signs posted on telephone poles, the found shoe. She prattles on, telling her mother about water holes and carousels, and as she listens, Natalia sorts through what is real and what can only be imagined, sieving the information as one might flour.

"Eva thinks she was *raped*."

"Oh, Jesus," Natalia says sternly. "Don't listen to your sister."

"Do you think she'll come back?"

Not knowing what to say, Natalia takes to the window again. She can only imagine what Ginny must be going through, what toll this must be taking. She thinks of her mother, how when the soldier clutched Natalia's neck as though she were a duck ready to be slaughtered, her mother screamed and spat at the ground. Still, even children can go through horrible events and survive. Anything can change—if for the worse, then also for the better. In a moment, a new story might unfold—the girl found, Ginny's house restored to harmonious order. "Anything in the entire world is possible," she says to Sissy. "Forget what Eva says. What story do you tell yourself?"

"I don't know," Sissy says. "But the one thing I *do* know is that if Vicki would have had a *dog* with her, on that day, I bet nothing would have happened to her. The other thing I know is that we're going to need to cut an onion, too, for Dad, so he won't yell at you so much when he finds out you're back."

7

If anyone can soothe Eva's wounded sensibilities, it is Peter, whose voice when he's comforting turns to velvet, cushioning her. If anyone understands that the tensions of a house are sometimes too much to bear, it is him. She imagines—she has always imagined—that it is the same for him, that they share a mutual desire to shuck off confining rooms, to be away from the demands of the people in them. They've been talking a lot lately, him sneaking furtive calls when his wife is away, their conversations sometimes brief and sometimes extended, sustaining her for the day like a pleasant meal.

Now she dials a number she hasn't yet dared to call, but one that she still knows by heart, having run her finger over "P. Fulton" in the phone book so many times, it borders on absurd obsession. When Peter answers, Eva blubbers out, "She came back. Can you believe my mother came back?" She tries to keep her tears in check, but it's no use, her emotions always betray her. "Peter?" she asks, sniffling. "Are you there?"

There is an awkward pause on the other end, a muffled, deadened noise, and then Peter calls to someone else—his wife, Eva suddenly realizes—telling her that he's got the phone, that it's no one. Hearing this, Eva becomes even more upset. "I'm trying to tell you something," she begins again, more stridently, "and you say I'm no one?"

"Eva." His voice sounds put-upon and burdened. He breathes in, waits. "Jesus Christ, don't call me at home." Then what follows is a click, a complete silence. She is suddenly as inconsequential as the day her mother left—cast off, adrift. She bites her lip, confused momentarily and, above all else, hurt. It seems she must make a decision then— to stay locked away in her room as she has for so many days, or to take some decisive action. She rummages through her jewelry box and slides on a tigereye ring. She changes into fresh clothes, a long white dress. Resolved, she takes her keys from the dresser, vowing that she, as much as her mother and father and Peter himself, can do as she pleases. Downstairs she finds Sissy in the kitchen, still upset, Eva thinks, but subdued, possibly stunned. Her mother, changed into work clothes, is down on all fours, cutting into the kitchen tiles with a wire brush. She looks up, eyes her daughter, the dress, the sudden need.

"Where are you going?" Natalia asks.

"What does it matter?" She opens up the phone book and writes down the address, just so she makes sure she remembers. "Where were you when anything mattered? Where did you go?" Eva thinks of saying more, but when she sees the look on her mother's face, the deep crease between her large eyes, she stops.

"Go, then," Natalia says, scraping harder across the floor, her muscles straining. "Be alone."

It is a twenty-minute drive to Peter's house on the other side of town. She gets lost twice and stops for directions at the gas station, the attendant finally drawing her a map before sending her on her way again. The winding streets around Peter's house daze her slightly, as do the idle park benches and newer houses. On Arbor Place, she turns and drives slowly, studying the numbers etched into brass fixtures on the mailboxes and front doors. She slows and parallel parks across the street from a blue colonial. The windows are open, the curtains flapping in the breeze. Wind chimes clatter. In the front yard a plastic kiddy pool lies abandoned, the slide shaped like an elephant's trunk. It all seems so practical, so mundane in a way, that it hurts Eva to witness. She expected Peter's house to be an altogether different shape, perhaps round with solar panels and Grateful Dead music blaring from smoky rooms—something hip and cool, but not this. Not this at all. She expected the house to have a different temperament altogether. She checks the slip of paper she clenches in her moist hand. Written there is "247 Arbor Place," a number that matches the one etched on a brass plate next to the windowed door.

She has imagined herself here so many times. She has constructed all the rooms of Peter's house, imagined herself moving through them, opening his drawers, running her hand over his tweedy smoky clothing, opening his refrigerator, lying down in his bed, the nutty smell of him on the covers. But she has never tempted the fates before in this way. She beeps the horn, waits, but no one pulls back the curtain. No one opens the door and steps outside. An elderly couple strolls along the sidewalk, eating ice cream with a pleasant laziness. A chubby boy jogs down the street, his cheeks pushing out air like small balloons.

She plans what to say, what to do. A sense of alarm grows in her, a sense of danger. She knows he is married. She knows he has a daughter he's talked about frequently in class and once or twice, more tentatively, when he was alone with her. She knows all of this, and yet in light of her mother's return and his callous response, her mind turns over new questions: Why *should* his wife have all of him? Why, if he and Eva are together, shouldn't he be there for her when she most needs him? She's filled with a sense of undoing and daring. What would happen if she walked up to the door? Knocked? Rang the bell? Announced herself as Peter's lover, told his wife about their exchanges, their bodies pressed together slick with sweat? She might say, *Do you know where he goes when he says "to the library"? Do you know the things that happen behind your back, when you aren't watching?* Thinking of all this gives her amused satisfaction. How liberating it would be to say these things aloud. If he thought he could keep her from his life, if his wife thinks their life so perfect, so immune to hurt and disruption, how wrong they both are. Eva lacked the bravery to say what she thought to her mother—her mother who in one moment managed to silence her yet again—but she could say what she thinks to a stranger, to this wife. The thought is simply tantalizing.

Resolved, Eva primps her hair and checks her face in the mirror. She gets out and sprints across the street, smoothing her dress as she ascends the walkway. She passes the kiddy pool, realizing that sand, not water, fills it, along with two plastic shovels and a bucket. *What kind of mother would let her little girl play in dirty sand?* Eva wonders, her sense of entitlement and swagger growing. She inhales deeply, hesitates only for a moment, and presses the doorbell. She waits, peering in through the columned windows on either side of the door. She views the front entrance, the curved wooden railing that leads upstairs. To the right, she catches sight of a dining room that has, in the corner, a desk with a reading lamp and envelopes stacked in thin slots. She imagines Peter sitting there, back turned to his wife, his attention consumed with his poetry, his sestinas. Around the desk, toys lie scattered on the floor. She holds her hand up to her forehead, cutting back the glare.

Impatient, now fully committed, she rings the doorbell again. She turns and looks at the view from this angle—the bushes pulling out, her car across the street, the empty-looking houses, the wide road. She hears a woman call from inside, "Hold on."

After excruciating seconds, the same woman appears, a child on her hip and phone cradled in her neck. She opens the door wider and motions with her finger. Eva braces herself and steps into the foyer made bright in the day. She puts her hand to her throat, the words ready to pour out from her. But the woman places her finger to her lips, and Eva waits, immediately comparing herself in attractiveness: Peter's wife is stout, with short permed hair, a pug nose, and a weary look. Passable, Eva thinks, but not beautiful by any stretch.

"I love you, Mom," she's saying. "Tell Dad I love him, too. Make sure Peter holds the ladder when Dad goes up on the roof this time, will you? We don't want a repetition of events." Unconcerned with Eva entirely, she turns and walks down the hallway and goes around the corner, disappearing again. Eva inhales, smells rose-scented perfume. She peers into the living room, taking it in full view. A puzzle on the coffee table remains only half-composed—a clown's face appears appallingly white, his eyes dark and serious. Against the wall, there is an ugly worn love seat with wooden inlay, a ficus tree with brown leaves collected in the base of the pot. Peter's wife comes back into the foyer a moment later, the baby still on her hip in a diaper, no shirt, a mass of red-yellow hair. "I'm sorry," the woman says, her breath exasperated. She shoos the cat from under her feet before setting the baby down in a children's swing next to the sofa. "Right," she says, turning, placing her hands on her hips. "So, what are you selling?"

Eva feels her stomach turn. "Me? Nothing."

"Oh. I thought you were selling something. You wouldn't believe how many people have stopped by in the past month, selling magazine subscriptions, cookies, wrapping paper, Avon, books. I can't keep up."

Eva shakes her head and puts her hand to her chest. "I'm not selling anything."

"What can I do for you, then?"

Eva tries to sound assertive, but she feels her swagger lessen suddenly. "Is your husband home?"

"Peter?"

She smiles. "Peter, yes. Peter."

The woman seems to regard her finally. Her eyes travel down over Eva's dress. Later, when Eva will replay this moment, she'll remember the wary look, the cautious handling of the conversation, how for a moment Peter's wife crossed her arms and paused. "He's at my parents'—

just left," she says, and it seems to Eva she stammers a bit, in the same way Eva might. "I'm his wife, Amy."

"That's sweet," Eva says. "That's nice of him to help your parents, I mean, to care like that."

Amy pauses for a moment. "Why do you ask?"

Eva tells herself not to flinch, not to miss a beat. She stands up straight, puts her hands on her hips. "I know Peter," she begins.

"Do you? Well, then, if Peter knows you, I should know you. We have the same friends, mostly, the same acquaintances . . ."

"You seem surprised." A moment more passes, and Eva sees something register in Amy, a quiet alarm. There is a broken quality to her expression, a tense hesitation. And, seeing this all, Eva suddenly hesitates, too. She wanted to feel invincible. She wanted this woman to be mean-spirited like she always believed her mother to be. The baby starts to cry. Amy sighs and pulls the child from the swing, pudgy legs kicking. She holds the little girl close, kisses her head.

"I talked to him before," Eva says, adjusting. Her cheeks flush; she can't think of the words to be so cruel. "About babysitting."

A sudden relief seems to come over Amy. "Oh," she says, patting the baby's head. "We've been discussing a sitter. You know, maybe once a month so we can get out. I didn't know he'd talked to anyone already. I don't suppose you'd do light housework, too?"

Eva bends her leg and tries to take on an air of complete casualness. She can feel the words failing her, the stutter in the back of her throat.

"I guess not," Amy says, waving her hand around. "The house is always a mess anyway, as you can see. I guess at some point it's ridiculous to bother at all with cleaning. But do you have references?"

"What?"

"You know." She scribbles an imaginary note. "Someone who could vouch for your reliability?"

Eva hesitates again, thinking. "Yes," she says, nodding, in what she will remember was a desperate way. "I can bring you names and numbers, I guess."

"People in the neighborhood? Are you the girl who sat for the Johnsons down the street? Rita Johnson? Their son's name is Henry. They were so happy with that girl; they said she was a dream."

Eva shakes her head. "No, I didn't sit for them."

"Who do you sit for in the neighborhood, then?"

"I don't," she says, straining now. "I live across town."

"That's far to go, then, isn't it?"

"Not really." Eva's hands drift upward, into the air. "I love being here. This side of town is so pretty. And the people here, they're nice. You're very lucky. I'd give anything for what you have."

Amy winces and rocks the baby. "What did you say your name was?"

"I didn't."

"Well, I should write it down. I'll talk to Peter when he gets home."

A few moments later, Eva hastily scribbles down the first name that comes to her, Brenda Armstrong. She gives the paper and pen back and then watches as Amy studies the scrawl.

"Are you still in school?"

"A senior this year. I'm almost eighteen."

"Big year." Amy glances at her again. "Well."

"Well," Eva says, "I should go." She turns, in that moment, victorious despite everything. It is so easy, she thinks. To slip into someone's life, someone's house, and imagine yourself in their rooms. A sense of gloating overwhelms her, thinking how easy it is to fool this woman, how much prowess she herself holds. Her face flushes with the knowledge, too, that it's a secret, that Peter will never know, that he'll wonder why on earth Brenda Armstrong would stop by to chat and offer services. She steps outside feeling, for the first time that day, for the first time in many days, a sense of empowerment.

8

After Natalia sends Sissy out to play, she vacuums and dusts the entire house and arranges the *National Geographic*s according to date, making a thick fan of them across the table. Upstairs, she cleans the toilets, both of which are coated with a red algal film, and she wipes dried toothpaste from the girls' shared sink. She empties a trash can that has been left to overflow with empty toilet paper rolls and tampons. She makes a quick sweep through Sissy's room, surveys the posters on the wall, the photographs of television stars around it. She is still a child and, short of her hesitations with Natalia—that awful look of distrust and doubt that Natalia caught earlier—Sissy is mostly the same, a little taller perhaps, a little more gawky and longer in the face, but still a child nonetheless.

In Eva's room, Natalia sets the laundry basket down. She absently pages through the marbled notebooks left on Eva's dresser, the copied pages of poetry by Whitman and Yeats. She rummages through the closet, pushes the blouses and skirts across the metal rod, a bouquet of scents wafting toward her as she does. She looks on the floor under boxes and yearbooks. It feels pitiful to do this. No one wants to have to piece together their child's life, to search for problems, to find out—in a desperate way—who she has become when you weren't looking.

From the window she sees Sissy playing, collecting rocks and skipping them down the sidewalk.

"Dad doesn't want us running around," Sissy said with a despairing look when she was sent out to play earlier.

"Get air," Natalia insisted, so tired was she of having to explain what she could not. "Go."

"The madman," Sissy said indignantly.

"Don't talk to strangers," Natalia told her.

"That's it?" Her tone was incredulous. She stood with her hands on her narrow hips.

"You're going to stay inside every day?" Natalia asked. "Is that how you see your life?" She saw a flicker of hesitation. "Fine, then help me scrub the kitchen floor. Inside there's always work to be done."

With that Sissy darted into the backyard, calling for the neighbor's dog.

Now Natalia opens the drawers and combs through Eva's cotton and lacy underwear. She feels dirty doing it, intrusive, terribly so, and yet something is confirmed for her when, in Eva's jewelry box, under the foam where Eva has laid her lapis ring, she finds a plastic bag filled with marijuana, which makes the candle on the bureau make sense— scented like cinnamon and burned down to a waxy, messy pulp. She breaks the dope into small pieces, flushes it down the toilet, and scrubs the rim again with a brush. She never would have expected drugs. As a child Eva was brace-toothed, pretty in pigtails, neither timid nor overly demonstrative, worrying Natalia that she hadn't given Eva enough of what the girl needed. Back in those days, Eva would ask Natalia to read to her each night, preferring books to made-up stories, as if the book, by virtue of black lettering and printed, ordered images, were more truthful than Natalia's musings. "These stories are boring," Natalia told her once, of Eva's fairy tales. "They never change." And yet, now, as Natalia looks around the room, to the posters (she recognizes the cathedral in Italy) and the records and notebooks, she sees so little of the girl she knew, of the harmony that once existed between them.

She collects clothes and takes the laundry downstairs. In the kitchen she wipes the glass in the door again, removing the flat palm print Eva left when she stormed out. She shouldn't have derided Eva, but she is still Eva's mother and it is still her house. The girls will strike out eventually, grown, to go out into the world and find their own places. They will make their own ordinary lives, not ones with magic and husbands who change into bears, not worlds where women flutter about, wearing colorful skirts and twirling around a campfire, in time with drums and harps. They will not dance over white moons or swim across oceans. What she spoke to Sissy was always a lie, wasn't it? A fabulist's tale. What is idealized is doomed to be unrealistic. Whatever dreams the girls have will be given up to the practicality of the day. They will be changed as in one of Eva's old stories from a book: the bucket, the mop, the broom.

She collects Sissy's drawings from the table, the ones done before Natalia grew weary of Sissy's questions. There are girls riding bikes across a blue backdrop, a yellow sun peeking out from the corner, spotted by a foreboding cloud. A second drawing renders lions in the jungle, and orange horses grazing by water, their nostrils hidden in the bright grass. She gathers the remnants of crayons, the worn-down yellow and indigo. She places them in the tin lying on the table.

Outside, in the glare, Sissy stands atop the ladder, holding the limp garden hose, pretending to spray water into the pool. She dances back from it, to avoid getting wet. She drops the hose. She leans over, pretending to measure. She climbs to the lip of the pool and walks. Natalia raps on the window. Sissy looks up, toward the kitchen, and inexplicably smiles. Natalia motions that it's time to come inside. When Sissy doesn't, Natalia opens the door and yells before Sissy jumps down, land-

ing with a heavy thud on the grass. She holds her arms up as if performing. "We've got to go out," Natalia says.

"Out, in!" Sissy yells. "Make up your mind!" She runs by her, her
body smelling of sun. She comes back downstairs a few minutes later,
dressed and ready. She eyes Natalia, who is holding Sissy's drawings in
her hand.

"I made them for you," Sissy says, suddenly shy again.

"I think we should give them to Ginny instead. What do you
think?"

"I made them for you. They're *originals*," Sissy explains, her voice
rising.

"All the more reason," Natalia says, "to share them with Ginny.
After we go grocery shopping, we'll stop by her house and see how she's
doing. You don't think a drawing will make Ginny feel better?"

Sissy stares fiercely. Another hole burned into Natalia's body. Sissy
grabs the pictures from her mother's hand.

"Do you think she's dead?" Sissy asks, struggling to keep next to her
mother as, later, they jaunt down the tree-lined street to Ginny's house.
The heat hits Natalia, flattening her like a bulldozer and melting the
chocolate chip cookies she bought from the grocery store. A pleasant
day, yes, were it not for the humidity that she didn't notice when she got
out of the cab earlier, the mugginess over everything that reminds her of
so many summer days. She looks up at the sky, the big clouds over her,
bright, heartbreakingly still. *Is there never a good medium?* she wonders.
Is there always a drought or flood? All or nothing? And how awful to be
caught between extremes, with not enough choices, with not enough
reconciliation between disparities. Natalia holds her free hand up
against her neck, wiping the sweat from it.

"I told you not to listen to Eva," she says.

"Eva's never lied to me."

Natalia glares at her daughter, catches herself. She's positively un-nerved by Sissy's new affection toward her sister, her irritating defiance. Before Natalia left, Eva spent most of her time ignoring Sissy, refusing to let her come into her bedroom, screaming when she'd find that Sissy had gotten into her lipsticks again. "Your sister used to lie to you all the time. She told you you were adopted. She told you that we brought you home from a church. Now she's some moral authority and compass?"

Sissy dismisses this altogether, tucks any cruelties away in the past. "Well, do you think Vicki's dead then?"

"Don't you dare say that, Sissy Kisch. Particularly in front of Ginny." She stops, turns, and grabs Sissy's arm suddenly. "I mean that. Don't be sassy."

"I'm not sassy, but you did *leave,* after all. I don't know anyone who's died, but I bet a madman did it. I bet that's what happened to Vicki. Or, my favorite *theory* is this: She ran away. I can guess why, if you care. She didn't like her mother. She thought her mother was a real bitch."

In this Natalia hears an accusation leveled against her. She eyes Sissy, tells her to watch her language. "I hope you didn't say that when Ginny visited our house, did you?"

"No." Sissy stares for a moment before pulling her arm away. "She hardly ever talks to me."

Natalia falls silent. She opens the gate and climbs up the porch steps. Before she rings the bell, she says, sternly, "Remember what I said. Not a word. Talk less, Sissy, not more."

When Ginny opens the door, Natalia simultaneously extends the plate of cookies, announces that she's returned, and goes to put her arm around Ginny in an awkward, loose embrace. She steps away then, brushes back her hair, and raises her chin without meaning to, aware once again of a distance. There was a time when she wanted Ginny's friendship more than anything. She needed a confidante and yearned for conversations. There was a time when the women were like thieves, spending Saturday afternoons together, awkwardly hatching plans against the neighbors, sipping martinis. Shouldn't she have expected that a woman like Ginny would sense, in Natalia's departure, an opportunity? That she would be grateful for a man who, despite any flaws, always provided, without complaint? Natalia might have imagined Frank with another woman in that time she was away. But when she did, the faces were inconsequential: a girl picked up over a drink; someone he met casually; someone who, in the days and weeks afterward, he would have difficulty remembering at all. But that Frank might have taken up with a woman Natalia believed to be a friend—and she must reconsider this now—is something she had not expected at all. Frank and Ginny were never particularly close before Natalia left, though it was true they were cordial and it was true Frank could always make Ginny laugh with a light joke now and then. Still, it was Natalia who took Ginny in when she first moved to the neighborhood. She was the one who defended Ginny against the rumors and admonishments leveled by the other women: Ginny's husband's suicide, the drinking that ensued, Ginny's failure to hold a job, her subsequent applications for disability. Then there were the screams the women sometimes heard, the fights with Vicki that created more animosity and disdain, particularly from those women who prided themselves on being good mothers.

She waits, watching Ginny, wondering. Only a moment passes, but it feels like an eternity.

"Thank you," Ginny says, taking the plate, not bothering to look to see what it is. She sets it down on the living room table, atop a pile of newspapers and flyers. When Natalia is left to linger, she ushers Sissy forward and shuts the door behind them. She surveys the disarray: a vase on the table filled with wilted flowers; the ashtray next to it that overflows with cigarette ends. Ginny's photograph of Vicki—long-sleeved red shirt, a gold locket around her neck, a dimpled smile, the backdrop blue like a clear sky—stares out from the table, eerily. There are countless photos of Vicki around the room, on tables and chairs. Natalia picks one up and holds it, remembering the girl who tormented Sissy, the girl who was unruly and always in trouble, the girl who, as if taking after her mother, was prone to a recklessness and disorder that matches this very room. "Sissy told me," Natalia says, not knowing what else to say. She realizes her hands are trembling. She believes if she tries to make pleasantries, she'll only seem unkind; but if she says nothing, the moment will continue this way: awkwardly, with an unsettling quiet.

Ginny gives her a look—sullen, suppressed. Natalia understands this loss. Every complicated feeling held in check and buried deep would erupt if Vicki were suddenly found, sending Ginny into hysterics, like the old women whose children were taken from them, while they stretched out their arms and screamed. "You should try and get dressed," Natalia begins. "It'll make you feel better."

Ginny looks down at her housecoat. "I haven't felt like going out." She sits down, places her hands between her tight knees.

With her pictures in hand, Sissy moves over to the high-back chair in the corner of the room. She regards the drawings. Natalia can't fathom why her daughter would put up such a fuss over a few simple sketches, or why she seems wholly incapable of sharing. She is grateful that Sissy is at least being quiet.

"It's my fault," Ginny says, not bothering to look at Natalia directly. "I should have watched."

Natalia tries to ignore the lamp shade that's askew, the faint layer of dust over everything, the trash, the lip of a bottle tucked in the couch cushion. She sits alongside Ginny. "Lots of things can happen whether you watch or not," she says, not unkindly. "Things can happen outside a house or in them. You can't hide children away. You can't stick them in front of the TV all day and deny them play and fresh air. What would happen if we did that?"

Ginny looks over at her then. Her tone is almost cruel. "And look what happened when I didn't do that, when I didn't make her watch TV and stay inside."

"It was bad luck," Natalia says, surprised by the resentment she hears. "A one-in-a-million chance."

Ginny says nothing, and Natalia rights herself. How many times did she spend with Ginny, mulling over recipes or discussing the girls' elaborate pool rituals, their habit of make-believe and conspiracies? Were their children the reason a friendship was formed at all? In the absence of the girls, did they really need anything from each other? She doesn't know. "Sissy has a gift for you, too," Natalia explains.

She waits as Sissy stands and pulls her T-shirt down. In the end, back at the house, Natalia had to bribe Sissy to procure the pictures. Now Sissy hands the drawings to Ginny. "I made them," she says. "They're originals." Natalia catches the evil eye. Her daughter looks out the window, at the same thing she stared at when they waited at the door: the bike parked up on the porch, leaning against the railing. How pale Sissy became, seeing it, how contemplative she suddenly grew.

Ginny runs her hand over the drawings. "That's very nice of you. You were her best friend." She catches herself. "Are her best friend."

"Yes," Sissy says, nodding, unsure.

"I'll clean up for you." Natalia does not wait for a response. She immediately sets about gathering up the flyers and stacking them neatly on the table. She concentrates on the task at hand, pushes away any thoughts that disturb her. "Has Frank been over to help with the yard?" This is said perhaps too lightly.

"We've always been friends, haven't we?" Ginny looks up at Natalia, and Natalia cannot tell whether she is speaking of them or of Frank.

"You must be tired," Natalia says. She runs her fingers over the burn mark on the couch, the circular black shape made from an unattended cigarette. She does this so that Ginny sees her do it. She straightens the pillows.

"You don't have to clean," Ginny says. "I'm fine."

"Nonsense. If I don't, who will? You've got enough going on."

"Vicki always thought of you as her best friend, Sissy," Ginny says. She pushes the plate of cookies forward. "Do you want one of these?"

"Okay," Sissy says.

"No, that's for later. That's for Ginny. You're getting ice cream, remember?" To Ginny, Natalia says, "We don't need anything. We came to help out. Sissy told me Frank comes over, too, to help."

"Frank 's been a help, yes."

"Of course. Did you—"

"What?"

Natalia shakes her head. "Nothing." She brushes the ash from the table, into the tray.

"He said Vicki would come home," Ginny tells her. "Frank."

Something shifts in Natalia, though she doesn't want it to. A tension mounts in her shoulders, a wildness pushes in her heart. Her look grows cold, serene. "Do you believe that?"

"I have to."

"A ten-year-old? On her own?"

"Mom," Sissy says. "Don't."

"She's very smart; she'd find her way home," Ginny says. "You did."

"Really?"

"Mom," Sissy says.

"Anything is possible," Natalia tells her, "but what is likely is an altogether different story."

"Less talk, Mom."

The moment Sissy says this, Natalia regrets her words. "You're right," she says, composing herself. She smooths her shirt. "I'm sorry. I'm tired and not thinking practically. Of course Frank's right. Of course Vicki is going to come back." Breathless, nearing tears, she retreats to the kitchen and surveys the broken glass on the floor, a partial footprint, a shocking smear of blood on the dingy tiles. She can only imagine what Ginny must be like after emptying a bottle, staggering around, her home unfamiliar. On the table a fruit basket has been left to rot—the grapes have withered on their vine, the apples have grown blemishes, and the oranges sicken the air. A note from Milly reads, simply, "Everyone is hoping for the best and keeping an eye out." How jarring, Natalia thinks, to live off scraps, on the things other people throw to you. How jarring to think people watch because you don't. There is always such a fine line between a statement meant to soothe and a taunt.

She finds the dustpan, cleans up the glass. She wets a rag and wipes the floor.

"You're her best friend," Ginny says, forcing a smile.

The words come to Sissy again, from out of the ether. "Best friend"—the implication of the phrase a light burden.

"She was so nervous her first day in school, being in a new place, and you were kind to her, to sit with her at lunch. Remember all your sleepovers?"

Sissy nods, remembering most everything: the first day of class and Vicki's stories about her father's Purple Heart; the many instances when she picked Sissy for volleyball or dodgeball before those who excelled in such arenas; the long searches for ghosts and conversations under the covers; the posed questions: *Did you ever kiss a boy?* How Sissy would blush, thinking not of a boy but *Greg,* Eva's friend with the dreamy gaze. *I haven't kissed any boy yet,* Sissy explained. *Me neither,* Vicki said. *But it's a goal for next year.*

Sissy isn't even sure she likes the girl who was once a friend and was then hated, and who is now, in absence, elevated to the stature of beloved, cherished. Mrs. Anderson's words allow Sissy a reason to *mourn,* in much the same way she sees on television: dramatically, with tears she only half possesses. An odd thing. Even if it is all true, that they were best friends and that because of that fact alone they are still such, she can't say she likes Mrs. Anderson, the same woman who, after the incident with Precious, came over to pick Vicki up a full day in advance of her scheduled departure—the sleepover cut hastily short. And when she saw the damage done to Vicki's hair—while ignoring the damage done to Sissy's doll—she yelled, causing Sissy to cry from embarrassment, from the shock of another mother acting like her own. That this was also done publicly, in front of Natalia, who did nothing to come to Sissy's defense, and that Vicki could witness Sissy's humiliation, made the entire event unforgivable. Only Eva seemed to sense in Sissy the extent of the damage. "She deserved it, that little shit," she told Sissy when, for the first time ever, Sissy begged entry into Eva's room and not their mother's.

And then, too, there are the kept secrets, the things Sissy knows about Mrs. Anderson, things told to her on those days Vicki would become somber and quiet, kicking stones down the road with an alarming force. All this makes Sissy leery of the woman in front of her now, the woman who is holding her drawings.

"Come sit," Ginny says, patting the pillow beside her.

"I'm fine sitting here." She hears her mother in the kitchen.

"Don't be silly." Ginny adjusts her housecoat, pulls it from where it's caught under her. She moves over. "Here," she says, "next to me. I need you next to me."

Reluctantly, Sissy obeys. She sits on the edge of the cushion, and before she can maneuver away, Ginny catches her suddenly and pulls her close in an embrace. She holds her there, her chin against her head, Sissy against her housecoat. Sissy smells cotton, the earthiness of it, and smoke. She can hardly breathe. It is painful for Sissy to sense an adult's world is crumbling before her. When an adult's world falls apart—like her father's, in the weeks after her mother left—there seems to be so little space for children, so little room to hide anywhere.

Still, she thinks: If she doesn't writhe around, she won't die, and if she can sit still long enough, she won't die, and if she can stand to have her hair stroked by a woman who months ago yelled at her, who embarrassed her, and who is really all in all a stranger, she won't die, and if she can accept the breath on her forehead, if she can do this—if she can withstand all this—it will be over and she will not die and she will be fine, she will live through it. And she thinks about her mother's stories of dancing bears and carousels, and she thinks about Scooby-Doo, and she thinks about Lake Paupac with its crystal water and women who try to touch the moon, and she thinks about Eva, who she wishes were here, and she taps her foot violently, though the rest of her body is mostly still, and she thinks of secrets, and she thinks of Vicki Anderson and how they were always pretending to run away. She stiffens more. It is a balancing act to be what an adult wants and needs you to be—to be a baby or to be a grown-up, depending upon whether they want you close or far away from them: *Come here, baby, be a baby,* or *No, no, be a big girl,* and she taps her foot harder.

"I can't breathe," she says finally.

Mrs. Anderson releases her and pulls back suddenly, a look of shame crossing her face as if she's just betrayed someone. She holds Sissy's hands. "You miss her, don't you?" she asks.

Be a good girl, she thinks, nodding.

"That's why you drew the pictures?"

"My mother told me to draw the pictures," Sissy says, "because she said I was staring a hole right through her back. I didn't think about the pictures—I just drew them. My mother said you would like the pictures."

"Yes," Ginny says, nodding. "I do very much. And you miss her, don't you?"

"I guess," Sissy says.

"I think about her all the time."

"Mrs. Anderson—"

"I know what you're thinking," she continues. "I know what Vicki probably told you."

Her voice in Sissy's ear, her warm breath. She thinks, *Be a good girl. Be a good girl.—Tap, tap, tap . . .*

"When she punched her hand through that window, on the dare. You remember."

Sissy doesn't tell her that she was the one who dared Vicki. She sits still, taps her foot, says nothing.

"Did she say anything to you?"

"No." *Tap, tap, tap, tap, tap.*

"I didn't mean to hit her," Mrs. Anderson says.

"Okay," Sissy tells her.

"She told you?"

"She never said anything, Mrs. Anderson. She never said anything at all." Sissy inches away, wishing her mother would come out from the kitchen. "Mrs. Anderson—"

"What, baby? What can I do for you? I'm here."

Sissy bites her lip. She bites again, harder, and tastes blood. Confusion fills her, a desire to run. She looks outside. "If Vicki doesn't come home," she asks suddenly, "can I have her bike?"

9

At midnight the house is always quiet, the girls asleep—sometimes alone, sometimes together. How fragile his girls seem, sleeping. Though they don't know it, Frank checks in on them every night, just as he did when they were babies. He opens the door a crack, lets a thin slit of light fall into the darkness. The light glides across their backs and covers, and, seeing they are safe and home where they belong, he feels happy enough and has a sense that all the hard work, that all the scraping by, is worth it. He stands for a moment, and he feels content. He does this before retreating downstairs again to eat, or sometimes to read the newspaper, or, if he is horny, before going to bed with a *Playboy* stashed under his arm, his date a brunette with smooth curves and pink nipples. Occasionally he'll read books on car maintenance, or he'll sit outside on the front steps and take in the night, the illuminated streetlights of the town he loves, this town he has lived in all his life.

And tonight he is so tense, he needs this grounding. Chaos erupted at work, after one of the blast furnaces was shut down for maintenance. The gases locked in the chamber, all of which were combustible, came in contact with the hot air and exploded in flames and choking and blinding smoke. The burns. The seething fire. A new kid's error, some eighteen-year-old. As the foreman, Frank had gone over all the proper procedures with him several times, in exacting detail. He'd guided the kid through the ordering of switches, the steps he needed for safety, the same protocols Frank had taught new hires time and time again. The new kid, a doughy-faced boy with a thatch of yellow hair, didn't wait and took to working alone. And then the building pressure, the heat, the blast throwing him back off his feet, the fire scorching the kid's face and hands while the alarm sounded. When the boom rattled through every pipe and shook the floor under Frank's feet, he and his friend Lennie came running. Frank pulled the emergency switch and set about extinguishing the fire. He secured the furnace while Lennie rushed to get a first aid kit and applied ointment. He wrapped the kid's hands. A piece of flesh had peeled from the kid's face. They didn't know what to do about that, and debated for a few minutes before Frank lifted the flesh up and placed gauze on it, with tape. They waited until the ambulance came. And, as if this incident hadn't set him off, later in the evening, toward the end of his shift, that medical truck from a hospital pulled in as it did on several nights throughout the year—they never knew when—and two men dumped body parts into the furnaces: arms and legs from amputees, tossed into the blasting heat. The workers—Frank included—were told from higher-ups not to ask questions, to keep their mouths shut if they valued their jobs. Still, as he watched the severed arms fall—the smooth cut of bone from the saw, the jagged bits of flesh illuminated in the heat—he thought it was wrong to condone this, that so much was wrong with this practice.

As he gets out of the car now and raps on the hood of his Chevy, he tells himself: *Forget it. Lay it down.* The night has cooled to mild temperatures. Tree branches break the moon into jagged pieces. The leaves flutter like small hands.

Inside, he sets down his thermos on the table, along with his lunch pail. The smell of garlic and cooked cabbage assaults him almost immediately. On the stove a pot simmers on low. He lifts the lid, feels the billowing steam and earthiness, and knows instinctively that Eva would never make this meal in a million years, and that Natalia is back. He catches sight of an onion laid in the corner of the kitchen—small-looking, quartered. He doesn't need anyone to tell him what, in twenty years of marriage, he has learned about his wife: that Natalia must have grown restless. He always knew she'd come back, that she would tire of the doctor if the doctor didn't tire of her first. Frank doesn't need anyone to tell him that for however assured and stoic Natalia might seem in the public eye, she has been and always will be a woman privately riddled with self-doubts, the same uncomfortable girl he met in high school, despite her pretenses. And he doesn't need anyone to tell him that she's there now, somewhere in the kitchen behind him, perhaps lingering at the doorway. He can feel her, like a shock wave that causes first a heightened sensibility in him and then tension. His jaw clenches.

He replaces the lid. He hears her register a breath, anticipating him and what he might say, or what he might do. How is it, he wonders, that he should suddenly feel as though he's done something wrong, that she should dread him, fear his anger? Why should he feel like this when she is the one who left? Why should he have to justify his reaction and have it be held to Natalia's scrutiny? He could, if he wanted, throw her out right now, out of the house that he pays for, out of the rooms she has abandoned. He could leave her with nothing. It would be reasonable. It would be undeniably fair. Many times when he imagined this day, this night, he thought he would lunge at her immediately. He might hold her down, rip at her throat. Taste blood.

"Frank." She whispers this in the almost girlish voice he remembers from long ago.

She stands by the kitchen chair, rigid, dressed in her plain nightgown, her breasts sagging, her hair pinned back. Seeing her, his molars press together. He opens the refrigerator, takes out a soda, pulls back the tab, and releases the pressure with a quick pop. But soda doesn't please him tonight, so he walks outside to the shed without saying a word. For the first time since Christmas—Did his hand reach? Did he press his lips to Eva's neck? Was there more? He barely remembers, the world was set to a dizzying, indistinct spin, his mind bleary and diffuse—he decides upon a beer instead. As he walks past the pool, he fails to notice for the second time that there is a glimmer of moonlight against the inches of glassy water, fails to notice the hose hanging over the rim—Natalia making good on another recent promise to Sissy. When he enters the kitchen again, she's sitting, her hands against the table, folded tightly.

"Your silence is the worst," she says. She will not look at him now, not register his disgust. "I wish you'd say something, anything."

He takes a swig of warm beer, his calloused, large hand encircling the can, pressing it like a vise—firmly, so he can just feel the give. He places the rest of the six-pack in the refrigerator, then leans against the counter, staring, content to make her feel uncomfortable. It seems the least she deserves: this stiff, protracted silence. He will not confess—he will never confess—that after his rage, and after all the angry nights lying awake, thinking of her and the doctor together, after all the time anticipating a moment such as this, he has missed her. He will not confess the moments when, instead of looking at the brunettes with soft curves, knockoffs of Hollywood stars, he pulled out an old photograph: Natalia shy at twenty-one in a one-piece bathing suit that hugged her hips, her head back, unaware that he had snapped the camera. Finally, he will not tell her that the most compelling thing about this very moment, the one thing that might make him speak to her, is the food simmering on the stove that he will not eat.

He swigs his beer, finishing the can. She begins to seem ridiculous to him, foolish, worthy of his contempt, sitting there, her gaze not holding his—his is an iron lock on her, how he could crush her. He knows his strength in this moment is her inability to quell his anger. She's looking out the window, to nothing. Perhaps, he thinks, she doesn't glance at him because he holds the day's sweat, the grease and grime, perhaps in this moment he disgusts her as well, his thick hair and body, the grizzled stubble. But she's still back again, still back in the house—for what, then, or whom? The girls? Only the girls? And this thought makes him angrier.

Natalia drums her hands against the wood. For the first time he realizes her knuckles have gone pale. She says, "Say something."

He will give her nothing. He will give her as much as she has given him over the past months—not one iota of care. Finally, after a long pause, he says, "I was thinking that I should have kicked you out years ago, when you first got knocked up. Would have saved me the hassle."

She adjusts her nightgown, pulling it upward, her hand to her chest. "You're angry," she says. "I know that."

"You think?"

"It wasn't easy to come back home. You don't have to make it harder."

"It feels good to make it harder," he says. "It shouldn't be easy. I don't know what you'd expect, what you want from me." For the first time since being home he notices that the house is clean, that there is an order to everything he has almost forgotten. "Why did you go, again?" he asks. "You never said, did you?"

"You know I didn't."

"You left apples. What the hell was I supposed to think? Crazy is what I thought. You went fucking crazy, leaving apples."

"I wasn't crazy," she says.

A fan hums in the hallway, circulating warm air. He notices the way her voice trembles as she speaks, while his quakes. "You know after you left, Lennie was on shift with me. He got transferred from days. I hadn't seen him in months and he asked how you were, and you know what I told him?"

Natalia rubs her neck.

"I told him, without even thinking, that you were dead. That you died in a car wreck."

"Did that make you feel good?"

"You're damn right it did. You have no idea how good it felt."

"I needed something," she says, still looking out the window, still quietly refusing him. "Something that wasn't this."

" 'Fucking dead,' I told Lennie. I said, 'Geez, that bitch just died on me.' "

She studies her hands then, rubbing her thumb over her finger. He has a perfect view of her profile.

"Did it make you feel better to say all that?" she asks, finally glancing over. She holds his gaze now. "The girls are so angry. Eva, especially."

"They're old enough to draw their own conclusions. They're old enough to figure out things. I didn't need to say anything. Both of them were wrecked. We—" He stops short of his last thought.

Natalia waits. "It was my mistake," she says finally.

"Is that what it's called these days when you fuck someone else?"

There is a long, anguished silence that makes Frank want to get in his car and leave, just drive for the night. Natalia starts talking then, making small talk first, and next trying to explain everything. She prattles on, in Frank's estimation, seeking reconciliation when there is nothing he can forgive. It all strikes him as insincere. It all strikes him as excuses that aren't grounded in anything concretely real, as if he kept her from her life, when the simple fact was that, prior to the doctor, and out of either ostentation or diffidence, Natalia had only kept herself from things and people. It wasn't Frank who'd shortchanged her, held her back. He hadn't held her hostage in the house. It never bothered him much, short of his pride, which even he knew to be foolish, that she got a job. There was no reason that she couldn't go and *find herself.* What self-containment she felt was born of the simple fact that Natalia finally didn't know what she wanted. She had never known herself, and she never would. And the more she talks now, the more he denies her, arms crossed. There is nothing—absolutely nothing—she can say to assuage him.

"Shut up," he says, suddenly. "Just shut up."

"I can handle a lot of things," she says, "more than you can guess, but I can't handle this from you." She gets up, pushes the chair in as if *she* might be finished.

For the first time since he's been home, it registers: that she knew he wouldn't insist she leave, that she had already settled in, that she was as ungracious as the girls often were, bent on somehow making him feel as if he didn't deserve a place in his own house. As if she was the one in control. He's furious at this thought. In a rush, he moves toward her and pulls her around before she enters the bedroom, his arm pressing down on her flesh, hard, drawing her near. He can smell her, the warmth of her. "I don't know where you're sleeping," he says. "But if you think you're sleeping in here, you've got a hell of a thing coming."

It is something of a spectacle then, the escalation of an argument. The words spoken bitingly, the shouting and Natalia's demand that Frank keep his voice down, but Natalia, her nerves frayed from waiting all day, also begins to yell. She pushes Frank away. And when Frank pushes back, he stops himself suddenly and takes to the bedroom, ripping up the covers, the sheets, the mattress, throwing them to the ground.

The next morning and for the next two weeks, there will be a silence so stiffening that it will be painful for anyone to be around anyone else in the house. Sissy will spend days reading in her room, alone. Frank will spend the morning tinkering outside before going to work. Eva will disappear from the house for the entire day, and no one will think to ask why. But for now there is a spectacle, this screaming and noise.

Thank God, Natalia thinks, *I shut the windows.*

Upstairs, through the thin walls, Sissy lies awake, straining to hear but not wanting to hear anything at all. Her clock—a plastic cat and mouse that, on every hour, engage in futile play, turning in circles, the cat never catching up—ticks and ticks, and the half hour sounds. Outside, the tree branches scrape against her window like fingers, and the leaves, black in the night, press against the glass. She concentrates on the ticking, not the sound of something hitting the wall. *What was that, though?* she thinks. *A body?* She thinks, *Is someone really dead?*

She knocks on the wall. Hearing the muffled sound in response, she slides out of bed and sneaks over to Eva's room. She finds her sister lying on her side, her hand tucked under her cheek, listening. Eva lifts the covers, takes Sissy in. Eva threads her hands through Sissy's hair. She pulls, gently, through knotted strands, separating them. "If life were perfect," she whispers, "we would find a cure for all these split ends."

"I know," Sissy says, taking her strand from Eva's hand and staring at it. She lets it drop against the pillow. "But no such luck. I'm cursed."

"You are," Eva agrees. "We both are."

"Eva?"

"What?"

"Are you okay with Mom being home?"

"No," she says. She pushes her own hair back, rests her chin on Sissy's head. "Maybe. I don't know how I feel."

"Me neither," Sissy confesses. "I hate it when they yell."

"Don't listen, then," she says. "Just think of something else. Think of anything else."

"Mom filled the pool today. Started to."

"She's a fucking miracle worker."

"You didn't do it."

"I didn't have time to do it," Eva says, lifting her head. "I've been watching over you, remember? And by the way, there's a drought, moron."

A crash, another dead body.

"Why do they do that? Why do they yell?"

"I don't know," Eva says. "Because they can't get along."

"Eva?"

"What?"

"Was it always like this?"

Eva thinks. She pulls her fingers through more of Sissy's hair. "Not always," she says finally.

"Were you happy then?"

Eva pauses, thinks, her thoughts far away. "I think I was."

"Was I happy then?"

"Yes," she says. "You definitely were."

"I thought so."

"Do you remember those fights they had when I started dating?" Eva asks.

"Yes," Sissy says, though she barely remembers. "Eva?"

"What?"

"Can you tell me a story? Can you tell me a story about the two of us, one that you remember?"

10

"Does everything just fall off the face of the fucking earth?" Amy wants
to know.

Peter refuses to ponder the implications of such a question and instead watches as she reaches under the couch, groping, her frayed cut-
offs riding up on her every time she moves. She curses again, and Peter
thinks to remind her about language but decides that would only be
wise if Sophie weren't in the kitchen, screaming, her gums worn raw.
Exasperated, Amy reaches deeper, looking as though she's being eaten
by the cushions and ribbed fabric. He kneels down beside her and
gropes under the sofa, too. "What are we looking for, anyway?"

"Sophie's pacifier, Peter. I already said. Didn't you hear?"

"Doesn't she have more than one?"

"That's not the point," Amy says, still intent on the task before her.
"The point is I can't find it and this is the third thing I've lost today, and
now I feel fairly cranky, like I'm incompetent or something. Do you

know what I mean? I *have* to find the crummy pacifier. I'm hoping it'll set the world straight."

Peter reaches farther and ignores the early August light. He wishes that he and Amy could be outside on such a day as this, passing time in pleasant ways—a trip to the zoo, or a leisurely lunch. He wishes she'd say, *Forget it, we're incompetent, yes, but let's just get out.* His hand brushes against Amy's—the smooth line of thumb, the rough cuticle. He apologizes, though he doesn't know why, really. He finds a toy mouse and thinks again of how, two weeks ago, when he came home from helping his father-in-law repair his shingled roof, Amy told him that Lear had gotten lost, escaped out the front door when she'd gone to retrieve the mail. Though Peter left cat food and milk on the front step in the following days, the food remained uneaten and the milk turned into a sour graveyard for gnats, their minuscule wings spread, their lifeless bodies clinging to the sides of the bowl. He felt such abject guilt. He imagined that the cat might have been hit by a car, or be stuck up in some tree. Lear's image haunted Peter as he composed a particularly brutal poem about accidental death.

Amy curses under her breath. "Finally," she says, pulling out the pacifier. She wipes dirt from it. "I knew it was under here. Sophie was playing on the couch today." She walks to the kitchen and beneath their child's sobs Peter hears a blast of water from the faucet. He sits on the floor, resolving himself to the tension he can't break of late, the lingering silences and tentative looks. In bed at night, Amy tucks Sophie between them, letting her sleep while she reads and Peter wrestles with another failed poem, one he plans to enter into a contest sponsored by the local college. He hopes Amy might address his sullenness, his own lack of conversation that often matches hers. He even hopes she might uncover his affair, which he wrote about in his third sestina of a planned sequence of twelve. He hopes the poem might afford them an occasion to air their grievances openly. Then, if they are lucky enough, they might emerge on the other side of their marriage, still intact. But Amy only views his work casually, informing Peter that his poetry always seems to be an act of verbal masturbation.

In fact it seems that all his hopes of late have been dashed, that he
has made the wrong choices. Even at school his students seem bored
with him and his anecdotes. As he gazes from face to face, he realizes
that he's failed them, and that they know this all too well. He wants
fresh faces. He wants to erase the board, walk out of the classroom, and
forget.

In the kitchen, he finds Amy atop a stepladder, stenciling lacy borders of ivy around the window frames—and once again he feels choked
up and weedy. "Why so much ivy?" he asked, when she started this
hobby. He told her it was becoming a bit ridiculous, that they didn't live
in a jungle, after all, but she responded, not unkindly, "I need something for me. You have the library, your poems, and I have Sophie and
my stencils."

He cannot argue with this now.

Age has caught him. His affair catches him as it becomes increas-
ingly complicated and when Eva's emotions become finely limned.
When he and Eva lie together in his van after sex, her stare often grows
too intense, her need overbearing—sweetly simple, in a way—and, in
that moment, he is frightened and ashamed. And how bizarre that, despite knowing all this, he still continues to see Eva, still continues to
sneak out when he can, or call, yearning for a break in the day. He cannot reconcile the contradictions he feels in his heart. He doesn't understand, really, why people—himself included—risk so much only to be
reminded of what matters most—to somehow feel love press more ur-
gently. Everything, absolutely everything, has taken on a quiet, conspiratorial air.

Amy leans back slightly and regards the wavy outline, the veined
pattern of leaf. Peter looks for his keys.

"Where are you going?"

"Library."

"Another library excursion? What is that, twice this week? You must
be a genius, with all you read."

He ignores this. "I might also look for Lear."

Amy positions a small brush on the container of paint. "We should talk about Lear."

"I already know you think the cat poses a health hazard," he says. He searches the junk drawer, which is stuffed beyond reasonable capacity with birthday cards, packets of lavender, tomato seeds for the garden Amy wanted but failed to start in spring, and, inexplicably, a pack of razors. He looks up. "Where are my keys?"

Amy descends the ladder and sits down at the kitchen table, next to the playpen. She offers Sophie a small rubber toy. "How should I know? They're your keys."

Peter doesn't answer. Already he's thinking about the phone call he's made, the proposed meeting, the frenzied tangle of skin that is to come, along with the afterthoughts, the sweet longing for so much—how pronounced it all is, after he risks.

"Lear is gone, Peter."

"I *know* that. That's why I'm looking for him. And my keys. Yes, to answer your question. Apparently everything in this house falls off the face of the goddamn earth."

Amy becomes quiet. She looks down at her toes, wiggles them, and looks up again. "Lear—I took him to the shelter."

"I checked the shelter, and what do you mean, you *took* him?"

"The one in Jersey. I drove him out to Jersey and dropped him off."

Peter shakes his head, unwilling to embrace the slow realization that comes to him. "You told me that Lear got out," he begins, almost tentatively. "You said he ran under the bushes . . ."

"I already know what I said. I'm not an idiot." Her tone is short. "The cat wasn't getting enough from *either* of us. It's better this way."

Peter can't help but think of Lear fated to a cage, sentenced to an early demise by lethal injection. He remembers better days—the cat just a kitten, Amy and Peter making the wide, rugged journey across the states, their vision for the future optimistic and wonderfully bright— the two of them holding hands, music playing on the radio. "No," he says, his voice flat. "It's better for *you*."

"I'm not in the mood to fight," she says, though it's clear to him she is.

Peter grows silent. He slams the drawer shut and opens another, which causes Sophie to cry more.

"Don't be bitter," she says.

But he is suddenly very bitter. He finds his keys tucked in the bread drawer, behind the Stroehmann's. Under them, there's a scrap of paper, the handwriting recognizable and thickly looped, but still not matching the name or number. He picks it up, thinking of what to say to recuse himself. He crumples the paper before tossing it into the trash.

"Why do that?" Amy asks. "What's so upsetting?"

"It's junk," he says. "Nothing is upsetting."

"No," she says. "That's not junk, that's the name of a girl who stopped by the other week. She asked for you, by the way."

"Did she?" he asks too casually. "And what did she want?"

"She *said* she wanted a job babysitting. But I'm just not sure. I don't know how we could trust a young girl with our baby, with our house. Just exactly how well do you know her?"

What is he to say? The plain truth and absolute lies are both bad in equal measure, his reasons for lying in the first place mercurial at best. He studies Amy, her thin lips, her questioning expression. "She's a girl from class," he says finally.

"That makes sense."

"It's not like that," he tells her. "Look, she's got a crush. Frankly, she's got a lot of problems."

"What kind of problems?" Amy waits.

"I don't know—domestic things, the usual stuff. She's looking for someone—for something—to cling to. It's nothing at all, nothing I've done."

"You blame a girl?"

"I don't blame anyone," he says, gripping his keys tighter. "You asked. I'm just saying."

There is silence, then, between them, too long, too pronounced.

Amy gets up and takes her paintbrush in hand. "Go," she says finally, waving her hand. She smacks the brush against the wall. "I need to think about things. I need to be alone. You can take Sophie with you. You're not the only one who needs a break."

Expectant, hopeful, Eva waits in the lot next to an elder-care facility that is situated away from the main roads and nestled behind a pond that geese frequent in the summer months. In the distance she sees a figure in white—a hospital attendant—shoo the honking geese from the road. She watches as the geese flap their wings violently and move into water littered with down and feathers. She plays with the fan vents on her driver's panel. She unsticks and sticks the masking tape that holds the radio knob in place. When she tires of that, she goes through the junk on the floor—a few fashion magazines, a receipt from the grocery store, a bag of half-eaten potato chips. She wonders if she misheard Peter when he told her the time to meet. She looks at her watch again, realizing it is an awful activity to engage in, the measuring of time—and only a minute has passed since she last looked, anyway.

If she could convince herself that it didn't matter, that Peter was just like so many boys she's known, she might turn the key again and leave him to find an empty lot and no one waiting for him at all. She might go and find Greg instead, whom she was to meet today before the phone sounded and her plans immediately changed. She might, if she didn't care, leave Peter to his regret, to the knowledge that, by making her wait all the time, he risks losing her.

Within the hour, a few drops of rain spot the macadam, and then a crack of thunder sounds. She tilts her head, taking in the line of trees. The breezes whirl and lift the leaves, whipping them into nervous motion. Eva cracks the window, grateful for the thunder, surprised by how much she missed its occasional forcefulness and grumble, its seeming accusations. Drops of rain slide down her window in erratic patterns;

she listens to the thudding sound on the hood. There is a sudden damp chill, the smell of earth made moist again, mud and grass.

How she desires Peter now, wants him to be near. How she wishes to slide into his van, gather him in her arms and feel his tongue in her mouth, his hands on her skin. How she wishes to shut everything out but him and the rain. To her growing relief, Peter has not mentioned her visit to his house that day. It is just as well, Eva decides. She herself began to regret the action almost immediately, the possibility of Peter finding out about her ill-planned, impulsive scheme. She cannot even inhabit the memory of that day without wincing at her own actions and behavior. The first time she and Peter were together, after that day he chastised her for calling and they spent considerable time arguing before he told her that if she ever did that again—if she ever called—everything between them would be over. But he said nothing of her visit, nothing at all, and so she assumed Peter's wife must have discarded the scrap of paper, or perhaps lost it amid the activity of the day.

After the argument Peter was slow to rouse and Eva found she had to coax him, gently, as she might a boy, weaning him from his anger until he relented, towering over her, his legs pressing hers then pushing them apart, all while his teeth pulled at her skin. When sex was over, they lay quietly, the rug scratchy under Eva's bare back, Peter's pale arms around her, her hip touching his. She rested her chin on his chest and went on about her mother's return and he listened, stroking her hair as she recounted everything about that day, up to the point where she left to find him.

"Have you forgiven her?" he asked, his own anger by that point entirely exhausted. He ran his hand down her neck, then along the line of her bare shoulder and breast.

"Not yet," Eva whispered. Eva moved from him then and concentrated on the worn books Peter didn't bother to return to the library. She sat up, naked, Indian-style, the smell of them mingling between her legs. She picked up a book and paged through it absently.

"Hey," Peter said to her. "Come back here."

"Will you be there when I need you to be?"

He looked up toward the ceiling and waited. "When I can," he said, finally, but it sounded to Eva like an untruth, and for as much as she didn't wish to hear hesitation, it seemed to lie under his words.

"Thanks a lot," she said.

"We're not married."

"Well, obviously." Eva rolled her eyes.

"Come here," he said again.

She looked at him—naked, his lean legs and stomach, his limp penis curled against thick hair. She would take any moment she could get, she decided. She convinced herself that whatever they had—however fleeting each encounter—she would cherish. And she did come back to Peter then. He touched her forehead, pressing it lightly with his thumb, and she settled down against him again. She closed her eyes.

The attendant is gone. The geese, too, have vanished in the now almost blinding downpour. The cool air teases her skin. Perhaps it is the weather that's kept him, the fog-ridden windows, the surely congested roads. She will never know about Peter's day, how he dreaded facing Amy again, how, once in his van, Sophie pitched a tantrum, how her screams reverberated in Peter's brain. She will never know how, at the SPCA in New Jersey, he described his cat to the attendant. She will never know that as he passed the cages, Sophie writhed and struggled and Peter blamed Eva for everything. She will never know any of this.

Instead, Eva plans what she will say, already coming up with the friendly complaints she will level—the amount of time wasted, her curls that have tightened and frizzed after she spent so much time primping. She'll tease him, telling him that he only thinks of her as a diversion—a bit of fun—then she'll wait for him to reassure her that it isn't like that, that she's got it all wrong and she knows it. She sits idly for another hour, until the rain turns into a faint drizzle and the last remaining drops of rain slide slowly down her window in drippy waves. She breathes and waits just one more moment—one moment longer, and then a few more—before turning the key and heading back home.

II

The summer continues unpredictably into mid-August, bleeding out moments. A forgetfulness sets in. The neighborhood meetings gradually diminish; searches at the park lessen, then cease. The police presence once felt dwindles as the officers' attentions turn toward drug problems on the south side of town: a planned raid, a chase through the city. There is, as is the case of those closest to an incident, the lingering effect of absence, and there is talk now not of the girl who went missing, but of how to best help the girl's mother. Ginny Anderson is seen out less, once—as reported by Milly Morris—wandering aimlessly down the street at night dressed in a housecoat and sneakers, and once—as reported by Edna Stone, who told a group of women at her card club—down at the park, sitting on a bench, staring out into the woods. The rumors amplify with each retelling, so that soon most people believe Ginny to be a woman made mad by waiting and doubt. The women in the neighborhood whisper at the mailboxes that something clearly needs to be done.

On Saturday, Natalia steps outside. The breeze blows gently, causing the branches outside Sissy's window to dance. Natalia blinks hard in the morning light, still smelling the lemony wash on her hands and arms, the soapy blend from her morning shower. She collects a copious amount of junk mail from their mailbox. Across the street, Ellie Green and Jenny Schultz sit out on Jenny's porch, and before Natalia can avert her gaze, Ellie, a small woman with dark short hair and olive skin, sends up a wave, beckoning her. She's been neighbors with these women for years. She's sat with them and exchanged pleasantries at those occasional summer picnics. She's passed them watermelon on a plate and done so with a smile, but she has never really entered into the cliques, never divulged too much of herself for fear of recrimination. Rather, she has kept a courteous distance that she considers necessary, with neighbors especially. She has never talked about anything of importance, nor has she since she's been home—Frank and the children, her struggle to find a place within the house again. Since she's been back, she's avoided most people, managing to slip indoors when she sees someone out, retreating until people have passed by on the sidewalk. She has even of late avoided Ginny—how ashamed of herself Natalia was after the last visit, the things she said about Ginny's child, the quiet accusations leveled. Still, she felt that same pinched hardness and jealousy return in her stomach when Frank called Ginny last night. Without saying a word to Natalia, he walked over to Ginny's house and came home an hour later, sullen and quiet.

"Is she okay?" Natalia asked, feeling something raw in her throat.

"She's what you'd expect."

"Any news?"

Frank shook his head.

"Are you and Ginny—"

"What?" Frank said, his tone genuinely surprised. He stood waiting.

"Nothing," Natalia told him. She went into the bedroom alone. "Never mind."

She didn't know what the neighbors thought, about her, about Frank or Ginny. She didn't want to know the gossip.

"Natalia!" Jenny calls.

Natalia sends a reluctant wave back and walks over, slowly, knowing it is impossible to pretend she doesn't hear or see.

"Glad you're out," Jenny says, leaning forward in her lawn chair. As she does, her pearl earrings dangle like small white moons. She smooths her hands against her tanned knees. Natalia thinks how attractive a woman Jenny is, always poised. "We wanted to talk to you."

Simple enough, and yet Natalia hesitates. Awkwardly, she shuffles through her mail. "Junk," she says. She's aware her hair is still wet and, with her free hand, she touches it absentmindedly, feeling the cool thickness of it against her neck. "It's always junk, isn't it?"

"Oh, I know," Jenny says. "Catalogs and credit card offers, right? It's the same over here. We were just talking about mail, actually. Sit. The dog's inside. I remember you don't like dogs—that husky loose at the park last year made you scream."

Natalia stands on the first step, leaning against the railing. "Dogs can be aggressive." She nods back to the house, trying to think of an acceptable lie. "I have to make breakfast, for Frank, for the girls. My hair, too, has to be dried."

"Of course," Ellie says. "Hungry mouths, always. We won't keep you. We were just saying that the postman stopped me the other day and asked about Ginny. He's tried her door several times, but she doesn't answer. When it rained a few nights ago, all the mail in her box got wet. Quite a mess, apparently. You're friends with her, aren't you?"

"We're neighbors," Natalia begins. She hesitates. "Yes, friends, I suppose."

"Have you talked to her at all?" Jenny asks.

"I've been a bit busy at the house."

"Of course. You don't have to explain. We've been hoping to see you out. We've been wanting to know if you need anything, if you need someone to talk to—"

Jenny's voice sounds sincere, but Natalia always has trouble gauging the depth of sincerity in others, particularly when they urge disclosure. These women might be like thieves after she leaves them, leveling assaults at her. She looks blindly down the street. "I mean, I haven't seen Ginny." She would like to say she's made a firm resolution to take care of her own house before others'. Each house, she would like to say, has its own problems and its own grief to manage. Ginny's house isn't her house. To claim that would be presumptuous, even foolish.

"And you?" Ellie says. "How have you been?"

"What can I say?" Natalia responds, smiling unnaturally, unable to lie. Although Frank has given Natalia back the bedroom, he has taken, as if in stubborn retaliation, to the basement, where he has erected a cot next to the upright piano bought years before for the girls, the same one abandoned first by Eva in boredom and then later by Sissy, who showed no acumen for the instrument beyond a sheepish rendition of "Mary Had a Little Lamb." Could she tell them this? And though the outright fights between them have lessened, and though on Sunday they can force themselves through dinner and the strained small talk, there is still tension between Natalia and Frank when they are alone, there is still the sound she's overly aware of during dinner—the knife as it digs into the plate, scratching it. Would they care to know that small detail that weighs on Natalia? There are days when she calls Frank only to have him ignore her entirely. There are days when he refuses to get out from under the car, days that, hearing her, he'll throw something onto the pavement—a wrench, a pipe, a bolt. She is only too aware of all these minute gestures, and what they might mean in a man like her husband—he is still angry. He is still debating about Natalia, and she might still find herself alone, without a roof over her head. And she is sure that, to lesser degrees, others are aware as well. The lights are always on in the basement, the small slits of windows illuminating his new room late into the night. She's certain someone has noticed this, passed by, talked. So, she wonders, what do they really want to know, other than for her to confirm their suspicions? She picks up her advertisements. "It was nice talking, but I really should be going."

"I guess we could collect the mail, put it in a bag, and leave it for her," Jenny suggests, content to change the subject. "That would be the simplest thing." She looks down the street and seems to focus on the white picket fence, Ginny's car parked outside, as it has been parked for days and maybe weeks.

"Hm," Ellie says. She gets up, leans over the railing. The breeze flaps her loose shirt, making it balloon. "That's a good idea. We can't get in trouble for that, can we? Just moving the mail?" She rests her elbows on the railing and lets her chin fall on folded hands. Each finger is adorned with rings. "Honestly, you don't think she's dead in there or anything?"

Jenny laughs uncomfortably. "Don't say that. Though, God knows, if something like that happened to a child that was mine, I can't imagine what I'd want to do to myself."

"No," Natalia says. "It's hard to imagine losing a child."

"We don't want to be overly nosy, you know," Jenny says. "We're just worried, that's all. We're worried about you, Natalia, too, about you and Frank and the girls especially."

"I'm sure Ginny's fine," Natalia interrupts. "Just keeping to herself. It's difficult sometimes when everyone is watching. She probably feels hemmed in."

"Hemmed in?" Ellie raises her eyebrows. "We're her *friends*."

Natalia is aware of the look that passes between the women, and she hears, too, the busy chatter of birds on the wires and in the trees. They talk a bit longer, about the upcoming year, about the possibility of Natalia partaking in the PTA and the annual bake sale in September. Natalia nods, assuring the women that of course she will help, though secretly she wonders if the women are just asking her, in a polite way, if she'll still be here, or if she and Frank might separate. "That sounds wonderful," she says. "I'll be there with bells on."

"Well," Jenny says, hesitating, "if you need anything, don't be a stranger."

"Never." Once back inside the house, Natalia leans against the wall and feels as if she is receding into it. Her heart beats quickly. She peeks out the curtain, seeing the women there, still talking, though now probably about her, probably about the demise of her marriage, her affair, her inadequacies as a mother. For the rest of the day she cannot shake the women off, their comments, what their comments might have meant—they cling to her, like tiny hooks thrown at her flesh. The evening is made worse when Eva struts out with Greg, a boy Natalia doesn't approve of—a boy she thinks smells like the bag she found in Eva's bedroom. Natalia stands and asks questions, waiting for Eva to tell her where she's going, but with Eva, as with Frank, her credibility of late has been ruined and though she fusses, Eva refuses to answer her because she knows she can.

"I'm going out," Eva says, vaguely. Her tone is causally neutral. She's dressed all in black—a halter top and skirt.

"Be back home by eleven," Natalia reminds her, though even that has the meek sound of a request, and what she really wants to say is *Please stop hating me.* It seems to her she is always looking at the back of Eva's head these days, the long wave of hair, the rush of her daughter out the door, the flurry of rather secretive activity that makes Natalia yearn to follow and spy on her daughter, were it not for the counter-impulse that always accompanies this thought—to leave Eva alone, to respect her need for space. *Does she need guidance?* Natalia wonders. *A sense of God and faith?* Only once did Natalia take Eva to church as a young girl. Eva knelt the entire time, fascinated, raking her hands over the red velvet cushions that lined the kneelers. She tried so hard to be good, but after the benediction, she yelled out, misunderstanding the phrase "Thanks be to God," and thanking God that he was *speedy,* instead. "Thanks speedy God," she said, her voice rising to a clamor. Natalia, who was herself trying to be as reverent as possible, buckled over with laughter. She doesn't know why she thinks of that story now. Eva is gone, out the door—and the Eva she remembers is gone, too.

Within the house, Natalia takes care of other tasks: Sissy needs to be driven to a friend's house, her first sleepover of the dwindling summer. Sissy descends the steps with two too many suitcases and her rolled sleeping bag and fusses when Natalia makes her take less—less clothes, less games, less stuffed animals. After she returns, Natalia passes the time by reading a book, her thoughts made worse in the quiet. She thinks about Frank, and how she wishes they could have a life as frivolous as that of the young protagonists—lying idly on the beach, spending hours in bed. She makes it through thirty pages, then puts the book down. By eight, once the house lights around the neighborhood have flickered on, she decides to take a walk. The night is warm, appealing. She stops in front of Ginny's house; the porch light remains extinguished, though through the curtained window she can make out the flicker of the television and movement—alive and well enough. She imagines Ginny in her own quiet rooms, her thoughts pricking her like briar. She stands, still unable to decide whether she should knock and make an impromptu visit.

Natalia continues walking. The streetlight above her flickers.

When she comes home, she finds Frank in the living room, back unexpectedly from work. At first she sees him in shadow, the living room illuminated only by the window. She jumps slightly, taken aback, but then, as her eyes adjust, she makes out the still-familiar contours of his wide shoulders and neck. He sits in his favorite chair, his cigarette dangling with a slow burn and orange flame. She turns on a light, sees the age in his face, the deep crevices across his flesh. "You scared me," she says. She smooths her hair, suddenly worried about how she looks.

Frank leans back, and it seems to her he is deciding something. It is the same look he had when he returned from visiting Ginny, and it is a look that caused an inexplicable though quiet alarm in her. "What is it?" she asks.

"Work," he says simply.

"Yes?" She sits down, across from him.

"A layoff."

She folds her hands and waits for him to explain more, though she doesn't really need the explanation in more detail. "In all our years of marriage, there's hardly no other reason you're ever home early," she says. To her surprise, she's relieved to know it's not them, that he hasn't decided to give up on them. "Do you want something? Coffee? Are you hungry?"

"The steel industry is dying, you know," he tells her. "I never thought that day would come when I started. When I was younger, steel was everything. It was all anyone goddamn talked about."

"They'll call you back in a few weeks, a month at the most, like they always do. What would they do without that plant? I think the town must have been built around it."

"What would they do?" Frank grins in an embittered way. "Fill up the hole, bury it, I guess."

"I've been looking for work."

"I know."

"I think there's a good chance I can get hired downtown, maybe at the florist's, or at the fabric store. I sent in applications. I could do books, numbers, if I had to."

"I saw the paper," he says. "The ads you circled."

She falls silent then, not knowing what to say to soothe him. She hates to see him this way, to see how his calloused hands rest idly on the arms of the chair, how without his job Frank Kisch is a man suddenly so very lost and without purpose. She senses his disappointment, his defeat. She could tell him she knows he's a good man. She could tell him she's sorry for the fact that he was forced to take a backbreaking job so long ago, all because she was pregnant with their son, the boy dying just at the moment Frank seemed to be anticipating him most, just when he was finished with painting the extra room in their small apartment a powdery blue. She could tell him that it's not them or even the world that's bad, it's just periods of bad luck. She says nothing.

"Natalia?"

She looks up, stands, and shakes her head. "I'll get you a coffee."

"Don't bother." He gets up and walks to where she stands, feeling absurd in the moment. He stops and they are close—so close she can feel his breath on her forehead. They haven't been this close since the night together in the kitchen, when she came back home and there was that terrible, rancorous fight. How warm his skin always seems, how the heat emits from his body. Or maybe it's her. She feels a wave of desire come over her. The moment seems sharply lined, entirely clear. She looks at Frank—his eyes serious in the moment—and wonders if he even remembers the two of them together, their bodies tangled in pleasurable ways. He places his wide hand behind her neck and draws her closer. He kisses her hard, with a measure of contempt, or anguish, or love—it is impossible for Natalia to tell, and perhaps it is everything, everything hitting them both all at once, all the years. The force of it all is crushing, tangible, a desperate need pressing in them both. Even if his kiss holds contempt, she takes him to her, thinks, *to be touched at all.* He is there, like someone lost that she's managed to find, someone once at great distance but now near. In the bedroom, his hands are rough and quick, his body rank from the day, his pants only half off the entire time. Her skirt is lifted above her slender thighs, her cheek against the pillow. She sees only a blind whiteness, hears only a low moan, a quickened breath. Still, she thinks, *to be touched by him at all,* to have his firm hands around her, familiar as he lifts her rump, to have him so near, the flesh of his belly against her. There is nothing to hold back. There is everything to risk.

She says nothing when, later, he pulls from her and composes himself, zipping up his pants and tucking in his shirt. She watches him, wondering if there is always inequity in any relationship, if there is always one person who loves the other more, even if by barely a perceptible amount. She decides only that any love matters, the binding of years. She decides only that she will do anything to keep him close, to not lose him again. "Are you through being angry?" she asks.

He doesn't look at her. "No."

"How long, then?"

He ignores her question. "I thought of you when you were gone. I missed you."

"You can sleep here, if you want," she continues, her voice urgent, pressing. "The cot must hurt your back. The draft—"

But he leaves, closing the door behind him, and she hears him shuffle through the kitchen. She waits, thinking he might come back to their rumpled bed. He might forgive her everything. It strikes her that Frank is still a handsome man, his thick head of hair, his strong features. She thinks of his face up close to hers—close but not touching—the small, complicated spaces that exist between people.

The next morning, she finds a dollar bill on the kitchen table alongside a note that she suspects Frank penned before he retreated down to the basement. "For last night," she reads, and then crumples the paper and throws it away. It should hurt—it is meant to hurt—and it does. She stares at the bill for a few moments, folds it and unfolds it in her hands, and then finally places it in the jar she keeps in the kitchen, one filled with spare change.

Still, if on occasion something good happens from something bad, Frank later apologizes, and there is, in the week that follows, an easing in him if not exactly an acceptance or a forgiveness. On days when they are both home and around each other, they parcel out activities that mostly leave Natalia to the house. If he is not at the unemployment office or out helping his friend Lennie with landscaping work for which he is paid under the table, Frank busies himself. He cuts the weedy grass, which the rains have made long again, flushed with new color. He paints the porch railing and sands down the screen door to keep it from scraping the porch. He washes out the shed and stacks his tools, paint cans, and cement buckets neatly. Over a few days, he rips through the tree in their backyard after judging it deader than dead, an act that practically sends Sissy into hysterics and leaves Natalia to wonder why her daughter has such an unnatural, worrisome attachment to absolutely everything around her. When the chain saw roars to life, wood chips spew out from under its bite and land in the pool, floating idly on the surface. Eva, in an effort to make Sissy feel better, skims the wood chips out and into a bucket. "We can plant something new in its place," Natalia hears Eva say, with a maturity and consoling tone that surprises her. Frank stacks the wood, piece by piece, next to the shed for winter. He covers it with a tarp, to keep it dry. Natalia pulls down laundry from the line and catches Frank watching her between the fluttery dance of still sheets, flapping like swan wings. She considers this a slow progress between them. Some days she even feels hopeful, the house finally breathing properly again.

Except Eva. Over the week she seems more and more sullen. Natalia can't discern what's wrong, and when she asks, Eva refuses to answer or pretends not to hear. When Eva doesn't go to work, when she isn't out with Greg, she takes to her room, the harsh rock music pouring outside the open window, pulsing like a violent heartbeat that sends shock waves through Natalia's body. If Natalia asks Sissy, Sissy only shrugs or becomes quiet and suddenly dumb, or she awkwardly defends her sister. Eva's entire attitude assaults Natalia, leaves her at first worried but then more persistently angered. She believes that Eva's moodiness is retaliation, an irascible reaction to Natalia herself, that Eva is only trying to intentionally disrupt whatever fragile order has been accomplished.

On Wednesday, Natalia wakes thinking of this all. At six she hears Frank rustling around before letting the back door slam shut, and she knows that he's taken to his car again. In the kitchen she finds he's left enough coffee for the two of them, and, though the gesture is a small one, she feels a childish longing come over her. She decides to dye her hair the same color it was when she was young. After she rinses and showers, she plucks her eyebrows, surprised by how much she and Eva look alike— the same arched curves, the same darkly concerned eyes. Only the lines of age separate them, the faint ring around Natalia's neck that she covers today as she did when she was younger, draping a silk scarf around it, knotting it loosely. She puts on a dress—a flowered voile, knee-length, trimmed with black ribbon and set off the shoulder—and inspects herself again in the mirror: thin, with a curved stomach, her arms a bit more stretched by extra flesh and gravity, but otherwise trim. She isn't so old, she thinks, that she can't wear a dress like this—one that her daughter might wear. She pins her hair back with bobby pins and applies a coat of lipstick.

The pool water glistens at this hour, just catching lazy morning light. At seven, the girls are still upstairs, sleeping. She raps on the car door and stands over Frank's legs, straddling them between her ankles. He pulls himself out from under the vehicle slightly, squints, and wipes an oily wrench with a rag.

"What's wrong?" If he notices the dress, he doesn't let it register beyond a quick glance.

"I've been thinking," Natalia says, her voice crisp. "I've been thinking for days, actually, that we should go for a ride in this Chevy, and I'm already promising I won't drive and get in an accident. I know that all you do is take this blasted piece of metal apart and put it back together again so that you don't have to talk to anybody. I've watched you. I figured it out years ago."

He squints again and pushes himself back under the car. She hears metal hitting metal. "Maybe that's true," he says finally, "and maybe it isn't."

"Do you like the dress?"

"You look like a kid."

"Let's drive," she tells him, nudging his leg. "I'll make some sandwiches."

Under the car, his voice remains muffled. "What about the girls?" he asks. "They're asleep."

"Eva's off today, which means all she'll do is mope and I'm tired of that. We won't be long. You can put up with me, can't you? With my being next to you in this dress?" She flounces, even though he doesn't see.

Frank says nothing. She hears a bolt drop to the ground and roll slightly before settling. "Maybe," he says after a few moments pass. "We'll see."

Natalia waits in the house, uncertain and slightly dejected. She pours a glass of iced tea and stands at the back door, watching him tinker. What's a few hours to claim? There are days and days of work, of tending to the house and children. To her surprise, he eventually pulls himself out from under the car, collects his tools, and places them back in the shed before heading inside. As he walks by her, he strips off his work shirt so that she can see the dark hairs on his back. "Okay," he says, going into the bathroom. "Make some sandwiches, then."

In the car, a little later, Frank doesn't buckle up; he never does. Once he told Natalia that in the case of extreme accidents it wouldn't matter and that in the case of a fender bender, it wouldn't make a difference. The statement itself was designed to make her laugh, and it worked. Now he stops to get gas before turning onto the highway, the same highway he sometimes used to race on with his buddies from high school, late at night, before the road became more traveled, before malls and neighborhoods sprung up out of nowhere along with strings of car dealerships. Natalia keeps the windows open, the air rustling her dress. In her mirror she catches the long strip of asphalt behind them, the blurry sun, the expanse of sky and clouds blossoming like white roses. Frank turns on the radio and fiddles until he finds a good station, but Natalia turns it off, hoping to talk. She reminds herself that he dressed up for her, too—clean shirt, plaid shorts. The thought pleases her, emboldens her. "So," she begins, "what should we talk about on our ride?"

Frank takes a swig of soda, rests it between his legs. "You only said you wanted to drive, so I'm driving. There's nothing worse than talking in a car going fifty-five miles an hour. If the talk isn't good, your only option is to jump out the window. It gets messy."

"I see," she says. She turns the radio on again, leans back, and looks out at the newly constructed houses that whiz by. Things have changed, in some ways, a fact that leaves her slightly disoriented today, though in other ways they remain unchanged by time, too, and she chooses to focus on these things instead: the ice-cream parlor they pass, one that opened when they first married, the row of shops that still advertised the same attractive discounts, year after year. "Do you remember what it's like?"

"What?" he says.

"To feel peaceful? Or to have a peaceful conversation?"

"Is this a conversation?"

"Maybe," Natalia says, adjusting her scarf. "Maybe it's the start of one."

Frank ducks his head a little, peering out to the landscape and the road. He adjusts the mirror. "It's a good day for a ride."

They fall into another silence, not so strained, not so painful. She waits, trying to think of how to bring him to the place where they might remember, where they might connect again. How long it seems since they first met, the night now clouded in nostalgia. Where would she and Frank even be without her high school friend Frannie, the heavyset girl with a leg stiffened from polio, Natalia's lab partner? When Natalia turned gray-faced during dissections, it was Frannie whose steady hand made the intricate cuts in frogs and pigs. She cut away the rubbery skin, peeling it back to reveal the intricate organs: the hearts, the lungs, the livers, the reproductive parts and stringy intestines. It was because of Frannie that Natalia met Frank. The girl, she supposed, had as few friends as Natalia did back then, and halfway through the year she invited Natalia over for dinner. It was a spring evening, and because Natalia didn't drive, because even in her junior year Clara said a car was an unnecessary luxury, Natalia walked the ten blocks to Frannie's house. She wore a full skirt, a conservative blouse that buttoned to her neck and had a lace collar, one Clara insisted upon and that Natalia herself hated. She had already opened one button by the time she found Frannie sitting on the porch swing. Frannie's brother, Benjamin, a broad-faced, thick-bodied boy, leaned against the railing, and Frank, next to him, turned his head when Natalia sent up a hello. Seeing her, he grinned like a Cheshire cat, but he turned quickly and went back to his good-natured ribbing of Frannie, who blushed shamelessly and sat with her leg uncomfortably jutting in the opposite direction from which her body leaned.

"You could sure cause some damage with that leg on a football field," Frank said. "Yow."

They continued joking until they were called inside. After a long dinner during which Frannie's father mused about politics and music, the four of them discussed school in the backyard. Benjamin and Frank passed a football between them, while Frannie and Natalia sat on the steps, watching them. Benjamin planned on obtaining a scholarship and had plans to go into the major leagues, while Frannie longed to become a vet, even though her mother was pushing for her to work at her father's law firm, where she had it on good authority that several young men were recently hired as junior lawyers. "She thinks I need someone to take care of me," Frannie said, fiddling with her brace. "She told me that a girl like me should be thinking of marriage." When it came around to Natalia and what she wanted, Natalia drew a complete blank. She played with the hem of her skirt. She thought, in a silly way, that what she most wanted was the moment itself, and that this very moment she wanted to dance. The air felt good on her skin. "I don't know," she said. "I just want to feel free."

The boys erupted in laughter, and Natalia laughed, too, realizing she sounded foolish. Frank threw the football back to Benjamin and looked over to her. "How about Hollywood? How about fly me to the moon?"

Natalia shook her head. "I guess after school I'll get a job doing something."

"Not dissecting frogs, I hope." Frannie got up, limped over to the boys. "Throw it to me."

"A movie star," Frank said, looking up.

"Please," Frannie said. She fumbled with the ball but caught it and happily lobbed it back, spinning it in the air like an acorn. "She doesn't want to be a movie star."

"Your plans?" Natalia asked Frank, blushing, changing the subject.

He grinned. "Everything. The moon and stars and whatever is between them."

"He's smart enough," Frannie said, announcing that Frank had skipped an entire year in high school. "He's a whiz. A person like that could do *anything*. A person like that might even become president of the United States." Frannie saluted him, stood up straight.

"It's still not football," Benjamin said.

Frank laughed. "Not much is." He threw the ball to Natalia, who, surprised, caught it with both hands.

When it came time to go, Frank offered to give Natalia a ride. She glanced at Frannie and caught her shift uncomfortably.

"It's not far," Natalia said, getting ready to excuse herself. She straightened her skirt. Sometime during the night, she had unbuttoned her shirt again, and now she rebuttoned it. "I can walk."

"It's a beautiful evening for a walk," Frannie agreed.

"Nice night for a drive, too," Frank said, raising his eyebrows. That Cheshire grin. "There's no reason to walk."

God, how he adored that car—black, sleek-looking with leather interior and chrome wheels. Later, after they were dating, Frank would teach her to drive in that Chevy, and she, nervous to the point of shaking, would hit reverse instead of forward and slam into a tree. She'd shrieked, realizing that she'd caused considerable damage to the back end—the metal completely crushed from the impact, the fender leaning at a bizarre angle. But that night driving her home with the car still intact, Frank bragged and told her it was the first thing he'd saved for in his life, bought with money he'd made working at the country club after school and on weekends. "The pay at the club isn't great," Frank confessed. "But the tips, Christ. It's a shame the old guys can't find their own balls, but I'm not complaining. Got the car used, a good deal. Fixed it up myself in the old man's shop."

When Natalia inquired about Frank's family, she was surprised that he told her so much about his father, about his father's temper. She didn't know why—perhaps the night itself, the sky deepening over them, magically; or perhaps it was that he'd risked something with a stranger when he had no reason to—but she told him, too, about her life, about internment, about her German parents. She told him—the only person she ever told—about the camp, the wires, the burn around her neck. "I'm a Gyp," she said, half ashamed, half ready for a rebuke.

"Must be why you have that look."

"What look?"

"I don't know," Frank said, grinning. "That pretty look, I guess."

"You won't tell?" she asked, suddenly nervous and blushing.

"I won't ever tell."

"I don't like to talk about it."

"Then we won't," he assured her.

"Frannie thinks you could be president."

"Frannie," Frank said. "Frannie's like a kid sister. I've known her forever. So where should we go? I'll drive you anywhere you want, Natalia. Anywhere at all, even to the moon."

Natalia glanced out the window and felt herself blush again. "I have to go home."

"All the better reason not to. Want to go for a swim? There's a pond out by a farm I know."

She smoothed her skirt. "I don't have a bathing suit."

"Never stopped me."

She hit his leg playfully and turned. "Forget it, Frank Kisch."

"You don't have to worry about me. I'm a gentleman. I won't even look."

"You would, too!"

"I wouldn't look," he said solemnly. "Even a little."

"I would be offended," Natalia said coyly, "if you didn't look a little."

They laughed and headed out the highway. At an exit on the other side of town, he turned off and traveled out roads populated with farms and orchards. "I always like it here," he said, pulling into a small grove with a pond, the wheels hitting gravel. "It would be nice to own a place like this." He parked. Though she would normally have felt uncomfortable in a strange place, she felt oddly protected with Frank that night, as if nothing in the world could harm them. She allowed him to put his arm around her.

They threaded through the orchard. In the distance there was an old house, the lights on the bottom floor illuminated like eyes. The crickets sang, and Natalia swung her hips as Frank talked. She unleashed a thread of stories on him, telling him, happily, that she once knew a boy who would turn into a wolf at night just to howl at the moon, for the pleasure of it. "Are you like that boy?" she asked. "Free like that?"

Frank howled then and climbed up a tree. He reached across a branch and picked her an apple. He inched down, presenting it to her, transformed again, not a boy but a gentleman.

Remembering this, she thinks to place her hand on his leg now. How much she loved that boy and that sweet promise of a man. She wants to say time doesn't really change us, that she knows that boy is still inside him, waiting. "The thing about memories," she says instead, looking over, "is that you can pick which ones to hold on to, and which ones to let go of. You can keep the good and leave the bad. Remember that time in the orchard, after Frannie's house?"

Frank laughs suddenly. He pushes in the lighter. He leans back, drives with his wrist. "Frannie and Ben, God. We were young then. We were kids."

"We're still those same people."

"We're not kids anymore, so there's no point pretending, dressing up like kids." His tone isn't gruff, but earnest, truthful.

"Still," Natalia insists, "a part of us is, the part that remembers us that way. I still love you, you know, despite everything. I still love you like that girl did." She glances out the window and focuses on the highway: the rock formation that rises up to her right, the spring that trickles down it, the bits of peeled rubber lying by the side of the road. "We were so young when we got married. If I hadn't gotten pregnant—"

"I've only ever regretted a few things," he says, peeling out another cigarette from the pack. "That wasn't one of them, Natalia."

"We had to borrow money from your parents, and that tiny apartment."

"I found work."

"Steel . . ."

He says nothing. He tips his cigarette on the side of the window. He looks over for the first time since they've been in the car. He picks a piece of filter from his mouth. "I knew you were lying all those months, each time I asked about him, the way you'd turn your head. I thought it would pass."

"My home," she says, "is with you. You're the only one in the world who knows me. You're the only one to be with."

His gaze returns to the road, and she cannot tell what he's thinking. Perhaps he's thinking about the time when they were younger. Perhaps he's thinking about the doctor, or even Ginny.

After a pause, she says, "You and Ginny—" She stops, feeling something catch in her throat.

"What about me and Ginny?"

"Nothing."

"You're right," he says, flicking his cigarette out the window. "There's absolutely nothing between me and Ginny. She was someone to talk to when you were gone."

"We never seemed to talk."

"We knew each other," Frank says. "What was there to say?"

Over the next half hour, the houses thin out to long stretches of land, flat fields, farms with dilapidated roofs and bent, twisted barbed-wire fences. Hex signs for good luck and harvest are painted on the rickety barns. Silver silos loom in the sky. She realizes he's headed toward Amish country, the long drive that would end at the farmers' market where people would be idling about, shopping for groceries or getting a bite to eat. She listens to the sound of the wheels humming on the highway. They turn and head straight, to the rolling pastures that spill out on both sides of them, the fields planted with corn and alfalfa, the white solitary houses and grazing cows spotting the hillsides, trees that shoot up here and there, giving shade. A horse-drawn carriage eases its way down the road, a yield sign fastened to the back. The day is made beautiful by men and women and children dressed simply, in bonnets and hats, young girls in plain blue dresses. "I wish we could get Eva to dress like that," Frank says.

"Eva," Natalia says, more to herself. "She's always so angry."

"She's angry with me."

"Why?"

"I don't know," he lies, not looking over. "Ask her."

"I've tried," she says. "She won't talk to me." Natalia studies the long white fence that stretches down to the valley. Behind it, horses graze lazily. A man in the field works a plow. "I wish everything could be simple," Natalia says. "Simple and green and easily tended."

"Life is what it is," Frank says. "Different seasons, different gains and losses."

12

That her parents think it unnecessary to explain, that they believe they can do as they wish and charge Eva with their unwanted tasks, infuriates her. She reads a note left by her mother, looks outside to see the Chevy is gone, and she feels her stomach turn again in nauseating knots. She is already tired, she is already moody, she has already thrown up today, and now this. She crumples the paper. She wants to call Peter, but whatever desire she has is lately replaced by hesitation. There is too much to say, too much to tell, and none of it tantalizing, all of it plainly bad.

She slams the door in the kitchen and walks outside, holding her hand to her forehead, wiping sweat. She's still dressed in her cotton pajamas, a T-shirt. By ten, Sissy has rediscovered the pool—each day brings a new love affair with it—and she floats facedown on the water, her dark hair undulating around her while she bobs across the surface like a dead fish. Eva can only imagine what her sister's fingers and toes look like now, if she still has them, if she hasn't somehow miraculously, like in one of their mother's stories, grown fins and learned to breathe under chlorinated water. Down the street Eva hears screams of children, the infernal noise. She raps on the lip of the pool, three times—hard. Sissy lifts her head, the water pouring from her bangs and down her tanned face. She presses her lips together.

"Just checking," Eva says. "Why didn't you wake me?"

"I can swim by myself."

"You could drown." She swats at a fly that buzzes around her face.

"You might drown," Sissy says. "But I won't."

"Parents are MIA, I see, again."

The phrase strikes Sissy as odd, one that Vicki Anderson often used to refer to her father, in that time he was lost in the jungle. Sissy imagines her parents lost in a similar weedy place, somewhere far, far away, slogging through dense vegetation with a machete. She spits out water and says, "I saw the note."

"Then you know you weren't supposed to go swimming alone."

Sissy ignores this. "Where did they go without us?"

Eva shrugs. "You read the note."

"Come in."

"No."

"Why not?"

"You still pee in the pool."

"Do you think they'll stay together?"

"No."

"Me neither," Sissy says, imitating Eva's casualness. She dives down and then comes up to play dead man's float again. Her hands rise to the surface, waterlogged and wrinkled. Then she swims across the pool—a seal, a sea lion, a fish, a streak of silver, finally just a girl. She reemerges, spits out water again. She studies Eva. "Actually, it makes me scared."

"Being with Dad?"

"Dad isn't bad," Sissy says.

"Yeah," Eva tells her sarcastically. She flips her hair over her shoulder. "Watch your back."

"Why are you mad at Dad?"

"You wouldn't understand."

"I would," Sissy says, offended. "I heard you fight."

"When? We always fight."

"After Christmas. Late at night, when he came upstairs."

"What did you hear?"

Sissy shrugs. "Stuff. You were crying."

Eva thinks about this and waits, debating. Finally, she says, "I would tell you, but you're a total Neanderthal."

"Thanks a lot."

"How long have you been in there, anyway?"

"Forever."

"Well, it's time to get out."

"I don't think it is." Sissy sinks down, underwater, and comes back up. She refuses to get out of the pool and come inside. This retaliation quickly descends into an outright power struggle, Eva fussing and raising her voice and Sissy content to play sides, to claim their mother when it suits her, and to claim Eva when it does not. Any ounce of authority Eva might have gained disappears in the dwindling weeks of summer. Though she always thought she would relish not having to watch over Sissy, she now finds herself missing that time, when the summer was freer, when there weren't as many lies and secrets. *How easy Sissy is,* she thinks. *How fickle.*

"Fine," Eva says, turning to go inside, wiping her hands clean of any responsibility. "Drown, then, for all I care. I think you're ridiculous and overbearing anyway."

Eventually, Eva hears Sissy slam the back door. "I'm *in*!" she says, calling upstairs. "Okay, are you happy? I'm in already." Then Eva hears the living room television blast at full force.

In her room, Eva, now showered and naked, stands in front of the mirror and turns sideways, examining herself. The morning light makes her feel ghostly, invisible, wholly accidental. She hoists up her breasts, which are sore, letting them rest in the spaces between her fingers. She releases them, turns frontal, and runs her hand over her smooth, dark stomach. She tilts her head. She sees nothing but the rounded curve of herself. Her skin is electrified by touch. Still, under no circumstances will she put on a bathing suit. She is ripe with a secret, ripe with a story, ashamed. Ugly. The thrill of expectation, of getting what she wanted, does not match what she knows now: Expectation does not always produce imagined results, like so much else this summer, like so much having to do with Peter.

What did she expect? she wonders. Love, a life away from this one, but certainly not this. She imagined the two of them traveling to a distant, provincial countryside, meandering through quaint towns and haggling over antiques, an image Eva finds both achingly simple and yet finessed somehow—full of refinement and worldliness. She expected that Peter would help her to forge a greater sense of the world beyond her own room, beyond this town.

What she didn't expect was that Peter would become a great disappearing act.

Not that she hasn't tried to find him. Over the past week she's driven by his home several times, not in her car but in Greg's. She made Greg park down the street on one such outing. "Eva," Greg told her, rubbing his boy stubble and then pushing back his owl-shaped glasses. "You're insane." She made Greg promise not to tell, and she knew he wouldn't tell, that he might be the only one left, short of Sissy, who Eva felt somewhat assured wouldn't betray her. Her and Greg's friendship was solidified in the torture of middle school, when they'd sit together at the lunch table, sharing parts of sandwiches. Everyone teased that there was surely a romance budding between them (the two of them sitting in a tree), causing both to inch away from each other and then take to bickering.

They waited in Greg's car until the sky darkened and pale stars peeked out. No lights came on at Peter's house. She opened the door, her face warm with moisture, her pulse racing. She stalked around the house, peering into a darkened window, and saw only shadows, the shapes of ghostly furniture. She felt along the side of the house to the back. Every time she heard a noise, any noise—a car driving by; a woman and man out for a walk, their conversation drifting to her—she crouched down suddenly, her knees scratching the bushes, holly leaves scraping her skin. She held her breath and waited. She raced back to Greg's car eventually, but only after stealing the gardening hat and gloves left at the side of the house. It pleased her to take them, just as it pleased her to later dump them both into the trash.

Today, when she woke, she hoped, as always, that Peter would call. She washed and shaved her legs, her bikini area. She lathered coconut butter on her skin until she felt slick. But already the morning is almost gone, and the phone hasn't rung. And the phone isn't broken.

She looks at herself, turns again. What will she say when Peter finally does call? She doesn't want to think about how she sat on the toilet, the piss streaming between her legs. She didn't know what to do with the apparatus or the box, so she brought it back to her room and buried it under old papers from school, old report cards and valentines she had stacked on the top shelf in her closet. She will not tell Peter any of this. She'll tell him instead that she checked the indicator several times, that she read the box over and over again. She'll tell him she triple-checked. How many times, she wonders, did she accidentally forget—one pill, two, a row? She'll tell him she was careful but life so often is unexpected. Perhaps she wanted it. Perhaps she believed it would help solidify something between them, something she sensed was precarious and easily broken. She mills through the possibilities now, the truths, the lies. It would be a lie to tell him she was utterly careless. But lies of omission, she believes, are not lies at all but merely blank spaces, silences in a conversation. She dresses and goes downstairs. She passes by Sissy without so much as a word. Still in her wet swimsuit, her sister sits on a beach towel eating a hot dog.

"*You're* ridiculous and overbearing," Sissy says. "I came in because I'm hungry and I wanted to be fed."

"Like I care." She goes into the kitchen, pours a glass of soda, and drinks it. She steps outside, walks out to the alley. Nothing. Only the black strip of road, the overhanging weeds from the neighbor's fence, trash cans so full that their tops have popped open. Whatever tenderness she is capable of feeling, whatever tenderness she has felt, dwindles in the day.

Sissy calls outside for her. At the front door, Greg leans against the frame, his hands shoved into his jeans pockets, his shirt untucked under a leather vest, the peach shell necklace he bought at the shore hanging around his neck, close to his Adam's apple. He pushes up his glasses when he sees her. Eva can't remember when he didn't have that annoying slouch. "Hot outfit, Evie." He says this in a calmly placid tone. It is as if a pale light surrounds him and he is suspended on a dreamy cloud, skimming across the sky.

"You're soaring," Eva says.

"You're *way* too low." To Sissy, he says, "Doesn't Evie look hot?"

"She looks ridiculous and overbearing," Sissy says confidently. "I got a new bathing suit." She models, spinning in a circle. She doesn't tell him it was from the second-time-around shop.

"Cool," he says. "I like silver on you."

"Me, too. I feel like a fish."

"Let's go," he tells Eva. "There's a bunch of us at the beach."

"I don't feel like swimming."

"She hasn't been swimming *all day*," Sissy tells him. "All *week*."

"They're not swimming," Greg says, pushing back his long hair.

"I've got to watch Sissy."

"So, bring her."

Excitement floods Sissy, and, without waiting, she runs upstairs to her bedroom. Eva hears her rummaging through her drawers. A minute later, Sissy is back, her navy shorts and a green T-shirt over her bathing suit. Still barefoot, she holds a towel and her new sandals. A pair of sunglasses is pushed up on her head, an effect Eva only assumes is meant to be glamorous.

"I didn't say you could come," Eva scolds. "I didn't even say *I'm* going."

Greg rights himself, pushes his glasses up again. "You got a hot date, Evie? Your hot date finally come through for you?"

"I know her date," Sissy says.

"Can it," Eva tells her.

"A few hours, Evie." Greg scratches his arm. "Can't wait on an old man forever."

"One hour," she says, grabbing her things.

For decades it has been called Depression Beach, a testimony to the thirties and those times when teenagers spent their summer days idling away on the man-made strip of sand that lines the westernmost edge of the creek, on the other side of the park where the Anderson girl disappeared, the two-mile stretch of woods between them. Back in a time when there was little to do and little money, local teenagers would gather here to sunbathe and pass around stolen cigarettes. They would sail small wooden boats or set their rafts onto the water and float for a mile, all the while knowing that they would have to eventually stop drifting, and then lug their rafts back to the beach and waiting friends. There were those older men, too, those who would meet here for late-night games of craps played under the glow of flashlights, all before the police inevitably came with the intention of hauling off only the slowest of runners, those who couldn't quite make their way to the woods to hide, or those who, laughing and usually looped with liquor, didn't think to run off down the street and back home to their wives. And then inevitably there were also those wives, annoyed, embarrassed, who would have to drive downtown to the courthouse in order to bail the men out of jail.

Eva has always loved this beach, even without knowing its history.

She loves the alcove that nestles up against the waiting trees, away from the view of the road; she loves the heat as it bakes the orange marmalade sand; she loves the sunlight on the muddy water, the pebbled shore. In spite of everything, she is cheered to be outside. In the parking lot, across the street from the beach, she listens to Greg as he talks about his plans to get an apartment this year, to expand his business and move to the city. New York, maybe somewhere in Jersey, by the boardwalk. His parents have taught him how to cultivate plants in the basement under high-wattage special lights. Eva has seen the clusters of weed firsthand— as large as bouquets and just as fragrant, all picked and strung the length of the entire room, hung to dry. He carries such spoils in a brown paper bag that is additionally weighted with beer. She hears the bag bump against his leg as he walks, languidly, behind her. "I'm rolling in it now, Evie," he says. "An apartment? Can you imagine? It's the most lucrative business I've ever operated."

"The only other business you've operated is trading baseball cards in grade school," Eva reminds him. She catches sight of a parked convertible, sleek, a pair of furry dice suspended from the mirror. Her brisk pace lessens so much that Sissy is able to catch up and then bypass her. She glances back to Greg. "God, you invited the *Armstrongs*?"

"Among others," Greg says. "It's all the same love, all the same business."

Eva stops and places her hands on her hips. "You have a crush on Brenda? That's rich. What does she do, put out for you?"

"You're the only one who puts out, and not for me." Greg grins. "What would you care, Evie, if I had a crush on Brenda?"

"Who is Brenda?" Sissy asks.

"Exactly," Eva says. "Brenda isn't anyone at all. And I wouldn't care, regardless." She lifts her chin in a purposefully haughty manner and wonders if Greg sees any difference in her. It bothers her that he thinks, and has told her several times of late, that Peter is a joke, a passing fancy. It bothers her that he thinks she has only a girlish fascination, and that Peter has only a taste for young skin. And in this, there is a dismissal from Greg, a failure to remember his and Eva's own history: the awkward moment years ago when they sat next to each other, pecking out notes on the piano in the basement, the dim light making them both feel slightly bold. The electricity of their first kiss, how Eva hadn't a clue what to do with her tongue and so let it hang there, idly, worried the entire time that peanut butter might be plastered against her wiry teeth. Afterward, she ran her tongue along the metal, checking and rechecking for hours. He never said anything about the kiss, though she supposes it's because she told him that if he mentioned it at all, she'd positively deck him.

"You're such an asshole," Eva says to him now. "Inviting the Mafia sisters."

"Pissy, pissy."

"That's not even the half of it," Sissy says, taking Greg's side. "She's been a real *jackass* lately."

Eva ignores this as they cross the street. She glances up and down the road, imagining that Peter's van will come speeding by and that, seeing her, he'll stop to apologize. She waits, but nothing happens.

They head down the dusty knoll and trudge across hot sand, Eva's feet digging in deeper with each step. Around the bend there are also others from Watson High: Phil Keefe and Andy Glass. Andy lies on his bare belly, white like an onion, while Phil sits Indian-style with his shirt off, the red from his hair gleaming in the sun, his entire body spotted with freckles. He plays a six-string acoustic, plucking Neil Young songs with his long fingernails. Next to them, the Mafia sisters, the Brenda wannabes, lie on separate blankets. Both wear bikinis that tie on each hip and shoulder. Brenda sits, wearing a razor-thin wedding dress, one sequined at the bodice and layered at the edges with tulle.

Greg waves when he sees them, and Eva lags behind. Sissy follows on her heels, chattering to Greg about the summer and days in the pool, the tan that, after seeing the Mafia sisters, she is suddenly working on. She prattles on to the point where Eva feels disgusted, to the point where she'd like to tell Sissy to go home. Sissy's foot catches Eva's sandal. "For Christ's sake," Eva says sharply.

Greg sits down, looks around to see if anyone else is in view, and then he hands the bag over to Brenda, telling her to pay up. "All of you." He waits for the flutter of money to be extracted from pockets and beach bags. "You look tortured," he tells Brenda.

"I'm more tortured than I've ever been," Brenda says. She pulls out a bunch of rolled joints and passes them around. She pulls out the six-pack. "Where'd you get this?"

"South side," Greg says. "The guy at the liquor store never cards. I swear I could tell him I'm Jimmy Carter and he'd just say 'Here you go, Mr. President.' "

"Well, thanks, Jimmy." Brenda raises the open can before tipping it back.

"Why are you dressed like that?" Sissy asks. She crouches down uncertainly.

"This?" Brenda says, picking at the tulle.

Eva, still debating, finally sits alongside Greg. She leans back on her elbows and turns her head, angling it toward the sun, content enough to feel the pleasant heat on her face. She closes her eyes. She buries her feet in the sand, up to her ankles. "I feel underdressed," she says. "Maybe I should have worn chiffon or a tiara."

The Armstrong sisters erupt into a chorus of laughter and throw pretend rice at Brenda. They ease into a rendition of "Here Comes the Bride."

"Very funny." Brenda bends her legs and lets the frilly material fall to her mid-thighs, the particles of sand evident on her bronzed skin, sticking to the coconut oil. "I was waiting for Prince Charming to come along, and look, I got a beer and Greg instead."

"Every frog is a prince," Greg tells her.

Eva opens her eyes again and sees Sissy has settled back, half on the sand and half on the edge of a blanket. Eva catches Sissy's blatant admiration of Brenda, of her dress and slender arms, long like willow branches. Eva, however, prefers to ignore this all: the silly dress; the Mafia sisters and their duplicated hairdos, blondes made whiter by summer. She inhales, dreaming of what she will say to Peter when she sees him again.

"You look beautiful in the dress," Sissy says, still marveling. "You look like a queen."

"So what's up with the dress, anyway?" Greg says, taking a drag and passing it to Eva. "Or do we have to guess all day?"

Brenda sits up and makes an exaggerated face. She crumples the empty bag and tosses it into the woods behind her. She passes around what's left of the six-pack.

"Drama," Eva says without looking. "It's intolerable."

"Funny from *you*. If you *must* know, it's my mother's, actually. She *starved* herself to fit in it. I had to fucking drive her and husband-number-three-Gary-what's-his-name to the airport so they could go to *Hawaii* for their honeymoon. It's like a serial occupation or something, marriage, going to Hawaii. She does it *all the time*. I keep telling her she's better off on her own, but does she listen? She tells me I wouldn't understand. And this dress? Well, I'm feeling just messed up and just pissed off enough to wear it to shreds, if you really want the truth, because there's no way in hell she's going to wear it for marriage number four, is what I think."

"Christ," Eva says, rolling her eyes. She stares at the clouds above her. "Get over it already."

Brenda laughs shrewdly and takes a hit. "I'll take your advice to heart, Eva. I really will."

"Well, I think you look hysterical in the dress," Andy says.

Brenda flops back down and spreads her arms wide. "I don't care what you think."

"I keep waiting for her to say she'll marry me, but she refuses," Phil adds, still working the guitar strings in his fingers. "All dressed up and nowhere to go."

"*Au contraire,*" Brenda says, drinking more beer. "You know they're sending me to France after graduation as a payoff, and I might just stay there and go down on some French guys."

"Go down where?" Sissy interrupts. She stole a beer when she thought Eva wasn't watching. She's already taken in a gulp, practically choking, and now she's wiping her mouth before taking another sip. "Eva?"

"Go down to nowhere. Go down to mind your own goddamn business," Eva says. She stretches her legs like a lazy cat.

"I think you should take me to France," Greg says. "I bet I could get a business going there."

"You?" Eva says, turning toward him again. "You don't even speak French, Greg. You got a D in French, remember?"

Greg grins. "Irrelevant." He passes the beer back to Sissy. She takes another swig, continues drawing circles in the sand with a small branch.

"Take it easy," Eva warns, but, amused now, Greg passes a joint and Sissy inhales. She starts a coughing fit before trying to blow smoke like Brenda does.

"You got to hold it in," Andy tells her, mimicking the action. "Like this."

"Don't," Eva says. "She's just a kid."

"I can do it." Sissy inhales, and Eva sees her register a haze, a sweet exhaustion. Her cheeks flush like peonies. Sissy inches closer to Greg. She lets her knee brush against his, holding it there for a second longer than she should, an illicit gesture, practically intercourse.

Eva laughs suddenly. "You better be careful. Dad might be watching. That murderer might be watching, too."

"Vicki?" Sissy looks confused.

"That was awful," Brenda says. "My mother gave me a curfew over that nonsense."

"She was my best friend," Sissy tells them all.

"Tough luck," Brenda says casually. "My condolences."

The group makes small talk about Neil Young and Lynyrd Skynyrd.

Over the next hour, Sissy sways in time to Phil's strumming rhythm, as enchanted as a snake, her eyes half-closed. Eva feels the pot working through her, that distance that brings with it an enchantment, as if she were outside of everything, watching. She's happy that it has settled her stomach. Happy only to feel a diffuse love.

Eva lets the sun bake her face. Sweat drips from her forehead and slides down her neck and onto her shoulder. The sand boils beneath her. She takes another hit and looks up at the plane that flies high above. She could fly like that. She is flying, she is flying so high now that she thinks she should never stop, that nothing can stop her and what she wants to accomplish. She waves at the plane, says, "Bye,"

"Am I high?" Sissy asks.

"Oh, you're fucking high," Phil says, cracking up.

In the distance, on the road, a car passes. Eva hears, too, a distant sound, a train whistle. Everything comes to her in subtle, gradual waves. Everything feels pleasant, even the sand that scratches her legs and clings to her back and her rumpled towel knotting up under her calf. She exhales, into the air, into the clouds, remembering a poem Peter once read in class. For some reason, the thought of him reading—too serious, too engrossed—now sends her into a hysterical laughter.

"Something funny, Eva?" This from a Mafia sister.

"Something you want to share?"

"Shut up and give me a hit," Eva says, still laughing. "I was thinking about wandering like a cloud. That poem."

"Oh," Brenda says. "Must be the inspiration of Mr. Fulton, I bet." She lathers oil on her arms. She wipes her hands on her mother's dress.

"Evie's got a date with poetry," Greg says, inhaling. "She loves it."

"Her sister isn't the only one with a crush," Brenda says.

"Maybe you could loan Eva your wedding dress," a Mafia sister suggests.

Brenda grins now, her pleasure evident. "You know, Mr. Fulton had me stay after class once. The day of that big pep rally, remember? He wanted to know what types of books I liked to read, but I think he just liked my cheering outfit."

"You're lying," Eva says. Her laughter fades too quickly, as does her certainty. She feels insulted and bullied. She tries to regain her composure, save what of her self-pride she has. She tries to imagine the Mafia sisters at thirty and forty and fifty, how their lives will be filled with boredom and fat husbands, how they will fawn over pool boys and young mailmen, regretting their spoiled youth, all while she and Peter will still be—somehow, miraculously—fresh and bright.

"I think you're the one lying," Brenda says simply, interrupting Eva's thoughts.

"I don't lie," Eva says.

"Well, then, tell us. Let us in on the secret. It's not like everyone hasn't already guessed, you know."

"I have a secret, too," Sissy interrupts, giggling like a lunatic. "I love Greg."

With that there is first a lingering silence and then snickers from the girls, from Greg himself. Confused, slightly out of sorts, Sissy looks around and then gets up and brushes sand off her knobby knees. Wobbly from the beer, swaying from the joint, she marches away like an ungainly soldier. Eva sees this and senses her disappointment. "Oh, Christ, Sissy. Come back! They don't mean anything."

Greg laughs again. "I love you, too!" he teases.

"Shut up," Eva says. She watches as Sissy marches with an uncharacteristic bravery, her feet pounding into the hot sand. She will preserve her pride, such as it is, Eva thinks, and prove that whatever is said means nothing, really, that nothing in the entire world bothers her, even their laughter. Her walk says, *Leave me alone.*

Eva thinks about running after Sissy, about running away with her, down the beach, into the cool woods. She looks around and senses everyone is waiting for that, and she senses, too, that if she leaves, she will only become the butt of their conversation and ridicule. She remains seated on the blanket, the longing to go after Sissy dwindling as her sister moves farther from sight.

"We're dying to know," Brenda says, lifting her dress.

Eva leans back and takes a slow drag, the dizziness coming over her in greater force. She feels as though she is on a ledge. If she says nothing, they will think she is making up a story. If she says nothing, they are already swelling with conversation, eager to fill in anything that Eva herself does not say. Feeling the sense of risk, she pushes forward. She waits while the silence grows so tangible it holds under it a growing buzz.

"Well?" Brenda says.

"Well," Eva says knowingly. "Here's the story with Peter Fulton. Here's what happened the day I bumped into him at the library . . ." She tells them of things she should not know, describing Peter in much the same way she imagines she has been described by if not Peter, then the boys—the shape of him, the way he moves when he comes to her, the way his stomach muscles tense up when he's over her. "He's wonderful," she says, inhaling. "You have no idea."

"You're lying," a Mafia sister tells her.

Brenda raises a slender eyebrow. "Scandalous," she says.

"The guy is a dick," Greg says. "And you, Eva, you're fucking stoned."

Eva, quiet now, senses a sly subterfuge of the moment, and her excitement, her secret pleasure at the telling, wanes; her thoughts turn ruinous. She registers Greg's caution. But still it feels so good to make mistakes. It feels so good to tell people what she's held inside, what she's wanted everyone to know. She wishes everything could be like that.

"Don't say anything," Eva tells them all. "I mean, if it got out, it would require the United Nations to intervene."

"Oh, no, we won't tell," they say. "We promise not to tell."

13

It is bad enough to be embarrassed publicly, to suffer humiliation in front of one's beloved. It is bad enough that the adult world remains mired with inconsistencies and complicated discussion, that the world outside Sissy Kisch's fingertips is incongruous and unpredictable. But that she will also now have to commit the moment to memory—her utterance of love, followed by their snickering laughter—is nothing short of horrific. She only spoke a truth, and in doing so, she felt the wonder of lightness grow inside her. And then, from those she believed to be new friends—the glances from those girls, and Greg's bemused expression—looks that said a defense or denial from Sissy would have been futile and would have rendered the point even more amusing.

She can no longer bear to dwell on the moment, and yet as she marches along the path, through the overgrown brush, as she pushes away the occasional low-slung branch that lashes at her, thin as a whip, she can do nothing but think on the moment. The path in the woods appears to her as a graveyard: a discarded buggy to her left, old newspapers, some empty water jugs long ago forgotten. Beyond the warm breeze that catches the leaves and tosses them like wishes, she hears—almost imperceptibly—the sound of her heart, still beating despite everything, still clinging to love because it is the heart that is assigned the burden of such a task. So often forsaken when it risks, when it favors not *tomorrow* or *someday* or *once upon a time* but the moment—the actual, unfolding moment—it is the task of the heart to uncover itself and break and mend. It is the task of the idiot heart to recover.

But now Sissy believes she will never recover. It is all too difficult, this process of growing up. Thinking on this, puzzled, she is a girl suddenly too proud for tears. Pollen drifts up from the disturbed branches. She sneezes, wipes her nose with the back of her hand. Smoke clings to her T-shirt and she is dizzy, the woods around her a twirl, a blur, a high spin. For the first time since she left the beach she realizes that not only is she brokenhearted but she is also terribly, ravenously hungry. She is so hungry she could snap a branch and gnaw on bark and pulp.

Still, no matter how hungry she is, no matter how thirsty she becomes, she vows not to go back to the beach and their smoke-screened laughter. She would rather be ravaged by wild boars. She would prefer to be lost in the forest than face the horrible, confusing repertoire of teens.

Just let them come and find her—she will be gone, just like Vicki, her best friend! (How mythic Vicki Anderson becomes in the light of memory, how reinvented.) Sissy will hide in the woods forever, and never go back. Thinking on this sweet victory, Eva and Greg suddenly regretting their selfishness, regretting the loss of Sissy Kisch, future performer, future ghost detective, keeper of a hundred dogs and cats, tamer of everything wild, she feels immensely satisfied. Emboldened, she lets out a barrage of curses that improves her stride and momentarily firms her resolve. But, when she hears a noise—the flurry of squirrels over leaves, the break of twigs—she stops, suddenly worried that Eva is correct—that their father may indeed be omnipresent, or that maybe a madman lurks by the water, waiting to grab her suddenly and make her scream. She looks around and tells herself: *No one is here. No one will care.* The fractured light pours down through the branches and the clouds dot the sky, a spattering of thumbprints.

She does not stop until she follows the path back toward the park, to the swimming hole that she and Vicki Anderson visited—empty today. She bends down, plucks some ferns and jack-in-the-pulpits that carpet the banks under willows. She finds berries that are bloodred, positively poisonous. She picks them anyway, careful not to squeeze so hard that juice stains her fingers. She takes all these things to the river's edge, letting her feet sink into the mud as she releases them. She says an incantation, garbled but well intended.

She will never go back. She will journey onward, forever. She thinks: *I am never, ever going home again.*

"Fuck them all," she whispers.

The thing that happens when you denounce the everyday world, the thing that happens when you deem everyone except yourself irritating, is that you are faced with the prospect of an incredibly lonely existence. Sitting on a limestone, Sissy listens to the birds that sing eerily overhead and to the rippling water that pools into rapids. The slanted light dances on the water, speckles it like a luminescent wing.

She pulls a thin branch from the overhanging limb, checking to see if it might support her weight. It snaps easily and falls into the water. Across the bank, the peeling birches form shapes of lids and dark chestnut-colored eyes. The knots lapse into uneven circles. The tall grass trembles.

If the everyday world fails her, there is still another under the water, a pulse of music, an ancient place that always beckons, a world not like her mother's swirling ash, not like the gray moths that float into nothingness, but something else, a world Sissy is already creating for herself, a world she is already shaping into existence. Sissy closes her eyes, and there, on the facing bank, stands a majestic white horse, its harness adorned with a feathery plume. The horse whinnies and snorts before galloping off into the woods, between the thick trees. There on the facing bank, below the trees with their ropey vines, there in the tall grasses, she spots the shape of the golden, chatoyant eye. A lion rises and paces before bending its head over the river and lapping up water. It roars. A thrill moves through Sissy, electrifies her skin.

And there, again, Vicki Anderson appears from seemingly nowhere, thin and pale in the light, stranger and more ghostly but also perhaps more beautiful, an alabaster shape, a moving statue. It seems as though she has always been here, waiting for Sissy in the ferns, somewhere near the edge of the water. "You're not dead," Sissy says. "I didn't want you to be dead, dead. I haven't forgotten you."

Vicki bends down and picks ferns and jack-in-the-pulpits, tossing them into the water. She pets the lion, running her hands through its fur. If it is a dream, if it is play, the dream is still elusive. Sissy senses it might be pulled from her, easily, as one might pull a thread and unstitch a garment layer by layer, piece by piece. She wants to slip off the rock, swim over to the adjacent bank, and touch Vicki. But it is a growing knowledge that holds her here and keeps her hands planted firmly under her buttocks. If she moves, everything will be broken. If Sissy reaches Vicki, Vicki will disappear. Instead she tells her, quietly, the things she's wanted to say, which is finally, mostly, only that she's sorry—sorry about cutting her hair—it *was* an accident; the blade seemed to go down on itself and that was that—and sorry that she didn't call to Vicki that day she saw her on her bike, heading down to the park. "Would it have made a difference at all?" she asks. "Would you have even turned around?" And she asks, finally, about God and if death really does or doesn't exist and if heaven looks like Valley Forge, the way she always imagined. She wants so many answers, she is breathless. She wishes she had someone to talk to, someone who would talk back.

This is the way the story goes, Sissy thinks. Vicki Anderson walked through the forest. Vicki Anderson marched down the weedy paths to the river, sad because of a boy, sad because of her mother. She wanted to hurl herself into the cool water and let it take her in completely. She wanted to drown in the water. She heard a bird's sound and turned to find a crow, fluttering its wings, hopping along a nearby branch. The crow had muddy eyes. She reached for it and it disappeared. She looked at herself in the water, her face rounded, her freckles gone. She dove into the water, but instead of sinking she floated, the force of the water lifting her until she floated above it, until she realized that she didn't have arms anymore but wings. This is the way, Sissy decides, the story will go.

She sits quietly for an hour, composing a tale she can believe. She sits until she hears noises and sudden laughter: high-pitched, squealing laughter, and for the first time, she realizes that it has started to rain. "Sissy!" she hears in a chorus of voices. "Sissy Kiss," she hears from Eva. Their tone not unkind. "Come on, Sissy Kiss," she hears. "We're coming to get you. We're coming! We're coming to take you home."

three

14

They are always traveling. In early September, they come by train along tracks that once transported coal to the region, along rails that hum in the heat, a low metallic sound that gradually ascends into a rumble as the train passes, metal hitting metal, the wheels flattening pennies left by children who wait to collect the thin copper and then wear the shiny discs around their necks, medallions for good luck, coins that transform them into kings.

A whistle. Blue cars and red cars emblazoned with gold lettering, lavish wagons with carved windows and flower beds—Gypsy wagons that transport performers who swing on the trapeze, dancers who twist upon wires—as well as flatcars and boxcars painted pink with waves of peach undulating like psychedelia. On the beds sit massive chunks of machinery, pieces of the carousel and Ferris wheel, the tilt-a-whirl and whip, the spider and bumper cars, the maze of mirrors. Tractors, too, sit idle, waiting to pull and haul equipment. Eighty beds in all, snaking down the tracks, towering against the sky. Around the corner the train chugs into town and slows, finally, to a halt. And with the arrival on an otherwise ordinary day there is crazy hoopla, ascending conversations, fluttering activity. Crowds gather to watch; couples with children point and chatter happily, snapping photographs and instant Polaroids as burly men unload equipment and escort llamas and horses and elephants down dusty ramps. Work crews and teamsters descend with ropes and harnesses. Three men—one red-faced with a wiry-looking beard; one with an octopus tattoo curling down his arm; the other with a cap and black vest—bark out orders about where equipment should be taken and erected. One of them ropes the wagons to tractors and carts them across the field, the smell of wood on his hands and bare back.

On this same day, others suddenly appear in town, arriving in campers and motor homes. They park at the edges of the field, near the tracks. Rosary beads and dice and coins hang on rearview mirrors; state stickers plaster the windows: ten, twenty, thirty states, from Florida to Maine and out to Wyoming. There is noise then, more noise: banging pots and Coltrane's jazz blaring out the windows. Women appear in trousers and T-shirts, silver bracelets littering their arms, turquoise rings on every finger. They string lines from trailer to trailer and hang out wash. Others appear, performers dressed noticeably well in tight shirts and pants that hug their slender curves.

The world's fattest woman—four hundred pounds of impenetrable, dimpled flesh—the wolf boy, a horse two feet tall, a midget who swallows fire and spits it out again, a lion trainer looking for a lover in the belly of a mangy beast. A spectacle for all to see, this circus, this circus hired to celebrate a town that was established two hundred years before, to celebrate people, those who first came from overseas, mothers and fathers and aunts and uncles and children with dark eyes and empty stomachs. All those who crossed borders and oceans for steel and coal, to work in mines and plants that would, over time, catch fire and burn or shut down completely. Long ago, they came with their hope inside them. They settled and rooted, gave birth to more children, those who grew and stayed in this same town and rooted in it again, like seeds scattered outward, in circles, from trees. They told stories to their children, stories of small towns and things remembered across time, they gave hope that their families held within them, dreams they kept.

The crews move quickly and efficiently. The men lug out canvases worn from age and lay them flat on the ground, like faded suns seeping into the grass. They erect tents on poles, snapping them up in the air, securing them with cross-wires and metal. Teamsters, some of whom consist of local hires made quickly, without question—men who range from the unemployed to the transient, drunk, and indigent—help haul equipment, and then collect pay. A few children play nearby with blocks and sticks. Later, as the tasks of the day are completed and the circus tops and stands and rides are assembled, men roll barrels from the train and place sheets of plywood over the rusted lips. They sit around these ready-made tables on folded chairs and play stud. Some of them, in a boozy swagger, will ante up their wives instead of quarters.

Downtown on this Thursday afternoon, on the ordinarily quiet cobblestone streets left to pedestrian traffic, activity heightens in anticipation of the bicentennial celebration. Natalia leaves Sissy to congregate with girls from school: Beth Trexler, Dana Salazar, and Dawn Grath, children of mothers Natalia knows distantly from sporadic school functions. "Behave," she says to Sissy. "Don't get lost." Then she heads into Orr's for their basement sale, and Sissy watches as her mother strides away, the line of smooth underwear showing through her white pants, her flats clicking against the pavement.

The girls walk to Toys and Magic on Main, marveling over the circus advertisements that line the telephone poles—clowns with red bulbous noses and dunce caps juggle balls into perfectly ordered arcs; an Asian woman in purple tights and a tutu flies on a trapeze; a blonde, skinny as a candlestick, poises atop a wire; a lion jumps through a ring of flames; a man with charcoal hair and a sinister mustache curled up at the ends shouts into a microphone. One poster obscures a photograph of Vicki Anderson that, in the heat and rain, has grown shredded and worn. *Gone,* Sissy thinks, *almost the entire summer.* There were times, in the unending quest for possible career paths and worldly achievement, when Vicki spoke of joining a circus and swinging high above the ground like a daredevil. Sissy loses herself in this thought momentarily, but then is swept up in the girls' chatter—the plans for bumper car rides and dunking booth attempts, for cotton candy and funnel cakes. The weekend will bring not only the circus but also craft shows on Main Street, stands with crocheted dolls, wicker wreathes, knitted boots, and wooden signs engraved with street addresses. Whitewashed rickety booths have already been erected on the square with signs featuring pierogies from the Polish church; kraut, kielbasa, and bratwurst stands; apple fritter stations. At the close of the weekend, fireworks will pop and crackle in the sky, a hiss of fire raining down like spent stars. In honor of the celebration, Mr. Morris, owner of Toys and Magic, has erected a giant LEGO Ferris wheel in the window. The entire wheel spins, making it a desired object among the girls today, though the sign next to it clearly reads NOT FOR SALE.

The girls prattle on and make animated displays with their hands. Beth tells them all about a circus she went to in Florida and how her father slipped into a tent to watch a girlie show late at night. As she speaks, her top rises over her plump stomach, and her pink glasses slide down her nose. "That's nothing," Dawn, the most worldly of the girls, exclaims. "I got stuck in the house of glass once. It was *dreadful.* I thought I'd die of embarrassment."

"Dreadful," Sissy says, marveling over Dawn's creamy complexion, her obsidian hair and strikingly blue eyes.

They plan what rides and amusements will be of most interest, what prizes they hope to win. Sissy impulsively partakes in all this, though there is still the task of asking her mother if she might go at all. Things have been busier of late: Her mother has been working at the florist; her father has been working odd jobs that sometimes keep him out until all hours of the morning. She and Eva have been sent on errands, paying for things at the grocery store, the last dollar counted in change.

"I saw them," Michael Massit calls. He pedals fast on his bike, his lanky form upsetting his center of gravity. His blond hair shines, as does his pug nose. Although there is a collective effort on the part of the girls to ignore him, he stops, finally, breaking up their huddle. He grins. "I saw them." For no earthly reason, he flexes arm muscles he doesn't have.

"Saw who?" Dawn asks, narrowing her eyes. She stands with her body kinked, one hand on a hip like a model.

"Carnies. That's what my dad calls them. Performers, drifters. They all used to come by train, you know; now only one or two do."

"What happened to the rest?" Beth asks, her interest piqued. She pops a huge bubble and peels it from her mouth.

Sissy leans against the toy store window and folds her arms haughtily. "He doesn't know. He's only *pretending* he knows."

"I do too know." He says this with such authority that Sissy doubts herself immediately. She slumps more, acting as though she can barely be bothered to listen. She lifts her hand and inspects her fingernails. Michael pauses for several moments before speaking again, knowing that, regardless of Sissy's newly found nonchalance, he has everyone's attention. "Well, some of them were sold and some of them went broke and some of them come by bus and truck now." He lowers his voice, which causes two of the girls to lean in. "Carnies are tricksters and thieves. My dad says if anyone comes to the door saying their car broke down, it's a trick. They keep you busy at the front door while the others sneak in your back door and steal from you."

"That's a lie," Sissy says, even though her mother once told her the same story.

"It was in the *paper*, moron. My dad read it to me. Crazy stuff!" Michael shakes his head, mulling it all over.

The girls exchange glances, their excitement visible and imaginations running wildly ahead of them like galloping horses. Sissy pictures women in long skirts and bandanas swooping into the house like vultures, sneaking out with her television and diary in hand. She opens her mouth to argue, though she doesn't know why she wishes to argue with Michael at all. She doesn't even read the paper; she doesn't know what he's said that's true or not. She watches as Dawn lifts her sweet-smelling necklace and nibbles candy from it. She bites one off for each of the girls and passes it to them, speaking now of the *carnies,* saying it as though it is a dirty word.

"My dad is what you'd call a *minor enthusiast,*" Michael continues. "Back in seventy-two one of the trains was even flooded right here in PA. Some flipped off the rails, killing people and animals. Some disappeared, and now they're here again, and I've seen them."

Sissy takes all this in, thinking that if it's true about the accidents and about the disappearances then they are a cursed lot, all of them, and no amount of crossing could possibly change their luck. Absurd and outlandish permutations of Michael's story race through her mind: a doomed people, drifting from town to town, searching for lost family, wandering like Gypsies. She bites her nail, horrified by the last thought, wondering if she'll have to take extra precautions with her bedroom window, or perhaps spend the weekend tucked in Eva's bed.

"I wouldn't go to the freak show." Michael flexes his arms again. "You could be eaten by that wolf boy, or maybe even by that fat woman. What else do you think a woman that fat eats but us kids?"

"A boy?" Sissy asks, wincing. "A fat woman?"

"There aren't kids there," Beth says, popping another bubble. She glances over to Dawn, who raises her arms.

"You're lying." Still, Sissy is no longer sure. Didn't her mother also tell stories of this, stories of people who wandered the countryside, tricksters with children who ran barefoot, their faces smudged with dirt, their bellies tanned and thick? Is it possible, she wonders, that all the Gypsy children were stolen away from other places and other homes? Given over to the fat woman for dinner? Changed into wolves, along with other unseemly shapes: roosters and bears and mice? Or put to work performing manual labor, lugging buckets across dusty fields, stumbling as the water sloshed around? The thought of it all sends her into a small, shrill panic.

"I hear they keep that wolf boy locked in a cage for his own protection, and for yours."

"Go on!" Dawn says.

"He's lying."

"Is there really a wolf boy?" Beth asks, excitement overtaking her.

Michael kicks back his stand and lets his bike lean, one sneaker positioned on the ground now. Sissy notices he's drawn triangles on the scuffed rubber rims. From his shirt pocket, he pulls out a candy cigarette and sticks it into his mouth, rolling it over his tongue first. "Crazy-looking men, too," he continues. "You get a little bit of every sort."

Beth takes a step back, debating. "We need protection."

"You should think about something," Michael says, "because you'll never outrun them. You all run like girls, that's for sure."

"We can run," Sissy says. Her tone is snotty and dismissive. "We can run faster than you."

Michael pulls out another cigarette and snaps it before popping it into his mouth. He grins at Sissy and then takes a bite of it, right in the middle.

"You're awful," Sissy says, staring at the chunks of pulped candy he shows her on his tongue.

Bells jangle against the door, and Mr. Morris sticks his head out, his white mop of hair brushed back in a wave. "Don't lean against the glass," he says. "You can look, you can buy, but don't lean, Sissy Kisch."

Sissy apologizes and begins to tell him how much she likes the Ferris wheel, a compliment issued in the hope that Mr. Morris might see fit to gift it to her right then and there, but his head is already gone and she hears bells singing as the door closes.

Michael stands on tiptoes, suddenly alerted. From the market down the street, three women emerge, their wrists cluttered with silver, one of the women with a knotted handkerchief around her neck. They hold bags stuffed with radishes, cucumbers, and carrots. When she sees the women, Sissy jolts up straight and nudges Dawn. "They're here!" she says.

In one quick moment there is a rush of feet, and the girls run in the opposite direction. Michael pedals behind them, screaming, "*Faster . . . faster . . . faster!*" He looks back once and, in doing so, almost crashes into a trash bin. The girls run around the corner of the eyeglass store and stop in the alleyway. They pant, squatting now, their backs leaning against the brick. Beth wipes her mouth and then holds her sides. Michael peers around the building.

"Are they gone?" Sissy asks, breathless.

Michael snickers. "You're always scared," he says.

"So are you. Look at you, back here with the *girls*."

He ignores this. "I can't believe you ever even leave the house, you're so scared."

Sissy leans against the building and folds her arms across her chest, an action meant to mirror his. "Michael," she says, offended, "don't be a *Neanderthal*."

Natalia woke this same morning with a blinding headache, a piercing pain through the right side of her skull—brought on, she assumed, by the noise the previous evening, the smoke, the shots of vodka consumed by everyone at the table but Frank. The men showed up unexpectedly: Lennie holding the booze; Jim behind him, already swaying as if hearing music; and Sammy, limping in, his cane scuffed at the bottom around the rubber nub. Sammy nodded at Natalia as he took off his cap. They all sat and made small talk until work inevitably came up in conversation. A serious and towering man with a deep voice, Lennie kept pulling at his suspenders while the men discussed the plant, the possibility of returning to work, the rumors that had been passed around, those of outsourcing overseas. This necessitated that they find other avenues of employment. Jim, the youngest of them all, had applied for work at the fire company already. "Sure as hell no layoffs as long as houses burn. God knows you can't outsource flames." He said this in a swaggering way. He lifted a glass and drank to that. Sammy was nearing retirement anyway and thought he'd take the early option, get out while he still could. His hands were riddled with arthritis and had choked up on him unexpectedly, making any work difficult. As he spoke, Natalia saw how his fingers shook slightly, with a mind of their own. Frank was still helping Lennie with some contracting work, here and there, but both he and Lennie would need more permanent employment if the rumors sent around the plant were actually true. Natalia listened quietly as the men made plans, realizing that none wanted to say what was really on their minds—that they were desperate to make ends meet for their families. While Frank nursed his beer, shots got passed around the table. Their stories of work unfolded as the crickets sounded thick through the open kitchen window and streetlights blinked on like shocked eyes jolting open. The sky flashed with heat lightning. Thunder rumbled in the distance, in long waves.

It must have been the thunder, or the scraping fingers that woke Sissy up. She ambled downstairs, sleepy, rubbing her eyes, wanting not Natalia but Eva. "Bed," Natalia told her a bit too sternly. "No complaints."

Sissy stood and looked around at the men. "Eva's still out. Her bedroom is empty."

Frank finished the last of his beer before setting the glass down hard on the table. "Where is Eva, anyway?"

Natalia didn't know, of course—perhaps with that boy, Greg, or perhaps down at the beach with friends—and so she fell silent, not wanting to make any fuss in front of the men, for either of their sakes. Sissy slumped against Frank, then, waiting patiently until he pulled her onto his lap and tousled her already tangled hair. His chin rested atop her head as he shuffled the cards, dealt, and looked over his hand. He inhaled, his nose pushing into her hair. As he did, Natalia saw Sissy's eyelids flutter like small moths. Her head fell slightly. "Come on," she said, scooting her girl up. "To bed."

"Where's Eva?" Sissy asked again as she dragged herself up the stairs. "I want to sleep in Eva's room."

"Out with friends." In Sissy's bedroom, Natalia pulled up sheets that still smelled of sun and breeze. She sat down for a moment and waited uncomfortably, suddenly unsure of what to say at all.

"What time is it?"

"Time for bed." Natalia leaned forward, her hand pressing into the covers. "You know, you're getting too old to sleep with your sister. Besides, it's just some thunder talking back to the flashes of light."

"It's angry," Sissy said. "And Eva likes when I sleep with her. She says I keep her safe."

"Maybe so. Maybe the thunder is like an old man who curses at the light. What do you think?"

Sissy shrugged.

"Well, that's nonsense," Natalia said. She waited a moment before she got up and brushed her hands together. "You need to grow up and not be scared of everything, Sissy Kisch." Despite saying this, she turned on the clown night-light next to Sissy's chifforobe, illuminating its starkly white face and bloody-looking nose.

"Eva said clowns are possessed."

"Eva is trying to frighten you."

Sissy didn't answer. She turned her head toward the window and seemed to consider things.

"Want a story before you sleep?"

"No," Sissy said. "Not tonight."

Natalia studied her child, who was hunched down in the sheets, her eyes thoughtful, watching. She hesitated. Finally she shut the door and waited outside, but she heard only the rain tap against the window. She was losing both her daughters. She knew that for all the years she waited, yearning for them to grow up, for all the times she thought after they grew up, she could do anything she wanted, she would have a measure of freedom again, she was losing them and she was surprised to find it hurt. What would be left was her and Frank again, the two of them, as before.

Downstairs, Frank sat with his elbows on the table, fanning the cards. The rest of the men were laughing about something—a joke shared before she entered the room.

"Your wives are going to put out search parties for you," Natalia suggested.

"We should put out a search party for our kids," Frank said, looking up, still annoyed.

She couldn't tell if the beer was affecting him or not. She sat down, positioned her hands on her lap.

Lennie patted her arm in a way that made her feel like a man. "We're not praying, Natalia," he said good-naturedly. "Unless it's for sevens. I'd say a few Hail Marys for a straight. I'd say a damn rosary for more money."

"Oh, I know." Natalia smiled. "I was thinking about the girls."

"Play," Lennie said. "Deal her in, man."

Natalia looked over at Frank. A cigarette dangled from his mouth as he dealt to everyone seated. "You can do what you want to," he told her, concentrating on his hand, not bothering to meet her gaze. He inhaled and blew a line of smoke. "No one ever argued about that, either."

She pulled the chair forward and heard the irascible scraping of wood against the floor. Lennie held up the shared shot glass. "To money. To work."

After he slammed the glass down, Natalia poured a shot for herself. "To sleep," she told him, raising the glass again, realizing her arm felt simultaneously heavy and strangely light. The hot liquid went down her throat, burning it. She studied her cards: one short of a flush.

"You didn't answer," Frank said. "About Eva."

"You know teenage girls," Sammy said, intervening. "They never want you to know what's going on, where they are, who they're with. My oldest was the same way."

"When do they outgrow it?" Natalia asked, trying to lighten Frank's mood.

"Never, far as I can tell."

"People start to get ideas about girls who are running around the town," Frank said. His jaw tensed, and Natalia sensed that the more the other men laughed and made light of things, the worse Frank's mood became. He probably was worried that they might think he was unable to control his house—first Natalia, now Eva, the endless succession of womanly antics, the clever acts of subterfuge. Perhaps he even thought they were laughing at him, as she often thought the neighbors did at her. The men joked, but she detected in them no real judgment. If anything they probably thought it was Natalia who was the terrible parent, that she was the one who could not enforce Frank's rules and wishes.

The men made small talk—the upcoming football season, favorite quarterbacks, bets on which teams would do well. With each hand the table seemed to tip toward Sammy, his stack of change piling up so much that Lennie, slightly annoyed and more than a little drunk, asked him if he counted cards. Jim's tolerance for shots deteriorated completely; he excused himself and bolted out the back door, and Natalia heard a putrid expulsion into the bushes.

"Kid can't hold his liquor," Frank said. "Deuces wild. Ante up."

It was more than an hour after her curfew when Eva sauntered in through the back door, her long hair wet from the rain, dripping down her neck and chest. Her dark bra was visible under the wet fabric of her shirt. She was, in Natalia's estimation, obviously high, which at least settled for her the question of who Eva was with all night, and where she probably was. Frank's jaw tensed again; his eyes swept across her outfit, and Natalia wished only that Eva would remain silent and skulk upstairs. Instead, what happened was that the rest of the men stared at Eva, and Natalia became aware of their gazes, their faint desire.

"What are you looking at?" Natalia asked them. "Nothing to see."

"No one said there was," Lennie told her. He returned to his hand, made a bid.

Eva, swaying a little, laughed. "Take a picture. It'll last longer."

Frank stood up abruptly and slammed his hand down, causing stacks of quarters to tumble, roll, and then fall.

Eva didn't flinch, though the table fell to silence: Lennie studied his cards for an inordinate amount of time, and Sammy scratched his neck with a gnarled knuckle.

"Enough," Natalia said, rubbing her temple. "Go to your room, Eva. For Christ's sake, just go to your room. Do you live to disrupt things?"

"You always defend him, don't you?" Eva asked, not moving at all, her eyes as locked on Natalia as the men's eyes were just a moment ago. "He could probably do anything, and you wouldn't care."

"What's that supposed to mean?" Frank asked.

There was a lingering silence again, a void in the conversation that surprised Natalia completely. Then Sammy cracked a joke, one that neither Natalia nor Frank found amusing, and Eva hoofed down the hallway, the smell of smoke wafting from her. Natalia rubbed her temples again, got up, and emptied Jim's ashtray. She poured a glass of water. Of course she would defend Frank to Eva, to the men. Could Eva expect less of her, standing there reeking like she did and wisecracking? What was Natalia supposed to attend to but a girl with a smart-alecky mouth, a girl with exposed knees and thighs? And yet the look on Eva's face chilled her—the animosity, the evident disdain that left Natalia with new questions.

"Kids," Lennie said. He let a breath of air escape from his lips, long, with a small whistle. "I got nothing tonight, no Lady Luck for this man."

"Yeah," Frank said, settling down again. His face was flushed. He tossed down his cards: two tens.

. . .

In town, after leaving Sissy on the street with the girls, Natalia walks into Orr's and heads downstairs. She hopes the aspirin will take effect and revels in the cool air that alleviates, somewhat, the throbbing in her head. She takes in the long rows of overflowing bins, the parade of women clucking contentedly, the cheery music blaring through the loudspeakers. In the bath and kitchen section, she rummages until she finds new towels, ones the color of canned peas, but cheap and matching and good enough for their intended purpose. She catches sight of a few women from the neighborhood: Milly, Jenny, Ellie. Natalia imagines how news must travel from porch to porch, buzzing wildly like swarming bees. Milly, however, has been snubbing Natalia—at least Natalia believes—still harboring a grudge over the two-hour babysitting stint that turned into three more hours of worry, until Eva showed up, collected Sissy, and had to explain that their mother was gone. After Natalia arrived back home, Milly lurched over her railing and told her: "Don't expect I'll be babysitting anytime soon."

Natalia adjusts the shoulder strap of her halter top and watches as the old woman barrels down the aisle, her face red from extended walking. Natalia's mouth goes dry as she anticipates Milly's questions.

"Quite a summer," Milly says, pursing her lips together. She holds two frilly valances in her thick hands and regards them. "What do you think?"

Natalia glances over and makes a face. "Beautiful, should go with the house." She moves a step away, browsing. She fingers the velvet towels, their ends braided in golden thread.

"I guess you're right," Milly says, tossing them. "They are ugly, aren't they? Sometimes I just see the price and go a bit bonkers. These days I'm in such a rush, I'd pick anything up in a hurry. We've been busy, you know, Mr. Morris and I. The bicentennial, the extra business it means at the store. We don't just sit idly. I wish."

"I should apologize," Natalia says, though she isn't sure if the apology is for the statement about the curtains or more than that, and apologies to people she doesn't know well often get stuck in her throat; they feel insincere, always ill-timed. She wonders how long Milly has been waiting to dispense this comment about used hours, how much she's turned over in her head exactly what she would say. "The babysitting," she says finally. "I was grateful that Sissy was with you."

Milly's lips purse together again.

"I shouldn't have burdened you," Natalia continues.

"Well, I'm not a woman who likes disruptions like that. I am very busy most days."

Natalia notes Milly's flared nostrils, her heady hair spray and coifed hair. Around them women and children push past. "No," Natalia says, a little ashamed, "neither do I like disruptions, and of course you're busy. It was wrong of me."

"It was. And I appreciate you saying that. But, really, I wanted to talk to you, not about babysitting, but about something else." Milly leans closer, seems to debate.

"I haven't spoken to Ginny, either," Natalia says. "She hasn't spoken to anyone, really, for more than a few moments, I hear."

Milly shakes her head and sighs loudly. "Not Ginny. Though I agree, we need to do something there."

Natalia hesitates. If it is not about Ginny, and not about babysitting, then by the process of elimination Milly—this woman who has never quite been a friend and who certainly has never been a cherished confidante—wishes to speak about Natalia and Frank, or about Natalia's long months away. She feels her neck tense, her scalp itch. She busies herself with the towels, impatiently folding them. "Yes, then, what?"

"Your girls," Milly says softly. "I'm worried about your girls."

"What about my girls?" Natalia asks warily. She dare not look over now. She couldn't bear to see Milly's expression.

"Of course I don't mean to tell you what to do, or how you should run your house. But you'd have to be blind not to see things. Sissy was alone most of the summer. I'd see her go off down the road, and I'd try to stop her, call out, but she's flighty, she doesn't listen to *me*. I'm not her mother. What with everything that's happened—" Milly pauses. "I don't suppose Eva cared at all, and God knows no one else was watching."

Natalia feels the itch travel from her scalp down to her neck. She tries to keep her expression perfectly neutral. "I know all about this," she says. "My family is my concern. I don't know why people are interested in other people's houses."

Milly's fleshy hand encircles Natalia's wrist. "I was trying to help. Ask yourself: If we weren't keeping an eye on your children, then who was when you were gone? It wasn't Frank, working all the time. It was us, the women who were home, the women out and about every day. Your nosy neighbors."

"I never said I thought you were nosy."

"You didn't have to. It's obvious you don't like us."

Natalia ignores this. She inhales, smelling something vaguely new and plastic. She pulls her arm from Milly and scratches her neck. "We've taken care of it. I know all about this already. I watch and see, too."

"Fine, then," Milly nods. "Fine." She turns and wanders down to the end of the aisle, her fat rump pushing against people. She stops by Ellie Green and Jenny Schultz. The women try to find matching pairs of water glasses. Natalia hears them strike up a discussion about crystal and has a vague sense that everything is wrong. She leaves to find a new pair of loafers for Frank, even though twice he expressly said to not spend the money, but he can't just walk around with a hole in his heel. Upstairs she finds a simple pair marked down more than 60 percent. Her hand runs over the scratch in the grain of leather as she goes to the checkout line. She hears the women call to her, their voices drifting from somewhere behind.

"More news?" Natalia says turning with a desolate look.

"As a matter of fact, yes," Milly responds. Her manner is smug. She fiddles with her curtains. "I've decided—*we've* decided—that we'll have a picnic tomorrow at my and Mr. Morris's house. Nothing fancy. For

Ginny, really. She's got to know people are around her, worrying that she hasn't been out of the house in weeks. When is she sneaking out to get her groceries, I might ask. In the middle of the night? Maybe she's starving herself. I know of people who have done that sort of thing, starving themselves in grief."

"Most parents would do that, if it would mean their children's well-being," Natalia says.

"*Most* would," Milly agrees.

"Maybe Ginny wants to be left alone."

"No one wants that," Ellie says, her voice full of certainty.

"I wouldn't want to be alone," Jenny says. "Not with that much trouble."

"Some people do." Natalia picks up her bags.

"You'll come, though, won't you?" Jenny asks.

Natalia feels tired, exhausted in the space of an hour. The women wait while she hesitates and then finally agrees. With that, Milly takes to delegating responsibilities. She is to be in charge of invitations and phone calls and agrees to shoulder the responsibility of calling Ginny and persuading her by force if necessary, something she isn't looking forward to, she informs the women, but something that should properly be done by the host. Ellie offers to make ambrosia, while Jenny is assigned the task of deviling the eggs, and Natalia volunteers potato salad. As they talk, Natalia makes her way along the checkout line, barely listening while Milly reminisces about those long-past get-togethers—uproarious occasions when her children ran about the lawn with same-aged cousins and friends, and Milly's sisters and aunts and old uncles would talk for hours at the picnic table. Probably, Natalia realizes, the woman has no one left, really, but her husband and the neighborhood. Her children, grown and living in Florida, probably shun her overbearing ways, her presumption to give advice, her inability to relinquish control. She is surprised to find she feels momentarily sorry for Milly. She can't say she likes her—she's not sure she'll ever be able to say that, exactly—but at least, in this moment, she understands the way

Milly pushes forward with things, her busy resolve. *What else is there to do,* she thinks, *when you find yourself mostly alone?*

At home, the haze of smoke still hanging in the kitchen, Natalia takes two more aspirin and contemplates taking more. She could walk into her house backward to undo time. She could rub vinegar on her temples to quell the pain. She could light a candle and let it burn down, to rid the nebulous air of the negativity she feels all over her. Her head throbs even more, not only from the cheerless interaction with Milly and the women but from the car ride home and Sissy's incessant pleading about this silly circus. She's been nipping at Natalia's heels, tagging along behind her back, literally pulling at her clothes. Natalia takes a piece of paper from the drawer and makes a list of things to accomplish before Milly's party. There will be the task, of course, of getting Frank to come at all, at least to create the appearance of a unified front. She'll have to call upon his friendship with Ginny, his responsibility to Ginny, though this thought makes Natalia bristle with jealousy. And there will be the task, too, of getting Eva to come, particularly after the night before, and this morning, when Eva, drinking coffee, was as silent as a stone, and Natalia thought to ask her what Eva meant by her taunts and rebukes—to the men, more so to Frank—but somehow couldn't bring herself to form the words.

Natalia concentrates on what can be easily accomplished. Pie pan and apples, extra cinnamon, a bag of potatoes. Celery they have, but no bacon. Eggs are covered. She doesn't know how, in the end, she was assigned both the salad and a pie, but she agreed anyway, so eager was she to be on her way. In back of her, she feels Sissy's stare bore into her muscles and bone. "You're so *negative*," Sissy is saying, and in this, Natalia hears Eva, her thin impatience, her accusations. "You're so awful. How often does a circus come to a town anyway? Once in a million years? And we're going to miss it? Is that what you're saying?" With that, Sissy lapses into the reasons why she *must* go, how in a few dreary weeks school will resume and everyone will still be talking about the big top, how she will be left out from coveted conversations, and how, worse, when Mr. Chero has them write on the topic of what they did for summer, Sissy will have a blank page. She will have to stand in front of the class and make something up entirely. "I'll have to *lie*," she says.

Natalia writes through all this, her back turned. Absentmindedly she agrees, saying, "Hm."

"You never listen! You never listen to Eva or me."

Sissy's tone is shrill and cuts into her. Natalia turns and regards her daughter. "What, were you at the top of the stairs last night?" She speaks as softly as she can, not because she isn't vexed by temper tantrums today, but only because her headache is made worse by loud noises that reverberate like cannon fire in her skull. "I can't listen, not when you're whining, no," she begins. "When you're whining, I can't listen to you at all. We have a picnic tomorrow at Mrs. Morris's house. I told you that. I told you that ten times."

"Two days," Sissy says, disgustedly, spreading her arms out. "It's only here for two days. Eva's right. Living with you is the worst thing on earth. You're never there when we need you."

Natalia snaps like a brittle branch. She yells, "Eva, always Eva, yes?"

"I'll run away if I can't go."

"And where will you go?" Natalia asks harshly. She grabs Sissy's arm and pulls her closer. "How will you earn money to live? Will you run away to the circus? I hear they want girls who complain that their life is so horrible, that their parents are so mean. I hear they want little girls who don't think of anything or anyone but themselves."

Sissy casts a hateful look, one that is pure and piercing. Natalia can feel it, how it judges and holds things against her. A flash of contempt, cold and pronounced. It is a look that, in Sissy, she has never seen, but in Eva is always present. It is a look that at once annihilates Natalia, the rules of the house, a look that accuses Natalia of her own hypocrisy, her own mistakes.

15

The Morrises', situated halfway between the Kisches' and the Andersons' on Ellis Avenue, is a two-story with gabled dormers and white trim and a row of granite rocks lining the front garden. On the shed situated to the right of the house, a large stuffed bass hangs, its mouth angled toward the street in a wide *O* greeting, its once vibrant colors faded from weather and age and from the fact that Milly Morris won't let that awful-looking fish be displayed in her purple house with its new pink curtains. Late afternoon, the house runs ablaze with activity, and all along the street, families emerge from their homes at sporadic times, carrying baked goods and covered steaming dishes and plates of brownies and watermelon. Jim Schultz, Jenny's husband, calls their schnauzer in before opening the gate and puttering along in shorts and woven flip-flops. Jenny strides behind him, dressed simply, tiny compared to her hulking husband, her famous deviled eggs in hand. Upon arriving at the house, Jim salutes the fish and then ambles into the backyard. The yard appears more verdant than most, and some speculate in whispers that it's more to do with the sprinkler than the shifting weather and sporadic rains. Still, Jim puts aside small grievances and immediately sets to helping Edward Morris determine the proper number of feet between stakes, for quoits. The men have a good-natured argument about whether it is twenty or thirty feet between the poles, and settle, finally, on twenty-five feet as a neighborly compromise. A size-twelve shoe, Jim carefully draws out the distance, one foot pressed against the other. Edward follows, mallet and stakes in hand. He pounds the metal into the ground while the women who have gathered by the picnic table send up complaints about the ruckus. Mrs. Brandt, Laura Landing, Edna Stone, Jenny, Ellie, and Natalia help Milly set out refrigerated items from the kitchen. They emerge in succession, a parade of women with trays of deviled eggs set on ice, macaroni and potato salads, ambrosia, and corn on the cob. In her hands, Natalia's pie cools, the thick butter and Crisco scenting the air. She sets the pie on the picnic table, next to beefsteak tomatoes and onions cut so thin they appear translucent.

Everything is warm and there is an air of pleasant cooperation and tolerance so vital to community gatherings. On days such as this, Natalia tries to be grateful for simple things—for the casual conversations between the women, for the bright checkered tablecloths and the homey sizzle of the grill, the seared burgers and chilled beers. She tries to see goodness in the everyday—in the trees and gardens, in the scattering children and calm breezes—no matter what else she might be feeling.

Edward and Jim play quoits while the other men sit in lounge chairs, beers sweating on their knees, their hairy, pale legs stretching out over the lawn. In the back of the house, toward the alley, Eva stalks the perimeter of the yard before finally stopping to talk with a girl from school who is a few grades behind her, a freshman this year. Sissy stands at the side of the house with a noisy cluster of neighborhood children, taking turns filling water balloons. She's already stripped off her shirt and shorts and stands eagerly waiting, her silver bathing suit pronounced against her tanned skin. Sissy screams and then runs and tries to climb up Milly's apricot tree to avoid getting doused by the Massit boy, a bulbous, shaking balloon held in the boy's hands. There are more screeches, scuttling bare feet, muddy tracks through Milly's kitchen, mothers telling their children to *behave.*

Amid all this, the topic of Ginny Anderson arises in conversation— lightly, tentatively at first, and with a surprising sympathy and fondness. Ginny has yet to arrive, but even this hasn't managed to upset the host. Milly only checks her watch occasionally, while the women, gathered at the table, plan how they might help, one offering to invite Ginny to her book club, another volunteering to sit with Ginny each day if she wishes. The women become like those caregivers who are entrusted with the task of vigilance over sickened or dying bodies, their desire to bear a type of witness and help as they can. Natalia listens as they fret and talk and is surprised to hear a note of genuine concern that she has previously missed on those occasions when she shuffled away from the conversation too soon.

"Can you imagine the guilt?" Ellie asks Natalia. "We need to tell her it wasn't her fault. It could have happened to anyone."

"She's probably shy about coming," Milly says, checking her watch again. "I had to march over there and practically crawl through the window to get her to let me in. She promised. She gave her word. I told her, 'When things get bad, you need other people, whether you like to admit it or not.' "

"I can't help but wonder what's worse, knowing or not knowing?" Edna Stone says. She tidies the containers, her wrinkled hands diligently working the Tupperware.

"Not knowing," Natalia says. "It's always the worst." From where she sits, she can see Frank flip burgers and make small talk with Jim and Edward. At this distance, she can't help but feel her love for him again.

"Things better?" Ellie asks, noticing Natalia's stare. Ellie pushes her big sunglasses up into her hair. Her eyes, Natalia notices, are a brilliant shade of brown.

"Of course," Natalia says, nodding.

Milly leans in, her sides spilling off the bench. "You know, Natalia, I left my first husband once—the one before my Edward. This was back in the forties, during the war. Markus had flat feet, you know, and couldn't join the military. He was a miserable man because of it. I swear he spent his entire life wanting to kill someone."

"I'm glad I'm single," Laura Landing says, sipping a gin and tonic.

"My advice," Milly says, pointing a fork, "is always find a man who wears polyester. It's a fabric that you can trust on a man." She tells everyone a story, then, about how Edward refused to wear blue jeans because when he was a boy his mother forbade him to wear them. "She told him when jeans became popular, the country went downhill. How's that for love and premonition?"

The women, including Natalia, chuckle. She listens as the women lapse into stories about their husbands and first loves, their years of marriage, their gloomy days and happier ones. She thinks of Frank again, remembers him as a boy who lived in trees, who picked fruit with an easy heart and courageous howl. She closes her eyes and sees him in moonlight, arms reaching out across the branches, full of intention.

"When we were young, Frank was so sweet he used to pick apples for me," she says quietly. She's surprised when the women stop and look at her for a moment. She smiles.

"Frank?" Milly asks, not unkindly. An amused look crosses her face.

Natalia is surprised to find her eyes well with tears. "Yes," she nods, her hand to her heart. "My *kedvesem*. My loved. My Frank."

"It's a giggle show," Mr. Nealy says, licking his lips. He grabs a beer and sits down. Mr. Nealy is always one of the last to arrive to any neighborhood function; it takes him a good hour to put on his best shirt and slacks and tie. He presses each beforehand, letting his hand guide the iron to create perfect pleats. He points now. "The women over there, they're plotting."

Wearing his plaid shorts and new loafers, Frank shifts and mumbles an agreement he does not necessarily feel today. A quoit loops around the metal stake and spins, and he calls out to the men: "A ringer around a tomato is worth double the points."

"Good Lord," Edward says, pushing his hand through his gray hair. He acknowledges defeat and plops down in a chair, panting. "Don't let the missus hear you say that."

"Too late," Milly yells from the table. She points her fork accusingly. "You ring my plants, and I'll ring your neck."

Frank grins. "How's work?" he asks Edward.

"I own a toy shop," Edward says, shrugging. "How hard could it be?"

"Hard."

"Business could always be better," Edward says. "Things go in waves. This weekend has been good, hope it gets even better. Long hours, though. The missus made me take off for the picnic. Got some kid manning the store today." He pauses. "I heard about the layoff, read it in the paper."

Mr. Nealy turns and adjusts his hearing aid. "Plant's been there ages," he says. "No worries."

"That's what they tell me," Frank says.

"Things good otherwise?" Edward wipes sweat from his brow. He sips his beer.

"Burgers are good," Frank says.

"Not that," Edward says, laughing. "Home, Natalia, the kids."

Frank surveys the yard, the fence and hedges, the children running about.

"I'd be mad as a hornet," Mr. Nealy says.

Frank says, "I am. Not much going to change that, for a while at least."

"Sticking to it?" Edward asks.

Frank catches a glimpse of Sissy, a flash of silver. She's hiding next to the shed, bent down. Her head pops out, along with the top half of her body, before disappearing again. The children scream, too happy and excited to bother to eat. He looks for Eva and catches sight of Natalia instead, sitting at the table, talking to the women. She sends up a small wave, a questioning look. "Better together," he says, "than apart. Better for the kids. Better for me, too."

"True," Edward says. "Best call, I guess."

After she eats, Natalia finds Eva sitting out on the front step, sneaking a cigarette, her legs stretched out before her, an oversize T-shirt hanging well below her cutoff shorts. Eva squints into the day, out to the empty street, and seems to regard nothing in particular—the wilting hedges, the fire hydrant, the dribble of water snaking down its base. Natalia waits, debating what to say, but Eva ignores her and her offering of a plate of food.

"A dirty habit," Natalia says of the cigarette. She thinks of sitting down, but remains standing instead.

"Dad smokes," Eva tells her, without looking up. "You don't get on him for it."

"It's his house, and he can do what he likes. It isn't your house, so there are rules. You embarrassed your father the other night, in front of his friends from work."

"Did I?" Eva inhales and blows a line of smoke, casually in the other direction. She extinguishes her cigarette. In the sun, her head throws off streaks of chestnut and gold. She threads her fingers through her thick hair, pulling out a few loose strands.

"You don't have a right to make him feel that way, not after everything he does for us all. You can't just bring shame to our family."

"Shame," Eva says, without looking up. "That's all we have."

Her tone exacerbates Natalia. There is too much Natalia wants to say—her discovery in Eva's room, her knowledge that Eva goes out to get high, her displeasure with how Eva influences Sissy. She wants to tell Eva that every once in a while she might think to cover her knees or chest when she goes out to meet her friends. She wants to say Frank is right—it's Eva's problem. That Eva acts like a *szuka,* a dog. She wants to say all of this, and more. "Look at me," she says, waiting. "Why are you so angry with me, with your father?" In the backyard, children shriek with laughter. *It is a pleasant enough day,* Natalia tells herself. *Everything is taken care of. There are no small catastrophes. Everyone is doing the best they can.* Eva, she realizes, sees none of this. "Ungrateful," she says finally. "You're ungrateful for all that people do for you."

"Me?" Eva glares at her then.

It is this type of willfulness and defiance that only infuriates Natalia more. She opens her arms a bit, to let the incoming breeze cool her. "I heard from Milly. I know that Sissy was alone, that you just left her." Natalia pauses, letting this thought in, too—all the things that might have happened with a girl entirely alone in a house: grease fires and broken bones, slips in the tub, a head cracked on the porcelain. "You talk about me, and look at yourself. Look at your attitude, your lies."

Eva shifts uncomfortably, and Natalia feels a flash of victory. To her mind, Eva has asked for this—with her sullen demeanor over the past weeks, her cruel words. She doesn't know what else to say, though it seems impossible to her that a mother does not know what to say to her own daughter. If Eva were a young girl again, this argument might turn into a conversation, might end with Eva throwing her arms around Natalia in apology. Natalia stands, wishing that her daughter would apologize, but of course Eva does not. She will not apologize for anything. "Lies are bad habits."

"If that's the case," Eva tells her, "then everyone except for Sissy is screwed."

There seems to be more to say, more to ask and uncover, but Natalia hears a voice and turns to see Milly and Jenny come around to the front yard.

"There you are," Milly says. Worry shadows her face. "I tried to call Ginny. Her phone is off the hook."

Natalia eases her posture and pretends that no argument has happened at all. "Maybe she changed her mind?"

"We're going over to see," Jenny says. "You'll come, won't you? Maybe she'll listen to you."

"In a minute," Natalia says. "Yes."

The women walk away then, launching into immediate discussion on how best to handle what Milly has already deemed a delicate situation. "We'll wait for you outside the house," Milly calls, turning briefly.

Eva is still glaring. She pulls her legs up more and lights another cigarette. "Glad you'll go and help them," she says, her words measured.

"Spit it out," Natalia demands. "Whatever you have to tell me, spit it out."

Eva hesitates. She stares off across the street, to nothing in particular. "You didn't care what happened," she says finally. "After you left. You didn't care that Dad went out one night, that he got drunk, that he came home late. And what did he do? Call me by *your* name? Come up to me? Put a hand on me?" Eva inhales and waits. Then she flicks her cigarette and sends sparks flying to the ground. She pulls her legs closer and wraps her arms around them.

Her words feel like a smack, quick, across the face. Natalia stands, shaking her head. "All you do is lie," she concludes, pushing Eva's words from her mind. "All you do is make up stories."

Upset, barely able to register Eva's words, Natalia walks to Ginny's house and finds Milly and Jenny still standing together like an envoy, calling out, unleashing a relentless succession of knocks on the front door. The afternoon light pushes down through the trees and between the row of houses. Somewhere beyond the house, a dog barks.

"We've been at this for five minutes," Milly says in an exhausted way. She checks her watch, possibly worrying at this point about the dwindling food and ice at the picnic, the necessity of putting items away. She peers into the window and raps on the glass, her knuckles white from effort. "Ginny," she calls, trying to peer in. "You're missing the picnic."

Natalia goes to the door and feels it give without hesitation. She lets it drift open, intending to only call into the house, intending to remain a bystander, but it is the smell of burning food that hits her hard and the slight gray smoke that grows diffuse in the living room. Her feet react before her brain. All the thoughts she had of Eva on the walk over disappear in that moment and are lost to the day. Instinctively, she runs. Milly and Jenny follow close behind. In the kitchen, they find Ginny on the floor, slumped over, the phone cradled in her lap. There is a vacancy in her expression that startles Natalia, but she permits herself only a moment to let this register before she flicks off the oven and grabs a towel. She opens the door and bats away smoke and pulls out the cake, blackened, smoldering.

"They called," Ginny says, just audibly, nodding but not seeing any of them.

Natalia places the cake in the sink. She comes over and tries to help Ginny up, but her body is like a lead weight that won't budge. Natalia rests on her knees, feels the cool linoleum through her summer pants. "Who called, Ginny?" she asks. She looks over to Milly and Jenny.

"They found something, but I don't think— By the creek. They don't think it's her. They said they aren't sure."

"My God," Milly says.

Ginny nods. Her face is pale. Natalia senses that she is falling, that every word they say is tumbling in after her, into an abyss. She knows this look. She saw it in so many broken faces when they became ghosts, floating, finally lost to the world.

"Ginny," Natalia says.

"They said—" Ginny tells them, choking up on the words, "—they said the girl was raped."

Natalia picks up the phone from the floor, replaces it on its receiver. She feels numb, lost in things. She thinks of Eva, she thinks of Sissy. A shiver travels through her, even on this mild day. She is aware of the cuckoo clock above the sink, how it ticks and ticks away the hours, and she remembers that a cuckoo is a bird of bad luck, each call it makes sounding out the years the listener has to live. A heaviness hangs on her and she forces herself to breathe. "We'll go together, Ginny," she says, leaning forward to help her up. "We'll go with you to see." She places her arm under Ginny's. The women help. Together, they manage to right Ginny, just as Natalia sometimes saw men do—men holding each other up even though it was futile, really, a last defiance against death, a last affirmation of something defiantly, wholly humane.

Ginny trembles, her body tilting sideways. "I can't. I don't want to know."

"You have to," Natalia says, steadying her. "We'll do it together."

"They aren't sure."

"You'll be sure then."

"I should go back to the picnic," Jenny says, shaking her head. She wipes back tears with her knuckle. "To let everyone know."

"Frank," Natalia tells her. "Tell him I don't want Sissy to hear. Tell him to take the girls out. I don't want them home when I get back, particularly if . . ." She feels Ginny get weaker and pulls her up. She whispers into Ginny's ear. "We'll go with you. Milly and I are going to go with you, but you have to walk yourself. Ginny, you have to walk."

16

There was, in Sissy's estimation, a sudden disruption at the Morrises' house, after Mrs. Schultz arrived, her face blotchy, her pretty hairdo smashed against her thin face from running, and her hand resting on her chest. A distress rose in the neighbors and there was, subsequently, a whispered conversation as the adults gathered in a circle, away from the children. Sissy strained to hear until Eva—Eva who was included in the conversation, who stood opposite their father—caught Sissy by her bony shoulder. Seeing Eva's expression—suddenly blank, palpably shaken—Sissy became nervous, her foot tapping the ground. She scanned the circle and the empty tables. She ran around the house and searched for her mother. Then, breathless and more than a little beside herself, she pulled on Eva's T-shirt.

"Eva," she started, her voice quivering.

"Go. Go play." Her tone was like their mother's was on that day she was in no mood, that day she left them all.

Within minutes the picnic ended, the men and women cleaned up, and a somber air seemed to settle over the once festive activity. The quoit game ceased, the hose was wrapped up. Broken pieces of balloons were collected and thrown into the trash, along with the empty beer cans and paper plates. On the walk home, both her father and Eva were oddly quiet. Eva teetered on the edge of the curb in a fine line, her mind elsewhere, her head down. Inexplicably, she held Sissy's hand the entire way home, gripping it tightly. Sissy should have felt overwhelmed with newly found happiness when her father announced later that he was taking them to the circus that night, the outing itself that, in light of the picnic, she had all but given up on, and yet the entire arrangement had a conspiratorial air, the longed-for event no longer what it was the day before. It reminded her of the day she was sent to Mrs. Morris—exiled suddenly, cast off—even though she didn't want to go there, even though she sensed something was very wrong.

Now in the car, her father keeps his eyes on the road, and Eva, her body turned toward the door, watches the shops that go by on the square. Sissy, alone in the backseat, finds the silence unbearable. Her mind unravels possibilities, all of which end up in calamitous ruin. "Eva," she says again, frowning.

Eva looks back, tilting her head slightly, studying Sissy. "What?"

"She didn't leave again, did she?"

"Who?" For a moment she pauses, her mouth open, as if she might say more.

"Mom?"

"For Christ's sake, Sissy, no," her father snaps, though Sissy doesn't know what she's done or said to make him out of sorts. She doesn't know why he's been brooding the entire drive, the vein in his neck throbbing. His voice sets her back against the seat again, and she knows enough to be quiet. The passing lights illuminate her arms and legs in strange, eerie ways, making her feel like a ghost. She watches her father, not knowing what he thinks—how his mind at this very moment is going over all the things that might happen to a girl, how violence can be inflicted on the flesh. She does not know that, thinking about all this, he wants to kill the sonofabitch who would do something like that, whoever would hurt a child in that way. He wants to pummel the sonofabitch with blinding fists. Sissy only senses his fury—palpable, the energy of it shooting in all directions around the car, ricocheting off the windows, piercing into her heart. This, coupled with Eva's lack of any further response, only confirms for her that she is accurate in her perceptions, that her mother is gone again, that what unfolds now is a lie constructed by everyone and meant only to appease. In the distance, she catches sight of the taunting big top, yellow-white against the darkening sky, a red flag flapping in the evening breeze. The Ferris wheel makes its spiraling descent, mocking her with idiotic motion, each chair outlined in lights and swaying when the ride is started and stopped again. Yesterday such a scene would have filled her with awe and wonder. Whatever oddities she found in the day would have dwindled against the bright musicality of the night. But now, for whatever splendor there is in front of her, the air is also tinged with something else. She will hear only a tenor of sadness against the music, and the contrast will make the world seem strange, inverted, everything hinting of something Sissy can't quite see or touch. Is it always to be this way? Sadness lurking behind laughter? Something amiss in the appearance of perfection?

Frank scans the parking lot for a pay phone, eager to call Natalia and find out the news. His eyes follow the rows of cars in the parking lot, then move to the booths lined with banners and clicking turnstiles, the crowd of people funneling into the gates, the sudden noise.

"Come on, Sissy," Eva says. She grabs her hand so that Sissy can feel the pulse in the space between Eva's thumb and finger.

Their father walks behind them. He tucks his shirt into his shorts. He pays at the turnstiles and ushers in the girls. The smells assault them: buttery popcorn, steaming hot dogs, oil from funnel cakes. Around Sissy there are gleaming faces, bright with perspiration, some of whom she knows. Foreheads shimmer under the strings of light that are thread unevenly from stand to stand. Children, hoisted on their fathers' shoulders, peer over the crowd, strings of balloons trailing behind them, bumping against one another gently. In the distance Sissy sees two balloons drift above the faces and heads, above the lights, carried westward by the breezes.

"Stay close," Eva tells her. "You hear me?"

"Is Mom coming later, then?" Sissy yells this above the din, but Eva says nothing, and it's impossible to guess whether Eva hears her and chooses to ignore the question or whether Eva hasn't heard Sissy at all.

Frank watches Sissy, her startling silver suit catching every bright bulb, reflecting them like a prism. Even this angers him tonight and makes him think that this is exactly the type of thing the eye is drawn to—the play of light—this is exactly what makes a girl stand out and makes her suddenly vulnerable. He imagines Vicki that day in the park, how appealing a lonely girl might have seemed to whatever sonofabitch who watched and waited and sensed an opportunity in the quiet, placid day. He looks from side to side, past the faces, past the rides. His face pinches. He already has it in mind that, in this mood, he won't be able to stand this for long—the blaring noise, the flashing lights, the screams from children, people packed like sardines, the smells of their bodies intermingling: sweat and perfume, grease and dirt. The more he dwells on events of the evening, the more he thinks of the things that could happen. (A man attacking a girl, forcing her down. *My God,* he thinks, *what if she were kept alive? What if her death were slow, spanning across days, or weeks?*) When he first heard the news at the Morrises', his mind went utterly blank. He felt numb and distanced from everything, pushed back into a void that contained only oceans of dumb silence. But now he is slightly dizzy, hot in the crowd. His body tenses.

"Hold up!" he yells.

To his surprise, Eva obeys. She turns and waits, still gripping Sissy's hand. Frank pulls out his wallet and gives her the last of his money. Eva releases Sissy. She counts the bills and shoves them into her shorts pocket. Eva and Frank's eyes meet. And there is something that is shared between them—doubt, guilt, regret. Something seems to register in her face for a moment—he imagines forgiveness—but then it disappears entirely. "The ticket booth is over there," he says, pointing. "Take Sissy on what rides she wants; get something to eat, too. I'll be back; I'll find you."

"Where are you going?" Eva says.

"I want to see if your mother is home. I need to find out what happened."

Sissy takes this in, a panic rising in her again. It is true, she realizes. What is gone and comes back is surely destined to go again. All her thoughts, all her worries. She grabs Eva's hand and squeezes, but Eva doesn't look down to reassure her.

"I'll find you. If an hour passes, meet me right here," he says, pointing to the ground. "And Eva, you watch Sissy, do you hear me? You keep your eye on your sister."

With that, Frank leaves the girls to weave through the disorienting crowd. As they walk, they bump elbows and push against people, and the ground changes from a paved surface to dusty grass, worn thin from traffic. The air is tight, stale. Concession stands and game stands lined with red-and-white canopies are to the left of them, the prizes—stuffed animals and plastic blow-up toys and dolls—strung along the tops, hanging precariously by arms and legs. The shooting gallery. The ring-toss. The water guns. The hoops. Lights flash, like a disco, pulsing in time with the loud music. They pass the big top, where a wiry-looking man takes tickets from the line of spectators. The woman on the wire; the wolf boy; the bearded lady; the woman balancing plates—they were all true, Sissy realizes. All of them. Away from this, a carousel turns in circles, like Eva's dancer in her music box turns—slowly, with a measure of caution. Creamy horses lope up and down on their poles; the pipe organ in the center plays by itself, the keys pressed down by a phantom. A house of glass spins on a metal platform lit with green lights. To the right, a fun house lined with mirrors towers up, a painted figure—a monstrous woman with beer steins in her hands and Heidi braids—

looks curiously though absently down on the crowd. Behind this structure is a petting zoo, metal pens with llamas and horses and goats, and then the field, the parked tractors and RVs, and the stationary train, the boxcars emptied, the flatbeds vacant.

A pulse, a beat. Music. A hum.

All the people. What do they wish for?

Eva pulls Sissy as she might a piece of hesitant thread, walking toward the ticket stand. Sissy glances up and sees a man high above her, as tall as the woman with the Heidi braids, but thinner and in animated movement, a stick man dressed in long blue pants, a white-and-red-striped jacket, a top hat. He looks down at her and waves happily. Sissy squeezes Eva's hand tighter and looks away. She searches the crowd of Gypsies.

The lines snake from the booths, uneven, noisy. A pale girl about seven or eight passes alone and seems to float along with the crowd. Above her head, she holds a large crimson flower—delicate, airy, made of tissue paper pulled apart from a tight center. As she moves, the flower inches up higher, as if it is bouncing along the faces before being swallowed up entirely.

Not noticing any of this, Eva unclenches Sissy's sweaty hand and lets it slip away. Her mind is elsewhere entirely. For the first time she allows herself to think that in one regard, her mother was right, that she's been negligent, that Sissy was left by herself all summer, even on that day when Vicki Anderson disappeared and something terrible happened. Sissy was left to do as she wished while Eva met Peter in his van, while they talked about silly things and fucked on the floor, Peter undressing her slowly, peeling off her clothes, lifting her skirt and rump, putting his mouth to her, his smooth hands running over her thighs, his moist lips on her waiting skin. Sissy was left to everything, and Eva didn't even think to ask about her day, about what might have happened. The nagging sense of *what if* consumes her now, and her mind mulls out possibilities that leave her feeling sullen and slightly ill. To think she wished it might be Sissy who'd disappeared, Sissy and not the

Anderson girl—that she actually had that thought of coming home to find herself blissfully alone—that she could be so self-centered, so cruel. And how she tried to scare Sissy with tales of death, not caring if they were true, all without really thinking it might have been Sissy who was grabbed, sending a shock wave through the world. She shudders to think of this, yet it hits her forcefully like a fist. Her remorse cuts to the bone.

"I could win you a prize," Eva says. She tousles Sissy's hair. "We have some money."

Sissy follows Eva to a stand where dolls are left hanging, one after the other, blondes and brunettes and redheads all in pretty blue dresses with too much frill. "I don't want those," Sissy says, folding her arms. "I thought you didn't want to come, to the picnic or here."

"I didn't," Eva tells her. "But I wasn't going to leave you alone."

"Dad's mad."

Eva stands on tiptoes and glances around. "All the more reason," she says, "to not be alone."

"Why's Dad mad?"

Eva says nothing.

"Mom left, didn't she?"

Eva looks down at her. "No."

"Are you tricking me? Are you lying?"

Eva bends over and untwists the strap of Sissy's swimsuit. She straightens Sissy's shorts, pulling them up to her belly button. "I wouldn't lie to you," she says. Her face remains serious and somber.

Sissy registers a doubt. Why else would her father be so angry, why would he suddenly go off and leave the two of them if not to search for their mother, if not to try to bring her home? She gnaws at her cheek, the soft flesh. All the clues make perfect sense. Lost in the haze of the day, the confusion of noise and hoopla, Sissy thinks all this makes sense about the world and more. She remembers that this is the place of Gypsies, that this is the world of a doomed people. And after the Gypsies have taken what they want, they will recede into the woods again and disappear in the darkness. They will vanish into the mists, taking with them a few unsuspecting children. She sees her mother there, too, with all of them—a woman lost and disenchanted, running wildly in the night, telling stories of how she knows only strangers—and Sissy sees Eva and her alone again, tending to themselves, living off scraps of bread.

"I'll get you a balloon, then," Eva says, righting herself.

Sissy stares, waiting for something else entirely. Hot tears come too quickly, again.

"What is it?"

Involuntarily, she moves from foot to foot as if she might pee. "You're lying," she says in a desperate whisper.

Eva pulls Sissy away from the crowd, to the side of a nearby tent. Inside there are men's voices, a faint smell of cigars. The air settles. In the distance, traffic whizzes past and lights spot the road.

"Listen," Eva says, in a way that makes Sissy's head pop up. "It's not mom. Mom hasn't gone anywhere except with Mrs. Anderson to the police station. I'm going to tell you something, but you have to prom-ise to be okay, do you understand?" Eva holds Sissy's waist tightly, in a way that makes her wince. Her bathing suit scratches against her skin, making it raw. Above them another balloon drifts into the air. "Sissy?"

Sissy feels it, a jolt that shoots through her limbs, making her want to run.

"It's Vicki. It's Vicki Anderson," Eva says.

Confused, Sissy grimaces and readjusts. She pulls away, though not entirely. She hasn't thought about Vicki Anderson in what seems like days. She hasn't conjured her since putting her image in its proper place, one that satisfied Sissy and left the world unscathed: Vicki, her best friend who magically grew wings, Vicki the girl who flew away, happily, into another place altogether.

Eva's voice calls her back to the reality of the moment. "They *found* her," she says. "She's dead."

"Here?"

"You don't understand." Eva pulls her close and holds her tightly again. Sissy tenses as she hears the word she has never understood, a word that hangs lifeless in the air: Dead. Dead, dead, dead. This, finally, is what cements the moment—the thud of the word in Eva's mouth, the finality of it on Eva's tongue. She pulls, wrenching as Eva tries to hold her. She steps back over the wire cables, over discarded wrappers, sticky with caramel. She sees only her blurry sneakers, the dirty ground. Nearby a generator roars to life, the belts moving suddenly, making her jump. Sissy calls Eva a liar—she yells this, saying Eva is an outright lying liar—and then she pulls away farther, out of Eva's reach. A space widens between them, filled with the word that Eva said, and in that space the word grows and becomes frighteningly forceful, with its own sound, a low dead hum. She runs. As the crowd moves, she moves with it, away from Eva, away from everything that confuses her and everything that hurts. She follows the lights. She heads toward music that grows louder. She darts through the mass of people. She turns at the corner of a concession stand.

Exhausted, her breath spent, she stops at the carousel, sees a smoky gray stallion with its front legs raised in a gallop, its empty saddle adorned with grape leaves. As it glides by, its rump changes, not a horse but a mermaid's tail. A white mare raises her left hoof, prancing, and on her sides, suddenly, green scales. Above the murals, gilded mirrors breeze by, and she sees only repetitions of herself.

She runs over ground covered with sawdust and peers into the big top: the suspended lights, the interplay of shadows. People perched in the bleachers roar with laughter and clap and cheer. Against the canvas wall, a man with a pockmarked face stands, his skin tight and eyes sharp and small. A cigarette hangs from his fingers, which he then extinguishes under the heel of his boot. When he turns toward Sissy, she notices a bird perched on his shoulder. The bird bobs its head up and down. It flashes its wings and they open in a taunting way.

Sissy's heart races. "Do you work here?" she whispers.

"Today I do," the man says, looking away, back to the rings. "Maybe not tomorrow if I make a woman angry tonight."

She thinks to tell him she's lost but doesn't. She doesn't want to go back to Eva. She doesn't want to hear Eva say that awful word again, and not simply to say it but to say it in a way that made it seem all too true. Sissy inhales the sawdust, the deep musky scent of animals and dung. She listens as the man with a top hat bellows into the microphone: "Everything is a wonder here. Everything is a spectacle!" The magnetic pull of his voice, the magician's look about him, willing the crowd's gaze, directing it above him to where the lights suddenly flash on. Exuberant, in motion, a woman in pink tights flies into the air only to be caught by a man who falls backward, his hands grabbing hers. The crowd claps. Clowns weave through the bleachers with their wide-painted grins, their masses of bright red hair. They hold buckets, swaying them unpredictably. A drum roll sounds. And then not water but a burst of confetti, thrown high into the air, floating down like snow. Shrieking, wild laughter. In the ring, a poodle with a tutu walks on its hind legs. In the center ring a lion roars. Suspended above the animal, twenty feet in the air, a woman spins on a rope, a twirl of rhinestones, crimson peacock feathers. Sissy's heart races to see a woman dangling above the lion's mouth.

She feels the bird's eye on her. "Have you seen a little girl?" she asks the man. "Have you seen my Gypsy mother?"

"Seen lots of girls," the man says, keeping his eye on the woman, the waiting lion. The drum roll sounds harder. "Seen some Gypsy women, too."

Confused, Sissy squints. "Where are the Gypsies, then, the ones who take children?"

"Oh, those," he tells her. He grins and produces from his pocket a kernel of corn. The bird takes it gently in its long beak, flaps its black wings again. "I'm one of those. But they're all over, Gypsies. Take your pick."

"Is he your pet?"

"Him?" The man pets the bird's feathers, and under his fingers they turn black-emerald, black-blue. "Found him when he was young, practically dead on the road. Never heard a damn peep out the bird, doesn't ever sing. Doesn't fly off."

"I'm running off," she says. "I'm running away. Tonight."

"Suit yourself," he tells her. "Doesn't bother me."

Her chest restricts. She cannot keep up with the motion in the tent, the changing circles, the spaces that are emptied and filled again. She thinks of Vicki, how Vicki wanted to be a performer. What is dead, anyway? Not to shift shape but to be gone, gone and never seen, gone forever, with no hope of coming home.

Outside, Sissy runs, mulling over Eva's words, over the word "dead" and Eva's expression as she told Sissy this. How the worry held Eva's face. She wants to believe that her sister is a liar. In that moment she ran away, she did believe it. Still what Eva said was different from the stories of the summer; her delivery of the news serious, her hands pinching Sissy's sides as if she wanted to hold her there, to keep her from running. The way Eva spoke the words, the cadence of her voice, matched the lines of worry in her face, as if she didn't want to hurt Sissy at all.

She moves toward the field. Better the Gypsies, then, she thinks. Better the Gypsies who steal away children than children who go missing and then later are found dead.

Amy marvels as she surveys the crowd. She sways, almost hypnotically, as she strains to see past the entry booths to the attractions. After her mother came over to babysit Sophie, Amy surprised Peter by dressing up for the evening in new pants and a blouse that fell just off her shoulders. He takes this as a good sign, one that's hopeful despite everything. She's asked about Eva several times—mostly when they are in bed, when the lights are out and her mind wanders—and he knows she hasn't let go, that she is still playing out possibilities, doubting his explanations. Eva is no longer the girl who delighted him, the girl who made him feel new. Instead she is that girl with the crush, a girl out of hand, a girl with a problem. As he tells Amy this again and again, as he reinvents Eva, the story shapes itself as true; they both begin to believe it. His betrayal lessens. Through comforting lies they grow closer because—it occurs to Peter—neither of them entirely wishes for the stark, deliberate clarity of truth. The girl could hardly be trusted to tell the truth. If she didn't believe him, she could talk to the other teachers. She could talk to the teachers and they would tell her the same damn thing.

To soothe Amy, he's also planned an impromptu vacation before the start of school, away from the house, away from everything. He's spoken to her of white sands, skeletal strands of the barrier reefs, a house on the ocean where, at night, with the windows open, they would hear only the sound of water, the swelling tides. Amy agreed to this, wanting, he thought, to believe. "We need it, don't we?" she asked him, her voice straining.

Only sometimes when he is alone, after Amy has drifted off to sleep and he is there in that same darkness, do his lies hit him with a force and weight. In those moments a murmur escapes from him, a regret, a sigh, something absent of words altogether, something that, in the next moment, to survive, to keep what he loves close, he dismisses again altogether.

He watches Amy now as she takes in the crowd, her eyes never lingering on anything too long. Her body moves with the music and he sees her again as the girl on the quad, dancing from building to building, light, free. "What should we do first?" he asks, looping his arm around her.

"I don't know," Amy says, still looking. "I haven't been to a circus in years. I used to love them when I was a kid."

Peter agrees, though, in truth, he doesn't view things the way she views them. What he sees is a gathering place for the bizarre and for the slightly idiotic, the warped sense of everything—the fat, bloated woman who looks as though she's spent years taking up water; the man with snakes coiling around his neck; the booths that promise the greatest spectacles on earth and then, when you step behind the curtains, when you squeeze into the small, cramped spaces, reveal only a mirror, a distorted vision of yourself. He says, "Did you see that guy at the tilt-a-whirl? Some poor bastard turned bright red, and the guy just smiled and kept cranking the machine. They probably take bets on who they can get to vomit."

"Maybe," Amy says, still looking around. "It wouldn't surprise me. My cousin got sick on that ride once. She and I used to go to the circus every summer. There was one that came through, and it was all we could talk about for days. My poor mother, she couldn't keep up with us. We had to go on everything at least once, some rides we'd go on repeatedly, like we knew the minute the circus left we wouldn't remember the feeling, so we had to cram it all in, whatever we could, or we'd miss it." Amy's voice trails off.

Peter pulls her closer. He breathes deeply, glad to be in the night air, perhaps a bit giddy himself, to be following strings of lights that seem to ask nothing of him. He thinks again of his family, of all of them away at the beach, the newly rented house. He kisses her hair.

"The older I get, the more I have to look back on," Amy says. She pauses, looks around, for what, Peter doesn't know. "And the less I want to lose, I suppose."

She eyes him now, and he feels a tinge of discomfort, a question in her starting to form again. "The older I get," he tells her, "the less in my life I remember."

Her face changes again, and he shifts uncomfortably, promising himself he'll do better. He promises himself he will be better for Amy, for the baby. He will never be so foolish as to let a girl come between them. Eva. (He allows himself to say her name, though thinking about her fills him with a quiet embarrassment.) He tells himself a girl like Eva is bound to bounce back, a girl like Eva has so many options.

Amy climbs into a carousel carriage and watches as Peter mounts a camel with a long golden beard and black eyes. He snaps a photo of her as she leans forward, her hand resting on the scrolled artwork, a quixotic look on her face, the stuffed dinosaur he won for Sophie next to her. A metal arm extends from the edge of the canopy, with a series of rings.

"Let me," Amy says, taking the camera. "Grab one when we go past," she tells him. "It's supposed to be good luck."

The music cranks, and each time they whirl by the rings, Peter lunges forward, his fingers straining right to their tips. They slip by his hand, the cool metal taunting him. On his fifth try he snags one that releases with a ping.

"For you," he says, giving it to her. He holds it up. "I thought it was supposed to be brass?"

"Brass rings?" Amy laughs again, and he cannot tell what she's thinking. She snaps a photograph, hiding her face. "That's just something they tell kids, Peter. The rings are all steel, didn't you know that? It's just a story."

Away from everything, Sissy moves swiftly, to the field next to the firehouse. She doesn't know how she got here exactly, only that her feet moved and that her body, driven by the day, followed, and that it didn't matter to her that her father would be angry, or that Eva might be searching for her frantically, desperately. She stops, not yet aware that she is moving toward the train. Next to a darkened RV, two horses graze behind a makeshift fence. A bay gelding noses the remnants of molasses on the ground. A buckskin looks up inquisitively as Sissy climbs the first metal rail and feels the structure wobble. She isn't supposed to be here; she isn't supposed to be alone. She makes a *click-click* noise with her tongue and the buckskin reaches with its muzzle, toward her outstretched fingers. She feels velvet and coarse hair, a nibbling at her palm. She smells the urine-drenched straw. "I'm leaving," she says to the horse. Flies buzz around the buckskin's eyes and back. It lashes its tail from side to side and stomps the ground.

She looks back, toward the lights. Everything happens at a quickened pace, a blur. She sprints along the darkening sky, a flash of glittery silver, a girl. At the tracks, she jumps over the many zigzagging rails and onto the rocky surface between the ties. She works her way past the long cars and flatbeds that smell of tar and diesel. She runs her hand over the rough surface, still warm from the sun. One flatbed, two flatbeds, three flatbeds, empty. She looks under the cars as she might have once looked under the bed for monsters. She passes a closed boxcar. Sissy jumps, but she cannot reach the lever to slide the door along the metal runner. She passes another boxcar made from old barn wood, the shapes of plywood uneven and rickety. The car stands open, wide like a terrifying mouth—tempting tonight, such darkness. Her hands touch the wooden surface. She feels the prick of a splinter as it lodges itself under her flesh, deep, penetrating. She stands on tiptoes to peer in, debating. Here she might wait until she feels the train in motion beneath her, and then she will be gone, gone from everyone in this confusing summer, gone from death itself, gone to be with those faces who once frightened her, the waiting Gypsies who have always called her name.

Resolved, she hoists herself up as she might in gym class. Her legs dangle for a moment; her feet scratch the gravel, disrupting it. Her body strains. She peers in. Using all her strength, she lifts herself higher until her knees scrape along the surface of the car. She crawls and disturbs the resting flies. The air closes around her. She can see only shapes and shadows, and, frightened, she turns toward the distant lights again, the muffled sounds of music and people. She moves along the wall, inching along, groping the wooden boards. She moves cautiously, the hairs on her neck on end. She holds her breath and eases deeper into the car, the straw crunching beneath her feet. She squints, trying to bring shadows into view, and can sense it there—precise, raw—the presence of something waiting to devour her, to take her, finally.

Something hits the top of the roof, an acorn, maybe, or knocking fingers. This isn't the world of the swimming hole, she reminds herself. This is another world entirely—the world of the missing and of the dead, the mothers and fathers and children, turned here, to this waiting place, the caravan of Gypsies, the train. Her arms stretch forward, along the uneven surface. Scratches, which she imagines belong to all the children who are dead, who are taken away in cars that must be, she imagines, exactly like this: the air tight and musty. *They claw to get to the light,* she thinks. *How awful.*

She closes her eyes and imagines Vicki Anderson that day at the park, how a man was there waiting for her, how he enticed her to the woods. Perhaps he told Vicki he'd lost someone, or perhaps he told her his dog had run off. Perhaps he, like the strange man in the tent, had a pet bird that flew off, and she followed it unknowingly, trying to reclaim it and bring it back. Perhaps he took her by the arm and yanked her away when no one was watching. In the woods, the man, a shadow of a man, came toward Vicki. He loomed over her until Vicki was in darkness. And, like the man so long ago, on that day when Sissy and Vicki were together, the man who exposed himself, the shadow man did the same, the shadow man grabbed her, the shadow man laced his hands around her neck. He left her there, dead—dead, dead, dead—the dirt caked under her fingers, the dirt staining her knees and elbows.

Sissy breathes hard thinking on all this. She says something, inaudible even to herself, her voice small and hollow.

A pause. Outside, she hears footsteps, rushed, and then sees a shadow moving across the door. Sissy's heart races. She stays still, her palms sweating against the wood. The shadow stops, looks in, moves toward her. The shadow lifts itself up into the boxcar. If she runs, there is death. If she doesn't run, there is death. If she moves toward the shadow man, she will die. If she breathes, she might die. If she can't breathe, she will die. If she screams, the shadow might come in and grab her, silencing her forever.

Dead.

She crouches down, whimpers.

"Sissy?" the voice says. Her father's voice, raspy, grumbling.

She doubts, waits for the voice to sound again, this time angrier. The voice bristles, irritable, inflamed. Still, she waits, unsure. A third time, the voice booming now.

She steps forward slowly. "Dad?" she says. The word in the hollow car echoes.

He reaches forward and catches her shoulder, his thumb pressing into her flesh, biting, his fingers biting, too, sending a shock, a wave of pain through her. She winces. He yanks her into the warm night air. Dumbfounded, she moves. He jerks her arm again and marches across the rails and stones and into the dim field, pulling Sissy behind him, the pressure of his grip descending down her arm like a clamp, sending up numbness, pins and needles.

"Where is Eva?" he demands. Without waiting for her answer, he stops, turns her, and his hand goes back wide, hitting her bottom, hard, flat, the bone beneath the flesh already stinging, and then more tears, more hurt, the deadened ache. She hears a horse snort and whinny. A light in a nearby RV goes on but no one is really watching. Anything might happen.

"If I hadn't seen you in the light," Frank yells. "Do you hear me?" He shakes her, brings her toward him. She can smell the faint aroma of beer on him from the picnic. "Do you ever listen? Where is Eva?"

Sissy grows mute. If she tells the truth, she will be in more trouble—could she say she ran away?—and if she says nothing, her father will only growl more, but if she lies to save herself, she betrays Eva, Eva who on this night has been nice to her, Eva who offered to win her a doll, Eva who has done nothing wrong except speak of death, speak the truth, Eva who is, finally, in this unfolding moment, loved by Sissy best.

"Well?" he demands.

She blubbers. She chokes back sobs.

Her father lets go a barrage of curses, each worse than the one before. He smacks her bottom again, harder, sending another wave of pain through her, from the bottom up, jolting her spine. "Don't cry," he yells.

"I w-was in line," she begins, stammering. "I turned and she left. She's left all summer long with *that man.*"

"Who?" Frank demands, yanking her, pulling her closer again. "What man?"

Sissy bites her lip hard. She studies the ground. "I went looking for her. I was looking for her and the man—you're hurting my arm."

Her father's jaw clenches, but he lessens his grip. "Don't you know, don't you goddamn know, that if you're lost, you find someone who works here and tell them you're lost?"

Dumbstruck, Sissy nods. He pulls her forward again. Her free hand rubs her bottom as she moves. She doesn't look back, at the boxcar with its giant mouth, nor does she look up, to the stars. She looks down at the ground to her feet. Disembodied, they move across the trampled grass.

Children. She realizes she would never be able to deal with them—she could never be able to have one of her own. Eva believed she was making things better by speaking the truth. She thought the truth would assuage Sissy's panic, soothe her questions, and yet then, how suddenly her sister became more troubled, her fears amplified. How she wrenched away, a flash of silver lost suddenly in the crowd. Eva ran. She ran after Sissy. She weaved through people, eyed the stands, looked in the tents, peered into the bleachers. She glanced up at the swings, to the dangling feet. She ignored those she saw from Watson High, when they called to her. She scanned the Ferris wheel, waiting until the wheel made one rotation. She thought: *If something should happen to Sissy in this place.* She passed rides and saw the eyes of men watching her. She shuddered. She thought of someone pulling Sissy into darkness, attacking her.

She tried the fun house and swallowed hard—the heat finally hitting her, her stomach assailed by the need to rid itself of the food she'd eaten at the Morrises', the food that, after her mother had left, she'd downed ravenously. As she passed the mirrors, she suddenly turned short and fat, her legs mere stubs that could belong to a midget, her hair flat and wide. Her shape elongated, and then compressed. She called for Sissy as she ran down corridors. A train horn sounded, stopping her with a blare of sudden light. She burst out into the night air. Her stomach wrenched. Saliva coated her mouth, and then something acrid rose from her stomach. She ran to a trash can, beads of sweat dripping from her forehead. She threw up, in the discarded cardboard cups of french fries and half-eaten corn dogs, their smell making her stomach wrench again. She looked to see if anyone noticed.

It is not Sissy she sees now, but Peter and Amy. She stops immediately, dumbstruck, catching herself. The two of them walk away from the carousel, holding hands—*holding hands!* she thinks to herself—Peter leaning into his wife. Eva stands, momentarily paralyzed, watching him kiss his wife's cheek, the way his mouth touches her, not with ardent desire but the tenderness of years. How this action disaffirms everything Peter said during their times together, when he voiced his complaints about marriage, about his wife. She imagined them in separate rooms. She imagined an absence of conversation, and yet it was she and Peter in separate rooms, she and Peter with infrequent contact, their voices speaking over wires, their bodies occasionally slapping together. Always behind this was Amy. She was always present in the background. It doesn't matter what he said. He and his wife were together. Like her mother and like her father, they were together and alone sometimes, maybe, but still together nonetheless. She doesn't understand how he could still be like this, touching his wife, kissing her, after the times Peter and she were together in his van, their bodies slick with sweat, naked, entwined. The force of the thought sends her back.

Peter places an arm around Amy, the camera dangling from his wrist. He doesn't see Eva standing by them now, her crushed expression, her intent stare. It is only Amy who glances toward her, and then stops, recognizing her immediately.

"Peter," Eva says loudly, so that it registers with his wife, the informality of a first name, the implied intimacy. She starts to make out the words that Peter whispers in Amy's ear.

"I don't want a scene, Eva," Peter says, his tone overly teacherly and academic, quelling any arguments or disruption. Eva, however, wants to make a scene. She wants to unleash herself, to claw at his eyes and pull at his hair. She wants to rip the glasses from his face and crush them under her feet. She wants to scream, to scream about all the lies, all the betrayals.

"Eva," he says again, warning, making it seem as though she is a foolish girl.

"My husband explained everything," Amy says.

A wave of embarrassment comes over Eva, the same that she suffers through when the boys at school look past her or when they talk about her at their lockers, calling her a whore behind her back. "Did he explain? Did he really?" She shifts her weight, stares at Peter.

"There are people to talk to who are your own age," Amy says, her defensiveness registering. "But you can't just go around following adults and pining after them. Did you come here tonight looking for Peter? Are you trying to cause problems?"

Her words, her accusations, level Eva. What untruths has Peter told, what things has he said that portray Eva this way, in this light?

"You're a liar," Eva tells him, but her voice shrinks in the noise, and she realizes she has only mouthed the words and not said them at all. A useless anger drains in her and is replaced by something stony. She stands up straighter, still waiting for him to take everything back. Heat travels through her, cutting deep—her embarrassment in the moment, her useless rage. She sees him like a boy, childish, foolhardy, accusing. He would lie so that he might keep together what life he has. He would lie about everything.

Somewhere behind her now, another voice calls, and she turns abruptly and sees her father coming through the crowd, Sissy being pulled along. Sissy's cheeks are blotchy, her lower lip protruding.

Frank looks over to Peter. He is quick to assess the situation at hand: Eva's English teacher standing there with a guilty, useless expression; Eva's own look that betrays her—amorous, longing, angry. "What are you doing?" he says. He lets go of Sissy's wrist and watches as she scrambles closer to Eva. "What the hell is going on?"

Eva presses her lips together. She shakes her head. "Nothing."

"You're supposed to be watching your sister. Instead you're here, with him?" His voice startles her. Around them, a few people pause and look over before walking on again. Frank turns his attention to Peter, his neck twisting in provocation. "And you, what the hell are you doing with my kid?"

"I'm not doing anything with your kid," Peter says. "Your kid's been following me around all summer long. Your kid's been getting ideas in her head."

Frank debates, weighing the tension, the strained looks passing between Eva and Peter, and holding these against Sissy's proclamation in the field, her mention of a man, of being left alone throughout the long days. His hands clench at the lingering knowledge that he's been made a fool of by Eva—his own daughter—and her lies. He's been made a fool of by this man who stands in front of him with his self-important look.

Frank's movements are deliberate and quick. He thunders past Eva, and delivers a punch that knocks Peter back and sends Amy into hysterics. The men wrangle on the ground, Frank's anger erupting from some deep place inside him. There is an explosion, a pummeling force, and then strangers finally intervening, breaking the men up, pulling them apart. The last Frank sees of Peter is him righting his glasses, stumbling away, his wife calling after him.

In the parking lot, Frank opens the door and screams at his girls to get in. His blood feels as though it's on fire, and then, in the car, there is a smack, hard across Eva's face from Frank, a blow. Eva's shock, her hand against her cheek. Momentarily, she is speechless. Then her hand comes down, revealing a shine, a blush, a few broken vessels. The flare of nostrils. And there is a sense that this is bad, *that this is very bad,* that everything is different now, bone hitting bone, Eva's nose disjointed, odd-looking. Frightened, Sissy leans back hard against the cushioned seat.

Blood, dark like the color of cherries. Blood on Eva's forearm from where she wipes: a thin smear that makes the dark hairs more pronounced. Eva cups her hand to her nose. The blood drips down, red, the taste of iron, and a wheeze then: blood in the nostril, the air pushing out. If Frank has seen what he's done, if he regrets the blow at all, the blood, the impulsive action, it hardly matters now. There's no stopping the evening.

17

It is quiet in the house, which gives Natalia time to think of what to say. She must find a way to explain to Sissy not only death but the death of a child, a girl her age, a friend. She contemplates an outright lie—but she knows that the days of lying are over. She can no longer pretend with her children. Eventually Sissy will have to step outside, and she will hear smatterings of conversations. It is so hard to keep innocence in children, to cocoon them in stories and pleasantly benign untruths, to wrap them tightly, layer by layer, in an effort to keep them from anything harsh or unkind. It is hard to keep the world from them.

When Frank called from the parking lot of the 7-Eleven, Natalia had just poured a drink—a shot of vodka from the liquor cabinet. She was so shaky. The flush of liquid—raw to her taste buds, hot in her throat—soothed her nerves and kept her hands from shaking, as they had been for the last two hours, since seeing the girl. She delivered the pronouncement as a newspaper reporter might—distanced, her voice drained of emotion. She described the scene, and Frank grew quiet, listening. She knew how angry he was, hearing everything—the girl's bruised lower parts. "I'll get the kids," he told her. "Don't rush," she said. "I need a few minutes, to process, to let it sink in, to let some of it go. The girls—Sissy, my God! They were about the same age." He told her both Eva and Sissy were fine, that nothing was going to happen to the girls tonight.

After she hung up, she went from room to room and turned on all the lamps. The entire downstairs glowed, while upstairs the windows remained dark. It didn't exactly cheer her mood—it was unlikely anything would—but the light at least made her feel better, as if she weren't alone.

How awful that small room had been, how it had smelled of chemicals and bleach, and how, when she, Milly, and Ginny had walked down the hallway, everything around her had been held in suspension: the lights above them hanging from metal poles, the stationary exit sign at the end of the corridor, the tense hum from the wired equipment in a nearby room, a framed print of a forest and stream hanging on the wall. She couldn't help but laugh at that awful print. It was meant, she supposed, to cheer the place, to alleviate the stiff angularity of the building. At the door, Ginny's legs buckled. Still, at least Ginny didn't cry anymore. Natalia couldn't have handled tears. She sensed that all Ginny's tears had been spent already, used up in the two months of waiting, and that this was the last thing to do, the last door to close. Natalia held her up, drew her close, and whispered: "At least you'll know. At least you won't go on in life, wondering." Ginny had turned white. It was so cold, like a bitter cold of winter, like the snow crashing down on skin, except there was no snow, only a metallic light that hung over everything. Air pulsed through the vents, and Natalia imagined a chill on the metal tables. A policeman was there, too, the same man, Milly said, who first went over to Ginny's house months ago: a mere boy. Natalia judged him to be in his twenties. His manner was serious, intent on giving the news and showing Ginny the body—"a body," he said, and Natalia thought:

Just a body, and not a girl. You could see it in the officer, the dread and
weariness that his job caused, especially on days like this. She had seen it
before in the guards, in the camp, that desire to get through with a task
and to leave, to go home to family, if they had one to go to at all; or, if
not, to get through it and then go out, have a beer, have six beers, forget.
He grimaced and his voice turned over to a whisper. "This is the worst
part of my job," he said apologetically. He took off his hat. "I hate it."

Everything was metallic and edged. The sheen distracted Natalia,
gave her eyes things to wander to: the square table with instruments precisely laid, scissors and knives with thin, sharp blades; a wall of silver
chambers, a piece of paper placed in the name tag slot. The entire room
had the quality of something compulsively ordered. It emanated a sense
of control, an antiseptic distance. She whispered to Ginny, but Ginny
was gone, Natalia could see that. A man came into the room, skinny, his
forehead creased with age and framed by the thin skullcap that hugged
his head. He reminded Natalia of the bird man from so long ago, except
this man had a clean face and full lips and looked rested. Perhaps the bird
man had been rested, too, though, and Natalia made him tired only by
memory, forcing him to perform the same task over and over again.

"I don't feel well," Milly said to Natalia. "I'm sorry." Natalia watched
as she turned the corner down the flat corridor. Natalia concentrated on
the task at hand. It wasn't about her but about Ginny. "Ginny," she said.
"Just force yourself to look, and in a minute it'll be over." It was a lie, of
course. It would never be over. Ginny would play out the scene over and
over until, after years of exhaustion, she might finally be able to let some
of it go, maybe even learn to smile again, to laugh—how far away that
was, but how that time waited for her in the distance, another place altogether.

"Just one look," she told Ginny. "Just one, Ginny, and no more."

The man approached. The bird man. A faint dizziness came over
her—something chemical, perhaps, clinging to his scrubs, something
like bleach burning her nostrils. She refused to look away, for Ginny, for

the woman who, after all, was her friend. "We're ready," she said, helping Ginny forward.

Though she should have felt little shock at how horrific life could be, though it seemed her past might have prepared her for this, it did nothing to alleviate the shock, the quiet terror that filled her when the man folded back the sheet and life was reduced, in measure, by smaller scales: not an adult but a child there, the frail bones and thin arms, the unshaped, bloated body, the tilt of the head and soft line of the jaw, the marks by her neck, thumbprints that had turned black. The thin ribs, the small pucker of breasts not yet formed. The table swallowed the child on all sides. There were bruises on her body that even death didn't hide, and a snaking wound that peeked out from the lip of the folded sheet that covered the body. The man with the skullcap kept the girl's right arm covered, but Natalia could still see the jagged, torn flesh. No blood, not now. Even the girl's face alarmed Natalia. She might have expected the last pain of death, the twisted expression she'd seen before, how the dead's last moments trailed them into eternity, to the next life, to whatever was around the corner between here and there. But what she found was worse, ironic—a face that despite the ravaged body and bruises seemed only at peace, as if she'd simply shut her eyes and slept. That was a look that filled Natalia with a quiet terror. That was a look that would follow her into her dreams that night.

"Don't remember this," Natalia said. "Remember her the way she was."

She took in air. She held Ginny tighter, felt Ginny's entire body go limp again. She stiffened her hold. She waited.

"No, no, no, no," Ginny said. A whisper.

"Something," the man with the skullcap said, "got ahold of her arm. We think maybe an animal."

A wolf, Natalia thought. *The child was devoured by a wolf.*

"That's not Vicki," Ginny said, shaking her head. Her eyes had gone blank. Her voice was hard like a pebble. She stepped back. She shook her head again. Natalia let her go. "That's not Vicki," she said again. "That's somebody else's baby. That's somebody else's girl."

Both Natalia and Milly took Ginny home. They stopped first at Ginny's house and collected items from her bedroom: clothing and a toothbrush, a hairbrush, a few nightgowns, some creams and floss, shorts and shirts, underwear.

"Do you need anything?" Natalia asked Milly as they parted ways on the street.

"It wasn't my little girl," Ginny said, looking up.

"We'll take care of her," Milly said. "She can stay with us as long as she needs." To Natalia's surprise, the old woman reached for her, too, and hugged her suddenly.

The air felt good, the motion. She focused on her feet, on the sound of her soles as they hit the pavement. Everything around her was sharp, the sky not black but a deep velvety blue, the stars jeweled in the night. The streetlights hummed, teemed with small bugs. A breeze. A house light at Mrs. Stone's was on. The Schultzes' schnauzer was out in the yard. Natalia passed and it sent up a bark.

The drink. The lights. She was tired. She could have slept for a long time, hours, decades, millennia, but she couldn't stand the thought of closing her eyes and slipping into another world that might, if her dreams turned against her, be even worse than the day, made more horrific in the aftermath and amplified to cataclysmic proportions.

In the kitchen she cuts vegetables for soup, as her own mother did when she heard about the invasion. She cuts an onion, realizing how profoundly absurd rituals are, incantations to keep away sorrow, those small things we do to cushion ourselves from blows, to hope against no hope. The world could be torn to pieces, bombs could fall and cities could fall, and they often did. People could die. Children could die, too. There could be rubble left, dogs barking. It all happened. All of it.

She finishes her drink.

. . .

Sometime later, moments, minutes, hours, Natalia hears the kitchen door slam, then the rush of feet, the sobbing screams, the curses from Eva first, and then from Frank, everything garbled and fragmented. Natalia gets up from the couch and rushes into the hallway in time to have Eva push past her, her hand held up to her face, and there, in her nostril, crusted blood, a shine on the cheek, a net of red-black lines spidering across her flesh. "I told you," Eva is saying, her voice breathless and straining, "if you ever touched me again. If you ever." Frank is behind her, the force of his energy tangible, fisted, balled. How everything turns in him, how an unmitigated hatred fills him, momentarily, one that will change, over the following hours, to regret—immense regret. But now the line of his jaw clenches. The air around him burns with electricity.

"Everything that comes out of your mouth is a fucking lie," he yells.

Jarred by the broken silence, Natalia rushes instinctively after Eva, but Frank grabs her. The table in the hallway wobbles under her weight. Eva maneuvers away from both of them. There is noise—so much noise—Frank's screams, Natalia's questions, and the slam of Eva's bedroom door, the elevated pitch of "What did you do?" And there is Frank screaming about what Sissy told him, a truth she should never have spoken. And all this is heard through open windows, from the lit house on the street. In the confusion, Sissy is left to herself. She crawls under the kitchen table, feeling bits of dirt and sand against her palms as she does. She draws her legs up and waits.

The story goes like this.

The story goes like this . . .

"What happened?" Natalia is yelling. "What did you do?"

"I don't know," Frank yells. "What was I supposed to do?"

If the world were Sissy's, and if Sissy were wondrous and death a thing that hardly existed, she might be able to save Eva. She might run after her, screaming, *I'm coming for you! I'm coming for you, Eva!* If the world were magical, she would send her apologies over the distance;

they would rain down over Eva like hundreds and hundreds of flowers falling suddenly from the sky; they would soothe her, mend everything. But the world, finally, is not hers to bend or re-create. The world is something else entirely. She crouches down more. A drop of blood on the floor—she wipes it with her finger, makes a circle.

She closes her eyes and disappears.

It is sometimes impossible to measure the time, to order things and place them in the past and leave them there for good, as one might turn one's back to a fire and walk away. At some point, after the door to her parents' bedroom closes, after the voices recede into a thin wash of agitated whispers, Sissy crawls out from under the table and tentatively tiptoes past her parents' bedroom door, each step laid softly, a ghost. Cautiously through the hallway, up the stairs. Her parents finally as unknowable as the day itself. A dead friend, a bloodied sister, how everything in a moment conflates, and how her thoughts settle finally on Eva. Upstairs she knocks on Eva's door, a *bumpity-bump-bump* rhythm. Then, when it seems the door will never open, she hears a click. Eva's phone lies on the bed. Sissy stands dumbly as Eva flits frantically around her room, gathering clothes without any thought: only one pair of underwear, one pair of jeans, five different T-shirts, two skirts. She stuffs them into an army bag.

Sissy moves to the edge of her bed, her fingers touching the cotton cover. The blood in Eva's nose is caked now. Black streaks of mascara snake down her cheeks. Sissy bites her nail, making it bleed, too. She bites the inside of her cheek, to do the same.

"What are you doing?"

"You know, Sissy."

"I don't."

"I'm leaving."

Eva pulls rings from her jewelry box and slides them onto her fingers, one by one, until there is a succession of silver.

"Are you coming back?"

"I don't know," Eva says, crying now. She gathers more clothing. She opens her closet and pulls out a few more skirts, stripping them from hangers. She leaves her books on her dresser.

"Can I come?"

"No."

"Why not?" Sissy leans against the bed, uses it for support.

For the first time since Sissy has entered, Eva stops what she's doing. She stands at a distance, across from Sissy, and makes an indecipherable face, not knowing what else to say. Finally, she tells her, "I'd take you if I could, but they'd just get you. They'd probably accuse me of kidnapping you or something. They'd probably call the cops. They'd do that if I took the car. They'd sure as hell do that if I took you." Her voice trails off. Sissy shifts uncomfortably, leaning on her left side, trying to consider this. She smooths the bedspread, the roses that look like cuts.

"You can have my lip gloss," Eva says, tossing it to her.

Sissy looks at the orange tube lying in her open palm. She doesn't remember even catching it. "Thanks," she says, studying it, waiting.

"You can have whatever else you want, too." Eva gathers a few more items: a nightgown, a halter top, a pair of sneakers. Outside, somewhere in front of the house, a car horn sounds once—shrill.

"Don't go," Sissy says. "Stay."

"Not here," she says. "But I'll see you around, you know?"

If running away were a game, Sissy thinks. It is over—the fighting, the racket—though it still clings to her, still feels raw. And Eva is packing the last of her items. And Eva is saying goodbye. In this moment Sissy cannot think to reach for her sister. In this moment she can barely speak.

Eva stares at her, blinks hard. "How much do you love me?" she asks.

Sissy says nothing. She shakes her head, dumbly, and with that, Eva mumbles something else—a piece of advice, perhaps. Sissy barely registers it. Then Eva goes, sprinting down the steps two, three at a time.

Sissy can hear the thudding of footsteps, the rush of motion. The front door opens and closes—a squeak, a bang—before she can say anything else at all. Then there are more footsteps, Natalia, alerted to the front door, hurrying out from her bedroom to see what's wrong, then calling out into the night, "Come back." Sissy freezes at the top of the steps, listening. She scrambles down the steps and hears a screech outside. Natalia grabs her by the shoulder. "Sissy," she says. "Stay here."

Sissy breaks from her mother's grasp and runs down the steps, down the sidewalk to the narrow street outside her house. She smells rubber; the tire tracks snake down the macadam. The night is newly settled and quiet, the air still. A few lights go on, here and there, along the street. A front door opens; a neighbor steps outside. Above her stars sprinkle the sky. She looks both ways, down Ellis Avenue, past the sympathetic trees and parked cars lining the road. She stares out into everything and sees nothing.

four

18

Time passed and settled into place.

There were always those occasions when Sissy, thirty-two, made the trip back again through seemingly relentless hours and hazy miles, sometimes with her husband and her daughter if schedules permitted; and sometimes, like now and for shorter weekend visits, alone. The train station was filled with people, and over the haze of static and the noise of the bustling crowd walking by, suitcases rolling unevenly, Sissy took a seat and waited for the voice to cut through the loudspeaker and announce the departure of the express from D.C. to Philadelphia. From there she would disembark and catch the bus to her parents' house, to those same streets and places she remembered from childhood, places where the memory of Eva always lingered. To her side, a board clicked out arrivals and departures with persistent regularity. In front of her a line of people inched slowly forward to the ticket counter. And above her the vaulted ceiling depicted a painting of a locomotive, steam billowing against the calm sky, a conductor dressed in navy waving people into cars, a smile etched on his face.

There were always times to leave things behind, always times to return again, changed, tempered by the consciousness of memory.

Outside the station, a December rain fell, forceful and even. Sissy called her husband to let him know that even with the slick roads and bad weather, the train was scheduled to leave on time, and her baggage was checked and ready. Her eight-year-old daughter, Margaret, got on the phone, her voice still milky with sleep, and stayed on just long enough to tell Sissy goodbye and come back soon and be safe and bring her back a gift, please. She heard her husband issue a comment about breakfast and then there was a shuffling sound, a small muffle, and his voice on the other end of the line again. "I could still come," he said, his voice a whisper. "I could get Margaret ready—"

"Don't be silly," Sissy said. "It's only three days, and you've got work tomorrow. In and out; I'll be home before you miss me."

They spoke for another few minutes, about preparations and arrangements for the weekend: Sissy and her mother and the planned excursion downtown to hunt for slipcovers; her father's offer to drive them all out to the country. Sissy didn't mention the anticipation she held on these occasions when she came home, the secret wishes she still, after so many years, held inside her, nor did she discuss the dread that sometimes crept in and clouded her love. She hardly ever spoke about Eva, though she thought of her—and in that way held her close—most days.

That night, after Eva ran away and Frank's anger receded like a storm wave, it was Natalia who spent days and days calling around the neighborhood to those friends of Eva's that she knew, finally exhausting her mental list to acquaintances and relative strangers. And it was Frank who drove around town for hours, searching for Greg's car at the school and parks and at his home. The boy's parents refused to give Frank any answers as to where Eva went, but finally, after a week of Frank's showing up and asking, Greg's mother acquiesced and gave Frank a slip of paper with an address in New Jersey, a friend of their family. Of course he went. Of course he looked for Eva. When Frank arrived at the small apartment, no one answered the door, though inside a curtain moved. Once, when he lingered too long on the front steps, knocking incessantly, practically pleading, the police showed up and asked him to leave. There was a knowledge that gradually seeded itself, that those who do not wish to be found never are, that Eva stubbornly, adamantly, refused to come home and eventually left the apartment in New Jersey altogether, her emancipation finalized on her eighteenth birthday, just three weeks after that night. Eventually, when Natalia herself drove out to the apartment—convinced that if not Frank then she could bring Eva home—she secured only an address in California and was told Eva had bought a bus ticket there, though no one could tell Natalia why.

Both Natalia and Frank waited, hoping that Eva would call. They suffered through scandalous rumors and correctly leveled accusations, though no one ever really thought Eva would stay away forever. No one believed that. Eventually, they all thought, the girl was bound to need something—money, a loan, a favor, advice—but the phone never rang once, and Natalia's letters trickled back one by one, unopened, refused, and then finally, after another year, it was no longer a valid address. And that was it. It sometimes seemed to Sissy and perhaps to Natalia and Frank and maybe even to Eva herself, that there should have been more—more antagonisms, more debate, more filling in of questions that persisted across the long years. But there was, in place of all this, silence that blanketed the past and the Kisches' history, covering it like a dense snow. Through all the years, Frank never, ever, spoke of Eva, so final was his remorse. Unlike Natalia, he never would say he'd tried his best, though he never again raised a hand to anyone in the family, and he barely, as Sissy grew, even so much as dared an embrace. In time his resolve weakened with his body, everything seeming to drain from his flesh—all life, all vigor. Often, when he and Natalia watched television, there might be an alert that appeared, flashing across the screen—a child suddenly gone missing—and Frank would stop doing whatever he was doing and grow contemplative, and Natalia would get up suddenly and put on a pot of coffee and no words would pass between them.

Time had done nothing to alleviate Natalia's wounds. Her face took on a complex network of lines; the skin at her neck drew itself forward, rope after rope appearing. As Sissy grew, as her body shot up and outward and her face filled in, Natalia told fewer and fewer stories about Gypsies and distant lands and moths that fluttered about, escaping over the wires. Eventually, the stories ceased altogether and were forgotten; indeed in Natalia, all history became lost. Still, sometimes, years later, questions about that summer—about so many things—consumed Sissy. She would remember Eva's accusation leveled at their mother—*Aren't you going to do anything?*—and then her final pronouncement to Sissy before she left her bedroom, one forgotten and later remembered, a warning that Sissy should watch her back. *If anyone lays a hand on you,* Eva said, *you get the hell out.*

"A story," an adult Sissy would say, tentatively, to Natalia when they spoke on the phone. "Tell me more about Eva. Tell me more about my sister."

"What stories?" Natalia would ask. "I'm all out of stories. I cried all my tears," Natalia said, "when you weren't watching. Not even God sees everything."

Inevitably, Natalia would change the subject, or the conversation would end abruptly, and it was as if Natalia were closing a book, their collective history pressed like a flower between the pages. Sissy couldn't help but wonder if there wasn't more they could have done; she couldn't help but think that in a small way, with Eva gone, something between Natalia and Frank was finally resolved—an order in the house restored—despite the hole at the center of everything that Eva could rightly claim as hers. How they all circled around that space, each of them carefully maneuvering it, in their own ways; how they danced around the space in conversations; how they sometimes pretended it wasn't there, turning their backs on it instead.

Did it make anything better to speak of Eva at all? Did it make anything better to dredge around in the murky waters of the past, to lift Eva like the drowned are sometimes mercifully lifted? In lifting Eva up, was she somehow transformed in the light of day? It seemed to Sissy that a terrible injustice was done, not only that summer but in the summers that followed, in the gradual acceptance and forgetting, in the final failure to acknowledge Eva at all. Could it be, she often found herself wondering, that the final hope in anything lies only in a story, in the speaking of her, in the utterance of words issued against the silence, in breathing, *Eva, Eva,* into the open space, calling out for her, *Come home?*

The house remained largely unchanged over time, her parents fixed securely in place, waiting, living in the same city that grew and changed around them. The neighborhood took on new faces and problems, people no longer out in the summer evenings, no longer chattering at the mailboxes or neglecting to lock their doors and shut their windows at night. No one called on Natalia. No one was left to call. Often when Sissy visited, she'd linger on streets that were still familiar, after many years and changes, places that held the imprint of time. Sometimes she'd walk downtown, past Mr. Morris's toy store that was long ago sold and turned into a coffee shop. She might be thinking of something else entirely—an errand she'd promised to run, a gift to purchase—but then something might overcome her suddenly and she'd feel breathless and overwhelmed. She'd turn, searching for ghosts, expecting to find Eva walking along the cobblestone streets. Sissy's imaginings weren't grand anymore but simple, almost achingly realistic: Eva would catch sight of her and then turn and grasp Sissy's arm, the space closing between them. "I know you!" she'd exclaim, even though they hadn't seen each other once in more than twenty years. "I know you! I'd know you anywhere, you."

Even though Sissy had long ago grown up and weathered her own teenage years and days spent alone in her room, and even though she went on to college, where she met her husband and they married, and even though she cut her hair short and her face had aged, Eva would still recognize her. And, in the odd light of memory and time, it was always like this: While Sissy had changed, Eva would have not changed at all. She would still have that look, as if she were perpetually almost eighteen—a catlike, killer walk, a star earring dangling from each lobe, her long hair falling in waves around her smooth face.

"I know you," Eva would whisper, holding her there in time.

They'd sit, the two of them, outside the coffee shop. Around them glasses would clink and the air would be light and the breezes agreeable—the weather always fine. People would pass, unaware of what a grand occasion it was—such a grand occasion!—to suddenly find someone who had been lost.

"Just in to town," Eva would explain, marveling, looking around. "Haven't been back in years."

"Me, too," Sissy would say. "How have you been? Catch me up. Catch me up on everything. Did you marry? Have a child? Were you reasonably happy enough?" ·

"That's a lot." Eva would smile then—there would be a balancing of laughter and tears—and it wouldn't be as though Eva were merely surviving. She'd be vibrant, bright, despite being on her own. She'd be better for it—stronger, more capable. She'd look rested and happy, not a runaway but a girl who had the life she'd hoped for, a life of easy attainment and pleasant days. She would be happy. Sissy would swear by it.

"I've never forgotten you," Sissy would say. "I've always wondered what your story might have been if you were given a chance to tell it."

"What's there to tell?" Eva would say casually.

"Everything."

"Whoever does that, Sissy Kiss," she would say, "whoever tells every single moment?"

Sissy would shift in her chair then and wait. She'd listen to the chatter from nearby tables. She'd notice the diffuse light settling over everything, over her, over her sister.

"How's the old man?" Eva would ask. "How's Mom?"

"Still there, in the same place. Still together."

"A miracle."

"Defied the books," Sissy would say. She wouldn't go on more about her parents; during these grand occasions with Eva they would seem as outworn as old playthings. Instead she would tell Eva about the town and how, over the years, most of the trees were cut down, one by one, and house after house was erected. She would tell Eva that two years after Vicki Anderson's death, Ginny met a man who made her smile again—slowly, at first—and that the two of them moved to New Mexico, for drier air. She would tell Eva that gossipy Milly Morris died of a heart attack Sissy's sophomore year of high school, and then three weeks later, Mr. Morris went to bed and died in his sleep; she would tell Eva how the Morrises' house was sold and painted a glaring white, and that whoever bought the house kept the bass hanging on the shed. She would tell Eva that once, during her senior year, Sissy walked to the swimming hole, down the snowy path, and that, nestled against the base of a cypress, she found a sparrow that lay too still, frozen atop fallen leaves, that she thought of Eva then, and she thought of herself, too. She would tell Eva that she was wrong, that the dead did go on living as long as someone remembered them, as long as there was a story left to tell in someone's body and bones and blood. "There was so much I wanted to tell you," Sissy would confess. "There were so many things I wanted to say."

There were, in Sissy's imaginings, never distances or accusations but only amendments. There were only resolutions and a love that persisted in spite of time.

What else did anyone wish for?

On the train, Sissy settled into her seat and stared out the window at the newly appearing light. It was an early departure, and outside, the rain pelted down, shiny and silver against the city streets. People shuffled past, overburdened with luggage and children and complaints of the early hour. An elderly couple in front of her had already drifted to sleep. Behind her a teenager listened to hip-hop music. In a few minutes the whistles would sound, shrill and sharp, and they would chug slowly forward, past the station, past the platform and chairs strung together like pearls, past the people waving goodbye to loved ones. And then things would suddenly stretch out on either side of her and the cities would give way to blanched, rolling hills, and flashes of color: a child riding a bike, a few old men who, despite the advancements in technology and travel, still drove out to the small town depot to wave as the train passed. How Sissy loved those old men; how she envied them, the persistence of their memories.

She sipped her coffee. A woman came aboard and looked at her ticket before taking a seat next to Sissy. The woman, a stranger, looked to be in her late forties. She pulled off her wool coat, releasing a mass of hair. She took off her glasses and wiped them with a tissue. "I missed my flight," the woman explained, glancing over, clearly tired. "Only the tenth time in my life that that's happened, but this is the first time the rest of the flights were booked."

"I never mind if I miss a flight," Sissy said. "But mostly I don't schedule the flight in the first place."

"Fear of flying? Ah, who isn't afraid these days? And the security checks . . ." She pulled a newspaper from her carry-on and left it folded on her lap.

The whistle sounded, and Sissy felt movement under her. The women made small talk over the next hour as the train crossed bridges and cut through rocky tunnels. A fog clung to the ground. She explained to Sissy that she owned a small antiques shop outside of Crystal City, and that she was traveling to visit an old friend. The woman's husband had died recently, she explained, and her friend informed her—blatantly, persistently—that she wouldn't take no for an answer. "Truthfully, I'm happy to get out for a bit," the woman said.

"I understand," Sissy said, nodding. "I'm sorry."

"Don't be," she said. "It was the cancer's fault, not yours."

"When?" Sissy asked.

"Last month."

Sissy nodded and watched as the woman fidgeted with her newspaper; she unfolded it, regarded the crossword, and then folded the paper back again and put it down. Her mouth parted, to say more.

It always began like this, conversations with strangers. How the world itself, and the people in it, provided a sense of belonging, of home. The woman told stories about her husband, lapsing into those years they dated, the silly fights they had, his love of cooking. By the end of the train ride, Sissy would tell her that she was visiting home, and she'd inevitably talk about her sister—how she always thought of Eva when she went back to Pennsylvania, to the old haunts. "Though," Sissy confessed finally, "there are times when I go days forgetting, sometimes even a week. Then suddenly I remember Eva and there she is again, just where I left her, somewhere right behind me, tapping on my shoulder."

"What happened to her?"

"Oh," Sissy said, "I don't know. She was stolen by Gypsies, I guess, but I may have some facts wrong."

The woman nodded, and, for a while, they sat in silence. A voice came over the loudspeaker and announced the dining car was open for breakfast. People idled down the aisle and Sissy looked out the window to the bare trees tossed by the wind, to the parked cars littering the roads, the shapes of houses and buildings.

"You know it happens," the woman said after a time. "Forgetting. I've done it. Sometimes it's the only way I can get myself up and going each day, to not think about it, to put things in their place."

"I know," Sissy said. "But I never want to forget anything."

How fragile things became at a distance, when they were all but gone. How important was the love that lingered in everyone, the memories of those never completely forgotten. How important were the stories issued around those lives. The stories were a song leveled against the darkness; the stories were a threading of hands around the table. The stories resurrected the dead and prompted the remembering. A story about this woman who told jokes when anyone was down; and this one who loved to dance even though he had a wooden leg; and this one who died in a horrible accident; and this one who rode off on a bike one day and disappeared forever. And there were stories of this one, who tended to orchids and was a delicate man; and this one, who loved to feel his hands in soil; and this one, who worried all the time. And there was this one with the marvelous singing voice and the collection of old records; and this one who held parties that everyone came to; and this one who sewed her sister's clothes before a dance, her veined hands pulling the thread. And there was this one who worked and died for his family; and this one who never forgot a name; and all of them are missed, and all of them are loved, and all of them are held for an eternity, alive and well and present. The stories came with hope and fell easily from people; the stories blew from great distances, like wishes. And the stories said *We are never alone,* that there was always a way home again, where everyone precious lingered there at the table, waiting.

acknowledgments

I am indebted to the following people, without whom this book could not exist:

My fabulous agent, Denise Shannon, has my utmost gratitude and heartfelt thanks. I also thank Laura Ford and Jennifer Hershey at Random House for their guidance, editorial support, and encouraging words. Thanks, too, to Dennis Ambrose, for his kindness and patience during the copyediting process, and to Jennifer Huwer and Sally Marvin, for their exceptional smarts and skill. Erin McGraw and Bea Opengart got me started and were wonderful teachers—insightful, full of wit. I am also lucky to have had tremendous mentors in David Jauss, who is as compassionate as he is wise; Douglas Glover, who instilled in me a sense of structure; and Victoria Redel, who, in one workshop, inspired me to love every word. I thank Fred Leebron at Queens University, who took me in when I needed it, and Mike Kobre for doing the same. Isabel Fonseca's book *Bury Me Standing: The Gypsies and Their Journey* was influential in shaping Natalia's character; Fonseca's accounts of the Romani culture helped shape the fictional world of *Precious*. Dr. Jozsef Palfy helped me with my Hungarian words, translations, and diacritical marks. I could not have made it through the writing process without the encouragement and cheer of Jean Free and Stephanie Bast—two old friends who are dear to me. I am thankful and grateful for my family— Mom, Dad, Tom, Chris, Jim, and Carole—all of whom I love more than words can express. I thank my husband's family for their continued support. I am blessed by the many people I've met in travel, those who shared their stories and in doing so taught me humanity and grace. And I owe all the thanks in the world to my husband, Phil: You are my best of everything.

Precious

SANDRA NOVACK

A Reader's Guide

playing hide-and-seek

with the truth

I'm often asked about the nature of truth in *Precious,* my debut novel. Perhaps it's because readers are familiar with the adage that first novels are often thinly veiled autobiographies, or perhaps it's because readers inherently understand that writers do not create entire worlds from thin air—there has to be *some* fodder, grounded in the real world. But for whatever reason, at book club discussions and at readings or over coffee, people want to know what events in the novel are real events. I always respond quickly. When I was young, I say, my seventeen-year-old sister Carole ran away from home, and I've never seen her again. After thirty years, it could be that the statement has become rote, or it could be that, through repetition, the feelings inherent in that statement—the sadness or shame or anger—are equally muted and dry. Because what happens next is generally this: The questioner pauses, hesitates. He or she might lean forward, as if expecting and sensing there is more to tell. It's always then that my own old, dumbfounded silence creeps in, for it always seems to me that truth is difficult for a variety of reasons. First, I didn't write a memoir or an autobiography. I wrote a fiction. And as fiction the work has to stand on its own; what I do or don't say about my personal life bears little to no real importance except as an aside or an endnote. Second, there is my family and their privacy to consider. My family is alive and well and there is the question of loyalty, which is something that always pulls me in various directions all at once: loyalty to my sister and to her memory, loyalty to my parents, and loyalty to myself. And there is also my loyalty to readers who, after all, only ask such questions after they have taken the time to become invested in the world of the book. "But is your sister okay?" they ask, genuinely concerned. "What happened?"

For this I have no good answer.

Then I think that I am the one who is hiding, because truths are painful for writers—truths are painful for us all—and truths, as I see them, are precarious things anyway, particularly when, as memories, they are hindered by the long years, fragmented by time. I was five, I remind myself, when my sister ran away, and even that is a statement that I have had to amend.

Hide-and-seek. The day Carole left was, to my still five-year-old and slightly criminal mind, a day of games. My sister was at work, but I had already decided (in the way I frequently made decisions for my older brothers and sisters) that when she got home we would play a game of hide-and-seek. Under the kitchen table I went. The kitchen was dim, the floor cold and smooth. I don't know how long I waited; for children, minutes can feel like hours, hours like days. I'm sure I felt anticipation at the thought of my sister's arrival. I'm sure I felt that peculiar sort of giddy dread of wanting to be found yet also wanting to stay hidden.

When my sister finally did come through the door there was no friendly greeting to my mother (whom I seem to recall was also there in the kitchen), but rather an explosion of yelling and tears. "That's it!" my sister screamed. "I'm leaving."

Next, where there should be more action—a succession of movements or some dialogue, or the escalation of an argument between what I eventually learned was my sister and my father, the details of which I still don't know to this day—there is, in my memory, only white space, blankness.

I once heard a writer talk about the notion of truth in fiction. He was relating an event from his life, one that later inspired a short story. He and his girlfriend of two years had had an argument, over all things, about how he stacked dishes in the dishwasher. The argument swelled in the way they often do. It was early and he hadn't yet showered and dressed. The fight made him late for work. In his anger and haste, he dressed quickly, and in the process of rummaging for clothes, pulled out one blue sock and one black sock from the drawer. Later that morning he looked down and discovered the mismatched pair. At the same moment, a song was playing over the sound system at the store where he worked. I have always imagined it must have been a sad song, because he said that for some reason the music, together with the mismatched socks, led him to a further realization, a very plain truth: The relationship would fail.

Years later, he wrote a story about the end of a relationship. Most details of the breakup were different from those of his own. The couple in the story was much older and long married. There was no argument over dishes or incompatibility. The reason for the breakup was not the same, though the feeling of loss was similar, I'm sure. However, there were two lines about, of all things, a pair of mismatched socks. The other lines—all of them, really—were crafted to bolster and sustain those two lines of truth taken from his personal life, that little detail that, for whatever reason, was long held in his memory and seemed to contain something worthy of a story. What the narrative afforded was a new context and meaning, a place to put a fragmented image, a way to breathe life into a single, lost moment again.

This is the truth: I don't remember how long I stayed under the table the day my sister left home forever. I don't recall if I scrambled out and ran after her, perhaps wanting to soothe her or perhaps even wanting a bit of gossip—to find out what exactly had happened to make her issue such a proclamation as *That's it! I'm leaving.* Or perhaps I simply kept waiting, magically willing away the chaos of the house, the tears, and the screaming. What I remember next is another fragmented image of that same day: I stood outside. It was a terribly hot day, very sunny. My sister rode off down the drive on her bicycle. That is the last image of her I hold in my mind, the last time I ever saw her. In reality my mother might have been outside, too, or my father, or my brothers, but in memory this scene is made very intimate—there is only my sister and me, her pedaling off, my watching her leave.

Then, more white space.

That day my mother, who was always well-meaning, didn't want me to be upset, so she called my oldest sister and charged her with my care for the rest of the day. After Carole left, my other sister took me and a friend to a local amusement park. I remember sitting in the back seat of our car, asking if Carole was going to come home, so I must have been worried. But I'm also sure that my worry quickly gave way to delight when we got to the park. I went on rides, ate cotton candy, had a hot dog. I must have forgotten about my sister at some point, dismissed the argument in a naïve way, as simply a fight that would blow over in time and not as the terrible thing it actually was: an altercation that would leave my family forever broken.

I must have laughed.

. . .

I never found out the exact nature of the argument between my father and sister, or discovered, at least in those immediate years following her departure, what could have been so terribly bad that she would have wanted to run away forever. Indeed, my sister's departure on that bright, sunny day was too painful a thing to talk about at all, and, when pressed, everyone in my family seems to have a different story surrounding those events, complicating the truth further and keeping it just out of reach.

In my family, we argue about the nature of truth and memory.

"You've got it wrong," my brother once told me at one of those rare moments when we actually talked about our sister at all. "You weren't five when she left home, you were seven," he said. "And I pumped the bike tire for her; it had a flat."

I cannot begin to explain how this one statement devastated me years after the fact, how it trapped me in a lie I didn't even know I'd committed. What was most upsetting was the realization that came with my brother's statement: I could not remember anything of those two lost years that I had suddenly recovered, that span of time between five and seven. Yet surely things must have happened. My sister and I must have joked around. She must have brushed through my always tangled hair. I must have accompanied her to the mall, played board games with her, bickered with her. Because I remember myself as younger than I actually was, I have effectively wiped out time and history with her; I have lost entire years I shared with my sister.

But why do I remember myself as younger? Was I particularly vulnerable at that moment, susceptible to the moods of the house? Is this why I remember myself as smaller? This error of memory leads to even more questions and doubts: Why, for example, do I remember that the floor was smooth and cool under me? Was it really so dim in the kitchen on what I also remember to be a sunny day? Most likely my mother or father had turned off the lights to help cool the rooms in those pre-air-conditioning days. But perhaps, too, I am adding details without realizing it, so that I can give this memory verisimilitude; the more detail there is, the easier the moment is to recall and the longer I am able to hold on to it. Perhaps I need to flesh in details to moments that, for me, are all I have left of my sister, ones that are inadequate at best. Or maybe this is the inherent problem of memory and of truth, that both exist only as fragments—mere moments—those isolated from the larger context and day. Who looks back over any remembered event, good or bad, and recalls every single detail?

I think that there is something in the brain that resists such fragmentation and that is the stuff of stories. What I can say are the following truths, these moments in a day that changed my life: My sister ran away from home and never came back. It happened on a very hot summer day. I was hiding under the table when she came through the door, crying. She rode off later on her bike, and I spent the rest of that day at an amusement park, playing with another girl my age.

Now, let's dwell here again, but with a new context, a new problem: A young girl has gone missing at a local park. Her mother grieves. Her best friend feels responsible. Down the street, in another house, a family is in crisis.

To say that the idea of a girl who goes missing is inspired by my sister is a true enough statement, accurate in a sense. But to say that the little girl is also me would be equally true, that I went missing on that day as well. Using images, ones taken from my own experience—the bike, the lost child, the hot summer, the amusement park—I have, in *Precious*, reordered them and given them a new context and meaning, woven together entire pages—entire lies—around what are a few true moments, those details long held in my memory. As a writer of fiction, I do this all in an effort to recover what is lost, to breathe life into something that is gone forever from view.

questions and topics for discussion

1. *Precious* is set in a small, blue-collar suburban town in the 1970s. Do you think this setting plays an important role in the story, or merely serves as a backdrop?

2. How does Vicki Anderson's disappearance mark "the beginning of fear"? How does it affect the course of the novel?

3. Sissy Kisch's beloved doll, Precious, figures strongly into her friendship with Vicki Anderson and the stories Sissy writes. Why do you think the novel is titled *Precious*?

4. How do characters in *Precious* cope with or mismanage their loneliness? Or feel "on the periphery of things"? How do loneliness and freedom become intertwined for many of them?

5. Consider Natalia: her childhood, her stories, her rituals, and the impact her absence, and eventual return, has on the Kisch family. How does she change? How does the family change? Does Natalia's return do more harm than good? Is it all "lucky or unlucky"?

6. Discuss the types of obligation in *Precious*: between parents and children, between husbands and wives, between sisters, neighbors, friends, lovers, and strangers. How is obligation enforced? Manipulated? How and why is this used as a means of control?

7. The day she leaves, Natalia tells Eva: "Don't give up your freedom. The day you give up your freedom, the day you lock yourself away is the day you disappear. In your own skin, you vanish" (page 27). What do you think she means by this? How does Natalia attempt to attain freedom? Eva? Frank? Peter? Is anyone in *Precious* free? Do you think this advice haunts Natalia?

8. Examine the characterization of the women in *Precious*: Natalia, Eva, Ginny, Amy, Sissy, Vicki. What similarities do you find among them? What differences? Are they victims, or something else? Do you identify with them? Why or why not?

9. How does Peter justify his relationship with Eva? How do their expectations differ? How does Eva's expectation that "Love, a life away . . . Peter would help her forge a greater sense of the world" (page 179) differ from the reality of the situation? Do you sympathize with Eva? With Amy? With Peter?

10. Discuss the characters who disappear in *Precious,* even those who just feel invisible, or "ghostly."

11. "There is always a story. No one leaves forever." How do stories and memories of those we've lost serve to "resurrect the dead"? Do you

agree with Sissy that "There [is] always a way home again" (page 270). Why or why not?

12. The final moments of the book mark a conversation between Sissy and a stranger she meets while traveling. Given the novel's trajectory and the Kisches's fates, how do you interpret this final interaction? Does it satisfy, or fail to? And how might that feeling work with the overall tone and theme of the novel?

SANDRA NOVACK's fiction has appeared in publications including *The Iowa Review, The Gettysburg Review, Gulf Coast,* and *Mississippi Review,* and she has been nominated for the Pushcart Prize three times. She holds an MFA from Vermont College and currently lives in Chicago, Illinois, with her husband. Please visit her website at www.sandranovack.com.